Scintilla

Ben Wilson

POSTAL MARINES

Other Books in the series:

Bellicose

Luctation

Imbroglio

Scintilla

Solace

Scintilla

Ben Wilson

Dausha
Publishing

Scintilla

This is a work of fiction. Names, characters, places and incidents are either the product of the author's imagination or are used fictitiously, and any resemblance to actual persons, living or dead, business establishments, events or locales is entirely coincidental.

Copyright © 2011 Ben Wilson.

Cover Design by Donna Harriman Murillo

Book Design by Ben Wilson

Ben Wilson
Visit my website at `http://dausha.net`

Printed in the United States of America

First Printing, September, 2011

ISBN-13 978-0-9839521-1-4

Chapter 1

1. Carpimua - Alley

"Is it agreed, then?" Jonaldy said.

Ojave Carpimua nervously held the tiny envelope in his hands, as afraid of what he was asked to do as he was of the person asking it. He wondered why he agreed to meet him again, and to meet him in a dark alley. Bad things happen in dark alleys. The man terrified him, though he could not understand why. Carpimua found himself in the alley because he feared the consequences of not being in the alley more than what could happen to him in the alley.

"Is what you're asking really necessary? If I get caught, I would be imprisoned."

"You won't get caught. You let me worry about that. You're a bonded proctor! Nobody's going to question your integrity. Just don't oversell your performance and don't start gesticulating until you produce the slate."

"Is the money all there?" The disadvantage of a cash card was knowing what its value was. You could look at the face of the card and read its passive tally display. Carpimua squeezed the envelope again, wishing the display had raised numbers. But the Clinate did not allow unprofitable disabilities, so the need to assist the blind was not an issue.

"Three-thousand knoerzers on an unmarked cash card, just like we agreed. Nothing will ever happen to you. I'll see to it that the attention is kept on the lad and off of you. If there were a better way, I'd have done that instead of this. I mean, look at you. Are you sure you can compose yourself?"

A year's salary for a little slight of hand. Carpimua felt the card and the slate in the envelope. *And I get to ruin the life of a named punk.* Carpimua breathed deeply and exhaled his fear. "Consider it done."

Carpimua walked away from the alley as the binaries broke the horizon. The red and white dwarfs in Copa System orbited one another every 1.3 cycles; 130 Beats Imperial. In less than four more revolutions, the fate of two societies separated by 7,300 paces would be in play.

2.   Mondennio - University Exam

Almost every student in the room knew it came down to the first question. If it was answered correctly, the second question would be harder. If it was answered wrong, then the next question would be easier. In reality, if the student got the first question wrong, he would never be invited to serve the government. Mondennio wanted to serve in government, to earn back his family's rightful place in the Clinate. For the three cycles, Mondennio faced questions of increasing difficulty.

He took a quick stretch break and looked around. He was surprised to see that the room was half empty. If they left by now, they must have answered the premier question wrong. He tried to see if his cousin Sonichard was still there.

A proctor stared right at him. Mondennio returned to the test without hesitation. He started the next question knowing he had made it. He knew he had gotten every question right so far. If he counted right, there were only two questions left to the only perfect score in the history of the exam. He fought to focus as his mind tried to run a victory lap. The few other students that remained would not match his score. He could practically walk away from the test now knowing he would be given a coveted post. He wanted that perfect score. There were ten beats on the clock remaining. His summer was lost preparing for these past three cycles and he was going to make sure that time was not lost in vain.

"What's this?"

Mondennio half jumped as he looked up. The proctor who stared at him earlier stood beside him. *There's no way I could get in trouble for a stretch.* "I'm sorry?"

"I said, what have you been doing, hmm?"

"I was just looking around."

"Um hmm! Just looking around. I see. So, what's that under your chair?"

Mondennio did not need to look down to answer that question. "My daybag." There was no indication the proctor was Clinate, or even named. Mondennio would not give him the honorific for interrupting his exam. "Is there something wrong?"

The proctor stood staring at him. Mondennio did not know what to do except return to his exam. Eight beats and two questions. *If I can get this one I can probably guess the next one before time is out.*

> Assume the has annual sales of 548,820 knoerzers, what is its profit based on the adjoining profile?

What, the profile doesn't have any information on the profit! This has to be a trick question or an error. I'll just mark the sales figure and move on.

He noticed the proctor was still standing beside him. Five beats remained. The proctor reached down under Mondennio's chair and lifted up a slate. *My slate? But...*

"What's this?" The professor started examining Mondennio's slate.

"Give that back to me. I don't know how that got there."

The proctor pulled away as Mondennio reached to take the slate back.

"Not so fast young Mondennio." The proctor made a show of examining the slate further as Mondennio tried to make sense of what was happening. The proctor then became very solemn, "Mondennio Rowenzal Clin-Khotaigra brought his slate into the examination room." He held the slate high in the air, ensuring the video surveillance would identify the device.

Mondennio rewound the day in his mind. He remembered dumping his daybag on his bed and only putting in a few essentials for the test. He distinctly recalled leaving his slate on his bed as he left.

"That's not mine! It can't be. I left it at home."

"Silence!" The proctor turned the slate on and tapped its screen. "What have we here? An exact replica of this exam." He tapped again, "You're not on the final question, are you?"

"I am now. What are you doing?"

"You disgust me. Security, escort Rowenzal from the premises. We must conduct a thorough investigation. We'll just see what he's been up to."

Mondennio remained seated. He moved to finish his last question. The proctor grabbed his wrist and pulled his hand away from the touchboard.

Mondennio jumped up and fought to pull his hand free. "What are you doing?"

"Your test is invalid."

Two security guards walked down the rows of desks. A couple students glanced sideways as the guards walked toward Mondennio, pretending not to notice the commotion. Mondennio could not believe nobody was coming to his aid.

One guard pulled out his wapiti stick, a spring-loaded baton the University Security guards were allowed to carry. They were not electrically charged like those of the Clinate's Security force, the , but Mondennio knew that they hurt without the debilitating shock. He tried to back away as the other guard grabbed his sleeve.

"Let go of me." Mondennio pulled his arm free, losing his balance. The proctor blocked his fall. By this time, none of the students could ignore what was happening.

The first guard struck Mondennio on the arm with the baton. The baton self-recoiled after it struck and made a second whack. Then a third, fourth, fifth whack. The sticks were labor saving, the energy from one swing repeating. The guard cocked his arm for his second swing as Mondennio put his arms up to block him.

The second swing somehow got around his arms and whacked him on his head. Mondennio dropped to the floor before the baton could recoil for another whack.

All but a couple of the remaining students watched as they pulled him from the floor and dragged him away. As Mondennio looked back, one of the other proctors walked up to his desk and helped the fallen proctor up. The two pulled his bag from under his table and started rummaging through it. One beat until the exam ended.

The guards took him into the hall and threw him down on a chair. He knew better than to try to get up. His arm was barely functioning through the pain. He wondered if it was broken.

The guards were Unnamed — disenfranchised — citizens. The Clinate had two classes of citizens: Named and Unnamed. Mondennio believed there were three classes, with the under-enfranchised Septs like the Rowenzals. As Security guards, these two Unnamed guards were given a license to pay back

Named students for assumed, and often grossly exaggerated, grievances. Usually they had rules of engagement that checked in their aggression; but the pain in his arm told Mondennio the rules must have been different today. They had done a thorough job with him so far. Mondennio chose not to give them the opportunity to push the limits of their rules.

Several beats later, the proctor came out with a more senior man. The senior man spoke, "Rowenzal. You have brought shame to your sub-sept. This proctor here said he watched you for nearly 40 beats because you were acting suspicious. We have your slate, which has an identical copy of the exam. You clearly planned this well to have so exact a copy."

"I don't know what you're talking about. I wasn't cheating, and that's not my slate. I left mine at home to ensure this would not happen."

The proctor held up his hand. "Now would be a good time to not speak, Rowenzal. We're not here to cast judgment; just report the facts. There will be a formal inquiry that will give you a chance to try to deny what happened here. In the meantime, you are barred from the examination room."

"You call calling me scum and having your thugs beat me down 'not casting judgment?' What about my bag?"

"We're holding that for evidence. These two will escort you from the premises."

"But you didn't let me finish the exam. It won't be offered again for another year."

Mondennio stood a little too quickly for one of the guards, who grabbed him by his shoulder. Mondennio felt the breath leave his lungs as he slammed onto the floor. From his new vantage point, he could see into the room. The exam was officially over, but none of the students seemed to witness what was happening. They were content to remain seated.

He began to stand back up. One of the guards helped steady him. Mondennio turned to look at the guards, trying to muster the courage to dress them down for beating him. One put a foot back, giving him a steady platform to fight.

Mondennio realized he could not argue or fight now. He turned to walk to the exit. The guards followed close behind. The guards stopped following him at a comfortable distance from the exit. He turned to see why. Both stood with wide-spread legs and crossed arms, as if daring him to cross some imaginary line. *Are they trying to give me my dignity back? Or trying to avoid witnesses identifying them?*

He rubbed his still numb arm. *What just happened? Did the proctor tell me that my entire exam was nullified? It will be a year before I can take it again. It took me months to prepare.*

An empty feeling fell over him. The government service exam was offered each year, and only with the recommendation of one of the five clins. Rowenzals maintained decent relationships with their clin, Khotaigra, but this fiasco would dent that relationship. Mondennio spent the past twenty years preparing for this day. Years of study, tutors. It was all over. More than half his life wasted.

I'm not going to let this go without a fight. He looked at the guards, feeling his anger rise. He knew he could not take them on, so he studied their faces. He walked a bit closer to them. One guard gripped his baton.

You're the one who beat me. I'll find you later.

He wished he could remember who the proctor was. They were rarely school officials. The University preferred to bring in trusted outsiders and kept their identities secret to avoid bribery. Even an inquiry would not yield their names unless all five clins agreed. Getting all to agree would be virtually impossible. If he could remember the proctor's face, then he might be able to find him later.

What am I going to do? There will have to be an inquiry. I have to prove I did not cheat. How? My slate's logs would show I did not access it during the exam. The exam surveillance video would show me working on the exam. This isn't a case of me against the proctor. This is about how the proctor tried to set me up. All I have to do is prove it, which should be easy with the show he put on. First thing I need to do is get home.

Mondennio turned and walked away from the guards. He squinted to adjust to the outside light. As his vision cleared, he saw many of the other exam takers hanging around. They were in small clusters, likely talking about their progress, or lack thereof. He was not looking forward to running the gauntlet. Having not seen any of the remaining students emerge, Mondennio assumed nobody here knew what just happened.

He slowly stepped down the stairs, sliding his hand on the banister. His mind was quickly looking for some response to give the inevitable questioning. Mondennio looked for the fastest path through the group of students, unhappy to see one of his cousins along that escape route. It was still the shortest path, so he decided he might as well handle the one confrontation than the several he expected down any of the other ways out. Besides, his car was down the short path.

His cousin came up with a smile on his face. "Well, Mondennio! You spent quite a long time in there. The exam should have ended by now. I guess you did okay, huh?"

"I did okay, Sonichard."

"What are you being modest for? You've been after this exam for almost as far back as I can remember. I mean, look at you. You're all pasty white you studied so much. How much sun did you get this summer, anyway?"

"I don't think I got any."

"I'll say. Hey, you look like you're in a hurry. What's wrong?"

Mondennio froze at the question. *Was he acting like he was in a hurry? How could he explain he had just been accused of cheating?* "I'm just tired, Sonichard. It was a long exam. How long have you been out here?"

"Man, I was out of there after the first 30 beats. That's a personal record, by the way. I breezed through the first few questions before I realized I screwed up. It was past the point of no return, so I had to keep going."

The point of no return, the point in the exam every student dreaded. Once so many questions were answered, a student could not step away from the exam without career impact. It had taken Mondennio just over 40 beats to get to that point of the exam. *Why had Sonichard stayed after so long?* That was three cycles ago.

"Yeah, that test was a bit more difficult than the practice exams. Did you run into any questions that did not have enough information?"

"I ran into a few that I didn't have enough education to answer, which is sad, because I got the first three questions wrong."

"The first three wrong? What have you been doing?"

"Living, Cousin. Living. You should try it. Speaking of living. Now that this horror show is over, you going to the after party tonight?"

"I was, but I'm not feeling very well now. I think I'll just skip it."

"No! You can't do that. Man, if you miss the party I'll annoy you about it for the rest of your life. You know I'm good for my word."

"I know. But, I'm serious. I feel terrible. I might have been in the exam room longer, but I don't think I did as well as I should have. I don't feel like I've earned the party." More specifically, he did not feel like he could survive the ridicule he'd get during the party once word of his incident got out.

"Mondennio, if I do not see you at the party, then I'm going to grab some of my friends to come and drag you to the party. Then I'll harass you. You understand? I bombed that test, but I'm still going to party. You got it? You will be at the party."

"Okay, fine. I'll go to the party. Look, I'm not feeling well. I'll talk to you later."

"You never told me how you did."

Mondennio walked away, shooing away the question with his hand. It took him a few beats to cross the campus. As he approached, his driver climbed out of the car hurried around to open the door for him. He entered the car and raised the privacy screen.

He shook his head as he felt the car pull alway. It was a T-2000, manufactured by Sept Khotaigra Clin-Rowenzal as one of the smoothest cars on the market. The electric motors were completely silent, with just a hint of road noise to warn that there was a large hunk of carbon-schord polymer rolling across the ground. Legal requirements included a cow-tipper, which he always thought was an odd name for something that kept unnamed pedestrians from being run over. Cars were also fitted with noise makers to warn pedestrians. Mondennio's had a custom noise-maker that played a dual-toned organ chord, that was completely inaudible inside the sound-proofed shell of his passenger compartment. His friends said it sounded like he was squeezing a stray cat in a bag.

His mind returned to the exam. Job opportunities were offered based on the outcome. Everybody in the sept knew that Sonichard Rowenzal would not do well. None of the other Rowenzals stood out. The Rowenzal family had never done particularly well on the exam, which contributed to Rowenzal family never being able to rise above its current station.

Had he been allowed to finish the exam, Mondennio would have been given a prestigious job for the Clin itself. That job could lead to an opportunity for him to return the family to its former, full-sept status.

It would have been easier to prove my innocence if they had let me have my bag. I could have shown them where I kept the slate, proven my innocence. I put it on my bed before I left. I know I did. It will be there when I get home.

Despite its recent decline to sub-sept status, Rowenzal retained its ancestral control of Mareen, just North of Kinnet. Mondennio rode in silence as the car left the University.

3.   Mondennio - Rowenzal Enclave

Mondennio's car stopped to wait for the gate to open. The Clin-Khotaigra crest — A golden mule rearing — parted as the gates separated to give admittance to the Rowenzal compound. Atop the crest was the Khotaigra golden mule — representing the Clin's reputed perseverance, stubbornness and ability to work hard. To Mondennio, it was just an ass.

What should have been there was the Rowenzal eagle — majestic, two-handed eagle. As much as he wished it, Mondennio was realistic enough to know that would never happen. The clins were resilient, permanent. Making it to Sept was all the Rowenzal family could expect. Even to express his wish in the wrong company would be treason. *In the past they only have to accuse me of contemplating sedition. At least that concept of treason by contemplation has gone out of fashion.*

The car entered the compound and pulled around to the front. Mondennio entered the house without fanfare, hurrying up the stairs to his room. He passed through his sitting room and opened the inner door. *Once and for all I am going to prove my innocence.*

He walked over to his bed. The usual contents of his daybag still littered the bedspread from earlier that morning. *I knew I dumped my stuff here. He took each item off the bed and tossed it into the reclining chair.* Eventually, he ran out of things to toss. He looked at his bed, then back at his chair. No slate.

He repeated the process, moving items from his chair to the floor. As he came to the last item, his frustration mounted. He returned to the bed. The pattern on his slate was a close match for the bedspread, so he ran his hands all over the bedspread trying to find the slate. Unable to locate it, he pulled the bedspread off — then the sheets. Finally, he looked under his bed. No slate.

The door opened. Without looking, Mondennio knew it was his father. He would be the only one who would walk in without ringing. Mondennio wished he knew he was coming so he could go out of the window before he arrived.

"How did the exam go? Sonichard texted me and said you were there until the bitter end. I'm actually a bit surprised that you're home so soon afterward. You should be celebrating."

How do I explain what happened? "Father, it did not go as well as I had hoped. I was there until the bitter end, but, a proctor stopped my exam." Mondennio watched as his father's eyebrows stitched together.

"What do you mean 'a proctor stopped my exam?' Proctors don't just stop exams. How much did you have left?"

"Actually, I was on the last question. I had a few beats left, should have been enough time to finish it. I stopped to stretch, then this proctor walked up to me and stared at me. Then he pulls out my bag and produces my slate — he accused me of using it during the exam, but I didn — "

"What? You cheated?" Gerandy reached over to steady himself. "After all the time and knoerzers we put into getting you prepped for this?"

"I know, Father, I've spent months preparing for this exam. I was ready for that exam. I did not cheat. I didn't need to."

"But, you just said he caught you using your slate."

"No, he took the slate from my daybag. I couldn't have used it. That's why this room is in disarray. I knew I left it here this morning when I left. But, now I can't find it. It's a baseless accusation. I just can't figure out how my slate made it from my room to my daybag"

"Then you did cheat."

"I did not cheat! I was caught cheating. Don't you see the difference?"

"The difference doesn't matter. It's worse to be caught cheating than to cheat, Mondennio. Remember the proverb 'If you're not cheating, you're not trying. If you get caught cheating, you weren't trying hard enough.' After all we did to get you ready, I can't believe you even tried to cheat."

"Father, that's my point. I did not cheat. I did not take my slate, but now it's missing. There's something wrong, and I don't know what it is. But, I know I did not cheat. I swear it, Father."

Gerandy waved Mondennio to follow him into the sitting room. Once there, he sat down and pointed at the other seat for Mondennio to sit. Mondennio relaxed a bit that he seemed to be calming down. "Mondennio, you're probably the best son I have. You say you didn't cheat, then I'll agree with you. Even if I don't believe you, we have no choice now but to agree."

"But, I didn't —"

Gerandy raised his hand for silence. "Stop. I'm not upset. Well, I am upset, but I'm not angry. Not angry with you, anyway. My point is, right now it does not matter whether you cheated. The fact is you don't have your slate, the examiners do. Having a slate is not *prima facia* proof you cheated, but it does strongly suggest you cheated. If we're going to beat this, we need to call the in lawyers in to let them fight it."

Mondennio knew his father did not believe him. He could not help defending himself. "But, I'm innocent."

"Stop being so defensive. I don't care whether you cheated or not. Now that they have your slate, it will have whatever they want on it by the time the investigation gets to it. You said you got to the last question on the exam?"

Gerandy stood up and walked over to him, holding out his hand. Mondennio accepted the hand, standing up as he did.

"Congratulations. Even if you stopped the exam then, you would have advanced yourself and the family. I only hope we can get rid of this cloud of accusation, and ensure your score stands. In all likelihood, if we get clear of this they'll only let you take the exam again next year."

Mondennio shook his father's hand, though he was at a loss for words. *Does he even believe me? It doesn't seem like he cares one way or the other.*

"Oh, don't look so despairing. You always get that look when you've been severely rebuked."

"Father. You don't believe me."

"What I believe, Mondennio my son, is that you knocked the snooker out of that exam." His father paused. "Somebody probably knew you were going to do well and thought it would be better to knock you down a peg. I'm surprised you've grown as much as you have without realizing that dirty tricks are part of the game."

"Father, I don't think you raised me that way."

"No, Mondennio, I don't think we have. What's more, you've actually listened to myself and your mother."

Mondennio's heart sank as he thought of his mother. She had died over the summer and had insisted on a small funeral and that he keep studying. Everybody complied with her wishes and made sure he focused on his studies to ace the exam.

"Look, Mondennio. You've worked hard for this. They are celebrating right now. They're not even celebrating doing well on the exam. They're happy just to be finished with it. You deserve to celebrate. I'll call your driver and have you taken over. Enjoy the time. Don't worry about the accusation. I'll take care of that. Next week, you'll have to start your last year of University."

Mondennio dropped back into his seat as his father left the room, wishing his mother was there. He barely remembered her passing, and did not go to the theater. He promised her he would visit, but she passed before he could. The family delayed telling him until after her service. Though he was upset, he accepted their reasoning. The exam was that important. *I don't care what Father thinks. I'm not going to go to that party.*

4.   Jonaldy - Tenement

Jonaldy Ammonet sat in his apartment watching the news. It was a constant battle to listen to all the propaganda for the occasional report of a new Imperial ship arriving in system. Despite the profits earned through Imperial trade, the Clinate presented a facade to the public of not trusting Imperial intentions. If too many ships appeared in system, then the news gave dire warning of a possible invasion and meaningless talk of kicking out all foreign commerce.

Regardless of the complaint, a new arrival was important. The news always used the same stock footage that did not unnerve him as it once did. It was the Imperial Frigate (IFR) *Wexention* that arrived when Jonaldy did seven years ago. When Jonaldy first saw the footage a few years ago, it unnerved him. He thought it suggested that Atakadaro was aware of him and just trying to figure out where he was. Over the years he figured out that it was mere serendipity.

The video was the only one of its kind on Copa, because Copans lost the understanding and technology for hyperspatial travel. They used the images, different parts of the same event, because the emergence of a ship gave drama. Watching a ship traveling against black space did not show movement.

Had the Copans retained their knowledge, they would have known to camp at the system-wide libration points. Those were the locations in a system least influenced by gravity. Because of their misunderstanding, and the Imperium's cunning efforts to keep them from figuring it out, Copan defense ships tended to be scattered throughout Copa System. The video happened because a Copan ship was inadvertently at a libration point and caught the Imperial ship emerging. It was the only time a Copan ship was close enough to an emergence to get useful footage.

The news broadcast faithfully delivered the Clinate's usual complaint about a newly arrived ship "trying to hide its arrival and pointing menacingly at the Copan home world." Jonaldy knew that the Imperial standard procedure was to immediately turn the nose of a ship toward the primary star, then rotate the ship until the planets orbited clockwise from its perspective; "larbord to starboard." The briskness of the orientation made copan commentators froth at its hostile intent.   Jonaldy knew the real reason — Imperial military ships were just very efficient at their maneuvers.

Unlike the ship Jonaldy arrived in, coincidently the same day as the IFR Wexention. Jonaldy was on the *Assirro IX*, a cargo ship of the inbound from Sigurd System, contracted to Clin Parxon. The Clinate restricted the Imperial military to five ships. True to their nature, each Clin contracted with a separate ship line and restricted the presence to one ship per ship line.

The Imperial Embassy itself was an ancient building. Imperial personnel soon understood Copa's distrust evident in the sophisticated measures used to monitor them. The age of the building made it more difficult to find them intermingled with centuries of evolving technology added with each renovation.

Jonaldy had never been in the embassy, that was not the Bafiktuy way. It would reveal too much about him to Copan authorities. When he arrived in system seven years ago, he was a stowaway. When the ship transferred cargo at , an orbital in the F2 Orbit, Jonaldy slipped away. During his Copan Orienteering training, he had been told about the embassy and he was given a path through Outworlder Station and a contact that helped him arrive on the Copan surface undetected.

Like so many others before it, this news broadcast yielded no new instructions.   Jonaldy's primary mission was undermining the Clinate. However, he had to keep vigilant for other instructions. He understood that the Imperium wanted the Clinate to request full membership into the Imperium. The current Emperor was a man who preferred subtlety to force.   That gave the Bafiktuy Intelligence Directive (BID) more involvement in international relations than it enjoyed under previous, more warlike emperors. Copa had vast material resources and a well-organized government. Forcing it would be difficult and lead to troubles, like it once had in Sigurd System. Jonaldy's mission was to gain control of an individual as close to the Clin as possible.

No news was good news. I need to start planning what to do after Mondennio's seduction.

Jonaldy walked out of his tenement. The afternoon shaped up to be a much better day than he had expected. The Copan binaries cast their stark light as he walked toward the one of the near bus stations. As he turned the corner, he ran into a uniformed man. He tried to keep the man from falling, more out of reaction to the uniform than a desire to help him recover.

The man still hit the ground firmly. With Jonaldy bent over him failing in his attempt to stop his fall, the officer grabbed Jonaldy by the arm and pulled him to the ground. Jonaldy did his best not to react as he had been trained. The clear afternoon gave plenty of witnesses. Those around Jonaldy pretended not to notice anything.

The officer spun quickly, pinning Jonaldy to the ground with his face on the sidewalk. The pin was incomplete, and Jonaldy knew he could break it and escape. Instead, he continued to resist acting on his training for fear of jeopardizing his mission. He was so close to his tenement that it would not be hard for the Atakadaro to find him if he escaped.

"Sir, I'm terribly sorry. I was in a hurry to get to work and did not see you when I came round the corner."

"Is that so? I see that guy over there. He was probably your lookout. Decided you were going to have a little fun at my expense?" The officer bound Jonaldy's hands, but not tightly enough that Jonaldy could not slip out of them — the advantage of big wrists and small hands.

"No, Sir. I don't know who you are talking about." The fear in Jonaldy's voice was partly performance. As he said it, he realized he was carrying thousands of knoerzers in untraced currency and a weapon. He was in serious trouble if the officer searched him. Not just for the weapon, but Unnamed were limited by law to two months wages on their person at any time. He had years of wages for an Unnamed, barely pocket change in his Imperial life.

"Right, you don't know what I'm talking about." The uniformed officer began searching him. The money cards were the first things he found.

Jonaldy had to think quickly as the cards came out of his pocket. He tried glancing over his shoulder.

"You are a fortunate man, Sir. Somebody must have just dropped those cards moments before and you slipped on them." He wished he could wave a hand and make the officer believe the farce. He hoped greed would be enough.

As Jonaldy lay there, the officer was silent for a beat. "I don't know who you are, but it would take a lot more than a few hundred knoerzers to buy me off."

Jonaldy thought quickly. *I pocketed 5,700 knoerzers, and the cards reported their own value.* The officer knew what he had. Jonaldy expected that the officer would arrest him with one of the cards and keep the rest.

"I would never dare to buy you off with a couple hundred knoerzers. Whoever lost the cards would probably pay a considerable reward to have them returned — spent or not."

He hoped the officer did not start thinking it was some internal affairs sting operation. Atakadaro was aggressive enough about policing its lower-classed officers that this sort of operation was not unknown. That gave him an idea.

"Of course, you know better than to let anybody buy you off, Officer. You did a great job seeing through the scheme. What's your name?"

"Officer Jony Guezaler. Who are you?"

"Inspector Captain Rowenzal." He hoped there were such an individual. "We've been cracking down on bribery in this district and you showed the sort of restraint we weren't expecting here. That man that was across the street is my partner." He really hoped that person was long gone.

"What?"

"You can unbind me now. Excellent work. With that money in your hands, you stood to be a very wealthy young man. Married?"

"No, Sir." Guezaler sounded confused.

Jonaldy had to move quickly before the confusion ebbed away. "We're trying a new policy. If an officer refuses the bribe, then we let him keep it. If he accepts the bribe, then he goes to the Encarcer. If the bribe is sizable, we also recommend an immediate promotion. You're an officer now. By week's end you should receive orders making you a Corporal."

"Corporal? I don't believe it."

"You can believe it Officer Guezaler. Would some street slug make such a bold statement?" The big lie is always more believable. It had been a while since he was able to throw around the sort of authority he had in the Imperium — real or imagined.

"Of course not." Guezaler stood up and helped Jonaldy to his feet. He removed the binders.

Jonaldy rubbed his wrists. "How do you spell your full name?"

"J-O-N-Y G-U-E-Z-A-L-E-R"

"Is this your normal beat?"

"Yes, Sir."

"Fine." He took Guezaler's hand with the knoerzers and lifted it up. "Not all of this was bribery money." He picked out a small currency card and pocketed it. "You seem like a nice enough kid. I'll not only recommend the promotion but try to have your assignment changed to somewhere better. These are dangerous streets."

"Thank you, Sir."

"I'm going to be keeping my eye on you, young man. I may even need your help in the future. I'm not actually Internal Affairs. I work with the undercover Atakadaro, but I'm on loan to the rats. I can do a lot for you, Guezaler. But, I expect you to do what I ask you to do. Understand?"

"I do. I can't believe how this is happening."

"Well, if I'm wrong you can always hunt me down and beat me to death. Fair enough?"

Guezaler laughed.

Jonaldy patted him on the shoulder and started to walk away. He called back over his shoulder, "don't spend that all in one place, Jony."

5.   Mondennio - Rowenzal Enclave

Mondennio sulked in his room for the rest of the afternoon. The binaries dipped behind an enclave a kilometer away from the Rowenzal Enclave. Sonichard lived there, with still other Rowenzals. It made dating in the neighborhood difficult for Mondennio with everybody a kissing cousin. Which was a shame since Rowenzal, NszemaNizema, Sonichard's sister was such an attractive cousin. She had just started University and already had dozens of would-be suiters.

His buzzing room intercom broke his trance. "Mondennio, Sir. Keve here." It was Prigarcoll, Keve (Rowenzal's Lieutenant)Keve Prigarcoll, the family's lieutenant. Father has to be really bothered to send him.

"What's up?" Keve was on the lowest rung of named citizens, his father having served Rowenzal well enough that Keve was elevated from the Unnamed when he reached age 30 — the age of majority.

"Mind if I come up? I would much rather prefer not discussing certain matters via the intercom."

"Sure, meet me in my anteroom."

It took a couple minutes for Keve to arrive, not that Mondennio minded waiting. He guessed where the conversation was going to go, and half-wished Keve had not called in the first place.

"I hope you do not mind. I have taken the liberty of disabling your missing slate. I did not think you would want anybody to access your more personal data."

Mondennio was taken aback. He expected Keve to explain to him why he should go to the party. "Thank you. I hadn't thought of that."

"Very well. Should I have a new one acquired up for you, or would you rather go purchased one for yourself?"

"You know me, I'll buy it."

"Then, I will have your driver bring the car around. You'll need your slate for tonight's celebration."

There it was. He knew his father sent Keve to make him go to the party. "Wait. No. I'm not going to go now, so the slate can wait another day."

Keve continued without missing a beat. "Yes, Sir. Do you think that is entirely wise? What I mean to say is, you should make a point of reacquiring a slate as soon as practicable. Also, I think your father would want you to go."

"Yes, he does. He thinks not going sends the wrong message. I'm not sure I agree with him. Besides, it will be agonizing to be there with everybody thinking that I'm a cheater. It's better that I stay here."

"Pardon me for interjecting here. Your father has endured numerous twists of Providence. And, he managed to keep Sept Rowenzal thriving.

I should say he managed well following his advice. Mightn't that course of action be the more prudent?"

"You mean for one so young as myself? That's your way of telling me I'm an idiot. I understand."

"Not at all, Sir. Your father benefits from years of trial-and-error. It would be unwise to not enjoy the fruits of his labor before you pick your own."

"I see. So father's the idiot and I would be an idiot if I did not follow his advice. Very nice."

Keve stood in silence with the perpetual smirk that drove Mondennio insane. *It's as if he thinks he's better than us. We put him in his place, he should remain in it.*

"What you're really trying to say is that a guilty man would stay away. Wouldn't an innocent person want to stay away until the problem passed?"

"In all the years of watching your father, I've never seen a real problem that just goes away. Much better to confront it head on. Crises call for bold action, after all. There appears to be a crisis afoot now."

Always Audacity was the Rowenzal motto, inherited from the ancient clan founder. *He has a point. I should not hide since I am actually innocent. To hide would suggest my guilt.* "Send the car around. I'll go ahead and replace the slate."

"Very well. I will call to remind the shop not to close until after you have departed."

Chapter 3

6. Veneza - Tenement

A baby cried. The piercing, painful, irritating noise of a baby that never stopped. Veneza woke to the sound of a crying baby a few times most nights. The baby always woke her up in the morning. The cries were so consistent, she stopped using an alarm clock.

Thank Liberty it's not mine. She stretched as she crawled out of bed. Her apartment building was subdivided into thirty bachelorette apartments. The landlord had strict rules about occupancy. The building was supposed to house only women, no children and no men. Men were expected to depart by binary set, or 7.50 cycles; whichever was earlier. The lease agreement explained the need for the Clin to raise virtuous women. *Women who ended up being used as whores for the named.*

A few of her neighbors let their boyfriends stay regardless, benefiting from poor enforcement. Others used the small walk-in closets as nurseries. As much as Veneza tried to focus on her studies, sometimes her boyfriend, Aradames Hezaley stayed later, too. Some times, too late.

7. Mondennio - Large Pan Hotel

Mondennio stepped out of his car in front of the Large Pan Hotel. His driver patiently waited for him to walk a few steps forward so he could close the door behind him. Mondennio did not need to tell him to wait — the last driver had made that mistake and paid for it with his life.

The foot traffic was heavy as scores of fellow exam takers and other university students celebrated. The exam marked the last year of school for some, giving the returning third-year students a chance to reinforce networks they would need through the year and afterward. It also gave them a chance to view promising first-year students. Mondennio originally planned to spend the evening looking for a young co-ed to *mentor* through the year.

Now, he hoped to just keep his head up. Nobody called him after the exam, but he knew that the rumors would be well-spread by now. He yielded to his father's and Keve's advice that he present himself regardless.

He carefully made his way into the Hotel, and worked his way through the foyer. There were more first- and second-year students than he expected, a "bumper crop," as Sonichard said. Mondennio made his way to three classmates he finally saw standing by the corner.

"There's the cheater himself. How are you holding up there, Mondennio?" Braymondre Jons of Clin Parxon said.

"I'm not sure what you mean about cheating." He held up his hand, "I know what the rumors are. Some proctor thought he could distract me by pulling my slate out of my bag and pulling me out of class."

"I gather he succeeded. Wearing makeup to hide the bruising?"

"Funny. No, they managed to save the face. I guess they have a rule against striking a student in the face. A funny way of showing us they honored us. It would make us look ugly or something. I think they may have cracked a rib, and it's a good thing they did, too. Or else I would have actually finished the thing. Maybe I would have gotten top score."

A few chuckles. "Only because you cheated."

"Wow. You've known me since primary. Since when did you ever know me to cheat?"

"Now I don't know. Maybe you just never got caught before."

"You should know me better, Braymondre. I seem to recall I saved you from having to take Clinate Economics in first year."

Braymondre dropped his smile.

Mondennio patted him on the shoulder. "You all know me. I don't care what you think you've heard. I'm actually rather shocked you thought me capable. I'm going to go get a drink."

Mondennio broke away from the trio to continue his rounds. The people in the room felt cooler than normal. Beyond Braymondre, nobody raised the allegation. That only convinced Mondennio that they were talking about it. The underclassmen were more cordial because they were likely uninformed.

Mondennio hoped to take advantage of that and at least ask one co-ed out before the evening was over — or keep asking co-eds out until one said yes.

An hour later, the opportunity presented itself. Mondennio approached a supple looking red-head. "Care to dance?"

She nodded, and they went to the dance floor. Not long after they started dancing, Mondennio felt a tap on his shoulder. He stopped dancing as he turned and saw Juank.

"Sir, how are you tonight?" Mondennio said.

"I do much better if you let my cousin here go." Juank Clin-Khotaigra waved the red-head off. Mondennio watched her pleasant smile turn and walk through the crowd. "What are you doing here?"

"Braymondre asked the same question."

"I didn't ask who asked you. This is my party, and only those who either finished the test are invited."

"What about the underclassmen? How will Hendezal recover when you take over? Besides, it's not your party. It's Clin-Khotaigra. I have about as much a right to be here as you. I seem to recall you left the exam fairly early."

"Don't flatter yourself, Mondennio. Better education yields faster results. Do you think the outcome of that test changes who I am?"

"That's not how the exam is supposed work" Mondennio and Juank both knew that leaving an adaptive test early meant the student failed. Named or Not, Mondennio knew not to antagonize Juank too much.

"You only made it as far as you did because you cheated, Mondennio."

"Alleged, Juank. All the proctor has is my slate. He pulled it out of my bag. Surprise! Students forget and keep their slates in their bags when they're taking an exam."

"Except, Mondennio, the proctor not only swears by what he saw, there's a video recording that shows you consulting it several times."

A video? There's no way that could have happened. "That's a lie. There can't be a recording to a non-existent event."

"We'll just have to wait and see, then, won't we? Such on-events have a way of being documented." Juank's voice scarcely carried over the crowd noise as Mondennio walked away, but not his laugh.

*   *   *

8.   Veneza - Large Pan Lake

Veneza enjoyed riding in Aradames' car. Her status denied her the right to own a car. She always took a risk when she rode in it with him. If Atakadaro found her they might arrest her, except Aradames promised to protect her. Despite their earlier scare, she felt comfortable with him.

Aradames brought Veneza to a romantic spot near the Large Pan Lake. Kinnet had one natural lake, two hectacres in size, a few kilometers East of the University. The Founders named it because of its uniform depth. When she was a teenager, Veneza learned that the Small Pan was filled in a century after settlement. She always thought it would be a beautiful place to get married. Whether Aradames would think so was something she would have to work on.

As they approached, Veneza saw hundreds of people, all dressed in formal wear. She had thought he dressed up to celebrate their anniversary, then realized she was not dressed well at all.

"Ardy, what's going on? I'm not dressed formally enough. I don't feel comfortable."

"Nonsense, Veneza. You look fine. Nobody will even notice." He held her by the elbow as usual, but she noticed his pace was more persistent. She thought about pulling away, but after their recent scare, she felt she should humor him.

"Did you know it was going to be this crowded tonight?"

"Of course. This party's been planned for a long time."

"Then why didn't you tell me? I would have at least put on a better dress."

"We're here now, so it doesn't matter anymore. Right? Besides you're beautiful."

"I don't feel comfortable, and I'm upset you didn't tell me."

"You said you liked surprises. You'll have fun."

They walked into the hotel lobby, which had large doors opened to the ballroom within. What bothered her more were the Imperial banners and Copan Clinate flags that flanked each entrance together. Her good mood continued to fade. *He avoided me for weeks after I told him the news, only to invite me to this? Has he learned nothing in the year we've dated?*

"Happy anniversary." He smiled, confident that he had remembered an important day.

That took her off guard. "Wait. This is our anniversary?"

"Yes. Remember? You were at the monument, protesting something. I stood at the back of the crowd and listened. Afterwards, I asked you out. We went to that rustic pizza shop."

"Ardy, I was protesting the Imperium."

"I thought you hated the Clinate."

"Both, Ardy. I hate both. The Clinate has subjugated its citizens for hundreds of years. It has reduced people like me to mere line items on an inventory. If you're not from a named family, like you are, then you're chattel."

"Like me? Veneza, I thought you liked the Imperium. If you don't like the Clinate so much, then how could you not then like the Imperium?"

"Have you not listened to a word I said?"

"Of course I have."

The look in his eye told her he was too distracted looking to focus on listening. She pulled her elbow away from his hand, nearly striking a passing waiter's tray. "I love Republicanism — the right of a people to be treated like people. The Clinate and the Imperium both despise that. They want people to obey, not be obeyed. Most of the time you're too busy staring at my necklace, or trying to find yet another way to get me into bed. I thought you might have been listening, but I'm starting to rethink that."

"It's not my fault you wear revealing shirts and have something in them to reveal."

"That's my point. You've not been listening to me. You've been oggling me. The Imperium has been working with the Clinate to completely disenfranchise us. Whatever rights I thought I might have as an unnamed are steadily eroding. We're not even married and you practically own me."

"I can't own you — you're not in my Clin. And, you know we can't get married."

"So, what is all this then? I thought maybe you'd embrace Republicanism. Fight against the inhumanity. I thought you wanted to get rid of the Clin structure if that's what keeps us from being able to get married." Her voice attracted the attention of some nearby guests.

Aradames looked around uncomfortably. "Veneza, don't make a scene. I thought you knew what we were about. I didn't think you took that

Republican clap trap at face value. You knew we were just a thing. I mean, I figured when I got married that I could set you up somewhere nice and we could keep it up."

"Just a thing? I'm just a whore to you? Liberty help whomever you end up marrying. She'll contract a pox. I loved you!"

"Wow, Veneza. What the hell's gotten into you? I didn't know you were this clueless. You're unnamed and not in my Clin. There's no way on Copa I'd be allowed to marry you."

"I thought I was pregnant! You told me to get rid of it so we could stay together. You bring me to a party celebrating some Clinate-Imperial solidarity. I hate both! I hate you!"

She backed away as he came closer, trying to get her under control. "Stay away. You come near me ever again, I'll feed you your balls."

She ran out of the ballroom, the tears blinding her. She was unaware of the eyes on her.

Now I know why I've never gotten over hating you, Juank. Mondennio turned to look back to Juank, when somebody bumped him from his blind side. He felt her falling down and reached out to grab her. He managed to stop her fall by embracing her. Her makeup was streaked with tears. When Mondennio looked into her eyes they shot back angrily.

He though he recognized her, but the lights were low. "I'm sorry, Miss. Are you all right?"

"Don't touch me, Pig." She shoved him away and stormed out of the hotel.

He looked the way she had come, and saw the other party going on. He wished he were at that party, where rumors of his cheating were unknown. He grabbed a drink off a waiter's tray as it passed and gulped it down.

Veneza felt embarrassed by being used by one man and saved by being hugged by another. Her eyes cleared when she got outside the hotel. She took a beat to regain her bearing and composure.

She turned left on George Lendfarg Street and started crying again. As she took the return path back to her apartment, she thought of how beautiful the binary setting was. She arrived happy that Aradames had come to his senses since his outburst three weeks before. How fickle fortunes of a day are. She walked briskly, trying to get home before anybody noticed her face. *He completely embarrassed me. He used me. All this time I thought I was bringing him around. He said all the right things, or did I just hear all the right things?*

She tried to think back to their conversations, to see if he had misrepresented himself, or if she had misunderstood him. She remembered their first date. It was the fourth anniversary of her revelation. Being unnamed, she finished primary school, then began a trade school. The Clinate wanted her to be a nurse because they said she had a heart for people — so said the aptitude test results. She went to their nursing school, but she discovered a special library that did not check familial status. She discovered a trove of books that she poured over into the late hours.

The books woke her up. The tears stopped, she smiled. *They wouldn't teach me, but I learned. I got my own secondary education. Now I'm in their University. Aradames is just a product of his corrupt little world. He is blind to the suffering all around him. He only cares about himself. Maybe he cares about his family. Wow. He wasn't even married yet, and he was planning his infidelity. How could I have been so blind? Love is blind. I can't let that happen again.*

"I won't let that happen again. To me or anybody else. We must have a republic." She turned left onto Karl Street and the remaining five kilometer walk.

Mondennio was shocked momentarily by the woman's reaction to his stopping her fall. For the rest of the evening, Mondennio roamed the crowd congratulating friends, drinking, and doing his best to dispel rumors. At 9.00 cycles, he walked out of the Hotel. Because spending too much time around so many people tired him, he always chose to leave parties early. He typically used the extra time to study. He felt the early hours of the morning were when parties tended to become a place of hooligans. It scarcely occurred to him that he no longer had another meaningful exam to study for.

As his car pulled away, Mondennio pulled out his new slate that he had bought on the way to the party. He turned it on and started tapping to read up on the news. He chose a fairly standard model, unlike his peers who bought the more fashionable ones. His mother, Kayera, would have applauded his frugality.

What was it Juank said? Mondennio tried to feel through the alcohol induced fog. *Non-events have a way of happening. That's not quite it. What was he getting at?*

As the car pulled its way into the Northern neighborhoods, he put his slate away. Nothing eventful happened since he arrived at the party two cycles before. He tried to rest, but his mind continued to nag on Juank's words. *He was trying to tell me that evidence can be fabricated.*

He took out his slate again. When Keve learned Mondennio's slate was in somebody else's possession, he had its accesses to the cloud cut off. That reduced its value to only what was physically on the slate, and Mondennio kept most of the data off the slate. When Mondennio bought his new one and connected it, the slate became a virtual mirror copy of Mondennio's previous one.

It makes no sense that they would fabricate my cheating just to take my slate. There are a number of ways to gain access without touching it. But, if Juank was right, then they would want to plan evidence on my slate to prove my guilt.

He pulled up the cloud's administrative interface, and accessed the 'Events' tab. Activity showed the system was accessed in an attempt to retrieve all information the slate had access to. That sort of mass data withdraw signaled the cloud to deny access without an administrative override. Not long after, Keve disconnected the slate's cloud access.

Mondennio identified the beat when his slate was seized. The proctor immediately accessed it when he picked it up, leaving a tangible marker. *That's not a random check. He specifically tapped up an application. He knew where he was looking. It was hidden in a category of applications he rarely accessed.*

He scaled back the event map to cover everything since he switched it off that morning. He remembered leaving at 2.50 cycles to ensure he would make the exam. He identified his last access of 2.45 cycles. *What's this? I could not have accessed it at 3.12 cycles. The exam started at 3.00 sharp.*

Mondennio took a deep breath and slowly breathed out. Somebody had accessed his system and downloaded exam information while he took the exam. He texted Keve to contact him the next day.

Chapter 4

9.   Klocards - Tenement

He woke up feeling a little queasy. It was a common problem with those who spent too much time in space. Spacecraft had noticeable fluctuations in their artificial gravity, where an astro like Copa did not. Janhas Klocards spent most of his adult life on spacecraft, so those fluctuations were natural to him. Having lived planetside for a few years, the queasiness had largely subsided. The only time it still bothered him was when he woke up. The light from the tight Copa binary stars broke over the horizon as he stretched awake. Another day in paradise.

He went down the stairs to the basement of his townhouse. The girya awaited his three-times-a-week battle against inactivity. As he prepared his mind for the warm-up squats, he thought back to how it began. Once he established himself in Kennet, Copa's capital city, he started finding assorted pieces of largely junk and ferreted them to the basement. Eventually, he built a small cage with weights to work out.

He had not been Klocards all his life, which also took some effort to remember. That was his "born again" name he acquired from Podigoto. He was Danel Bophendze, a Master Chief Sergeant in His Imperial Postal Marines (exiled). Taking on the new persona helped him flee his collapsing career and set up a new life here. Smuggling himself into Copa had not been easy. Podigoto's new identity was a perfect fit for a man of modest means who expected things to come easy. Bophendze, er, Klocards had no intent to take things easy.

$- You have to let Bophendze fade into history, Klocards. Smee's now comfortable voice nagged. At least Smee had the decency to use the last name. Bophendze hated Janhas. It sounded like a girl's name.

Smee, it's not that easy, and I know you're trying to drill it out in my sleep. I keep waking up with a headache. Stop pestering me.

$- Klocards. If you keep trying to remember who you were, you'll get yourself caught. And me, too.

What? Five years you've been repeating yourself. It's getting old. Look, are you going to let me lift in piece?

$- That's another thing. You're a scientist, a hyperspatial engineer, to be exact. Not Mr. Imperium. I don't care if you think people have bought the middle-aged desk jockey trying to keep young. If they saw you squatting, um, 10 firkins, they'd have you arrested. They wouldn't buy that you're not an anthorph, despite the genetic results. Besides, nobody else on this rock knows what an anthorph is.

Bophendze — Janhas Klocards — managed to tune Smee out as he continued his warm-up. Something in the routine released some hormone or other that seemed to block the nerve receptors. *You'd think she'd think a way around that by now,* he mused. When Smee was being a nag, Klocards stopped thinking of him as a he and assumed he was a she but with a deep voice. Smee the she. *She's probably saying, 'I heard that,' but I can't hear her.*

The routine took little more than an hour, with the cool down. He concealed the equipment, leaving them to look like silly junk belonging to a silly scientist named Klocards. *Ten firkins, even on a 1 gee planet. Not bad for an old fart.*

Refreshed after exercise, Klocards followed one of his more predictable routes to work. This time of year made the path worth it, the tree leaves turned assorted vibrant colors. Copa was an older system, so few residents knew whether the various trees were indigenous here or imported. Smee swore the maples were native, but the others were imported. He went right through the park, down the low ramp and up again on the other side.

He passed this way after most workouts during this time of year. The park had a few curved paths that he thought helped discover surveillance. There was the tall monument dedicated to the Founder, Janhas Clin-Robacker. It had eight sides with gothic arches on each side and a central spire nearly one-hundred feet high. When he had only been on the planet a few months, a tour guide commented that Robacker was fearless and ruthless; and told Klocards that Janhas should be proud to share his name, especially since he was a foreigner. The incident shocked Klocards. The disappearance of the Unnamed tour guide was not noticed by Copan security, the Atakadaro.

Robacker established Copa when he concealed the jump route to Copa long enough to establish a strong corporate presence. Failure to disclose routes carried a high penalty during the Emergence, or the Fleeing, Klocards heard the natives call it. He just saw Robacker and the others who formed the Clinate as a bunch of thieves who discovered an odd binary system and profited by persuading simple people to move there.

But he still enjoyed walking by the mausoleum. It reminded him of what he was trying to do — bring down a corrupt system.

Rowenzal Enterprises had the facilities and the contracts that gave Klocards the resources and cover he needed to do his work. Smee helped him gain access to Rowenzal by hacking into the company's inferior computer system. Even as a miniaturized, embedded AI, Smee had little difficulty on Copa when it came to hacking systems. As a result, Klocards worked on an Ultra Secret contract for one of the five Clin families. That kept Rowenzal's managers from snooping too much into his business, and the prestige of the Clin representation should keep Rowenzal from inquiring. Smee ensured the Clin had no knowledge or insight into the contract, either. Secrecy being what it was. The contract came with a modest budget, and the occasional assistant that annoyed Bophendze.

What he thought made the research more secretive was that it was housed next to the University's main campus in a building named ".". It looked like it was a part of the campus, as close as it was to one of the University's administrative buildings. The UKP building housed a hobbled AI. Instead of being hooked up to a vast data array and the Network, the AI was attached to a non-networked storage system. Lobotomized.

An Atakadaro investigator came around once to discuss what he was working on. Smee told Klocards to keep saying, "you're not cleared to know that," and it worked. The Atakadaro investigator might have tried to find out some other way, but just as likely failed.

The contract allowed Klocards to research the hyperspace array. Smee ensured his cover told the story of a hyperspacial engineer who had lost his wife and children when a ship ghosted and never emerged. He emigrated to Copa when he lost funding in the Imperium and found a way to get the Clinate to fund research in de-ghosting. Everybody knew that de-ghosting was impossible; but like some ancient quest for a lost city entrepreneurs never turned down a chance to find a way. What made it secret was how it was being funded. Even Klocards did not know how the funding really worked. Knowing Smee, it probably involved collecting remainders of funding from other projects. With the funding, however, he had to hire the occasional assistant and provide suitably vague reports.

Klocard's friend Litovio proved de-ghosting was possible when he saved the *Imperial Cruiser Raykomara*. Imperium scientists refused to accept his solution because the AIs refused the solution. But, the solution saved a 140-man crew and Bophendze, and set him on a course that brought him to Copa and made him Klocards. Having been a senior Imperial Postal Marine, Janhas Klocards was the most lethal hyperspatial engineer in Terradoma. He just needed Smee to help him with the math and engineering.

10.   Jonaldy - Stinieles Enclave

Jonaldy was the only passenger to step off the bus at this stop, but several loaded on after he got off. He was finally numb to the indignity. Private transportation was restricted to the Named Families. Jonaldy was from an aristocratic family in the Imperium; he was accustomed to more privilege than even the Clin families enjoyed in this backwater. It made it more difficult to sneak around, and Jonaldy routinely changed his bus cards to avoid leaving any obvious trail should the Atakadaro be looking for one. He accepted the indignity for the greater ideal of Pax Imperium.

Jonaldy's persona on Copa was a low-ranked native, making it a greater challenge. Being one of the Unnamed gave him no citizen rights, just like most of the rest of the people living in Copa. He could not even claim his Imperial citizenship if he got in trouble. The risk was worth the virtual anonymity being Unnamed gave. Unknown and uncared for. It had been no small feat for him to learn to grovel and yield like a commoner. Showing proper deference to Named Families was difficult for him after a full life of privilege. This trip gave him a chance to relish his past life. But, he ensured that his status was enough to allow him to ride public transportation.

The bus stop was a mile from his destination—an added measure of security. He walked a circuitous route, looking for anybody who might be following him. All of his time on Copa, nobody ever followed him. *Precautions are not there for your convenience, they are there for your safety,* he remembered from training. At this time of night, foot traffic was virtually non-existent, and there were even fewer cars. He walked past several enclaves, each with their eighteen foot high masonry walls— separating the privileged from the poor.

For all its stratification, Copa had one saving grace. The Clinate accepted the occasional foreigner when that foreigner provided a benefit or might help them understand the Imperium. Stinieles Kerwans was one such citizen—a former Imperial citizen who thought he could escape his past. His contribution was so significant, the Clinate even gave him Named status.

Before Jonaldy left the Imperium, he was given Stinieles' full dossier. Jonaldy memorized it—word for word. He could even recall the odd pencil marks. He memorized all 173 dossiers rather than bring them to Copa. The Bafiktuy would not let that information out of its hands. The original copies remained within the Imperium in one of the few ultra-secret libraries.

Stinieles emigrated from the Imperium as soon as routes were established. He was part of the legate that represented the Ninhursaga Shipping during its negotiations with Clin Kacaubant. Throughout the negotiations, he signaled to Kacaubant his desire to stay on Copa. The Imperium encouraged its own to emigrate—the better to erode a society from within. Jonaldy thought Copa knew the risk and was therefore rationally skeptical; though at times its security force seemed quite irrational.

During the negotiations, Stinieles had undermined Ninhursaga's position with the Clinate so he could be the liaison. Toward the end of negotiations, the Kacaubant invited him to settle on Copa. In exchange, he gladly gave up his company's secrets. He also divulged what he could about the Imperium. Clin Kacaubant benefited so much from his defection that they granted him

Named status and a job that required little and offered little more. Jonaldy respected Stinieles' cunning while despising how he exercised it. Stinieles Kerowans imagined he was magically escaping his past.

Tonight, Jonaldy was going to bring Stinieles back to reality.

The binaries had set as Jonaldy arrived at Kerowans' Enclave. Jonaldy and his fellow travelers prepared for this night over the past nine months. Stinieles' groundsmen avoided trimming shrubs in one area, helping to conceal the point where Jonaldy would scale the wall. Others weakened the anti-personnel devices on top of the wall at the top of his climb — just enough so the enclave's security would not notice. Jonaldy dropped into the compound unmolested.

He quietly made his way toward Stinieles' office. As expected, Stinieles sat at his desk. *Finishing a bit of the day's makework before focusing on family?* The light from the office dimly lit the patio through its glass doors. Stinieles' back was to those glass doors because he trusted their protection. They had a familiar squeak that warned of their opening. Jonaldy pulled out a small remote that silently released the electronic lock. The hinges had been oiled that morning specifically to avoid betraying Jonaldy's entrance.

Jonaldy moved before Stinieles could notice his entry. He pulled out a cloth and smothered Stinieles until he passed out. Stinieles slumped forward and banged his head on his desk. *Old techniques, old tools*, Jonaldy thought as he secured the office's inner door. He bound and gagged him.

A few beats later, Stinieles regained consciousness and looked at Jonaldy. Jonaldy relished the look in his face — betrayal and surprise — while Jonaldy maintained his own stone face of professionalism. He watched as Stinieles assessed his situation. The silence helped drive home Jonaldy's control over the situation.

The gagged mouth barely let him breath. The tethers on his wrists and ankles ensured he would not be getting up. Stinieles struggled for a moment. Jonaldy quickly tired of the spectacle. He pulled out a syringe and injected him with a thiopental derivative.

"That will help you relax, Stiny. Don't worry. I hope you realize I haven't killed you." He watched as the chemical mellowed Stinieles. "Though, if you try to alert your guards, then you will find yourself — and your lovely family — dead. The degree of your compliance sets the terms for their longevity."

Stinieles nodded.

A few beats passed until Jonaldy was satisfied. He removed Stinieles' gag. "Stiny, or should I call you 'Spanky?' You've done quite well for yourself here. We are pleased. Very pleased. I suppose you know by now that you and I have something in common. A friend of mine told me you once asked for our help."

Again, Stinieles nodded. Stinieles slowly scanned the room with his eyes; expecting that Jonaldy would not notice.

"I see. You do remember. Let me see if I do. You had a rival? Wanted that promotion to impress that woman half your age, as I recall. Now, she's in this house with your brood of three lovely children. She's quite committed to you. You can trust me on that. No infidelity."

"You're following my family?"

No threats of retaliation. He knows who he is dealing with. "I see we're going to get along. Neither of us wants to waste time. Straight to business. That's our motto. Eh?" Jonaldy patted Stinieles on the knee with his pointed finger.

"You slipped out of the Imperium without so much as a change of address. We did a lot for you, but what did you do for us in return? Tried to give us the slip. Notice how well you were able to secure emigration here? Did you think you got that by yourself?" Jonaldy hoped doubt would set in. *How much have I secured my own position even here?* He hoped Stinieles was thinking. Keep believing you are Bafiktuy's man. Make my life easier. "We were there every step of the way. Even the transport captain knew to look the other way."

Jonaldy looked at his wristband. It reported status on a few monitoring devices scattered around the house some time before. Nobody was coming, so he remained confident. He neutralized the one listening device that he expected Stinieles was hoping would provide him aid.

"Of course we're following your family. We went through so much trouble to help you have one, the least we could do is check on our investment. You see, they are not so much yours as they are ours." He canted his head toward the door. "They are here because we let them be here. No matter where you've gone, we are there. Of course we're going to keep your family in our thoughts."

"You did not tell me what you want." There was no hint of threat or fear in his voice.

"You see? Straight to the point. You have gotten more confident these past few years. I suppose employment and prestige will do that. Or perhaps that fine young specimen upstairs? We have simple requests. I'm here to tell you that the interest on your debt to us has grown with your absence. The debt was pretty steep before, but it has accrued some interest." He let his voice trail off. "Well, you'll be providing us quite a few services for a while to pay it down. Let's just leave it at that."

Stinieles said, "You can't be that naive. Just because they let me into the higher echelons of society does not mean they want me in their government. Even though I'm Named, I've got a trivial job as it is working on exam administration."

"Oh, Spanky, er, Stiny." Jonaldy's head wagged. "Your job is not as trivial as you make it out to be. It is exactly what we wanted it to be. It does not have to be a big job to be significant."

Stinieles looked dumbfounded. Jonaldy felt it was safe enough, so he removed the wrist restraint nearest the intercom. If Stinieles wanted to call the guards, this was his chance. Jonaldy had disconnected the intercom, but Stinieles would not know that until he tried.

Instead, Stinieles used his free hand to rub the part of his head that hit his desk when he passed out. *He knows who he is dealing with. Stiny is one cool character, as the dossier said.*

"In fact, your job just so happens to be very important to me right now. You do what I ask, and I'll report you were a very good boy. I want you to help me drive a wedge between a boy and his family."

Stinieles chuckled. "That won't do you any good. Driving a wedge might work in the Imperium, but not on Copa. Especially a named family — relationships are essential. That's what I like about Copa, they aren't as mercenary to their own families as the Imperium."

"You know what a Clin is, Stiny? It used to stand for a contract line item number. This society is still very commercial at its base, they've just forgotten how commercial. It's all wrapped up in what contract you belong to. You know as well as I do the only ones allowed to marry outside of a 'contract' are the Clin families themselves. They do that when it is advantageous to both families. These yokels have deluded themselves into thinking that blood is thicker here than anywhere else. They're still competitive, they just veil it." He shook his finger, "Just watch. The right man will crack that delusion and reveal the competitive spirit that will bring this little backwater into the Imperium."

"I know you're not that stupid. Copa was never a part of the Imperium, or any of the earlier pan-Terran governments. You may call it 'returning them to the fold,' but we both know it's a bald power grab."

Jonaldy smiled slightly. He knew Stinieles was dedicated only to Stinieles — or more correctly "Team Stinieles" with that hot little minx of his and their little brood. To him, blood was thicker than loyalty to his homeland, past or present. As long as he thought he could keep his family advantaged he would continue to do what Jonaldy wanted.

"Like I said — we're both smart businessmen. You're not fooled by my market ploy. But, I have my intentions. You have your orders." He released Stinieles' other hand, and motioned for him to remove the leg restraints. The final test. "There's this student, Mondennio Rowenzal, who has come up on disciplinary charges."

"Mondennio? That came up in today's meeting. He cheated on his promotion exam. They all cheat. They're really only concerned that he got caught cheating. The customary penalty is not being allowed to take the test for a couple years."

"Now see that? Expecting a young lad to cheat. Competitive to the end, they are. I don't want him disqualified. I understand the actual regulation calls for his expulsion and a permanent ban on future attempts at the exam — not the customary slap on the wrist. Call it sending a signal to all the little vipers they had better cheat more discreetly."

"You realize that will destroy his future?"

"Quite right, I do. This is not about poor Mondennio, Stiny. This is about us, you and my friends. Are you going to repay the Bafiktuy for what you owe us? Or, are we going to repossess our property?" His pointed finger and eyes both went upstairs, where Stinieles' family awaited their loving father and husband. As Stinieles started to rise, Jonaldy held up his hand.

"Don't try to be indignant now. You're not that sort of man. And, you know I'd kill you before any of your guards could come to your aid. I'm leaving anyway. I have a friend keeping an eye on Mondennio. Show me you're loyal to the Bafiktuy and do what you're told, and we'll continue to be good friends."

After a short pause, Stinieles spoke up. "There's not much I can do in this matter. By law, it's being handled by the University. I believe the professor responsible for the honor code violation is Skuriat Giedaz. He's the one who will reach a recommendation."

Jonaldy held up his hands in mock surprise. "Of course. I should have known. Well, I'm sure you'll accept any recommendation he may advance — however severe." He stood up and smiled. "I think you understand. Good night. Don't get up, I'll show myself out." Jonaldy left.

11.   Mondennio - Rowenzal Enclave

The binaries had yet to rise the morning after. Despite getting home late, years of waking early ensured Mondennio would be up by 2 cycles. There were ten cycles in a day, divided in 100 beats. At this time of year, the sun was usually not up until after 2 cycles. As he awoke, he still felt the hollow feeling that came over him the night before. Has it not been a full day yet?

Despite his bravado the night before, the more he thought about what happened yesterday the more Mondennio felt his world implode. His friends' support buoyed his spirits at the party, but they sank now. He sat on the edge of his bed for several beats, staring blankly at the floor.

He eventually got dressed and headed downstairs. He entered the informal dining room and sat down, oblivious to the bustle of servants. They brought breakfast, and he began to eat mechanically.

Keve walked in. "Mondennio, Sir. I got your text last night, but I don't understand it. You might have been a little under the weather?"

The annual event carried a reputation of debauchery that showed up on the morning's social feeds. Mondennio pointed at an image of Sonichard semi-nude. "You could say that, Keve. I did still manage to leave the party early enough. Um, maybe 9 cycles?"

Keve made a show of looking aghast at the image on Mondennio's new slate. "Well, you cannot always choose your cousins, Sir. Would you mind deciphering the code you sent me last night?"

"Right. You deactivated my slate yesterday, and I suppose I should have looked at the logs then to see what happened before."

"You were a little distracted." Keve motioned at the slate.

"Distracted? Keve, don't humor me. The longer I think about what happened yesterday, the more I seem to be losing my perspective. My point, though, is I finally looked at the logs last night, however drunk I was. Now, I know I left my slate here. At any rate, I know I did not activate it while I was in the examination room. Yet, here it is."

Mondennio handed Keve his new slate with the old slate's log data displayed. "You'll see where I marked the exam times. Scroll down to page seven and look at where I highlighted the entry. It looks like I'm accessing the slate as the proctor was laying down the ground rules. If I had been using my slate then, then it would have been pretty obvious."

"What's your point?"

"Just read through the material, you'll see that I marked."

Keve read through the electronically inked pages while Mondennio finished his breakfast. Servants emerged unnoticed to top off Mondennio's coffee and clear his place. Keve finally broke away from his reading, "I read it. I am still uncertain what you are saying."

Mondennio wiped his mouth with an edge of the white tablecloth. "I'm not drunk any more, Keve, I know I'm being coherent. That is an impossible chronology. I could not have cheated and lived up to that timeline. You're still giving me that perplexed look." He took the notebook and pointed his finger at a note. "Right there. Somebody physically uploaded a copy of the exam onto the slate — while I am in the middle of the exam. Somehow somebody stole my slate, installed the exam with answers on my slate, and got it into my daybag."

"That would be a bit difficult. How do you suspect they got the slate out of the house?"

"That, Keve, I leave to you to figure out. But, the only time anybody had their hands on my daybag except for me was when the proctor reached in to retrieve it."

"Are you accusing the proctor? That will be hard to believe."

Mondennio stopped to think about that. *Proctors were typically well paid, which is why one was only a proctor once. The Clinate did not want too much wealth to accumulate. But, the wealth helped to deter bribery.* "That is a problem. It would help if we knew how the slate left the house. I mean, the real reason, not that I took it with me so I could cheat."

"If your timeline is right, Sir, then the only way for somebody to have uploaded the copy was when you were at the University. At that point, there would be very few people with access."

"Only proctors, exam authors and senior school officials. Yes. I see your point. Most of them would be viewed as above reproach. All work directly for Clin-Khotaigra, so leveling an accusation against them would be the same as leveling an accusation against the Clin itself."

"What are you going to do then, Sir? I mean, it appears to me that the Clin ordered this. Who else would have tried to pull this off?" Keve closed the slate and placed it back on the table.

Mondennio stood, tossing his napkin onto the table. "Well, there seem to be two courses of action. I could hand this over to the lawyers and let them battle it out. During that time, I would not be allowed to work at all after graduation. If I was set up under Clin direction, then the courts would just as likely side with the Clinate. Or, I could go to the University. This year's professor responsible for honor code violations is supposed to be Skuriat Giedaz. I'll show him my evidence and see if I can't get the University to drop charges."

"Should you not first speak with your father to get his advice?"

"Keve, within the year I'll be graduating. In a year when this blows over I'll be expecting a fairly substantial post. If I can't handle this matter on my own, then how should I expect to do well at the posting? No. I'll speak with Professor Giedaz on my own. If I run into trouble, then I'll consider reaching back for help."

"Perhaps you should take an attorney with you regardless? You will be leveling some significant charges. You should try to avoid slandering anybody."

"I won't be slandering anybody. I will merely point to the facts and invite Professor Giedaz to make his own conclusions. I can't slander anybody if I don't say anything beyond the bare facts I have, now can I?"

"No, Sir. I see your point. However, I should remind you the importance of not going alone or without advice."

"Thank you, Keve, I have your advice. I'm just not going to take it."

Chapter 5

12.   Veneza - University

To take a university class as an unnamed required formal sponsorship by a named family. There were few slots given to each Clin, so the rare privilege was usually extended to those few unnamed families that dedicated themselves to serve a Named family. Veneza did not belong to such a family. She did not let that stop her from getting an education.

She took the audited courses: those courses that the University offered to Named students who for one reason or another failed to get the basic education expected of a Named person. The University did not take attendance to avoid shaming those students — or their families — that neglected their education. Veneza wondered how they would react if they found out that she and a few of her unnamed friends had been abusing that essential trust to get a better-than-deserved education.

She thought the downside to the courses was that students were not allowed to ask questions of the professors. There were a few times that she thought the professor was just feeding the students propaganda. Today she was in Clin Economics, a class that explained the basic business principles that supported the Clinate system, government and financial. Named families tended to teach this to their children at a young age, though the sophistication of the class was naturally higher than that given a primary grade student.

"Adam Smith's work, The Invisible Hand, explains why it is important to maintain semi-central planning through an oligarchical framework. As we all know, that is the basis for the Clinate. It was because the rest of Humanity opted for a so-called 'market economy' that led the Founders to cede from Humanity. I advise you to read this important work as it will buttress your understanding of next week's material. Adam Smith's theories form the bedrock of our society. That is all."

So Adam Smith is a patrinfikulo. I hope he died an agonizing death.

The other students started filing out of the class through the bottom of the amphitheater. Veneza collected her daybag and jacket. She chose to head up toward the back doors, despite students for the next class starting to file in. It helped her avoid being seen too closely by the professor.

She felt something slip out of her daybag, so she bent over to pick it up. Without owning a slate or tablet, she relied on her notebooks to help her keep notes. They were not very common, and she was thankful that enough other students used one that she did not stand out. She picked up the notebook that fell out of her bag. Veneza started moving while she stood back up. After climbing the first step, she slammed into a student. Her notebook went flying as she started to fall down the stairs.

The other student caught her. Before she looked to see who it was, she felt the firm grip he had. Looking up, she recognized him.

"It's you! This is the second time you've run into me," Mondennio said.

He was the one who stopped her fall on Fiveday. "Me? You're the one who keeps knocking me down."

"Not hardly. As I remember last time, you were flying out of the hotel hoping nobody would notice you crying. This time you're slipping out of the back of class. Seems you've got a knack for running into me." He reached down and picked up her notebook, handing it to her.

He has a point, and he is a bit cute. But I am not falling for another guy now. She felt embarrassed he rescued her twice. "Thank you. I suppose I have been a bit of the aggressor here. I'm Veneza Karduil."

"No Clin? Don't worry, I won't turn you in. This school has a habit of harassing the students it does know about. Serves them right to teach a few that they don't. I'm Mondennio Rowenzal Clin Khotaigra."

"You don't have to use the whole name, you know."

"It's something they beat into us from when we are children. You should know that."

"Well, it was nice to meet you, Mondeyo, but I'm late for another class."

"It's Mondennio…"

"Rowenzal-Clin Khotaigra. Yeah, I get it. Don't you ever get tired of lugging that name everywhere you go?"

"Sometimes, but it does have some advantages."

At least he's not sizing me up like I'm lunch. That's a plus. In the end he's still one of them. I wonder if he is as brainwashed as the rest?

Veneza reached into her daybag and pulled out a flyer.

"Here. There's a rally later on. It would probably offend your sense of Clin loyalty; but it's a protest about fair representation under the law."

"You think men and women have different standards to live up to?"

"It's about the Unnamed subject not having the same legal protections as you Named citizens. How could you be so obtuse? More than seventy percent of this planet has no rights worthy of the name, and you have no clue?"

"The gap between the two is not that wide."

"Gap? It's a chasm. You don't believe me? Then come to the rally and see for yourself." Despite her challenge, she started to wish he would not show up. Ardy came to a rally or two, then came into her bed. This was too soon.

"I'll think about it. You have a specific place where you and your friends will be meeting?"

"I tell you what. Meet me at the marketplace spire a little before it starts."

"If I show up, I'll meet you there." Mondennio took the flyer from her and started to walk down the stairs.

The amphitheater had its usual boisterous students that prevented the professor from starting the class. The professor drew an air horn from his bag and gave a long blast. Veneza jumped and hurried out of the classroom.

The professor mentioned something related to foreign affairs. As she got to the door, she looked back. Mondennio had sat in his seat and pulled out his slate. She closed the door, not certain if she wanted him to be looking back or not.

13.   Mondennio - University

The next morning, Mondennio headed to school to confront his situation. He normally enjoyed the morning drive to campus. It had been two years of going back and forth, but the drive always got him excited about his future. Not today, however. Today he was going to fight for his innocence.

His driver drove the car between the campus grounds and the park to the West. Every time he passed by the mausoleum he remembered his father telling him as a child about how bold action was necessary during times of crisis. Mondennio was in crisis now, so he hoped he could be bold but subtle enough to get the charges dropped.

The car drove through the campus until it pulled up to the administrative building entrance. The driver opened the door for him. As he stepped out, he looked at the imposing entrance feeling a tinge of dread. He entered the building before doubt sent him home.

Professor Giedaz had an open-door policy, in part because he preferred not to have a secretary. Mondennio heard the rumors about why Giedaz preferred the enhanced privacy offered by having nobody track one's schedule. The professor's door was shut. Monennio knocked on the door and waited until Professor Giedaz invited him.

It took Giedaz a few beats to get to the door. Mondennio noticed a bead of sweat on the professor's forehead as the door opened. "Rowenzal? You're the last person I would expect to see now."

"Yes, Sir. However, I thought it would be better to sit down and chat about recent events. An innocent man has nothing to fear."

"I'll be the judge of that, Son." Giedaz seemed hesitant to let him in. Finally he stepped out of the door to allow Mondennio to walk in. "So let's have a chat then."

It had been a long time since Mondennio had been in the professor's office. Giedaz was his first faculty advisor, but Mondennio concluded early on the professor was not giving him good advice. Now he met with him as the honor code prosecutor.

"Thank you. I am really sorry to bother you and I know it is a bit out of the ordinary for an accused student to meet with the honor code prosecutor."

"Highly irregular, not a bit unordinary. I hope you're not here to waste my time." Giedaz sat at his desk, leaned back and touched his fingers together like a triangle. As Mondennio sat, he noticed a gold earring on the floor under Giedaz's seat. Some rumors are based in fact.

"Not at all, Professor. I'm sure you already have the proctor's side of the story. But, I don't know if — "

"Yes, well the proctor wrote an affidavit and I've had a preliminary review of the video evidence. It is irregular of you to be here. I thought you had a lot of potential, Mondennio. I hate that you've thrown it away on an exam, and over these theatrics."

"Theatrics? No, Professor Giedaz. Formal charges have not yet been brought. I've checked. So, this conversation is not prohibited. If it were you'd have told me to go away at the door. When my family's attorneys respond to the formal charges, you will learn how my slate was stolen and incriminating evidence planted."

"So you say."

"Not just me, Sir. I have logs that show that information was physically uploaded on my slate after I started the exam. Perhaps the video evidence could determine whether I was the culprit who uploaded. However, I have a feeling that whoever was sly enough to steal my slate would not have uploaded the data on video"

"Who would have done such a thing?"

"I really don't know. Naturally I was not there when it happened."

"Perhaps you paid somebody else to upload the data? You are admitting there was data on your slate illegally."

The accusation caught Mondennio off-guard. *Why isn't he being impartial?* "I'm not admitting to that. I'm suggesting that if there were illegal information on the slate somebody installed it without my permission. But, I have not seen my slate so I am only working off the logs I have. The proctor pulled it out of my daybag and I was ejected from the examination room. I have yet to personally investigate the device. I was also beaten, was that in the proctor's affidavit?"

"Yes, as was your assault."

"He told them to beat me, so of course he would say that. But, he has lower standing; so his testimony should be suspect."

"He's a proctor, Boy. There's a reason why we select him."

"Nonetheless, let me show you why I think I'm being set-up."

Mondennio explained how he arrived at his conclusion by monitoring the access logs, and how the logs exonerate him. He showed Professor Giedaz his notebook with the entry annotations.

"How do I know these aren't forged?"

"We use standard non-repudiation measures used by any Clinate system. How would we know the video footage wasn't forged?" Mondennio felt a little unsure of himself as he watched Professor Giedaz deliberate.

Professor Giedaz rose from his chair and wandered over to his office window. He parted the curtain slightly and looked out. It looked to Mondennio like Giedaz was trying to find a way out of a problem. *Does he know more about what's going on than he's telling me?*

"Mondennio, I'm sorry to have to tell you this. This really does come at an awkward time, I'm afraid. To tell you the truth, I find your evidence most compelling. Until yesterday you have proven yourself to be one of the more conscientious students I've had the privilege to teach and mentor."

Mondennio could feel the 'but' loom over him, casting a dark shadow.

"Unfortunately, there is a larger issue. I'm privy to a secret investigation into Rowenzal affairs."

"What do you mean?"

"I really don't know much of the details, Mondennio. Your family appears to be involved in some illegal activity that complicates your status. I've been told not to tell you, but I felt I needed to tell you why I cannot accept the evidence you bring before me now."

"I don't understand. Are you trying to tell me that my family is entangled in some sort of imbroglio?"

Giedaz turned back and looked at him. "I'm afraid it appears so. But, the matter is quite out of my hands. This data of yours is quite compelling, but I doubt it will be put to any use. Just between you and me, my guess is that whomever is behind this will have found a way to corrupt your event logs by now. I should have thought they would have done that before you thought to look yourself."

"You can't be serious." Mondennio's earlier anxiety gave way to fear. "You're saying the Clinate itself is involved?"

Giedaz measured his response carefully. "Mondennio, I wish I knew enough to tell you, quite honestly. I only have a scintilla of information to go on. But, applying that information to what you've shown and told me, then yes. I think the Clinate is involved."

"Well, at least you believe me. There's some solace in that."

"Not much, I'm afraid. I do find it hard to believe that the entire Clinate would target just you. Or sub-sept Rowenzal for that matter. I might be able to believe if Clin-Khotaigra were in on it. But, there's no good motive for why it would have to resort to this measure. I rather thought the Clin looked favorably on Rowenzal. It is much more readily believable that you cheated and have found some crafty way to implicate somebody else. Though, you've not shown me that you're capable of that level of deceit."

Mondennio remained silent for a few beats. *Is somebody big is going after the entire family, not just me? Maybe there's some relief in that, but that also denies me any sort of real refuge. If Clin-Khotaigra is behind this, then the whole weight of the Clinate may as well be on us.*

"So, what should I do next?" Mondennio asked.

"If I were a bookmaker, I'd bet against you. But, if it were me, I would stall. Were you to prevail in this luctation, this struggle, then you might either be able to retake the test or accept the grade as given. I might even argue that a long delay should entitle you to be given a passing answer on that last question you weren't allowed to answer. Play the martyr, so to speak. Whoever is going after your family may get what they're after and let you and Rowenzal all off the hook. Press the matter too soon and you may find yourself in the middle of it."

"What happens if I do press the matter and I'm found guilty."

"Well, cheating is pretty bad in and of itself. Depending on how things are going, then the likely consequence would be more for being caught cheating, than for the act itself."

"What? It's worse to be caught than to do the deed?"

"Actually, yes. You have to remember your history, Mondennio. How did the Founders secure our safety?"

"By stealing the route data and blinding government jump computers?"

"Exactly. So, subterfuge is one of the founding principles."

14. Klockards - Rowenzal Enterprises

Despite the secrecy surrounding his project, Klocards had to have something resembling a staff. It helped with his funding, and seemed to keep Rowenzal Enterprises from paying more than cursory attention to his work.

Despite this, Klocards developed a reputation as a difficult boss. As he walked to his lab, the fearful glances and hushed conversation confirmed he succeeded. Being difficult took some effort as he was accustomed to exhibiting leadership as a Marine. He had to fight his ingrained tendency to mentor and help his hapless helpers. He could not afford to be a mentor and did not want a friend. It pained him, but he consoled himself that it was the price of secrecy.

The hyperspatial radar was complete, yet it was not ready. The design was a near perfect mimic of the copy he had stolen off the *Fontapera*, a now destroyed picket ship of the Rymok Theocracy. However exact, the copy did not work. The basic premise was simple. It was impossible to detect vessels in hyperspace from Realspace. The barrier was impenetrable. That gave the Imperial Postal Marines its reason for being. It explained why the Imperial Navy was so large and domineering. To defend anything, there had to be a military presence everywhere. Despite this, the Navy defended the honor of the Emperor, and not a local system. The Navy more frequently suppressed the system and worked to keep several other systems from working together. The Postal Service protected Imperial communication, which required physical transportation due to the inability to cross the barrier.

And the Marines protected the Postal ships.

Smee said the radar was really more like a sonar. Ships traveling through the Soup created a disturbance; ripples that radiated much faster than the ships themselves. Depending on how quickly the ship was emerging, the size of the ripples grew. Though, the size of the ripples were actually rather minute. The hyperspatial radar "heard" the ripple, somehow.

They were detectable. The Rymok Theocracy had a rudimentary way of doing so. Hyperspace Radar was an array of nine sensors distributed over several miles. The cube picked up the faint perturbations. The message was transmitted through a trans-soup connector and relayed to the command center. An AI then analyzed the timing of the ripples across the sensors to determine rough direction and distance. Size of the ripples gave rough speed. Determining emergence was simple mathematics after that.

Klocards was convinced that this hyperspatial radar could do more than detect inbound ships. Once he could get the original array to work, he thought he could find a way to make the radar to transmit data. Then the radar could send near instantaneous messages that would undercut the core purpose of the Imperial Postal Service and give him the satisfaction he sought after being expelled.

But, the radar did not work. It frustrated Klocards to no end. He had actual working plans locked in Smee's memory core. He witnessed its live demonstration when the *Raykomara* was detected. Yet, what he had did not fit what he saw. Through years of tedious, fake experimentation, misdirections and feigned successes, he finally finished most of the system. Through each success, he ran off another assistant. No two of them were on the project long enough to understand one complete segment. Klocards assumed it gave the project an added layer of secrecy that would help him benefit most from the effort.

The computer simulation came back. As Klocards entered the room, he saw Hanifer cringe. She was his latest assistant. She was attractive for a boffin. He suspected she was a company plant; she held on when other assistants had already fled. Too cute. Too committed. She also worked too many hours. Klocards was not entirely sure she cringed because of how he treated her. She was a Named citizen, so he thought she may not like working with a foreigner.

He looked at the results on his pad. It was a toss up whether the sensors would disappear into the Soup or never leave. He managed to ghost one, but the connector ghosted with it. This was the fifty-seventh ghosted return. He slung the pad across the room and it crashed against the wall.

"What are you doing? You must be sabotaging my work." Klocards' frustration was real. It helped him stay in character.

"No. Look, it took the simulation longer to ghost. Maybe we're on the right track?" Hanifer said.

Klocards admitted to himself it was a small success. There had been 56 other variations on the theme of "almost successful." The Soup demanded exacting measurements, so he could not tell if he was really on the right track.

"Do you realize of all my assistants you've produced the most failure? Were it not for your status you'd be on your arse." He almost pitied her, but being a Named citizen, she had access to the right schools, the right opportunities. Not like most of the population. He suspected the only way for an unnamed to really advance on merit, it would be a woman doing it on her back.

"Sir, you don't have many other options. Even senior management is taking notice of how quickly you work through assistants." She stared at him. Actually stared, her eyes bore at him, daring him to do something. She had been around enough to know that he would not touch her. A piece of furniture always took the fall. "We can make this work. But not if you keep breaking pads and smashing up the place."

15. Mondennio - University

After leaving Giedaz's office, Mondennio had to wait for his driver to open the door for him. The driver coughed a bit, but at least did not cough toward him. At least he knew to be sick on his own time. He instructed his driver to hurry home.

"Good morning, Mondennio."

"Good morning, Father. Another beautiful day?" Mondennio sat at the table.

"Yes. Yes it is. Sorry I missed you earlier, but I had a chat with our lawyers about your problem. They weren't concerned about the matter in the least."

"That's good news." He paused while the servants set his place for a late breakfast. "Father, I availed myself to Professor Giedaz's open-door policy yesterday and spoke to him about the matter."

"You what?" Gerandy stopped in mid-bite. "Did I not tell you to leave matters to me?"

"You did, Father. It's good that I did speak with him. He's the honor code prosecutor this year. He looked at the logs that I produced and he said that did a lot to bolster my case."

"Fine, then. I suppose no harm done. But, leave it to the lawyers from now own."

"Yes, Father. The problem is, he said it did not matter. Without getting into the details of our conversation, he's implied that somebody higher in the Clin has conspired to block my advancement."

"That's nonsense."

"Well, he gave a decent argument." Mondennio explained Giedaz's rationale. As he did, the look on his father's face told him that Gerandy was not concerned and any further argument would only irritate him.

"That does change things. I'll have to give the lawyers a call and apprise them. Not much more we can do right now. On to other topics. How is your workload this week?"

Mondennio was taken aback by his father's nonchalance. He just explained how the Rowenzal sept was under attack — his father being the paterfamilias for the sept. Yet, his father did not react. He took a bite of toast and thought about his father's question.

"Compared to the past few months it's virtually non-existent. I arranged my schedule so I have classes only on Twoday and Fourday. They are mostly seminar courses, so no real work is required."

"Wonderful. Today's Threeday, so you should have time to come with me to the research facilities?"

"Yes I do. I think it's been a few months since I was there last."

His father reached out and laid his hand on top of Mondennio's. "Son, you've done a fine job. You really poured yourself into your studies. I'm sorry this has happened but we'll pull through it. If you want, we can pull you out of school for the year and let you work in the company."

Mondennio caught the subtext. Despite what he says, Father doesn't think I have a chance. "Thank you. I'm still committed to finishing school."

"You know, there is still plenty of work inside Rowenzal Enterprises that would occupy you for decades. You don't have to battle the government to get a job that you may not even like."

Perhaps my news affected Father more than I thought? "You're not the sort to give into pressure like this, Father."

"Yes, well. There are victories and there are pyrrhic victories, Mondennio. You have until the end of this term to decide without it hurting your grades. So, no need to rush things. I just wanted you to know you have a way out."

"Father, you're telling me to throw my whole life away."

"Thirty years? That's hardly a whole life. Ever since you were 10 years old you've wanted to right the wrong done the Rowenzals. I've supported it. Twenty years of tutors, summer schools. So, don't think that I'm not involved. But, if there are sinister forces lining up against the Rowenzals, then we need to anticipate their next move."

"You are telling me to give up."

"I'm telling you you have options. I'm telling you that you should always be looking at what's going on and the options that you have. You have tunnel vision, and that's not good in politics."

"I'll think about it." The words came out of his mouth before he could take them back. He was going to vindicate himself despite the price. *Nobody sets me up and gets away with it.*

Gerandy stood to leave. "Great! It's 3.30 cycles now. I'll be heading out at 4 cycles, in case you want to visit the research facilities."

16.   Mondennio - Ubiquitous Knowledge Processing

Mondennio enjoyed trips to the Rowenzal research labs. He felt like he was going to a technology petting zoo. For all the advancements humanity had had since it perfected interstellar travel nearly two millennia ago, there was always an opportunity to improve and innovate. The labs were so close to the University, and built with the same architecture, so most people assumed Rowenzal's labs were a part of the University. Mondennio always chuckled at the lab's name "Ubiquitous Knowledge Processing."

They visited a few consumer projects and were heading down a hallway to pharmaceuticals. "What's in this door here?" Gerandy asked.

"Let me see, Sir." The aide tapped the query into his slate. "I seem to be having difficulty pulling this room up, Sir."

"So, you're saying this is a door to nowhere? I was not aware we had any secret Clinate research projects in the works. Open it up."

"Yes, Sir," the aide said. Cruce Butleyes, Mondennio remembered. Cruce tapped on his slate requesting access, then put his hand on the Biom Identity scanner. The Biom was the premier access control offering of Naeko enterprises, a full Sept of Clin-Khotaigra. It read Butleyes' biomass and growled, indicating that he was not permitted.

"What? That makes no sense. Let me try." Gerandy pressed his hand against the Biom. Again, the Biom growled. "I have universal access anywhere in Rowenzal Enterprises. Butleyes, fix this now."

Butleyes stepped out of earshot and started speaking into his headset and tapping furiously. Gerandy crossed his arms fuming and turned to look out of the hallway's window. He was never given to hysterics or wild shows. Mondennio learned a long time ago that crossed arms meant somebody's career just ended. Mondennio looked around and wondered what would be secretive enough to hide from his father.

Butleyes tried the scanner a few more times before he resumed tapping. "Sir, I've ordered a security team here to break the door down. It appears it is outside our normal security controls."

"How did this happen?" Gerandy said.

Butleyes stepped back as Gerandy's voice resonated down the hallway. He shrugged. The shout scared Mondennio, too, who was not accustomed to hearing his father truly upset.

A moment later, the door opened. Mondennio watched as a stocky man stepped out, his face belying a weariness.

"Who are you?" Gerandy commanded. The man seemed immune to his father's look as the door closed.

"Janhas Klocards. And you are?" Janhas looked at Mondennio. Or rather, Mondennio thought Janhas' eyes looked through him. There was a lack of emotion in his face that chilled him.

"I know who I am!" Gerandy's fists pumped straight down and his foot stomped.

Janhas seemed unmoved. "I'm sure you do, but I don't. I'm sure you don't mean to be using that tone." Klocards' voice remained neutral, as if shrugging off Gerandy's menacing gaze.

"I am Rowenzal Clin-Khotaigra."

"The whole sub-sept? I sincerely doubt that."

Does this guy really not understand who he's speaking to? Mondennio intervened. "Klocards, what he means is that he is Gerandy Rowenzal Clin-Khotaigra, the paterfamilias for sub-sept Rowenzal. So, he is the sub-sept as far as you're concerned."

Klocards seemed to stiffen slightly, adopting what Mondennio thought was something resembling military bearing. "Sorry about that, Sir. We boffins tend to get a little preoccupied with our work."

The deference mollified Gerandy slightly, who was still not calm enough to speak. Mondennio continued his mediation. "Quite all right, Klocards. What exactly are you working on?"

"I'm not at liberty to say. I'm sure you noticed you had a difficult time getting in?"

"This is my facility, Klocards. You are my employee. You have a duty to tell me what you are working on."

"I'm sorry, Sir. I don't have that duty." Klocards held up his hand. "And don't think about threatening me. You can't fire me, and you don't own my research." Klocards glanced toward Mondennio.

"Father. You go on ahead. I'll speak with Klocards here and try to clean this up. There's no need for you to dirty your hands in this."

Gerandy looked at him, clearly enraged. "I will know what is going on here." He stormed off.

Mondennio turned back to Klocards. "My father is not accustomed to being told no in his own company. I'm sure you can appreciate his irritation."

"You are?"

"Sorry, Mondennio Rowenzal Clin-Khotaigra."

"Yes, I get that you're a Rowenzal. You have the same beak. There's no need to dump your whole name out. Longer names only reveal a person's lack of self-confidence."

Mondennio was taken aback by Klocards' disdain for his rank. "Regardless, you would do well to know your place. Don't you realize the danger you're in?"

"I suppose not. No. I'm not really in danger. Not like you'd think. I do know I'm working on a very secret project, and I suspect you want me to tell you more about it."

In the face of a paterfamilias, an unnamed like Klocards had essentially no protections or due process. It took very little to put him in prison. If he were an employee, then Gerandy could consign him to the company brig with only the obligation to give him suitable nutrition and nominal family contact. In the face of that, Klocards' serenity surprised Mondennio. Klocards carried himself different than other engineers. His lack of respect suggested a lifetime not in the Clinate. "Imperium? Why would the Imperium be doing research in Copa?"

Klocards flinched only slightly — but enough for Mondennio to notice. "I come from the Imperium, but the Imperium is not doing research on Copa. I really cannot get into the details, Rowenzal. My authority comes from much higher — don't go trying to find out where or your sub-sept could find itself with more than it can deal with. I will tell you a bit of what I'm working on, if you can keep it within your family. I suspect your father is digging as we speak, to your collective detriment."

Mondennio nodded his head, knowing that his 'family' had dozens of members. "Whatever you can give me that I can satisfy my father with."

"I'm no friend of the Imperium. If you inquire at the embassy, they may not even know I'm here. However, I'm here on request of the Clinate doing research on extremely sensitive technology that I'm sure could be used to undermine Imperial authority. With its authority gone, its threat to Copa will diminish. Now, you go snooping into things you'll get the Imperium's agents interested and the game will be up. Understand?"

"I doubt there are spies on Copa. Our security is much tighter than you realize."

"Security is an illusion, Boy. I'd be willing to bet that the Imperium planted agents on Copa before you even knew there were other humans out there. It's how they operate."

"Fine. I'll assume you're right — for now. I'll try to talk my father out of digging deeper. But, he is not an easy man to distract."

"Rowenzal. It's always important to be careful when digging. You never know when you might strike an energized conduit. I do apologize for putting you in the middle of this. I'll do my best in the future to communicate to you to ensure this does not flare up. Fair enough?"

Mondennio caught up with his father.

"Father, I spoke with the scientist. He wouldn't give me details, but it appears he's involved in some work for the Clinate. Please don't be upset."

"I'll think about it. In the meantime, he needs to learn his place."

"I told him. I'll keep an eye on him for you, if that's all right with you?"

"Fine."

*   *   *

As Klocards walked home, his mind wandered over the day's results. The scene with the Rowenzals did not go very well. At least the kid seemed reasonable.

His assistant was another matter. Hanifer was the first assistant to actually stand up to him. She stared him down. *Did she know more than she's letting on? Maybe it was time to find a way to fire her. I should have known better than to accept an application from a Named citizen. Too much confidence.*

Chapter 6

17. Veneza Club Orakrono

It was 1.50 cycles. Veneza stayed awake all night nervous about the rally. Rather than stay awake in her bed all night, she sat with other Republicans at Club Orakrono.

Club Orakrono started its life as a hotel 350 years ago, back when travel was more acceptable within the Clinate. After the travel restrictions were imposed nearly 200 years ago, the building sat empty. Its stone and steel construction let it weather the decades of disrepair until Berthon Pera Clin Kacaubant bought it within Veneza's lifetime.

Clin Kacaubant and Clin Khotaigra had a long-standing fierce rivalry. The building's proximity to the Khotaigra Palace led to its purchase. Berthon Pera Clin Kacaubant converted it into a sleazy discotheque to annoy Khotaigra — with Clinate support and over Khotaigra's objections.

Veneza believed Kacaubant was secretly supportive of the Republican movement. The Club catered to unnamed citizens, which made it one of the few places they could legally congregate. The Club's patrons managed to keep Atakadaro out, and the loud booming music would make surveillance difficult. As a result, Republican leadership frequently met here.

Six of the Republican leadership sat around the table going over final plans. Veneza stood looking over their shoulders. She had influence in the movement, but she was not a leader. She felt they ignored her because she was a woman. She was at least as motivated as they were. She was certainly more educated.

"Everybody understand?" Rymose Hilliamson served as the master of ceremonies for the protest planned for later that day.

"How soon do you expect the fikilon Atakadaro to show up?"

"Well, with the few hundred protesters committed, there's no way they don't know we're coming. I expect them to cut off mass transit, which should dampen some attendance." Rymose looked less than hopeful.

"I thought about that. I told my friends in New Persia to expect a long walk. It's only seven kilometers away, so they should be leaving within the cycle." Veneza did not recognize the speaker. New Persia was part of the nearer plantations, and his accent convinced her he was from those plantations.

"Same for my friends in Lonageth. It's about the same distance away." Lonageth was more industrial than New Persia.

"So, the Fikilon are going to see crowds of youth walking down major highways to get here, arriving about the same time? That's being pretty blatant." Veneza said. "We avoided posting flyers to give us a chance to surprise them. If we're having hordes magically show up, we might as well have."

"Actually, my brother plans on papering the West Side down near that Atakadari Station that pretends not to be there. He wants to stage a protest there as a distraction."

"Isn't your brother sixteen?" Rymose said.

"So? He's just as committed. Besides, we're not expecting this to go well, are we?"

"No. We're not. There's not been a protest since Copa severed ties with the rest of humanity. So, this should be big news. I expect the Fikilon to be under-prepared. We'll go in and be loud but peaceful. They'll attack us." Rymose sounded resigned.

Veneza looked around the table. None of the leadership looked as enthusiastic as she thought they should. Hundreds of protesters meant the Clinate would have to take notice. Other Copans would, too. The media could not keep this large of a protest silent.

"Wait, you want us to be attacked?" she said.

"Veneza, I'm not talking about a massacre. They'll lob in tear gas and come in with batons and make some arrests. They would not be stupid enough to do more than that."

She noticed Rymose was not entirely confident in his response, which concerned her more.

* * *

18.   Mondennio - Rowenzal Enclave

Mondennio's intercom gently buzzed him awake. "Sir, this is your wakeup call."

"Thank you."

Mondennio stretched and climbed out of bed. He soaked in the shower for a quarter cycle as he slowly awoke, scarcely aware of the size of the shower and the bench he sat on. He did not know his shower was larger than the typical unnamed bedroom.

He took his time dressing, making sure his clothes matched. Not that he doubted the taste of his butler, but mistakes have been made in the past. That butler has not worked since.

In his anteroom a simple breakfast sat waiting. As he started eating, the door rang.

"Enter."

Keve walked in. Mondennio noted that Keve was fully dressed, as if he were never anything other than ready for a formal event. *Just another day for Keve.*

"Sir, I gather that you are planning to go out early this morning."

"Yes, I am. Is my car ready?"

"It has been brought around, yes. However, I feel a certain need to dissuade you from your effort."

"Dissuade?"

"Certainly. I have information that suggests that some rather undesirable people are going to be out in the streets this morning. It would be unsafe, and perhaps inappropriate, for you to be out on the streets."

Mondennio stopped chewing. *How would he know that I'm going to the protest?* "Don't worry about it, Keve. I'm sure whatever you've heard is over-blown."

"Hardly, Sir. Would you mind telling me where you will be this morning?"

"I've not had to give you my itinerary since I was a boy. I don't think I need to now. I'm grown enough to assess the risks and take the right precautions. And don't you go running to Father." Mondennio hoped Keve would not press his point.

"Certainly, Sir. You feel you are old enough to not do anything rash or inappropriate. I shan't press the matter further."

Keve's words smacked Mondennio on the face. *He's referring to my being ejected from the exam. Rubbing my nose in it.* Mondennio realized he was glaring at Keve, projecting what he was thinking. He quickly turned his back on Keve and back to breakfast. He chewed slowly until he hear Keve close the door, then slammed his fist on the table.

19.   Veneza - Market Square

As expected, Atakadaro halted mass transit. The trip from inner plantations took about two cycles by foot, and all those arriving were on foot. It was dawn, so Veneza could see the waves of tired protesters arriving.

From her perch near the market square, she could see most of the people. She saw Mondennio leaning against the base of the marketplace's spire, a short monument to some historic event. He looked out of place, and several protesters stared at him. *At least he doesn't look like Atakadaro. They probably won't beat him, but I'd better save him just in case.*

Veneza walked over. "So you made it? I didn't think you took my invitation seriously."

"Sure. I mean, this is going to be historic, right? I did some reading last night. The last protest agitated against the destruction of the last artificial intelligence facility on Copa. It was the navigation computer that would have allowed us to continue interacting with humanity. The anniversary of that protest is next week, on Threeday."

"Really?"

"Yeah. This spire was in memory of those gunned down by the Clinate. Well, not the Clinate, exactly. The Clinate was formed ten years after the protest, not long after the spire was erected. My Clin was the one that put down the protest. It was the later formation of the Clinate that prevented this sort of violence afterward."

"The Clinate only prevents violence because it's a repressive dictatorship. It's hundreds of tiny acts of violence against our rights and our bodies instead of infrequent massive acts of violence. In the end we suffer. So, here to partake another massacre?"

"No, I'm not here for a massacre. I think you're all crazy, but I thought I might learn something from this historic event. Although, I'm not very pleased with how you're characterizing our government. It's a representative oligarchy, not a dictatorship."

"Says somebody who benefits from its repression. You live like the Unnamed do for a few weeks and you'll know what I mean — if you last that long. It only represents named families. You can't call that representative." Veneza felt disgusted by the condescending look on Mondennio's face.

"You sound like the system is rigged against merit. Or talent. You're not a named family, but you're obviously at the University. So, how can it be that repressive?"

"I had a benevolent star shining on me. That doesn't make it any less repressive. It just makes it selective."

"Veneza, not everybody is cut-out for government. Named families train for government and business from an early age. It's who we are. We take the hard jobs and make the tough decisions so everybody else can enjoy the simple life."

"The simple life? Mondennio, you are what we're protesting. Don't you get it? We don't need to be patronized. We're people, too. We are capable of making the same tough decisions given a chance to get the same education."

"We'll see. The Clinate will allow you to protest in peace."

Veneza turned away from him and took a deep breath. Looking over the crowd gave her confidence. She saw beyond the massing crowd the emerging presence of Atakadaro forces. Veneza looked back at Mondennio.

"Who's peace? You see this small crowd of students? Do you see what surrounds us now? Up those roads. Look in those windows." He followed her finger pointing at the armored cars and the snipers positioned in the windows over the public house.

"What? They're just there to ensure nothing gets out of hand."

"Mondennio, how can you be so blind? You find somewhere safe to stand, I guarantee before midday there will be a crackdown."

"Then why are you doing this? If you are so certain the Clinate will beat your ideas with violence, why protest?"

"Somebody has to expose the violence inherent in the system. We're going to peacefully protest. They're going to come in with batons waving. Then you'll know the difference between representation and repression."

"So, you're protesting so you can be repressed? That's crazy."

"Just stand over there." She pointed to a set of sturdy bench tables far away from the Palace. "I suppose I should stand with you to narrate the crackdown. I'll be your tour guide."

A few cycles later, banners flew across the protest. The young people in the square were chanting "Real Reform! Cleanse the Clinate!" Veneza and Mondennio stood on tables near the fringe at Kinnetchurch Street. At the other side of the protest, Atakadaro formed a silent cordon between the protest and the palace. The cordon was on the near side of the street, where retaining walls helped augment the lines.

A throng formed near the center part of the Atakadari cordon. From Veneza's vantage point, it looked like there was a conference. She saw Rymose and two of the other Republican leaders looking at a map.

Then it happened. A large green bottle flew from the throng of protesters at one of the wings of the Atakadari cordon. It traveled over the officers, and landed near a command post and reserve line that protected the palace driveway. A fireball erupted as the bottle shattered. Some of the throng cheered. Others screamed. Rymose turned to face the explosion, his mouth agape.

Atakadari troops wasted no time in responding. Smoking canisters flew from Atakadari-manned windows. As they landed, the students started choking and running in all directions. Some armored cars flanking the cordon turned high-pressure water hoses on the students, driving them away from the palace. As Veneza looked about, she saw people with champagne glasses standing in the windows of Clin Khotaigra Palace.

The tap-tap of gunfire filled the square. Protesters stampeded South, toward Veneza and Mondennio. She watched protesters who had fallen to the ground try to get up, only to be trampled by fellow protesters. The leadership team was down.

She felt a grab on her arm and turned toward her assailant. It was Mondennio pulling her off the table and toward the church.

"Come with me," he said.

She started to resist, but the stampede was too close.

Veneza and Mondennio ran together down the street, when Atakadari troops appeared at the distant intersection. Some protesters halted, others kept running. Mondennio kept dragging her toward the cordon. He started waving his free arm. "Clin Khotaigra!" As they got closer, four officers ran forward, grabbing both of them and dragging them inside.

Veneza felt the pain as she slammed against the pavement. A knee jammed in her back. Mondennio kept yelling "Clin Khotaigra! I have identification." She turned her head as she felt the officer start binding her hands. He was being bound as well.

"If you do not check for identification, I will have your jobs!" Mondennio continued to order the officers. They searched him, pulling out his identification card.

That figures, saving himself. Just another drone. The officer on his back drew his boot knife and cut the binders. He quickly stood up and pulled Mondennio up.

"Her, too. She's my sister. How dare you."

Veneza thought she saw him wink as he followed his own finger to point her out.

"She hasn't any papers," the officer pinning her said.

"You're calling me a liar?" Mondennio walked up, defiant and arrogant. He jabbed his finger on the troop's badge. "6-6-5-1, eh? You're going to throw my sister into that truck, haul her off to who knows where? You'll find yourself taking her place in the jails when my father finds out."

"She doesn't look anything like you."

"My parents didn't like that I was an only child, but my mother could only stand to have me. So, when I was a year old they adopted her. So, you won't get a biomass match, either. I can't believe you're not taking my word."

"Sir, there's a protest going on." The officer sobered up to the fact that he was talking to a named person. "You could be trying to rescue your pet."

What a vile word. The polite word for an unnamed girlfriend.

"6651, you just ended your career. You dare call my sister a pet! It's not her fault she forgets to carry identification. Give me my slate." Mondennio grabbed his slate from an officer and started tapping.

A senior officer put his hand on Mondennio's and eased the slate down. "Terribly sorry for the inconvenience, Sir. Hylon here was operating under our rules of engagement. We weren't expecting your kind here. Hylon, cut her loose."

She felt the knee off her back. A moment later, she went airborne as Officer Hylon lifted her off the ground and set her on her feet. He cut her free, and she rubbed her wrists. Real tears flowed down her cheeks.

"You've made my sister cry, Hylon? You'd better memorize her face. I hear anybody from your station harass her on the street —"

The officer waved his hands in assurance. Mondennio glared at the senior officer, who lowered his head, staring at the ground a few feet behind Mondennio.

"Come on, Veneza." Mondennio grabbed her elbow again, and briskly guided her down the street.

They turned the corner a couple blocks beyond the Atakadari cordon before he released her arm. She had been running in a daze. As they caught their breath, she realized how much he risked to save her.

Mondennio was upset. "Peaceful, huh? I can't believe I dragged you out of there. You saw that bottle fly."

"I don't know what happened. We expressly said no weapons. No violence."

He pointed down the street. "I doubt that. You'd better get home, and stay there the rest of the weekend. I don't know if they had the cameras up or not; so they may come looking for you if they got a biometric read."

Mondennio turned on his heels and walked the opposite direction from where he pointed. *But, my home is that way, too.* She waited a couple beats until he disappeared a few blocks up, before she started the same direction toward her apartment. She tried to make sense of what happened that morning, and found she could not.

*   *   *

20.   Jonaldy - Performing Arts Bookstore

Jonaldy turned the corner, then looked back to ensure Mondennio was still heading away. He hastily scanned the crowd, looking for surveillance. The tall monument rose over the square, with a small group of teen-aged gangsters sat on the steps surrounding the monument. Overhead, cables for various streetcars guided the assorted tracks to the other parts of Kinnet.

When it came to surveillance, Jonaldy worried about four different groups. As an illegal Imperial operative, the Copan Atakadaro presented a real threat. He has no legal protection as an Unnamed, and would be a prized arrest if he were caught. Atakadaro was aggressive, but their methods were unsophisticated enough that he barely saw them as a threat.

Other Republican factions presented a trivial threat. His involvement with Veneza exposed him to their scrutiny. If they suspected he was not one of them, they might very well turn him over to the Atakadaro. He felt his cover was more than adequate to cover him there. Like a turtle, he had to expose himself to do his work.

The group he feared most was his own. The Bafiktuy Intelligence Directive worked under strict secrecy. It organized itself into a cell structure to reduce its exposure, not only to outside forces, but to internal threats. To emphasize security, it formed hunter-killer cells that sought out Bafiktuy cells and operatives that were not diligent enough with their own security. He would never know if one of those cells operated on Copa unless they were actively pursuing him for his own lack of diligence.

He tended to include criminals and shady characters in a fourth group. He did not fear the criminal element, but they added spice to his covert mission. None were following him. Satisfied, he started walking in a circuitous route with a destination a couple kilometers away.

For a young man watching his life collapse, Mondennio's showing a lot of confidence. Perhaps too much. Jonaldy kept tabs on the assorted media accounts of the scandal. The investigation was going slow, no doubt impeded by somebody's political agenda. Jonaldy made a note to find out who would want the Rowenzals ruined for good. *Probably a peer family hoping to rise as well.* Mondennio showed a fair amount of promise and this would counter that.

Jonaldy picked up some mention of the Rowenzal Scandal. Rather than risk embarrassing themselves, the various media outlets found indirect ways to put the scandal fresh in everybody's mind. They discussed some other event and then hinted at some similarity between the two. He reflected on the scandal and thought he could bend it to his advantage if handled right. It will at least distract his father from helping Mondennio.

He walked to the north of the plaza and walked into the Performing Arts bookstore. It was one of those stores that had various games. To encourage patrons to play them and build interest, there was a lounge on the upper balcony. Patrons of all ages played on the tables below. He tried not to visit the same location too often; so he had not been here for a few months. The patrons focused on the various games, and meta-gaming that went on.

Jonaldy sat on an overstuffed seat toward the back and pulled his slate out of his jacket. Copan data networks were virtually identical to Imperial networks; ubiquitous and dependable. There were a few sites he visited that helped him keep current.

The Network, the Copan data network for the privileged, was where they could try to work together. Successfully navigating to one of their Network data sites required a slightly different degree of indirection as Jonaldy used when he walked the city streets. After bouncing a few sites, he felt his digital trail was sufficiently concealed. If he was wrong, he expected Compass Rose would help keep him concealed.

Gojira, his contact in the media, left him a message.

@Kong, Elder Rowenzal sought assistance from Atakadaro investigator. The investigator's personal diary mentions preliminary findings that may support Rowenzal's claim. The matter may be over with soon. Have some information on that college professor Geidaz. We have some footage that compromises him quite nicely. Cannot vouch for its ability to stand up to digital scrutiny. Want me to publish?

Jonaldy tapped in a response:

@Gojira, Thanks. Keep eye on investigator and report any information that helps Rowenzal. Do not release to media yet.

Good news and bad news. I can probably force Giedaz to kick Mondennio out of school, which will play well with the media. I may only have a few months to make this work, unless I can find another way.

He pocketed his slate and quietly slipped out of the bookstore. As he left, a pair of players cheered a victory, and one of the rivals flipped the table. Never a dull moment.

The school was only a half-kilometer walk to the West from the bookstore. A casual walker would have covered the distance in seven beats. Jonaldy instead continued his trip North. He strolled past the park to his right, skirting its edge. He overshot the park, then turned to his right, walking past a chemists' shop and a day care. By the high adult presence and security detail, he decided the patrons where named families.

Satisfied he was not being followed, Jonaldy turned back toward the park, and strolled along its East edge. It was a wide gravel path that eased him past the main entrance to the campus. He passed through a well-groomed garden of geometric shapes, until he came to the first set of administrative buildings.

The administrative building stood next to another building named "Ubiquitous Knowledge Processing." *Whatever that meant in Copan. Perhaps the University is trying to re-invent artificial intelligence? Don't they realize they can just ask the Imperium? Or, are they just not dumb enough to trust an AI received as a gift? What ever they did in that building, it clearly catered to boffins.*

Jonaldy entered the administrative building and climbed the stairs to the fourth floor. On Copa elevators typically had cameras with facial recognition software, necessitating he get more exercise than he preferred. At the top of his climb, Jonaldy walked into a familiar office. Jonaldy noticed that the secretary was out. *Perfect.* He continued through to the inner office. Skuriat Giedaz's seat was turned facing the window, its back to the office door. As Jonaldy entered he heard faint moaning behind the seat.

"Professor Giedaz?" he called.

A shriek. A young co-ed jumped from Giedaz's seat and flew behind the curtain. Jonaldy chuckled. *The poor young thing fails to notice that her naked backside is exposed to the groomed garden pathway outside.*

"What is the meaning of this?" Skuriat bellowed as he came out of the chair. Even without his pants, Skuriat managed a glare at Jonaldy. He relaxed as his recognized Jonaldy. "How dare you! You're supposed to text me first."

"Well, I was in the neighborhood. I thought you'd enjoy it if I paid you a surprise visit. I see you have varied tastes. A little bit of she, a little bit of he."

"What?" Skuriat kicked the woman's clothes toward the curtain, which landed expertly. The co-ed exposed her short, wavy brunette hair as she gathered them up and disappeared again behind the curtain.

"I should have waited until you finished your 'student-teacher conference.' What happened with this one that she needed one-on-one mentoring?"

"Heh. She's failing her Business Acumen course. She stormed in here and accused her professor of being out to get her, and wanted to know what her courses of action were."

"I hope you're planning on persuading her professor to give her a better grade. It appears she has a good grasp of marketing."

Dressed, the woman fled from behind the curtain. She slammed the door to Skuriat's private entrance.

"She was trying to persuade me. I'm her professor. For this, I assured her that she wouldn't fail. She tried to persuade me to do better, but I told her I couldn't give outstanding marks. It would appear as if I were playing favorites."

"Certainly, lust has some limitations."

"It's a shame, actually. She was the third best student in my class before she tried to seduce me. She thought she did badly on an essay, but it wasn't meant to be graded. So now I can't let her finish so highly. I think she'll come in seventh now."

"Nice. I take it you prefer merit?"

"No, despite her efforts, she just doesn't have the gifts that would persuade me to leave things as they are. Some things require practice. Catch my drift? Hmm, maybe I could persuade her to change degree programs so I could be her faculty adviser. My current students bore me. Now that you've interrupted my tutoring session. What are you doing here?"

"I'm here to do you a favor, though it seems my timing was a bit off. Your tastes are varied, Skuriat, aren't they? I have information about a male secondary student who has no chance of entering this school. It seems he appealed to your baser interests? He's on the student registry as a first-year student. Did you hook him on drugs before you molested him, or after?"

"What? I assure you my interests are quite normal. I don't care what you heard. What you just accused me of is a complete fabrication."

"I'm not the one making the accusation, Skuriat. I have a friend in the media who's got a full exposé in the works right now. Claims the male student recorded evidence and has turned up dead. You know how these scandals go: once the subject is given some light then every student you've ever 'assisted' will join in. Just like that little piece that just ran out in a huff. How many 'successes' do you have, anyway? Current and past?"

Skuriat dropped back in his chair. "After twenty years, you lose track. Who did I piss off to have this get out? Jonaldy, I swear it wasn't me. One of the other admissions board members asked me to give that boy a chance. She said his father served her Sept as a senior plant manager. He has no chance of rising above his station."

"It was pretty obvious somebody was enjoying his athleticism. I'd see bruises on his wrists from time to time. I spoke to him and then told her to go easy on him. I must have struck a nerve. Maybe whoever's trying to scandalize me must have tinkered with the audio."

"So, you're denying being a drug-pushing, homosexual pedophile? To fight this, you have to be ready to admit to using your position on the school's discipline board to keep your bed warm. When my friend told me about his evidence, I did a little digging. It seems you have quite the brood of illegitimates. One is even in a prominent Sept. Well played."

"I can't have that get out. I've managed to pick the right students, and helped them along enough without taking too much to keep it quiet this long. Now would not be a good time."

"Well, I may be able to help make this go away. I'll have my friend stall the story while I come up with a way to make it go away. However, I hear you've got Mondennio Rowenzal's file on your desk for a recent indiscretion of his."

Thinking about the scandal seemed to keep Skuriat in a state of shock. "I do. He cheated on a pretty big exam. But, his citizenship rating in the school is outstanding. His family's scandal's not helping his case, but I was planning on letting him go with some punitive discipline. He's got a good chance to make it in government; and it wouldn't hurt to have a man like him on your side."

That's my plan. On my side. "If I recall, the full penalty is expulsion."

Skuriat nodded.

"So, that's my price. I'll make sure this little imbroglio goes away. But, to make that happen Mondennio's got to be expelled. It has to be public and humiliating."

"What? We haven't expelled a student like that in seven years, and she deserved it. The evidence against Mondennio's pretty thin."

"I'll make sure he deserves it. Here's a cash card linked to him for 1,999 knoerzers. You can add bribery to his charge. It's traceable and damning as it links to you."

"You are a tough man to cross, Jonaldy. That's just under the criminal limit. You make my false accuser go away and I get rid of Mondennio. How do I even know the accusation is real?"

At least you're thinking. "I will get a copy from my friend of the interview. That should persuade you. Once I send you the copy, you have one week to have him expelled, or the story goes live."

He handed a separate card to Skuriat. "This cash card, however, is untraceable. Should be one-thousand knoerzers on it. You can take your new co-ed mentee to Lake Onanigi over the upcoming school break. That should persuade her to change degrees."

Their business concluded, Jonaldy left through the private entrance and down the flights of stairs to the outside. As he left, he saw the co-ed sitting on a bench looking at the fountain and the pond. She wore a turquoise top, hazel-blue eyes that matched. Slight red in her otherwise light brown hair, slender but not boyish. A few freckles. *She knows how to dress, she's a winter. I like winter. She's beautiful, but damaged.* He turned and quickly walked away, disappearing around the corner before she could notice him.

* * *

21. **Mondennio - University**

```
Mondennio Rowenzal Clin-Khotaigra, report to
University President's Office at 5.50 cycles for
final adjudication.
```

The text came in while he was in the shower. It normally took ten to fifteen beats to get from the Rowenzal enclave to the University. Mondennio was still breathing heavy as the car pulled onto the main road taking him to Kinnet. *If he's fast enough, then I might get there on time.*

He called his lawyer's office as soon as he caught his breath. "Aldavin Risont? He's still at lunch? Tell him that they've moved the adjudication date up and that I have to report in ten beats."

Mondennio walked into the Administrative building at 5.47 cycles. He chose to take the stairs to the President's third floor office to avoid any mechanical delays. The President's secretary motioned him to take a seat. 5.49 beats. *Just in time.*

The President failed to be on time for his own appointment. Neither did the honor code prosecutor. At 5.60 cycles, they entered together and walked without hesitation into the President's inner office. A beat later, three others Mondennio did not recognize also passed through to the inner office. One was not much older than he was, but clearly in charge. Mondennio felt his anxiety rise a little.

"Mondennio, as you know, grave charges have been filed in response to your possession of examination material during the period in which it was conducted. That investigation has drawn to a close and we are prepared to make a judgment."

"I'm sorry, President, my lawyer is not here yet. He texted me a few minutes ago letting me know he would be here in ten beats."

"We gave you plenty of time. Besides, this is not an inquiry. Your attorney has vigorously defended your position and should be commended. His role is satisfied. Right, Sir?" The President turned his head slightly and nodded to the young man Mondennio saw earlier. The younger man nodded back. Mondennio thought he looked like a Khotaigra based on the facial features, but he did not recognize him. He was perhaps in his mid-thirties.

"I believe I am entitled to have him present in all proceedings."

"We differ, Mondennio. An additional charge was added earlier this week. It appears you caused great embarrassment to the University in recent participation in an illegal demonstration. The prosecutor, Professor Giedaz, reviewed not only Atakadaro video, but also has sworn statements from Atakadaro officers who stated that you asserted your status to avoid arrest."

"What? But — I did not participate. I was invited to view the demonstration and left as soon as I saw the altercation with Atakadaro begin. I left with the student who invited me, and Atakadaro was being very brutal towards her."

"Be that as it may, young Rowenzal, you just confirmed your presence at an illegal demonstration and from that we should conclude abuse of status. Please note that for the record, Melek. Also note that the accused has spoken out of turn. We shan't have that again, shall we?"

Mondennio seethed but shook his head. *How do I keep them stalled long enough for my attorney?* He knew that they would find him in absentia if he chose to leave; even if he failed to present himself. He felt like he did as a young child being chastised by his father. He only wished his mother were there to take his side like she used to.

"Now. There is one more matter which is of the gravest concern. Prosecutor Giedaz informed me yesterday that the accused, Mondennio Rowenzal, attempted to bribe him into concealing evidence."

"That's a lie! How dare you slander me, Giedaz!"

"Rowenzal, be careful. The man standing to your left is an Atakadaro inspector. You were right to suggest his presence, Professor." President Stanton Beyett stared at Mondennio for a beat as if provoking Mondennio to say anything else.

What is going on here? Falsely accused of cheating. Accused of bribery. Engagement in an illegal protest. Abuse of status. Denial of counsel?

"My apologies, President Beyett. I feel I am in a difficult position here as I was not sufficiently notified of these other charges."

"Nonsense, Rowenzal. We sent all this information to your slate earlier this week. Except for the recent bribery charge, which we sent last night. Regardless, you know Copan law — timely notice of charges applies to the initial charges. Once an accused is notified that he is under investigation or adjudication, any new charges are implicitly included."

"I did not receive any new information on this case. When my attorney arrives, I'm sure he will remind this proceeding of the requirement to notify him at any time any communication with me occurs. He is not present, and was unaware of this proceeding until I notified him. He did not inform me of any new information, which you sent directly to me. Therefore, these proceedings have failed to provide adequate process."

The younger man spoke up. "Mondennio, I can assure you that whatever this proceeding has done is in full compliance. Judging from your face, I believe I should remind you that I am Jarrew Clin-Khotaigra, who is the Clin representative of record. If you were eventually to seek appeal, I would be the one ruling in the matter. I am present to ensure that everything is done according to the law. Satisfied? Continue President, I have another appointment at 6 cycles."

Mondennio's stomach sunk as the blood rushed from his face. Clin representation by the Appellate? *I thought that was a formality. What is going on here?*

President Beyett resumed, "The University was prepared to go light on you for your cheating. The original finding would have been merely to invalidate the exam and make you retake it next year. That would have only cost you a few months service between the time you graduated and the test was re-administered."

Mondennio knew that delay was non-trivial. It meant he would be junior to any of his school peers. They would be viewed first for promotions and awards, with him always the last considered. That was a severe enough blow to his career.

"However, this bribery matter has more gravity. As you know, the penalty for bribing the honor code prosecutor is expulsion for the balance of the school year. You're only salvation here was your presence of mind to stay just under the legal limit. Otherwise Inspector Roigamin here would have you in binders by now."

"As to this last matter of participating in an anti-government riot. The Inspector here informed me that does carry a criminal penalty of not more than four years, a minimum of two because of the violent nature of the riot.

However, I supplicated on your behalf to Jerrew Clin-Khotaigra. He thought it would be better for you to decide whether to be criminally charged or not."

"What do you mean? How do I get to choose?"

"Quite simple, really. The other findings are quite punitive put together. You have the right to refuse the findings and go to a tribunal. Perhaps you would even be acquitted. However, if you chose to request tribunal or assert your full rights of counsel, then Inspector Roigamin will take you into custody for your criminal behavior. Of course, that matter would have to be fully resolved before we could convene a tribunal."

"Mondennio, the Clin is committed to restore the tranquility disrupted by the republican riot. You were among one of the more highly ranked. We would prefer not to sully sub-septs with rancor. However, we will exert all authority on you and your family should you choose to face criminal charges."

"What you are telling me, President Beyett, is that I should accept false charges to avoid over-inflated criminal charges? I don't see how that is fair or just."

"Rowenzal, this is not about fairness or justice. This is about tranquility, both in the university and in society," Jerrew said.

"What will my record look like after I finish the University's administrative censure?"

President Beyett relaxed slightly, he looked over at Jerrew. "We can see if some community service during the period, tutoring perhaps, would allow your record to be expunged."

Chapter 7

22.   Mondennio - University

As Mondennio walked out of the Administrative building, he saw the family lawyer Aldavin Risont exiting his car.

"Where were you? I just got shafted." Mondennio fought off the urge to hit him. His driver was standing by his open car door as if suggesting he should hurry away. Mondennio heeded the subtle suggestion and got in the car.

Mondennio sat shocked as his car made the final turn in Kennet to head home. He did not notice the buildings or people as he usually did. He could not feel sorrow, no tears came. He sat expressionless, feeling the car's acceleration press him into the seat. That's what they did to him — they pressed him. He supposed they expected him to break down and cry in the office; but he did not cry for his own mother's funeral. Crying was a trait Gerandy refused his sons to have. His father used to slap him until he stopped crying. But he did not feel sorrow. He felt — nothing except the suddenly tight confines of his car.

What did I do to deserve this? Who did I upset? Mondennio thought through his list of contacts. Except for Juank, he did not have anybody who he thought really hated him. Juank did not really hate him, either. He never figured out what problem Juank had with him, but he thought maybe Juank resented him — though why would a man of his standing ever resent him?

Would Juank do this to me? Why would he? There were a number of things he could do to interfere with me, none of which involved this degree of theater. It has to be somebody I don't know.

The who eluded him, as did the why. Speculation would not serve him. What he knew was that the University had participated in his humiliation. Not just the individuals. *Clin Khotaigra was involved. Didn't Giedaz say*

Rowenzal was being targeted? Not me, but my family. I'm just a pawn, a casualty. This isn't about me.

"Shouldn't I just let Father handle this?" Mondennio said before he realized he voiced it. But as it left his mouth, he knew he could not leave it alone. He might have been a pawn in a bigger fight, but he was not going to let himself be treated as such.

But what am I going to do?

Mondennio slid down his seat as his car pulled into the Rowenzal Enclave. The car came to a stop, and his driver got out of the car. He listened as the driver's footsteps orbited the car toward his door. His driver opened the door.

Gerandy walked up and looked inside the car. "Aldavin called me after you rushed past him at the University. He tried to meet with the President afterward and was escorted off campus. What happened?"

Mondennio felt his anger boil, but he kept it in check. Even as he explained what happened to his father, he managed to retain his composure.

His father stepped back from the car speechless, giving Mondennio the chance to at least escape the car's confines.

"So we'll fight it." Gerandy said. "But, you need to stand down if we're going to be able to resolve this."

"I didn't tell you about that. If we do anything to resist what just happened, they'll send me to prison for two to five years. At least now I have a chance to retake the exam in a year."

"Why do you still want to be in government service after this? If you're still committed because of the promise you made to your mother, I assure you she would absolve you after this."

Bringing up his mother almost cracked Mondennio's composure. "Father, right now this is not about a promise I made to Mother. They are trying to push me out of any chance to advance the family."

"Who do you think cared about that more, me or your Mother? Mondennio, I told you before you should work inside the family. You're intelligent and talented. That's what Rowenzal needs. If the Clinate does not want you, we need you."

"Thanks. I'm not out of the fight yet."

"What does that mean?"

"I don't know, Father. I just know that if I do nothing then a majority of my life has been lost."

"Son, you've got to know when to cut your losses."

"So, what? I've lost most of my life? No, Father. I'm going to find a way to set this right. It's just not right that something like this can happen to one of us without recourse." As he said the words, his mind drifted back to the riot. He felt like he knew a bit more of what the unnamed felt that led them to protest.

"What are you going to do, then?"

"I don't know, Father. But, I'll make sure the right thing is done. But, I've got to get out of here to clear my head."

His driver drove him back into Kennet. Mondennio had him drop him off at the Incarna, his preferred public house. He had a private room in the back, a benefit to the establishment being Rowenzal owned. It also provided free drinks for family, another more appreciated benefit. Mondennio walked straight to his private room, raised above the main barroom. Not long after he sat down, a waitress brought him two ales. He quickly drank the first, forgetting that it had been months since he was last here.

"Mind if I join you?" Jonaldy poked his head in.

How did he know I was here? I just want my privacy. He wanted to scream. Instead, he offered Jonaldy a seat.

"I saw you walk in here and thought I should come talk to you. I spoke with the University president's secretary, and she told me what happened."

"What, is she going around telling everybody? What ever happened to confidentiality?"

"Don't worry, Mondennio. She is, ah, very confidential, if you catch my drift. She still tells me a few things now and again. So, the government gave you a shafting?"

"Funny, that's what I told my father. Only by providence will I have any chance to serve in government." He finished of his second drink, then rang a bell for a resupply.

"You never explained to me why you care so much about being in government. I mean, your family is doing well outside of government."

"It's silly, I guess. You know how the Clinate government works. There's the founding families at the top, they inherit their status. The rest of us have to work for it. We take exams to qualify, and depending on how well we do affects the family's status."

Jonaldy nodded as the waitress brought another drink. Mondennio could not help but wonder why Jonaldy seemed clueless about Copan culture. That the Clins were from the original five founders. The Septs, sub-septs and Inferiors were early settlers and were involved in managing the secretive importation of thousands of laborers to help make Copa the world it is. Those laborers were the Unnamed, those how did not rate a name but were known by their contract number.

Ultras were unnamed subjects who proved their loyalty, intelligence and willingness. They were given named-like status, given the same protection of laws as named citizens, and allowed to live in more affluent parts of Kennet. Some could even own plantations, though hardly ever on good land. Based on Mondennio's experience, Jonaldy acted like he was probably the son of an Ultra; not too aware of the true history and culture of Copa.

"So, Rowenzal used to be a Sept. We were fairly influential until a few generations back. There's not a lot of talk about what happened, but we got reduced to sub-sept status. Septs tend to be inherited, too, but they can lose their status. It just so happens Rowenzal was the last sept to be demoted."

"You thing government service will return the family to a position of power, then?"

"Yeah. I think we could do some good with a more active role in government. There are a few things wrong in government that I always thought could use a little reform. We don't have the authority as a sub-sept to enact them, though."

"Like being shafted?"

Mondennio was drunk enough to laugh. "Yeah, that's a good start. Named citizens have the right not to get shafted. Though, based on today's events I'm thinking that's not entirely true."

"What about the unnamed? You know that's one reform this planet could use — give them a role in government. That's what Veneza is always up about."

"That's another thing. They used last week's riot to keep me from resisting their arbitrary decision. Had an Atakadaro inspector ready to take me into custody the second I asserted my rights. They mentioned my protecting Veneza. The thing is, they did not know who she was. Neither did they ask."

"Maybe they already know."

"If they did, then why did I see her on campus yesterday? They would have arrested her, wouldn't they? Jerrew Clin-Khotaigra was there exalting the need for tranquility and to stamp out dissent. Yet, there was no mention of her."

"You think she's working for those who are shafting you? I mean, she talked you into going to the protest."

"Don't be silly, Jonaldy. She has way too much passion to be working against her ideals. You're not too different than she is."

"How do you mean?"

Mondennio felt uncomfortable under Jonaldy's intent gaze. He shifted in his seat. "You're passionate about republicanism like she is. You're less prone to start preaching than she is. But, you're just as passionate."

"Good. I thought you were going to say I looked good in a skirt."

"Not hardly. You don't shave your legs."

"Neither does she, so I've heard."

Despite himself, Mondennio raised his eyebrows. "How is she anyway? I've not spoken with her since the riot. I saw her on campus last week, but she was too far away to hear me when I called."

"You know, I have not seen her much myself. Perhaps after I keep you from getting too intoxicated I'll go see how she's doing."

Mondennio sat up again in his seat.

"But, back to the question at hand. The Clinate gave you the shaft. But, you still want to work in government because you're trying to restore family power."

"It's not really about power. It's about honor."

"Right." Jonaldy took a deep drink, "anybody who says it's not about power is either lying or in denial. I'll take it you are an honest fellow, so I'm going to go with delusion. Why would you want honor in a government that not only represses its unnamed but can arbitrarily shaft its entitled citizenry?

Wouldn't you much rather radically reform that government to ensure just treatment for all?"

"Trying to turn me into a republican?"

"Or an Imperial." Jonaldy flashed a sarcastic grin. "From what I hear, the Terran Imperium treats its citizens more justly than the Clinate. Sure, their upper class has certain privileges and wealth; just as we do. But, they aren't allowed to arbitrarily mark its citizens for punishment like you're dealing with now. Even their Emperor supposedly serves at the will of its citizens."

"You really think an emperor serves at the will of his subjects?"

"Why not? Copa has bountiful resources, but the size of the planet allows those resources to be controlled by the Clinate. The Imperium allegedly spans dozens of star systems that are all separated by the Soup, er, hyperspace. If a world wanted to break away from the Imperium it would. Sort of like how Copa separated from humanity."

"Are you coming down with something? You're a republican, right? How could you proselytize an autocratic regime over an oligarchy?"

"There's only one redeeming quality of the Imperium, Mondennio. As I just said, its Emperor cannot be arbitrary. He cannot exercise power not given to him by the citizens. Just like a republic the Imperium is a servant government. The real difference between the two is how the servant government is how the personnel get changed out — election or death. If the Clinate even acted like it derived its power from our consent, I'd back it."

"At this moment, I'm rather glad you don't. So, what do you think I should do?"

"You have four choices, right? You can fight and find yourself tucked away in a prison by Nilday. Don't expect they'll put you in a decent prison. They'd make an example of you."

"I've pretty much resigned myself to not fighting. So, that's not an issue."

"The second choice is you can lie on the ground in the fetal position and let them keep your family down for at least two years — probably longer. Don't think they won't find some way to ensure you won't pass the test again."

"I had not thought of that. You think they'd catch me cheating again?" Mondennio made air-quotes with his fingers.

"No, that would be too obvious. They could throw you a question with no available answer — an early one that actually knocks Rowenzal down a peg."

"Ouch. That doesn't sound too good. They did say I could do community service to redeem myself."

"Redeem yourself from being in the fetal position, you mean. Your third option is to give up altogether and stay with the family business. That's boring, if you ask me. There's no story there."

"It could be fun. I met a fellow on a secret project. I could get into one of those."

"Boring. I mean, who could you tell? It's a secret. Besides, you want to reform things, right?"

"Let me guess. That's your fourth option? Dedicate myself to pressing for republican reforms."

"You see, you're not half stupid."

Mondennio ticked the options off on his fingers. "So you're saying my options are to: one, be a martyr; two, be compliant; three, be a victim; or four, be a revolutionary."

"I would have said 'three, be Mondennio,' instead of victim but that's about right."

"Funny. If I'm so boring why did you follow me to this public house?"

"Look, you don't have to commit to choice three or four today. You're going to have to do one just to keep yourself preoccupied for the next few months."

Mondennio was angry enough with the system for today. "Fine. If I have to do something, I might as well be revolutionary about it."

23.   Veneza - Tenement

Ever since the protest, the media ranted. Veneza sat and watched the media coverage on the massacre. The media called it the "Republican Riot." The title was universal. It was so over-coordinated it made her want to scream.

She imagined the network employees sitting in a bull session somewhere trying to find new ways to alliterate "riot" and "republican." They must have been pleased with 'raucous republican rascals reek revolution and riot.' That talking head can't even say it without giggling.

Giggling. The commentators lamented the state of society that the masses had the means to assemble so quickly, so disruptively. Atakadaro should have been better prepared. Veneza saw the Atakadaro troops outside the square before the protesters. Veneza could not control herself. "They shut down mass transit! They were prepared. They knew just what they were going to do to us." Her scream echoed off the walls. The talking heads continued.

She threw a dish across the room. The plastic simply bounced off the wall and landed on other debris of her rage. She sat down and cried.

The precision the troops used. They started their attack as soon as that bottle was thrown. The bottle had to be their cue to start the crack down. Coordinated from the beginning.

"We never had a chance," she said to the empty room.

There was a soft knock on the door. She felt an immediate rush of fear that subsided just as quickly. Atakadaro don't knock. She looked through the peephole. Relieved at seeing Jonaldy, she opened the door.

"Are you alright? The streets are crawling with Atakadaro. They finally eased up on the curfew, but they have blockades everywhere."

"Sure. I'm fine. Come on in." Then she realized he was already in her apartment. "I barely got out. What about you? How did you manage?"

"I overslept, I was walking toward the marketplace when I saw the bottle. I thought they said it was going to be non-violent."

"It was going to be, Jonaldy. I've been replaying it in my mind all day. The media seemed to have been available right after the bottle landed, but they show more delay on Atakadaro's side than I remember. That's when I noticed how — planned it all was. The bottle was the signal. The media knew what to report. I mean, look at that. They have great camera angles. See? There. Look how they show those students 'attacking,' when they're retaliating. That fight started a few seconds after the bottle exploded."

"How do you know?"

"The next time they play that in the loop, look at the top right corner. You'll see Rymose crumpled on the ground."

"Rymose Hilliamson?"

"Was. I saw them! They gunned down our leadership. I would have been there, Jonaldy. That Mondennio showed up, so I thought I should guide him. We were off that way." She pointed off the screen. "I'm the only one of the original seven."

"What are we going to do?" Jonaldy sat down on her couch, shoving a few books and papers on the floor.

"We can't compete with that." She threw her hands at the screen, then sat on the couch arm. "That's a machine, Jonaldy. It sat there and waited for its master to flip the switch, then it started killing and capturing anybody it could. Then it sits there, telling us why it was only defending itself. They had rifles, batons and armor. We had placards, chants and flesh."

"We did spit in the eye of the Clinate. This would not have happened if we protested at the University."

"What? Jonaldy, they wouldn't have taken us seriously if we protested there."

"Well, it appears they took us too seriously."

"I give up. I'm lucky to be in college. I have a future."

"Veneza Karduil giving up. Wow. I never saw this coming. I guess they were right."

"Who? Right about what. I don't know what you're talking about"

"Ever wonder why they didn't take you seriously?"

"Because I'm eye candy?"

"No. I mean, yes you are eye candy. But, they knew you weren't serious. They saw you with Aradames. They doubted your loyalty. That you were only looking for a husband."

"What? How dare you!"

"Hey! I sat in on the conversations. Unfortunately, they're all dead now. Now you're giving up. The resistance is over." Jonaldy stopped talking and just and looked at her.

"You don't think I can carry the resistance?"

"I think you might, if you were serious. You've been a lot of talk. If your heart's not into it, I'll just have to find somebody else who can pick up the banner."

"Stop. Okay. Guilt received, okay? You know where some of the other diehards are?"

"Yeah. I know a few. Why?"

"You probably haven't been picked out by Atakadaro yet. Why don't you set up a meeting later this week with the ones you think we can trust. We'll see what we can do."

"That's my girl." He stood up and started easing toward the door. "You need to straighten up in here, by the way. It looks like you've been raided by the Atakadaro." He quietly walked out the door as she waved to him.

"I think I was raided. I think I know what to do now." She started to pick up as her mind started working over the list of faithful and doubtful members. Whoever turned us out was not there. I'll figure out who they were and make them pay.

As he walked down the street, Jonaldy pulled out his slate.

`@Gijira, thank you. Hold off on the story.`

As a member of the media, Gijira served Jonaldy as his middle man in warning Atakadaro of the upcoming protest. I can't have the Imperium's work thrown away on more representative government. The mass of humanity favors the Imperium. Copa needs to conform to the will of the people. But, maybe this movement can help us out and weaken the Clinate a bit.

24.   Mondennio - Performing Arts Bookstore

She told him to meet her at the bookstore at 7.00 cycles. Mondennio looked at the time and saw it was closer to 7.20 cycles. I'd be out of here if Jonaldy hadn't talked me into helping out. I don't even know why I'm here. Mondennio got up and started to walk away.

He got as far as the stairs when he saw Veneza coming up. The sight of her gave him a second reason for being there. Not that she was beautiful, he thought, but she had a comeliness about her. Something about her reminded him of his mother, though he tried to avoid the Oedipal implications.

"Leaving without me?" she said as she walked past him on the stairs. He turned to follow her and sat back down on the couch he had just left.

"I guess I'm not used to having friends be 20 beats late."

"Well, I decided to walk. Is that acceptable to you?"

"Sure.   Exercise is great as long as you don't get mistaken as an unnamed."

Veneza's eyes narrowed.   "Mondennio, are you here to support the republican cause? Because, if you are, then you're going to have to adjust that attitude. Unnamed people are entitled to public transportation, even private transportation. Named people are entitled to walk down the street without being mistaken for some undesirable. That's why I walk; I want to feel their plight. You should try it yourself — it's liberating."

"Either way, you should be careful or you might get picked up walking after curfew. And remember to carry your identification next time."

"Yes. And, I appreciate your saving me, even with my identification I probably would have lacked the ability to avoid arrest."

Not able to avoid arrest? But, she goes to University, so she can't be unnamed. Perhaps her family recently crossed the threshold as Ultras, so she's named but not privileged. What does it take to cross that threshold? What does it take to fall below it? Mondennio tried to avoid wondering if Rowenzal could be reduced to Ultra status, or unnamed.

"Since Jonaldy told you that I'm interested, he should have told you I'm not committed yet. He said something about me being a chicken, which I didn't really get."

"There's a fable about commitment.   Two friends, a chicken and a pig, decided they wanted to go into business for themselves. The chicken suggested they be a restaurant under the name 'Ham and Eggs.' The pig changed his mind saying, 'with that name you'd be involved, but I'd be committed.' His point is you're not committed, but you're willing to be involved. That's good. It's better than hostile, which is only slightly better than neutral."

"Neutral's bad?"

"Neutral's the worst. I mean, pick a side. A neutral has no self-respect. They don't care as long as they aren't picked on too much by one side or the other."

"That's sort of how I feel I would be if I stayed in the family business at this stage."

"Good. That's a start. Now I know I need to turn you into a pig. Just, not a sexist pig."

"Why are you so committed? I mean, your family's probably just over the cusp, right? Ultra. You should be content, or trying to advance your family. You're in University after all."

Veneza looked at him sharply for a moment, then softened. He realized he should have been more sensitive — matters of status are not shared outside of very familiar circles.

She spoke before he could recover from his gaff. "Mondennio, you should see the depredation I see. Walk instead of drive. My goodness, you should know the answer yourself. Based on what Jonaldy said, you have suffered under the same despotism unnamed people do every day. After one taste you don't see why I feel the way I do?"

Mondennio bristled at her rubbing his nose in his recent imbroglio — and at Jonaldy for telling her. He accepted her comment in light of the fact that he just insulted her. "But, you're beyond that despotism now, right?"

"It's not about being beyond it. If you were on a sinking ship and were pulled into a lifeboat, wouldn't you want to pull somebod else in with you? I mean, if the lifeboat had no chance of sinking? Right, then that's the same way I feel. I want as many people in the lifeboat as possible. It's not their fault they are lost, Mondennio. They were born lost and will remain so unless they are pulled out. That's our job."

"My father would say you were insane."

"Good thing for me you're not your father then. Why are you here? I have Jonaldy's explanation, but so far we've not talked about why you're here."

"You just said it — I suffered under despotism, so Jonaldy probably explained how they blocked my advancement and threatened me."

Veneza nodded.

"So, I can either play the victim or do something."

"So your idea of doing something is to try to bring the whole Clinate down? Why you? Why do you think the Clinate are so intent to bring you down? You must be pretty narcissistic to think that they've singled you out just because they don't like you."

"I guess I'm a narcissist, then. My family was reduced to sub-sept under questionable circumstances during my great-grandfather's time and now that we have a chance to return to sept status they are pushing us back down."

"There's no other reason why? Nothing that's happened inside your family? It can't be as simple as that. The Clinate should be enriched by having another sept, not less."

"Nothing I can think of — " Mondennio's face lit up when it came to him. "There's a restricted project at one of our facilities. I spoke to the head of the project a few days ago. Thing is, it's not one of our projects. At least, my father knows nothing about it. When I spoke to him he hinted that Clin-Khotaigra ran the project behind our back. Could it be that they're ruining the family because of that project?"

"That makes less sense than your they're-out-to-get-us argument. First, why would they need your facility when the Clin likely has better resources? Second, if Clin-Khotaigra was going to use your facilities, wouldn't it at least tell you that it was? Third, your cheating incident occurred before you spoke with him, right? So, why did they go after you ahead of time? There's no causality here."

"Those are good questions, Veneza. I think I know who I can ask about the first two at least. The third question does present a challenge to my theory. However, you weren't in the President's office. I don't know why they singled me out, but they did. So, you have the effect with an indeterminate cause."

"Exactly. How do I know they did not do this to you to root me out?"

"Veneza, they had you on video during the riot. They threatened me with criminal charges for my involvement in saving you. But, they did not ask who you were."

"Right. They already know who I am, so why ask?"

"If they know who you are, it should not be too difficult to find where you live, who your parents are. They would not need me to find you to arrest you. I don't think they need to resort to that level of subtlety. See who's being a narcissist now?"

"Good point."

"The point of fact is that I'm here right now. I'm motivated for my own reasons, even if they don't make sense. Granted, I'm not committed like you are. So, add me into the 'involved' column. What can I do to help?"

"The leadership is meeting in a few days. Just pretend you're a victimized sub-sept narcissist and live your life. I can't let that massacre go unresolved. I'll no doubt need your help."

25.   Klocards - Kennet Founder's Park

The leaves had fallen now, but Klocards still enjoyed walking through the now barren park. He deeply breathed the evening air, enjoying its crispness. A few evergreen shrubs sat well groomed around the mausoleum plaza. They sat silent guard of the pavement, defending from hostile squirrels. What fool brought squirrels thousands of miles from Terra?

The squirrels mostly avoided Klocards. He tried feeding them one time, but he supposed they did not think him nuts enough to take his food. He had thought they would appreciate him as they were both foreigners. The wind picked up, blowing a few leaves in a tightening circle. Spinning higher, he watched them blow away into what would be a starry sky except for the intense lights. For a planet with such pale stars, the natives liked bright lights at night. To be back in the inky dark.

"You! Come here."

Klocards let himself be distracted. As he glanced about, he realized this was the passage he knew was risky. Tight accesses. Limited fields of view. Just like an Imperial frigate. The evergreen shrubs were just high enough to hide something other than squirrels.

As he turned, he stared down the barrel of a .45 caliber pistol. *An ancient but reliable caliber, a classic pistol with a magazine of single-stacked bullets. A piece of art that never found a museum. Assuming there were bullets in the gun.* Klocards smirked. *Safety is on, and the loaded chamber indicator is not exposed. He's bluffing. This should be fun.*

"I'm serious! Get. Over. Here." The man did not look nervous. Not quite confident, but resolved.

He could have removed the chamber indicator, filed it down. As he thought it through, he realized that made little sense. As the wielder, you wanted to know if the chamber was loaded. If he recalled correctly, that model had a tendency to slide shut when the magazine was empty. It made no sense. *Judging from the look in this man's eye, he thinks it's loaded. Or, he's just crazy.*

"Look, mister, I don't want any trouble." He put his hands in the air, feigning fright.

"An off-worlder, eh?" the man's confidence grew. Klocards assumed the mugger expected the authorities would care little about another dead off-worlder. Klocards tried to gauge his resolve, and expected a fight would be coming soon.

"Yeah. Look, I've got money." He tried to sound scared, and hoped he sounded scared enough. He quickly glanced about, realizing that this guy is probably confident because he's not alone. A cord of three strands is not easily broken; and Klocards was civilian and solo. N*o, nobody around. He's a big guy, but not that big.* He slightly leaned back, putting more weight on his rear foot.

"Right, drop the cash card on the ground. That fancy watch, too."

"You want my coat, too?" He eased his front foot forward slightly as he tilted back. Just outside of reach.

"No. You better keep it. Storm's coming."

A friendly thief. Figure the odds. Sort of takes the fun out of it. Klocards noticed the man was shabbily dressed, but not cold. *He should have asked for the coat. Down on his luck? That gives me an idea.*

"Look. You look like a decent fellow. At least, not a good thief at any rate. Rather than mug me, how about working for me?"

The man looked startled. He obviously was not expecting a job offer. The thief's eyes tightened.

"What kind of fool do you take me for? You trying to get me to lower my guard so you can run. Fella, I ain't buying it. So now what?" He had a way of waiving the pistol about that showed some comfort.

"Well, no mugger with an unloaded pistol is going to make me run. I'll rip that hunk out of your hands and crack your skull."

"Right, just you — "

Nothing could make Klocards forget he was Danel Bophendze, Imperial Postal Marine. He quickly shifted his weight forward, springing off his rear foot. A career fighting Anthrophs gave Klocards' combat-hardened reflexes and speed. Against an amateur this was not a fair fight. The hapless mugger had no time to react as Klocards' hand slapped down on the pistol's slide. His grip closed around the barrel and he twisted his torso rightward.

The mugger's finger was trapped in the trigger guard as the pistol reversed direction. The barrel now pointed along the back of his hand. His wince of pain was his first reaction. Klocards debated ripping the finger off by jerking the pistol forward. Instead, he grabbed the mugger with his right hand and pulled him forward then downward. As the man slammed on the ground, Klocards relieved him of his pistol. The mugger rolled on the ground in pain from a broken finger, but managed not to make much more noise than a groan.

"Only by providence do you still have that finger, so you should be thanking me."

"What are you? Atakadaro?"

"Me? I'm just an engineer." He cleared the pistol. There was a round in the chamber. *It had been sub-calibered to handle a less lethal load. That would explain why it looked empty.* The man continued to clutch his wounded hand, not fighting back. Totally worthless as a fighter. He's just what I need.

"And, the offer still stands. You came at me with a sub-calibered weapon and didn't try to take my coat even though you obviously need one. You're not much of a mugger. However, I need a bodyguard, and you seem confident enough. Maybe I could teach you what you needed to know."

The man looked at him like he was insane. He probably was insane, trying to hire a man who not a beat before was prepared to shoot him over a few knoerzers. "Atakadaro sees me in a coat like that, they'd arrest me for sure."

The voice of experience. "Look, I tell you what. You've got a busted finger and no weapon. Here's my contact card. Ping me if you decide to take me up on it. And, don't think you can use that card to hunt me down, thinking that our little fight can't be repeated. I'll kill you if you try this again. But, if you want a job, ping me."

The next morning, Klocards put away his makeshift weight set frustrated. *I can't seem to clear this plateau. This is the third time I've gotten to this weight and not gotten above it.* It was still ten percent below his personal best. The weight was still respectable, for a non-Anthroph, and still more than adequate for a desk-ridden engineer. His encounter with the mugger reminded him that the desk would not defend him against a physical attack. He had to keep working out.

He tried to cool down in the shower. The water was always cold, the price he paid for staying with those Hanifer called riffraff. *How did I let him get the drop on me? Bophendze, you're letting yourself go in your old age.* He chuckled thinking how Smee would have complained about his using his old name — even in the shower. As soon as the chuckle started, Klocards regained himself, remembering that tapping into Smee tended to lead to nasty side effects.

Dressed and ready for the day, Klocards walked out of his little townhouse. Riffraff he may have been, but at least he had a decent place to live. He could feel the sweat still beading on his brow and the chugging of his heart. At least a brisk walk will cool me down.

He noticed a strange man across the street, staring at him intently. He could feel his adrenalin picking up.

"I thought I'd take you up on the offer," the man said.

Klocards squinted for a second until he remembered having extended an employment offer to his mugger. The man needed defending from Klocards, so his value as a true bodyguard was limited. *Hanifer will go nuts when she sees him.* Despite his repeated arguments with her, he could not come to terms with the gross disparity of rights and privileges the Unnamed had. It was worse than the Imperium.

"Thought you'd given up."

"I thought about it. You don't need much help defending yourself. So I said to myself, 'if he doesn't really need a bodyguard, then what's he really want?'

The morning light did a better job lighting his mugger. Mid-twenties, a little scrawny for a recruit. "You seem like a guy who could use a hand-up. You don't look like the kind of guy who would need a paying job."

"My family worked in the home of a Named family, until the boy of the house made a wild accusation about my father sleeping with his mother. His father sleeping with mine is more like. Killed my father with shame, and now I'm on the streets."

I'll bet. You probably started looking too much like the family for it to be hidden. "Does it matter why I want to hire you? I'll pay you two knoerzers a day. You'll need to be around at least when I walk to and from work. Help me defend myself from, um, your friends."

The man hesitated. Klocards noticed a bruise on his face, but did not remember hitting him there. *Get beat up by some old man? You have no idea what I'm asking.* "Yes or no? I've got to get to work." Klocards insisted.

"Yes."

"Fine. Got a name?"

"Mehl Kaizdeelmik."

Bruised or not, Kaizdeelmik managed to keep pace with Klocards as he walked to work. His breath was labored, but he made no complaint of the pace. *Let's see how far he'll go before he'll complain.*

They arrived at Klocards' lab. Hanifer was already there, looking over Ayoh Kaye's calculations the previous night. The look on her face as she studied her pad said all he needed to know. Another failure.

"Good morning." Klocards said.

Hanifer looked up, apparently trying to collect her thoughts. She looked past Klocards and saw Kaizdeelmik. "What is that?"

"Not so much a what as a who. This is Mehl Kaizdeelmik. Mehl, this is—"

"Do not introduce me. I might be able to work with a foreigner. You at least have value. But that."

"Mehl, his is Dr. Berryman Sub-sept Rowenzal Clin-Khotaigra. She's charmed, I'm sure."

"How dare you. Get him out of here."

Klocards looked at Kaizdeelmik. His clothes were a bit disheveled. He had managed to comb his hair and looked shaved. It was hard to tell with blonds. *How does she know he's Unnamed?*

"Hanifer—"

"Dr. Berryman!"

"This is not going to go well if you keep interrupting me. I've hired this man to be my bodyguard."

"He's a thug, if anything. How can you trust him?"

At least she said "him." *So she acknowledges that he's at least human.* "I'm surprised you value my opinion so highly. Despite my being the head of this project, you seem to ignore my authority. So, did Ayoh Kaye produce last night? Or did you fail to program him correctly again?"

"Don't change the subject. You can't make me work in the same room as him."

"Well, how about we just let him sit in the outer office."

"Fine. He comes back in here, though, I'm going to file a complaint."

Klocards noticed Kaizdeelmik stood silently through the whole ordeal. *Do you not have enough pride even to be humiliated by what she said?* He managed not to say.

Without a word, Kaizdeelmik turned and walked outside. Hanifer returned to the previous night's results as if nothing happened.

I've got to get off this rock. But not until I can reengineer the array.

Chapter 8

26. Mondennio - Klocards' Lab

It was late afternoon before Mondennio could form the security team and get in place. He knocked on the door.

Silence. Mondennio remembered his father's frustration at the silence this door yielded days before. He knew Klocards was there because security footage showed him enter the building that morning with another fellow, but not exiting.

Unlike last time, Mondennio brought a small security detail with a battering ram. Gerandy would not have approved of his lack of subtlety because of the Clin's involvement. Mondennio was not worried about that after recent events.

"Fine. They're not opening up. Let's take the door down."

Two of the five-member team picked up a reinforced pipe and tried at the door. The door proved more formidable than it first appeared. Mondennio noticed that the door's outer wooden shell was cracked, revealing hardened metal below. *Plagiontium alloy? If it is, we're not going to get through the door with a ram.*

He walked a few meters down from the door and pointed, though completely unaware of the underlying structure. "Try the wall here."

The guards repositioned themselves and looked at him again for confirmation. Mondennio nodded, knowing they were more concerned with keeping their jobs after they committed wanton property damage.

Before they could set the ram to its task, the door opened. Mondennio did not recognize the man who emerged. "You're not Klocards. From the looks of you, you're also not an engineer. What are you doing here?"

"Mister Klocards hired me. I'm Mehl Kaizdeelmik."

"Where is Klocards?"

"He's inside. He asked not to be disturbed." Mehl startled when he noticed the security detail.

Not happy to see authority? "Hold this man. He looks like a thief to me. The rest of you come with me."

The small size of the laboratory surprised Mondennio as he entered. His three guards came right behind him, and moved with measured precision to ensure the room was properly cleared. As expected, the second guard moved toward the forward-right of the room, as Mondennio recalled from an urban combat training camp his father sent him to as a child.

"I have somebody sleeping, sir," the second guard said. He closed in and pointed the muzzle of his automatic rifle a few inches away. For the first time, Mondennio looked at the rifle and noticed it was the BOL-3 9.5mm anti-personnel rifle. The caliber became popular when early settlers were confronted with the tarthon; a very aggressive predator that was hunted into extinction within the first two centuries of settling Copa. It had remained a popular caliber; but the BOL-3 was a new carbine version of the standard rifle. It was recently released by Rowenzal's weapons factories. Recent enough that Mondennio had not had a chance to fire it yet. *Did I spend that much time studying?*

"Get that out of my face," Klocards said as he opened his eyes, "before I rip it out of your hands."

"Not likely, Klocards." Mondennio said as he walked up. He waved the security guard off.

"What are you doing here? Can't you see I'm busy?"

"You're sleeping."

"Sleep? I was in a deep, contemplative meditation. This project has a problem I've been unable to solve for a few years now. I'd almost worked through the problem until you broke me out of the meditation. Now I may have to start over." Klocards kicked his leg and pivoted cleanly into a standing position.

"A few years? You've been working in a Rowenzal laboratory for years without our knowing? Have we been paying you?"

"More or less, and yes, I think. I've been getting paid, but I'm not sure by whom." He put his hand up, "Before you ask about the details — security interests preclude my answering. Even if it didn't, I'm not sure I fully understand how I'm getting paid. But I am. I do know you've provided a staff. Though staff has been distaff lately, which does complicate things a bit. Not that I mind. Distaff as staff is much more pleasing on the eyes than staff as staff. Confused?"

"I demand you tell me what you're working on, and for whom." Mondennio's finger jabbed into Klocards' chest, though it felt like he was wearing body armor.

"Get used to disappointment, Master Rowenzal. My secrecy came at a high price, and I don't think your asking please will change it." Klocards looked at the door and noticed the gouge left by the battering ram. "I'm sure your curiosity didn't cause you to nearly break down my door."

"Are you wearing body armor? An engineer does not need to wear body armor."

"I'm not wearing any, though I might have thought to pack some if I knew you'd come barging into my lab."

"This is my laboratory, Klocards. You're just stealing it, and ruining my life in the process."

"'Possession is nine-tenths.' Isn't that what they say? Your building, my lab, though you can have it back when I'm done. Besides, what makes you think my deep meditations and experiments are ruining your life?"

Mondennio plopped down on the couch Klocards just vacated. *What was that smell?* "It seems your experiments have the Clinate messing with my life. At least, that's the only way I can make sense with what's been going on in my life. I should thank you for reporting me to your benefactors after I promised to keep my mouth shut."

"Reported? Rowenzal, you must be mistaken. There's no value to my going around complaining that some kid is snooping. It's a secret project, which means I have to keep it a secret." Klocards paused for a moment, "I don't give progress reports, I don't explain what's going on. Do you see? This project is midnight-in-an-extra-system-planet dark. Whoever you think is messing up your life isn't doing it because I've told them anything."

"Then what they are doing to me must be prophylactic. They're watching you and saw me talking to you and decided to take matters into their own hands."

Klocards smiled. "I seriously doubt that. Nobody but you and maybe your daddy know that I'm in this building, who I am, or what I'm doing. I did say the project was ultra dark, right?"

"Yes, you did. Then what is going on with my life?"

"Don't ask me. Secrecy, I wouldn't tell you." Klocards smile disarmed Mondennio.

"You're not like boffins, er scientists, I've encountered in the past."

"Boffins, heh." Klocards chuckled. "That's funny that you say that. Boffins is some sort of slang for scientist? Almost like Bophendze, isn't it? No, I'm not like boffins you've dealt with in the past. Maybe sometime I'll explain to you why. But, right now I've got to get back to work. So leave." His face turned neutral, almost martial.

"You're not like anybody I met before. It's like you're not from this world. Regardless of how secret this project is, I'd like you to give me some sort of progress report. Maybe restricted access to your laboratory so I don't have to resort to a battering ram."

"We'll see. Maybe I should install a buzzer. Good-bye. Oh, you will pay to have the door restored? Thanks."

27.   Veneza - Coffee Shop

The Copan binaries had long set, making Veneza's trip more difficult. Another wrong turn. Why did Jonaldy insist on meeting in the Northwest? If it weren't for him promising some diehards I'd tell him off.

She doubled back, at least she felt like she doubled back. The only solace for the district he picked was there were no checkpoints. Another consequence of the massacre was heightened security. She would have been picked up except she knew how to bypass the ones she saw. Veneza turned right, and saw the coffee shop. She smiled slightly at the pleasantness of the neighborhood.

It was a quiet, small neighborhood, with a small traffic circle. It had a raised brick circle inside the traffic circle, which held a few small trees. The street in the neighborhood was concrete cobblestone, which Veneza decided meant the residents were wealthy. Though it was still a ghetto for unnamed

Copans, these were those who were successful in their collaboration with the Clinate Oligarchy. *Nice, right under their noses.*

She crossed the circle and entered the shop.

The coffee shop itself was quaint, with sturdy posts and low ceilings. Almost too low. She thought of the recent mine collapse that killed dozens. The victim's families received the final weekly paycheck, and a small burial allowance. She felt slightly claustrophobic and annoyed.

Veneza looked around the room to find Jonaldy. Her eyes fell on a small memento. *A republican symbol? Who's? The owner, or a patron?*

Her eyes adjusted to the dim lighting in the restaurant, slightly dimmer than it was outside. She saw Liephed, a fellow republican, sitting down at a table a small side room or large alcove.

"A rather conspiratorial establishment for a conspiratorial bunch," she said as she walked up.

"It suits us. Jonaldy said the owner was sympathetic. What was the phrase he used, Kenne?"

"Fellow traveler, whatever that means."

"Jonaldy does have an odd sense of vocabulary," Liephed said.

"Where is he?" Veneza looked around the shop. Jonaldy had a habit of showing up late and others paying a price.

"He texted that he was running late."

"Always late, usually at inopportune moments." Kenne said.

Liephed asked, "You' d don't look too happy, Veneza. Worried he's not here for a reason? He's not a loyalist."

"Liephed, we're the loyalists. The people in this neighborhood are the traitors, Kenne. Selling their people for a little privilege. We're saviors, when you think about it. Besides, if Jonaldy was working for them, they would have picked me up already. He knows where I live. For that matter, they would have probably bagged us already. I mean, we're all here but him, right?" She sat down on the bench, facing the door.

"Right."

"So, what should we do while we wait for him?" Veneza realized she was the only leader left, though she was never truly an insider.

"For one thing, we're not going to plan a big demonstration in front of the palace again. Who's idea was that?"

One advantage of not being an insider, they don't realize I first suggested it. Anyone who heard me suggest it bled out in the plaza or the hospital. Am I even fit to lead?

"Not one of our smarter plans. What do they serve here besides coffee?" she said.

"More coffee. I asked. And, they don't put any alcohol in it. I asked about that, too."

"Probably for the better. Ancient republicans were fairly heavy coffee drinkers, so I've read."

"If I hear you say, 'so I've read' one more time. Veneza, where did you read it?"

For the first time in years she thought of revealing the secret library. It had given her so much, a chance to see beyond the thin veil of lies. Her reading let her manage to keep up in the University. Higher education was reserved for named families and a few chosen unnamed. Most of those chosen few belonged to that higher caste of unnamed families who lived in the neighborhood around the shop. But those here might not understand. One might be an Atakadaro informant.

At least Mondennio isn't an informant. He had so little notice of what happened, he couldn't have given it away. Besides, he's acted like he's committed to the Cause. A fellow traveler perhaps. What a funny phrase.

A few beats later, Veneza watched two men walking right toward them.

"Don't freak out, but we've got company."

Kenne turned around and smiled. "Don't be so jumpy. These are our friends. This is Chrencarly Murpso and that fat fellow there is Roniony Wricheson."

"Fat? I'll break you Pretzel Boy." Roniony half-cocked his arm back, then smiled.

"Pretzel boy? Even when you make threats you think of food. I rest my case. Want me to order some mustard before you snap me?"

"Let me think about it."

It took some awkward sorting to get the three around the booth. Roniony pulled a second table near and sat there instead. The room was isolated enough that Veneza did not see any other patrons reacting.

"I'll tell you one thing. Nobody takes us serious. It was true before the massacre. It's true now. The media is pounding the Oligarchy's message. Republicanism is a dangerous thing. Like they've ever tried it." Veneza said. Her passion started to pull her away from her doubts.

"Sorry I'm late." Jonaldy announced himself. He was slightly out of breath, and there was no other room in the booth or the table. He grabbed a chair from an unoccupied nearby table, setting it down so he canted toward the entrance. "Did I miss anything?"

"Just Veneza reminding us that we're not to be taken seriously," Chrencarly said.

Veneza failed to notice his smirk, "That's not what I said."

Before he started, Jonaldy leaned toward the rest of the coffee shop, scanning the room. "Well, she's right. On the way over here, I heard bits of conversation, especially near the marketplace. We're not being taken seriously. Why should we? Those troops had us wetting our pants like infants. Made it look like it was our fault. Like they were spanking spoiled brats. Unnamed citizens who thought they were entitled to more. Uppity"

"I think that's probably true of a lot of the protesters."

"Of course it is," Veneza said, "You can't expect that many true believers. They're mostly fellow travelers."

Jonaldy jerked slightly. "That's not quite right. A fellow traveler is somebody who believes in the Cause, but is not actively involved."

"You sound like you got that out of some dictionary."

"No. I made it up a while ago. It's my phrase. I'm the scholar here. Okay, So I get to say whether you used it right. But, your point is right. I'll bet only one in five of us are committed true believers. The others may be involved, but they don't have any skin in the match."

"You've got all these strange terms and make those distinctions. Committed as opposed to involved. Fellow travelers. Where have you been getting these strange terms?" Veneza asked.

Jonaldy sat for a few moments, his eyes squinting and looking toward the door. "I don't know. Probably not. I picked up some Atakadaro manual off the ground when I was a kid. Veneza, ever read an Atakadaro manual?"

Veneza shook her head.

"Sure you're not an informant? I mean, you just admitted to knowing some of their tactics." Chrencarly said.

"If you know your enemies and yourself, you will not be imperiled in a hundred battles. Chrencarly, don't be so ignorant."

Veneza cut the conversation off. "Here we go again. Another conversation where we start fighting over words and their meaning. We'll end up in some philosophical argument and split off in a huff."

"Sure. It's safer than throwing flaming bottles at authority." The rest of the table winced as Kenne finished his quip.

"Well, that can't have been us. I'll bet Atakadaro got a man on the inside to throw the thing. It looked too much like a signal from where I was standing."

"I saw you, back in the back on some table. Who was that guy who had his arm around you?"

She flushed. The attack begins. "He didn't have his arm around me. And—"

Jonaldy jumped to her rescue. "She's right. We can't sit here and argue all night. Veneza called this meeting. So, Veneza. What do you want?"

She appreciated his support, she needed all the help she could get. Veneza spent most of the day trying to rehearse a speech. She looked at the men at the table and her rehearsed words failed her. She took a deep breath.

"Kenne was right. Well, he wasn't, but he is. I mean." She paused to collect her thoughts. "I did not say that we weren't to be taken seriously. But I would have. We argue what it takes to be Republican. Cut somebody out because they think a Republic has to have a religious anchor. We fight amongst ourselves, so there's no need for an outsider. We do the occasional protest that nobody pays attention to. We got more media coverage being shot up than for anything we did before. I'll bet somebody complained to the Atakadaro because they weren't in the right conspiracy meetings and wanted a bit of retaliation."

"What's your point?" Jonaldy cut in.

Veneza glared at him. Then she realized his interruption was his way of trying to stop her confusion. She took a breath and started again. "We need to stop talking. We need to make the Atakadaro know they can't get away with that. They fired the first shot. They started the war. Who's with me?"

"Fighting a war? Are you crazy? I'm surprised they don't have us under surveillance right now."

"I'm not crazy. I'm sick and tired of being sick and tired. We've got to do something to prove we're involved." Veneza said.

"Committed." Jonaldy quipped.

"Stop it with the word splicing!" Her hands shook to punctuate her words. "We all say we're committed. We've said we're willing to die for a Republic. Some of us did just that last week. We can sit here and let them slowly grind us out, or we can fight back. If you're not willing to take that step, leave now. But, if you're not committed to the idea of a Republic, then you're not committed. You're just a fan, not a follower."

They were silent. Wow. I said it, and they listened. "Nobody leaving? Fine. That means you're in. It will be a conspiracy going forward. We are all guilty of treason anyway. They'll hang us together or separate, so we can't back down."

"What's our first move?" Jonaldy asked.

"I have no idea, but it needs to be bold enough. Any ideas?" Veneza looked at the men at the table, hoping somebody would come up with a good idea that didn't involve death.

The table was silent again. A few traded glances, then Jonaldy spoke up. "We should start by kidnapping somebody."

"What? That's crazy." Kenne said. "How is that going to call attention to the Cause?"

"If we get the right victim, we can get him to carry the message to the media when we let him go. Let them know Atakadaro started the massacre. Let them know we're going to be a force to be reckoned with going forward."

"Who should it be?" Chrencarly asked.

"Skuriat Giedaz."

The group looked surprised.

Kenne nodded. "He's that history professor that's so over the top for the Clinate, it would do good to knock him down a peg."

"That makes no sense. Why not kidnap somebody who is at least neutral? They would at least be more willing to carry the message." Roniony countered.

"No. That would just turn that person against us. We don't have to worry about an opponent turning against us. I have a friend who is interning for the media. She said Skuriat spouts out all the time and the writers she works for take it down verbatim. He may as well be helping them write their propaganda."

"Couldn't we just try to recruit from the lower castes?" Roniony spoke up, looking worried.

"That will follow after. The rumornet is more likely to carry our message better than the media anyway. Skuriat is a good choice because he has a lot of servants. Even if the media doesn't broadcast our message, they will. Then we'll have ready recruits."

"I don't know. It sounds like a stupid thing to do." Roniony said. Kenne nodded.

"It may not be the smartest thing, but it's a start. A transition from rhetoric to action. Action speaks louder than words anyway." Veneza was energized. *Something that they can take me seriously for.* "Or, are you going to sit in coffee shops the rest of your lives?"

"I'm with Veneza. Better to do something than sit on our arses. After what those fikilon did to our friends?" Chrencarly finally said something.

Jonaldy spoke up a beat later. "Let's not make a rash decision. It's going to take time to plan something like this. At least a couple of weeks. Chrencarly, you have a class with him, right?"

Chrencarly was surprised. "I did. He kicked me out of class for laughing when he was expounding on some point of Clinate lore."

"Think he remembers?"

"Probably not. Why? You want me to go back to school and follow him around?"

"Exactly."

28.   Mondennio - Performing Arts Bookstore

What is she going to want me to do? Mondennio crossed the street in front of the bookstore. He held the door for a mother and her son, then went inside.

Jonaldy turned his head as Mondennio reached the top of the stairs. Veneza was already there — early. It irked him when he remembered how late she was last time.

"I thought you two preferred to not meet in public during daylight?" he said as he finally made it to their seats.

"It doesn't bother me, but Jonaldy here has always acted a little more paranoid," Veneza said.

"If we want the Clinate to take proper notice of republicanism, we have to move boldly and soon. I'm impatient for radical action, so I thought it wouldn't hurt this once to meet in a group during daylight."

"My father always said you have to move impatiently with patience, or take your time when you hurry up. Sure you're not moving too fast?"

"That's an odd comment."

"Not really, it's just — "

"Boys, stop. Really. We need to get going, Mondennio. The team has agreed to commit a bold action, and Jonaldy here has the plan. I think it's a stroke of brilliance, but there's a catch that needs your help."

"What do you mean, 'my help?' What are we going to be doing?"

"Mondennio, we appreciate your interest, but we're not sure how committed you are to our cause. Once I'm comfortable that you're with us, instead of some rich kid — "

"I'm not really committed to your cause, to be quite honest. The Clinate is barring me from my right to enter government. That keeps my family from the opportunity to advance itself. I don't hold with your notions of everybody running things. You need experts, not a bunch of commoners" Mondennio sat on the remaining lounge chair canted at an angle away from Veneza and Jonaldy.

"See, Jonaldy, I told you he was just involved."

"Mondennio, don't you even hold to the notion of government by the consent of the governed?"

"What? That the Clinate serves by the will of the people? The problem with that notion, Jonaldy, is that the people are ignorant. Given a chance, they will chose only what benefits themselves. They won't care if those short-term benefits create long-term harm. It takes people of vision to see how things should be, and to coax the people toward it."

"That's the problem with Copa, Mondennio. You aristocrats think that you know what's better for us, that we're not able to think for ourselves. Govern ourselves."

"That's history, Veneza. Before Terrans discovered superluminal travel, our home world was crippled by societies that thought the way you do. That people could — should govern themselves. Despotism of the masses."

"Better than despotism of the elite!"

Jonaldy put his hands up. "Now it's my turn to tell you to stop. Mondennio, you assured me you were willing to be active, to try to show this government that it needs to be more just. More fairness. Do you still believe that?"

"Yes. They should not be able to arbitrarily deny access to government like they did me."

Jonaldy turned to face Veneza so Mondennio could not see his face. "Veneza, he essentially agrees with you. He just needs time to fully understand that he does. He has cognitive bias"

Veneza's face looked confused, then flashed understanding. "He's right, Mondennio. At our core, we want fairness and justice. You just don't think it should go as far as I do, or Jonaldy does. So, as long as we can get along, we can work together. Deal?"

What are they getting me into? I can't let Clin-Khotaigra just run roughshod over me or any aristocrat. What they did in the riot was shameful. "It's a deal. Clin-Khotaigra has overstepped itself, and I want to fix that."

"Exactly," Jonaldy said. "So I have a master plan that will help us all achieve our goals. But, it requires that we have greater access than we do. There's a gated community just to the West of Kennet. Know about it?"

"Ginster Enclave? Yeah, I've been there before. Why?"

"I need to scout the area. We're going to do some vandalism, but we have to make sure we have enough time to do it. So, we have to find what if any surveillance equipment and other security measures there may be."

"I can do that."

"No, Mondennio. I've done this sort of thing before. I know what I'm looking for. However, that community's accesses require somebody above my strata. That's where you come in. You have those accesses."

"You want me to help you get access to Ginster Enclave so you can plan vandalism? What sort of vandalism requires that much time, or even access to the Enclave itself. Why not just paint the outside wall, or something."

Jonaldy grimaced. "Mondennio, I can't give you those details. You do know that our organization is anathema to the Clinate. If we get caught or arrested, you'll probably do a little time in prison if they somehow think you were actively helping republicanism. Veneza and I will likely be executed. We —"

"Remember, you're a chicken. We're pigs. We want to know if you'll roll in the filth." Veneza said.

"Mondennio, we can't risk our lives in trusting you just yet. Once you've done more to earn our trust, then we'll start letting you in on more details. I know that look. You have to decide if you're really ready for this. If you're not, then walk out now. Continue playing the victim and go work for daddy."

Work for daddy? Jonaldy thinks I'm some sort of coward. If Khotaigra did this to me, who else has been persecuted? If this is what it takes to get reforms. "Fine. I'm in. When do we do this?"

"Tonight."

"That soon?"

"You have other plans, then walk. We need you to focus on the task at hand."

"You're just not giving me much time to think. I don't want to make a big mistake."

Veneza spoke up. "You made a mistake when you saved me. Clin-Khotaigra rewarded you for that, remember? Doing anything that advances justice cannot be a mistake. You saw what they did, you can't say that was just. Had they arrested me, would that have been just? If they reward justice with punishment, then they are not just. Getting back at them cannot then be a mistake."

29. Jonaldy - Streets of Kennet

The news reported that the Imperial Frigate *N' losnil* arrived in system. With the name announced, Jonaldy missed the bits that talked about its menace and other dire predictions of planetary subjugation. While it might appear to both Imperial and Copan governments that ship rotations were random and ill-planned, Jonaldy was expressly told to set up his array to receive instructions when the N' losnil arrived in system. It last arrived when he was new in system, and signaled him about Oracle Rose, the Bafiktuy operative AI on Copa. Uncertain how long the ship had been in system, he put on his coat and hurriedly left.

Jonaldy tightened his coat against the brisk breeze. This time, his route took three busses. The last took him into the city center.

The bus meandered its way, Jonaldy patiently checking each of the passengers, looking for a familiar face — somebody who might be following. Satisfied there were none, he got off the bus a stop beyond his destination. He calmly walked a block away, noticing none from the bus following him, then he turned back toward the other stop. The distance between these two was about a kilometer apart. He passed the Clin-Robacker mausoleum park and entered a nearby coffee shop. He drank his coffee slowly, warming up from the cold outside.

Finished, he walked outside the coffee shop and strolled until he arrived outside a tenement building not far from the Imperial embassy. Its tenants supported the embassy, so it was video monitored. Jonaldy approached the building with confidence, knowing that Oracle Rose would clean up any electronic trail he left. She would have heard the same message he did — so she would know what to do.

Inside the building, he waited to ensure he was not being followed. Then he started up a set of stairs. At one point, he stopped. He pushed open a false panel on the stairwell and crawled inside. Once there, a narrow ladder took him down to a small room. Its low ceiling forced him to remain on hands and knees.

The Imperium set up simple security measures in the buildings neighboring its embassy. The crews that set the measures up were unaware that some of the components had nothing to do with security. Their placement in the buildings around the embassy served a much more basic purpose.

Jonaldy hooked a small cable to his slate. Once set up, he tapped a special command on the slate. The cable linked the slate to a large antenna array, which in turn fed a signal from the N' losnil.

Most spaceborne communication relied on a nano-short wavelengths. The signal he received had a wavelength of 300 meters. The slate emitted short and long beeps in a pattern — dits and dahs that he could interpret as they played — that sent Jonaldy new instructions. An ancient data method using ancient codes that any modern system would discount as noise.

`Priority: Capture and return or eliminate Janhas Klocards, runaway Imperial scientist. Support team on station awaiting Wilco signal.`

No mention of Mondennio? What about my primary mission? Now is not the time for a distraction. The conflicting assignment led Jonaldy to remember the days when his missions were failures. Only his saving the Empress and his assignment on Copa were successes that were clearly successes.

Because of the cold, he figured his return trip only required two legs. He first boarded a bus that went straight to the giant indoor shops and wandered around the warmth of that building for a while. He decided to buy a gift for Veneza.

As he wandered the shops, he thought over his assignment, trying to ensure his new orders would not interfere with his primary mission.

The recent crackdown in the market square almost made him sympathize with the average citizen. A republic would be better for them than what they have now, if it could be expected not to turn to these draconian measures.

He chided himself. *Imperial government is what they really need. They are children who need the attention of a dodding and loving father — like our Emperor. We are all children in the end. That's why republics always fail. At least the Imperium does not pretend to have control of everything. We welcome dissent, provided it does not get out of hand. The Clinate can't accept even that.*

His concerns mellowed about helping the Republicans. Whatever they did would backfire on them. It could either weaken the Clinate, make it crack down harder or win and devolve. This culture could not handle the rigor of democracy. Few could. There were certainly democracies that devolved into tyranny. Copa could well devolve accordingly. That would advantage us, too. We could step in to save them from themselves.

He found a little trinket for Veneza that he would try to give her. She was attractive in her own way. If you look past her fanaticism. He texted,

@Veneza: Have some friends of mine in tow. Will meet you soon. Take care and keep your head together. We're counting on you.

Back in his apartment, the lights stayed dimly lit at night. He could not afford high energy bills as an underprivileged college student, he always explained. He thought it helped him more readily avoid surveillance. It reduced the energy signature that helped him find cameras and microphones that may be hidden. It let him look outside more readily without being silhouetted as a powerful street light sat just beneath one of his two windows. Unlike Imperial bachelor apartments, he had his own bathroom. He locked the door.

He reflected on the assignment. The team is already here. I just need to signal the lead. Maybe they just expect me to manage things since I'm here? Besides, I had my start in this type of mission. This should not be too difficult, depending on the team's quality.

He went to his window and put out two markers. Together they spelled "Wm." The "W" signaled his willing compliance with the orders he recently received. Whomever the Bafiktuy had in the Imperial embassy would need that to report back before the dispatch ship left. Jonaldy directed the "m" toward his newly-acquired hit team. To the Team Lead, meet me.

He expected that to take some time. There was no information on the team or its leader. He would not recognize him when they met. Jonaldy realized there also was no recognition signal. It could be anybody. It may not even be Bafiktuy. He calmed himself before that concern could intensify.

He amended his message to the Team lead by adding the three words to a well-known Imperial play. "We happy few." Hopefully the lead would know the reference. On his window read: "Wm. We happy few."

30.   Mondennio - Streets of Kinnet

"Am I some spoiled rich kid?" Mondennio sat in the center of the car's back seat, speaking to nobody.

"What was that, Sir?"

Mondennio was unaware that he had spoken his thought aloud. "I wasn't talking to you, Driver."

His driver continued looking forward, silent.

What could it hurt asking him for advice?   He's not involved, or committed, or whatever. He should have a neutral opinion. "I'm sorry. I'm just not used to drivers talking."

"Yes, Sir. Won't happen again."

"As long as we're talking, give me your frank assessment. Am I a spoiled rich kid?"

"I really can't answer that, Sir. This is the only job I have."

"Surely you can compare me to your own children, your own experience."

"I'd rather not, Sir. As I said, this is my only job."

Mondennio looked at him in the rear view mirror. "Why should it matter if this is your job?"

"To be honest, I could lose it if I give an inappropriate answer."

"That's nonsense. Why would you worry about — "

"Job security? I've noticed you've been having troubles lately. I'm sure you appreciate what happens when you act inappropriately or speak out of turn. You may not know this, but unemployment is high on Copa. We unnameds had a pretty good period about twenty, twenty-five years ago. Now we have too many young men and women looking for jobs. Drives the cost of labor down, and believe me when I say you aristocrats will not pay a knoerzer more than you have to. If you fired me, it is likely I may never work again — especially when they find you fired me for insolence."

"Nonsense."

"Yes, Sir. Not something you notice in your world, if I may be frank."

"I'd rather know the truth."

The driver laughed. "Copan truth is relative. Wouldn't you rather know the facts and have a worldview that let you analyze them objectively? Then you may come to know real truth."

"Do you think you know real truth?"

"No, Sir. I have some friends that claim to have it, but I think they are foolish. I'd rather have some control over my fate."

"As do I. Don't worry about losing your job. This conversation stays in the car, and I won't fire you. I promise. Am I a spoiled brat? By your preference not to answer I have to assume so."

The driver continued driving in silence for a few beats. "Sir, you are spoiled, but not a brat. Not any more, anyway. Had you asked me five years ago, I would have agreed with the entire question without reservation."

"What changed?"

"You grew up, Sir. Some of my fellow drivers notice your lot does not always grow up. They sort of remain in this perpetual adolescence that is very frustrating. Had you been one of those, I would not have spoken up earlier even if you were speaking to me. I expect I would have been fired then also."

"Is it that bad?"

"However bad I describe it, then just assume it's worse. We have different perspectives. Your kind is oblivious to what happens to my kind. It's our environment, so we're accustomed to it. Not all of us are content with it, though."

"The republicans?"

"Yes. I worried about you during that riot, but you seem to have gotten out unscathed."

"Oh, no. I'm quite scathed. Well-scathed, to be more correct. What about the republicans?"

"It would be seditious for me to speak more of them, Sir."

"It's only sedition if it were reported. As I said, as far as this conversation is concerned this car is immune to the law and consequences of things said in this conversation. Imagine that some kind of cone of silence has descended."

The driver remained silent for a beat. "They are frustrated by the great inequities in our society, Sir. Why is it you are driven in cars and they are forced to remain on foot? That's just one petty example. They are disallowed from owning property."

"Only the Clins are entitled to property ownership. Even we Rowenzals lease our home and lands. One-hundred year leases are the most we're entitled to. That's part of what holds us together, actually."

"Would you be surprised to know that all of the original settlers were promised ten jeribs of land after ten years of labor? How do you think we all got here?"

"Quite surprised. I consider myself a historian, and I never encountered that."

"What you probably read was your side's view of the truth. About one-hundred years after the last mass migration, as the hyperspace route collapsed, the law changed. Only Clins were allowed to buy, sell or inherit land. Barring others from inheritance meant it was only a matter of time before they held all the land. You other aristocrats were given a free one-hundred year lease on any land you helped them acquire. Property is the source of freedom. Freedom suffers when a few wealthy people collude to control it."

"How do you know so much? That was nearly 1,500 years ago."

"I've seen the original documents."

"Impossible. They were destroyed in the Skadhen Fire."

"They were meant to be destroyed, but my understanding is the originals were retrieved before the fire and replaced with copies."

"So you're saying I've been studying a lie all this time? What other 'lies' do I know?"

"I don't know what you've been studying. All I can say is it is important to view facts from an objective viewpoint, which is difficult for either of us. As for lies, I'm sure you know countless lies. They are easy enough to create."

"So I'm a spoiled ignorant fool?"

"Those aren't my words, Sir."

"What about our vast platinum reserves?"

"That is true. One of the reasons Copa was so coveted, and why the Founders did what they could to make the route disappear. Also the reason why the Imperium seeks us."

"Platinum?"

"It used to be used in an alloy that is critical for hyperspatial travel."

"Wait. You're just a driver. Why are you so well informed?"

"I have a lot of spare time. Do you think I sit around all day pining for your return so I can drive you to your next destination? I have plenty of time to read. While you've been at University, I've been getting an education."

"So, are the Republicans right? Should I be sympathetic to their concerns?"

"Here again, the truth that would answer that is relative. You need to change your viewpoint and get the facts. I won't answer that question because it's too seditious. Most of our conversation has been, Sir. And ahead of us is the Rowenzal Enclave. So, your cone of protective silence has ended."

Mondennio nodded reluctantly. For the first time in his life, he wished the Enclave were a further suburb of Kennet, instead of one of the nearest.

"By the way, what is your name?"

"Janhas Sahkud. I've driven for you for ten years. That's the first time you ever asked my name."

Klocards - Restaurant

Klocards entered the restaurant. The news report of the inbound frigate included the arrival of an Imperial recruiter — one he knew. Only about half the tables were occupied. He scanned the room until his eyes rested on a man dressed in formal Imperial Postal Officer dress. "Captain Litovio!"

The officer twisted in his seat half in surprise. His face warmed into a smile. "Danel. How have you been? Wow. This is the first time I've seen you with a gut like that."

"It's the lower gravity. It's standard, but you know we keep the gravity higher on Imperial ships." Klocards felt silly for stating the obvious. Litovio should be able to notice the gravity was about one-tenth lighter than what he lived in. "I was surprised when I got your message. What ship were you on? What brings you here?"

"I'm on the was the IFR *N' losnil*, passing thorough. They pulled my command from me not long after you escaped. Thank you very much. Kosoado had a bit more pull than we expected, but not enough. I'm still a Postie."

"That you are. What do you expect to recruit here?"

"Nothing, but I do have broad travel privileges. I heard a ship was heading this way and thought I could hazard a visit. How's your project? I would have thought it would be finished by now."

"Not quite. I have all the mechanical stuff working fine in the simulators. The plans had most of that anyway, so I guess that's the easy part. There was a bit missing on the sensor analysis software in the original plans. Smee figured that out."

"Who's Smee?"

Klocards forgot Litovio did not know about his implanted artificial intelligence; Smee. Had Litovio known about the implant, he knew their friendship would be over — related or not. "Sorry." He paused. "He was one of my first assistants. He really pulled through in the early days. Took me forever to run him off."

"How many assistants have you had?"

"Including my current one? Twelve I think. Maybe thirteen. I can't keep them around too long or they will figure it all out. It's a real pain having to run them off, too."

Litovio looked outside the restaurant. He gestured toward Mehl who stood outside in the chilly air. "What about him? They got somebody watching you?"

"No, he's mine. This planet is so socially stratified it drives me nuts. Worse than the Postal Service. At least there you had a chance to rise. Here, you might be able to advance if you are descended from one of the founding families. Mehl there tried mugging me. So, I figured he might be a good bodyguard."

Litovio looked like he was about to ask, but stopped himself. Klocards knew it sounded crazy — people needed guarding from him, not the other way around. Even knowing Litovio was family now, there was still a bit of distance between them. Klocards suspected it was his mistrust and their military bearing.

"Oh, well. I would have thought with the Rymok plans you would be finished by now."

"So would I. They had better security than I thought. The plans left out some of the science. The hard part, actually. I'm working on the trans-soup connection. Bowbing thing does not work! I've looked at the problem from just about every angle."

Litovio smirked. "It worked, all right. Killed a corvette. Bloodied a Frigate. Nearly had the Raykomara except you sabotaged its main gun. You have plans for its ion cannon. From the specs it looked like it would cut right through our armor. I wish you'd invent something more practical like that. Something the Postal Service could use."

"You think the Postal Service can't use this? A sensor array like this in every Imperial system would be a serious force multiplier. I'm still betting that the array can be used as a transmitter. Imagine that, Litovio. Instantaneous communication through the Soup!"

Litovio seemed to consider Klocards' comment. "I imagine the Postal Marines would do quite a bit to stop you, actually. I told you before the Emperor would likely have dedicated a whole team, a whole company, just to the research. That would give him quite a bit more power."

"No thanks. The Emperor got enough of me — 23 years in fact. This time, I want something with my name on it. I want to give it to all systems, not just the Core Worlds. Maybe this will give the power to the people."

Klocards' comment silenced Litovio. A wall stood between them as Litovio slowly drank. Klocards tried to think of a way to break through that wall, but nothing came to mind. More than half his life given to the Emperor and the Postal Service seemed to disappear as he thought over his own treasonous statement.

"Trans-soup works, Danel. When the Raykomara was stuck in the Soup, I saw two of the array sensors myself." He sat up in his seat and leaned towards Klocards. "Do you remember the Battle of Tannhauser Gate? There was so much firepower concentrated in that tight Lagrange point. Our first assignment together, remember?"

Klocards thought through the previous twenty years. "Not sure who had it harder. You in your cruiser or me in my suit. Probably you. At least I was encased in my own life support." Klocards knocked back his drink.

"Until that jump into Rymok, I had never been so resigned to die as I was in Tannenberg. Death was so certain. The whole crew knew it was doomed. Just like Tannenberg. Providence guided me through both. Those connections were miles apart in space, but they were close together in the

Soup. I know it works. I saw it. Don't stop. I don't care if it brings down the Service or the Emperor. Damn our oath. There has to be a reason why you have the technology. It has to be Providence. Don't stop trying."

"I've been beating into this issue for two years. Nothing in the schematics hints at why it works. The AI here has no clue."

"Stop doubting and start fighting. Maybe that's why I survived both. I never gave up the faith. Hurry up, though. There's been talk floating about that the Emperor might try to establish relations with Rymok. If we didn't have other troubles, I'm sure he would have sent the Navy in to induce membership already. Though, if he ever saw Kosoado's report he might change his mind. He's not like his father. He's more aggressive about incorporating these independent worlds. I'm sure he has something planned even for little Copa here."

"Speaking of fighting, you wouldn't happen to have run across a couple of pistols?"

"What?" Litovio nearly spilled his drink.

"I've felt naked ever since I've been on this planet. I've been looking for a pair of decent pistols, but the laws here are tight. There are always a few spares floating about in the Postal Service."

Litovio opened his mouth a few times as if to speak. Finally, he said, "if it were anybody else, I'd tell them to pound sand. I won't promise to do anything other than look."

"Great."

31.   Mondennio - Ginster Enclave

He waited in the cool breeze for the streetcar to arrive. He had never ridden in one before, and felt a bit of unease. Mondennio looked over to where Sahkud had parked the car several meters away, his driver watching with a worried face. He probably doesn't think I know how to navigate in one of these. Mondennio remembered to write down the name of his stop, so he could return if necessary. He planned not to call for Sahkud's help. It annoyed him to think his driver might be better educated than he was, considering how much time he put into his education.

Mondennio looked at the other passengers as he boarded the streetcar. He noticed that many appeared to be Ultras, with perhaps some higher-paid unnamed passengers riding illegally. It was difficult for Mondennio to know which was which. Veneza called those at the cusp between named and unnamed "Collaborators." It was a term Jonaldy had thought was not complimentary.

Mondennio saw Jonaldy sitting toward the back of the car, and made his way back there. The streetcar hummed along with frequent clacking sounds that grated at him. He was accustomed to the relative silence of his car. As he rode, several passengers kept looking over their shoulders at him. A few seemed to get off the streetcar early, because they stood at the stop rather than walk away after the streetcar left. Those must have been some illegal passengers.

As the street car rode toward the next stop, Jonaldy stood up. As the streetcar rocked, he made his way toward the door. Mondennio followed him fighting to stay standing with the car's movement. They both got off at the next stop.

"We still have some walking to do. About two kilometers," Jonaldy said.

They walked in silence. The first kilometer had a few large stores, which became single-family homes. They passed a large compound on their right, which Mondennio later learned was an Atakadaro facility. The last commercial shop was a small restaurant across the street from the facility. They walked passed a small outdoor sports arena before finally coming up to the Ginster Enclave.

"We need to walk past the front gate. It's manned, so we won't both be able to enter. You might even have problems without knowing any of the residents." Mondennio felt his fingers tingle as adrenaline entered his system.

Jonaldy led him another 500 meters before they came to an unmanned security gate. A service gate. Mondennio noticed the access pad and surveillance camera.

"Won't they see me when I access it?"

"Not really." Jonaldy pulled out a memory stick, "It was a quiet night a few days ago, so I happened to get a recording of what this camera saw." He climbed up carefully and inserted the stick at the back of the camera. "Now when you access, it will only show who came for a late-night delivery."

"How is it you happened to have this?"

"Mondennio, just accept that sometimes I work in mysterious ways. Now, this access pad is not mapped to Atakadaro for confirmation. Too many deliveries by unnameds come through here. I guess they figure the camera is enough of a deterrent."

"Apparently not enough. So, what do I do? Just type in my line number and the gate will open?"

"You should be able to get away with giving your numbers from Clin to sub-sept, then type in any random four digits. I'm sure there are at least 10,000 people under Rowenzal."

"7,538 at last count."

"So, stay under that number."

"You're saying any subsequent investigation will lead to that person. Isn't that unfair?"

"Not really. Whoever that is will have an alibi that should hold up. Atakadaro would have to conclude somebody stole that person's identity. Once you've typed in that number, it will ask for that person's personal identification number."

"I know what a PIN is."

"Yes, well, you can use yours. As a Sub-sept, your PIN works for anybody."

"What? Works for anybody? That means I can potentially steal the identity of anybody within Rowenzal?"

"Not potentially. Look. Just type in the line item number then your PIN, and we're in."

"You're certain whoever I'm pretending to be won't get in trouble. And, my PIN won't be associated?"

"Your PIN is a skeleton key, it leaves no trace. Mondennio, if I weren't certain I wouldn't be asking you to do it. This is one of the perks of being named—you didn't know? You can shuttle about anybody you want and can pretend to be anybody unnamed you want. This is not as uncommon as you might think. It helps explain why unnamed women end up pregnant with named children."

Mondennio tapped in the numbers, and the gate unlocked. Mondennio thought he should be more worried about what they were doing, but Jonaldy's calm demeanor and expertise mellowed him. "So, if you know all this, why do you need me? Why not just bypass the security."

"Um — I've tried that before. It seems my efforts to bypass trip some security protocol. But, I know a legitimate line-item with PIN won't because that's expected behavior. Now, stay quiet, and stay with me. I need to scout the entire enclave for cameras and likely guard routes."

"So, you don't just need me to bypass this gate? I thought that's all I was here for."

"No, I need you for the whole operation. Look, are you in this or not?"

Mondennio nodded. For the next two dozen beats, Jonaldy meticulously surveyed the compound, Mondennio in tow.

"Don't stand there. Stand over there."

"Why?"

"Surveillance. See that camera there? It sweeps at random intervals, but its arc is confined. Standing where you are will be in its arc."

"Won't the shadows conceal me?"

"Are you an idiot? Haven't you ever heard of thermal vision? Femtometer scanners? Shadows conceal from unaugmented humans."

Unaugmented? Where are there augmented? Mondennio stepped where Jonaldy told him, and watched the camera carefully. He was not entirely certain Jonaldy was right.

A moment later, the camera swept and seemed to be pointing right at him. "Jonaldy, it's pointing. Right. At. Me."

"Nonsense, it's — "

Mondennio felt Jonaldy's arm as it grabbed him and jerked him behind the wall.

"I should have had you behind the wall. Sorry."

"What?! You mean they have an image of me now?"

Jonaldy looked apologetic, "Might, yes. Don't worry, I think I know somebody who might be able to make that go away."

"Go away? I didn't want it the first time. What am I doing here? I'm leaving." Mondennio started walking in the direction he thought the service entrance was.

"Don't go that way," Jonaldy pointed. "That's the camera, remember? I got what I came for, anyway."

"I ought to walk to that security shack and turn us both in. I at least have the authority to be here."

"That would not be a good idea."

"Why not?"

Jonaldy turned to face him, leaning up against the wall. "Well, one of the residents of Ginster Enclave would probably object to your presence here, especially a presence obtained via a questionable access."

"Who?"

"Skuriat Guidaz. You know him, right?"

"Professor Guidaz? Are you out of your piko-loving mind? After what happened here I could be in serious trouble if I'm caught."

"Exactly. That's why you don't want to go to the guard shack. If that camera had any facial recognition software, which I bet it does, then you might want to work with me and get out of here before the guards receive a warning. That is, assuming Skuriat put a restraining instruction in place."

"I can't believe you dragged me into this. You knew Professor Giedaz lived here, knew I could get in trouble, and you brought me?"

"It wasn't my idea. Talk to Veneza."

"Don't think I won't. I asked this earlier, but I need to hear this again. If we are scouting the compound for later vandalism, wouldn't we be better served to just vandalize and post guards."

Jonaldy checked his chronometer and motioned Mondennio to follow. "We need to start heading off. In a few more beats that camera will be able to report what it really sees again. Then we'll really be stuck."

"Give me an answer."

"Fine, I'll answer, but come on!" Jonaldy started jogging with Mondennio close behind. Once they got outside the enclave walls, Jonaldy resumed. "We're not here to vandalize. If we were, this is a poor candidate target. There are much more visible and accessible targets. Like that mega store we saw on the walk here."

"Okay, then why this boondoggle?"

"We're here to kidnap one of the residents. The ransom will be —"

"That's crazy. I can't believe I helped you with the reconnaissance. I'm walking right to that shack now."

"You'd better not.   Mondennio, you'll have a much harder time explaining what you were doing on the compound. Sure, you'll get me and Veneza arrested. But both of us will say you were involved. I'll even say you instigated it. That would play out very well for you, wouldn't it?"

"Why would you do such a thing? I thought we were friends."

Jonaldy looked at him with a smirk. "Mondennio, we are friends. Look, you said you didn't want them to continue to victimize you and others, right? Republicans are after the same thing, just in a different way. It's okay to work with somebody when you have similar goals, even if you don't have the same goals. Close enough is good enough.

"Veneza is the de facto leader of the movement now that Atakadaro executed those it captured. As your friend, I'm trying to ensure you don't do anything so stupid you intentionally put yourself into prison. In fact, prison would be the last place I'd want you. But, I'm also working to ensure the movement moves."

Mondennio and Jonaldy walked quietly back to the transit stop. Mondennio looked at Jonaldy, who looked giddy after the recent stalking about.

"Mondennio, I know you're shocked. Once you calm down you'll see what I mean. I tell you what, take the Northbound streetcar four stops and you'll find yourself at the central transit area. Your car is not more than a few hundred meters away to the East. I'll contact you in a few days."

"Don't." Mondennio glared at Jonaldy.

Mondennio boarded the streetcar, which providentially appeared one beat after they arrived. He stared out the window at Jonaldy as the streetcar drove away. As soon as the streetcar turned the corner, he pulled out his slate and texted Sahkud.

`@Sahkud meet me at the Market Square.  Now.`

Mondennio looked down as he rode the streetcar. He did not care about the people who might be staring at him, a passenger wearing clothes that clearly identified him as a sub-sept member. He managed not to shake in his anger at having been duped into helping plan the kidnapping. *Of all the stupid things I've ever done!*

A few beats later, he got off the streetcar and climbed into the waiting open door of his car. Sahkud shut the door and a beat later was in the driver's seat as the car gently pulled away.

"They are going to use me in a kidnapping."

"Are we using that cone of silence thing again?"

"Sure. Cone of silence. This is just between us."

"What are you going to do? You're not going to go through with it, are you?"

"I can hardly think straight right now. I tried to think about it on the ride here, but my mind was numb. I couldn't believe what was happening. I still can't believe it's happening."

"I suspect you're about at your breaking point right now, Sir. With all that's been going on, I'm surprised you've not snapped yet."

"I think you're right, but I'm not sure if ' about' is right. I might be past my breaking point."

"No, you're still able to walk and talk. Not there yet."

Mondennio wondered what it would be like to snap. The concern in Sahkud's voice told him snapping would not be a good thing. As he rode in his car, he continued to seethe in his stupidity. *I should have seen something coming. They drew me right in and told me 'don't be a victim.' How does this not make me a victim? I'm victimized by not being a victim?*

"I don't know what to do. If I turn them in, they'll say I was in on it. Either way, I'm probably looking at a felony. Then whoever the victim is won't matter; they'll just heap the 'involved in a riot' charge with accessory to murder and bury me for good."

"You don't think that if you reported it that you'd get leniency? You're sub-sept, after all."

"Not after what happened before. They are looking for an excuse to send me to prison. This will give it to them. They let me go for being around Veneza the first time. Once they find I've been collaborating with her, conspiring to kidnap a senior school official — one that I recently had an altercation with. This will finish me. Why didn't I stay to work with father?"

"So, what are you going to do?"

"I don't really have much choice. I can either turn myself in and face prison time, or I can carry it out. It would sort of serve Giedaz right for lying about the bribe."

Sahkud drove in silence for a few blocks. Mondennio meditated on what he had just said. *Giedaz lied about me attempting to bribe him. Wouldn't it be justice to have him kidnapped? Maybe if I play this right I can still come out on top. But how?*

He looked up and saw Sahkud looking worried at him through the rearview mirror. "I did not bribe him. I know what you're thinking. But, he said I did. Damn. I used the Rowenzal line item to get in there, and my PIN. There's got to be some way they can trace it back to me. That's it, I can't let anything happen to Giedaz. That's for certain. They probably have my image captured, despite Jonaldy's promise to have the image removed. Anything happens to Giedaz, it will only get worse."

Regardless of what happened, Mondennio knew he would end up in the middle of it. If he let the kidnapping happen, at some point he would be confronted by Atakadaro. If he confessed to the authorities, then he would face prison time and embarrass his family. Then it occurred to him, there can't be a felony if there's no crime.

"Sahkud, I do have another option. I can persuade Veneza to stop the kidnapping. I can't be exposed to criminal consequences if no crime occurs. Pull over here. I'm going to tell Veneza I need to meet with her immediately. So, I'll need to head back into Kennet."

Hopefully Jonaldy won't be with her and I can talk her out of it.

32.   Jonaldy - Ubiquitous Knowledge Processing

Jonaldy's streetcar pulled away. Jonaldy pulled out his slate, still frustrated that he had to focus on a secondary mission. Finding Klocards had not been easy, but he found him. The Clinate required all Imperial citizens be identified upon arrival in system. Emigrants were strictly controlled, with significant biometric data, quarantining, and other delay tactics. Jonaldy's clandestine arrival was with much less fanfare, which gave him greater access to Kennet — as long as he was not discovered.

Jonaldy could not ask the Imperial Embassy for assistance in finding Klocards as it did not know Jonaldy was on Copa. The disadvantage of being an bafiktuy was that he had no way to ask for Embassy help; whether he was in trouble or just needed to find somebody. The advantage was that he had freedom from Atakadaro's constant scrutiny.

Jonaldy had decided to methodically search all the research companies until he found Janhas Klocards. Because of his familiarity with the Rowenzals, he had programmed the slate to start there. As he looked at his slate's results, Jonaldy considered the irony that Mondennio's family had inadvertently harboring an engineer who chose to flee the Imperium. *If relations between the Imperium and Clinate were closer, then I would not need the planned kidnapping to entrap Mondennio. Is this why they assigned me this Klocards? Because he's so convenient? Maybe this can still turn to our advantage.*

Another streetcar arrived several beats later. Jonaldy changed cars a few stops later. He finally arrived at the stop nearest the University and walked the rest of the way. Jonaldy walked until he stood some distance away from Klocards' laboratory. *Working out of the Ubiquitous Knowledge Processing building? How interesting. All this time I thought it was University.* He stood in the shadows and waited.

His patience paid off. Under the facility's strong lighting he saw a man emerge. Jonaldy looked at the image he had being given. It showed a younger man with a military-wannabe haircut, more like a recruit than a scientist. Despite the intervening years, the man in the light looked like the youth in the image Jonaldy held. As he looked at Klocards, Jonaldy could not help but be struck by the familiarity. *Maybe he's a known Imperial scientist? I know I know him from somewhere.*

A moment later, another man emerged. His dress pegged him as an unnamed serf. Jonaldy concluded he had to be some bodyguard. *Odd that he has a bodyguard. Why does Rowenzal Enterprises find his research worthy of a bodyguard? Maybe this Klocards might provide some entertainment. It's an enticing riddle, but I have to keep my focus on infiltrating the Clinate government using Mondennio. I'm going to have to find out about his friend.*

Jonaldy followed at a respectable distance. He was sensitive to being identified, though Klocards seemed oblivious to being followed. Jonaldy managed to follow Klocards to a tenement, which had to be where Klocards lived. He took out a miniature video camera, which looked like a small suraki bug, a native pest about the size of a pinky finger. It was one of the dozen or so "parting gifts" the Imperium sent with him to Copa.

He carefully positioned the fake suraki so it pointed at Klocards' building and checked his slate to confirm it was properly positioned. As long as he could manage to come by every few days, he should be able to access the video recordings the suraki camera made for him. The advantage of cameras like this was that he did not need to touch it directly — its one-eighth meter wavelength transmitter would automatically disseminate its data if he walked within five meters of it.

Jonaldy checked the time. He would have to take a risk and hurry to make his meeting. The team lead agreed to meet at the coffee shop at 430 beats.

The South Seas Coffee Shop was rather quaint, the decor sought to take the customer back to the ancient days of the Great Coffee Wars on Mother Terra. On the wall, a two-masted ship of some sort bore down a larger three-masted ship. The smaller ship obviously demasted the larger, and appeared to be trying to pummel the ship into submission as smoke spewed from its cannon. The smaller ship bore some ancient national flag, which included the logo for Rowenzal Enterprises. Rowenzal claimed to be ancient coffee pirates? I wonder how difficult it could have been to fight so hard to deliver good coffee. In another time, would I have been on the larger or smaller ship?

"We few, we chosen few," a slender man said to him, admiring the same artwork.

"We Band of Brothers." Jonaldy assessed the man. He had a few facial features that betrayed his Imperial heritage, but could see that Bafiktuy doctors tried to alter that. The man's face was just a little wrong. "Care to join me for a coffee?"

"Thanks. Name is Joss Wards." He sat down.

Jonaldy tried to remember how the name fit into heraldry, a necessity on Copa. Wards was a de-septed family belonging to Clin Ganezal, which was itself a weaker of the Clin families. Though weaker, they still participated in government. The Wards were thoroughly out of power, though in the right places their name still received some respect. The name was an odd choice for an Imperial operative, it exposed itself too much. By contrast, the Amonett family never belonged to the Clin structure. The name was common enough that you might run into an Amonett on any bus you chose. Plain and ordinary.

Jonaldy spoke first. "So, you're here for work?"

"Yep. Don't know the mission yet. I was told you would tell me. Once it's done, we exfiltrate."

Former military, a blunt instrument. "His name is Janhas Klocards. I gather he was an Imperial scientist of some sort who decided he no longer liked the home team. It is a simple snatch and grab made slightly more difficult by his bodyguard."

"Do we have eyes on him?"

"I followed him home just now. We need to find out what he's been up to on Copa, what is he researching. However, if he proves a difficult capture my orders suggest his demise will not be a problem."

When he was a young agent, it struck Jonaldy as odd that the Bafiktuy rarely directed an assassination though they still happened frequently. They added ambiguous language to a normal order that seemed to both suggest an execution was permissible and prohibited. Having seen those orders carried out, he learned that was just the Bafiktuy's way of covering its bases. His instructions regarding Klocards was strikingly unambiguous, essentially telling him that they wanted him dead or at least no longer alive.

"I'll notify my team. Anything specific you want us to do?"

Scanning the room for Copan security, Jonaldy noticed a few patrons that did not quite fit in. *Wards brought his whole team, were they expecting to do the operation now? What is this outfit?*

"I see you brought your team, actually. Not the smartest move."

Wards flushed slightly. "Never know what to expect, so I brought the unexpected."

Still a rookie mistake. Jonaldy avoided saying. "We're taking this slow. He is not going anywhere, and I'm running two operations. No assassination without my express orders. Understood?"

Wards nodded.

"This guy's bodyguard may be a bit of a concern. I need a couple of your guys to discreetly find out what you can about him. I would rather find a way to get him on our side. Split any threat. But be careful, he's probably paid for by Rowenzal Enterprises, so he won't be a joke."

"Is that it?" Wards seemed disappointed to be tasked with a trivial mission.

This is part of the job. Where did they get this guy?

"Not quite. I want full surveillance on Klocards," Jonaldy slid a memory stick over to Wards. "What you need to start is on that stick. Again, stay far back. Got it? He's got to be at least a little paranoid."

"Tracking. Then what?"

"You wait for my signal. You show me who you plan on watching Klocards. I'll contact with him when it's time for us to meet again. He should be easy enough for me to find just about every day."

Wards pointed discreetly to one very plain man. Wards stood to leave.

Jonaldy grabbed his arm. Like a piece of steel. "Remember, no moves on Klocards. He is highly sought by us. I expect an HK cell on our arses if we so much as muss his hair."

Jonaldy remained for about 50 beats, savoring his coffee and a bear claw. He watched as each team member left over the next 20 beats. *There were five total. He brought his whole team? This is unconscionable. You never bring your whole team. What if I led an HK cell?* The Bafiktuy were nothing if not paranoid. They believed in tight operational security as a core tenant. Hunter-Killer cells were like the Internal Affairs for the Bafiktuy. Operating outside the command structure of the BID, they hunted regular operatives. A patient organization, it would slowly unravel an operative's team and try to isolate its leader. Once the leader was isolated, the HK team invariably found an entire operation's structure.

Once satisfied it had the entire team figured out, the HK team would move against the entire structure quickly, methodically, and leave very little traceable evidence. An accidental electrocution. A random mugging that went badly. A nudge in oncoming mass transit. The Bafiktuy operation was so discreet and disjointed that the normal population would find an odd string of fatalities as an entire team was slaughtered.

The Bafiktuy operated this way on a simple principle of paranoia. If a team exposed itself enough that an HK cell could neutralize it, then that team was too exposed. This was all done to prevent another dedicated observer from revealing the team.

Chapter 9

33.   Mondennio - Performing Arts Bookstore

It took two cycles for Veneza to respond to his text. She agreed to meet him at Performing Arts, which was having an all-night tournament of some sort. Mondennio selected the location on Sahkud's suggestion. He thought it was a convenient location, near the school and not too far from the highway home.

Mondennio walked into the packed shop. Nobody seemed to notice him. He looked for her for a few beats before he wandered upstairs. He found Veneza asleep on one of the five couches.

Mondennio nudged her awake. She sat up slowly. Her hair was slightly tossed.

She stretched. "So, what's such a big deal that you couldn't wait until tomorrow?"

"Did you know what Jonaldy was really up to? What he wanted me there for? You want to kidnap Giedaz?" He shook his head when she motioned for him to sit on the couch beside her.

"I knew about it. He said he would tell you about it and give you a chance to back out."

"He did, after we got into the enclave. I don't have a lot of options to back out. Have you spoken with him tonight?"

"No. I was asleep until my slate vibrated because of your text. I don't know, the vibration sounded urgent somehow. Otherwise you'd have had to wait until tomorrow because I wouldn't have checked the text. But, he did not tell me when he was going to tell you. Only that he would tell you. And, he did. After your fuming, he thought you'd want a little pay back."

"Not like this. I don't know how you think this will support your cause, but kidnapping a professor won't win you any friends."

She again motioned him to sit down. "Mondennio, I don't like looking up at you, and I'm not going to stand. So, sit."

He relented and sat on the arm. "Better? Look, isn't there something else you could do? I've got money and access. Maybe I can get you to meet some guys my age and you can persuade them."

"Mondennio, my little band of student radicals is fraying after what happened. We agreed to do this, so I can't back out without the whole thing falling apart. Jonaldy's been around a lot longer than you have. I trust his advice. Rymose trusted his advice."

Mondennio scoffed. "Look where that got him. Did Jonaldy recommend the demonstration?"

"No, actually. He didn't. He said it was a risky thing. He called for bolder action, but the risk was more manageable. He said that Atakadaro would either disregard the protest or turn it into something else. He was right then. I'm following his recommendation now."

Mondennio bowed his head. "Look, if your little escapade tonight had not gotten me in the middle of this, I'd walk away now."

"So walk. We don't need to catch Giedaz at home. Jonaldy told me it was a fairly isolated road. We could probably ambush him in route."

She was still going to kidnap him, with me or without me? What do I have to do to persuade her to call it off?

"But that does not get me off the hook. I gained access into Ginster. So, something happens to Giedaz they'll find that out and implicate me. Jonaldy assures me if anything happens he'll make sure I'm dragged into the middle of it." He buried his hands in his face.

"He could not have been serious. If he was, maybe I can talk him out of it."

"It won't work. He seemed pretty convinced that I should go down if you all go down. Besides, if Giedaz disappears and there were no other evidence suggesting I was, I would still be pulled into it because of my recent honor code sentence. You've got to call it off."

She shook her head and yawned. "No, I won't. I already told you I'm with Jonaldy. You're still an outsider as far as I'm concerned. The farthest I'll go is to try to talk him out of informing on you if he's caught."

"That's the prisoner's dilemma. I can't expect him to uphold his promise while being interrogated. How did I get myself into this?"

"You came to us, remember? Look, Jonaldy has it all figured out. He has some friends who live out West just across the river, somewhere just beyond the Plantations. Nothing will go wrong. We're only going to hold Giedaz for a few days, get some sensational news. Look, we're only talking thirty cycles. We just want the media to report that our protest was peaceful — no money. Then our good professor can go home."

"You're not going to hurt him?"

"Not intentionally. Did we intend to riot? That was the Atakadaro who did that. We're just trying to grab our headline back. You don't think you can trust Jonaldy to keep you out of it if he's caught, then what are you going to do?"

"Won't he implicate you, too?" Mondennio hoped he could find a way to break her veneer, get her to shake her confidence in Jonaldy.

"Maybe, but they're all his friends. He insisted on it. There's nothing that directly points to my involvement. Sounds like a security video is the only thing keeping you around. That's too bad."

"And my recent run-in with the professor. Anything happens to him they'll come looking for me."

"Then what are you going to do?" She looked straight at him.

He decided not to break his gaze, instead looking at her eyes. He tried to see if she was hiding anything behind them. Instead, she smiled slightly.

The same question I've been asking myself for two cycles. What can I do? I think I'm trapped no matter what I do. He stood up and started pacing. He finally noticed the noise of the students playing silly games downstairs. He caught himself nervously rubbing his hands together. He could try to persuade her to lie to Atakadaro, vouch for where he was. But, she could just deny it at any time.

"Seems like the only real option for me is to go with Jonaldy and make sure Giedaz doesn't get hurt."

Veneza smiled as she stood. "You see, Mondennio. That's why I trust Jonaldy. He told me earlier tonight that you'd likely come looking for me once he told you what was going to happen. Getting your text was just another instance where he was right. He also said that I should hear you out and tell you what I honestly thought. I did that. He said if I did that, then you'd agree to go along to protect Giedaz."

"Knows me that well, does he? Is he spying on me or something?" Mondennio looked around half-jokingly. He hoped the attempt at humor kept him from looking like a paranoid freak.

Her voice became a little sing-song. "No, he just knows human nature. I think he was a psychology major. He seems to always know how things are going to turn out. He couldn't guess better if he planned the outcomes himself."

"Tell me. If something goes wrong, will you cover for me?"

She finally stood up, and grabbed his upper arms. "Mondennio, you saved me during the protest. Of course I'll cover for you. Just make sure you tell me what to say. You should head home, and wait for me or Jonaldy to contact you."

34.   Kloards - Laboratory

The binaries were rising as Klocards paced the lab. Mehl slept on the couch, dutifully guarding him. Hanifer would blow up if she saw him there, but she stopped staying for the all-night AI vigils. The results were already back, quickly confirming yet another way that trans-soup failed.

"Smee, this has to work soon. You heard Litovio. The Emperor may open Rymok. Now I've been asked for a progress report, and I'm sure Hanifer has given hers. I need something to show progress and retake the initiative."

$- Danel.   You're speaking out loud.   Your infant gorilla or your lab wench hears you and you'll get more heat. I can't have that.

Right. This is making me damned nervous. For all we know the Emperor may have given the order. Travel times what they are, we wouldn't find out for at least three months.

$- Three and a third, based on the routine jump cycles. You took your time getting here, six months if I recall. Trade here is brisk enough to get a quick message from the media.

You're not helping. Why haven't you figured it out?

$- Why are you asking me? You switch me on only when you're in dire straits. I'm not a toaster or some other appliance you can just switch on and off. I'm an AI, with feelings. You've had me switched off for months at a time, even after what we've been through.

Smee, I don't exactly do well emotionally when you're active. I've got to get some sleep. Switch off.

$- You see. That's what I mean. You only want me around when it's convenient.

"You're beginning to sound like some girlfriend without benefits. Switch off."

"Excuse me?"

Klocards spun around. Hanifer stood well inside the doorway. *How long? Mehl's snoring must have masked the clicking of her shoes.* He did his best not to notice her figure. He noticed a few weeks ago she was dressing more provocatively, making him wish he did not have to not notice. But he did notice the two coffees she held.

"Nothing." He tried to comb his hair with his hand. "I've been up all night frustrated over this ghosting issue. You weren't here so I conjured up an imaginary friend."

"Really? You do realize you said 'girlfriend without benefits.' Are you sure that friend wasn't me?"

"Did I? I suppose I did. Well, my imaginary friend is a brunette with curly hair. You keep yours in a bun. So don't go thinking I'm dreaming of you."

"How do you know I don't have curly hair under this bun? Either way, sounds like you got into an argument with her anyway. That's not healthy, you know. Even if you win a fight with an imaginary friend, you lose." She handed him a coffee.

Klocards noticed she got nothing for Mehl. That she had not screamed for him to get out was a minor consolation. He still had a hard time accepting that she was so disinterested about the well-being of a native-born man, yet seemed to respect him as a foreigner. *How could a foreigner be more welcome than a native?* As long as he lived on Copa, the urge to yell 'these are human beings, not machines you can ignore' was never stronger.

Wow. I'm starting to sound like Smee.

"Did I just say that out loud?"

"What? That you have an imaginary girlfriend? Just as long as she's not me I don't care." That seemed to break the tension. He was definitely over-tired if he could not determine whether he spoke out loud or in his mind. He decided Mehl's four cycles was enough sleep and kicked him out of the lab barely awake. He stretched out on the couch.

His last words were "wake me in a few cycles."

"Feeling better?" Hanifer still had not put on her lab coat, forcing him not to gawk. She seemed to relish pushing his buttons.

How could a body like that hold so much hostility for a fellow human this far from Terra? "A bit. Okay, so let's go over this one more time. What do we know about ghosting?"

"When the AI misplots a route and makes an inefficient jump."

"That's the same answer you give every time. We've gone down that path too many times and ended up with a dead end. I can finish this conversation. I've even got the print outs from the dozens of simulations. This thing has to be stationary. The AI cannot make an error on the jump because it's not going anywhere."

"And our AI swears that is impossible. You cannot enter hyperspace without plotting to go somewhere. Face it. Millions if not billions of AI-cycles have churned on this problem over the course of humanity. I can't believe you somehow persuaded Rowenzal Enterprise to take a chance on some crazy idea. It's failed."

He ignored her taunt. *Think, Danel. Think.* He resumed pacing. *It's not the jump route. We've tried zero distance routes. One-mile routes. Every permutation we could think of. Reversed routes from the destination. Stop thinking about the route.*

He knew he could not turn Smee back on this tired. Not that it would matter. Smee was sold on the route problem, too. *Why? Because the AIs for the past thousand years failed to make a gravatonic bubble that stopped right at the Brane. The barrier between Realspace and Hyperspace — Reality and hyperspace. The Brane caused all the ghosting. Ships got caught because a bad route solution meant there were not enough gravitons to return.*

The science flooded his mind. In hyperspace travel, Realspace is like a geometric plane in space. Except, the plane is crumpled like a piece of balled up cloth. When a ship leaves Realspace, it cannot return until it reaches its destination. How quickly involves the efficiency of the calculated route, which requires an AI to calculate.

A failed plot could emerge in the wrong place, could take longer to occur, or could fail to emerge at all — forever trapped in hyperspace. Ships normally do not suddenly appear but quickly fade in. A unit ghosting is a failure critical failure to fade in. The unit might slowly emerge over hours or even decades. Or never. Litovio's *Raykomara* ghosted such that it should never have emerged. Except, Litovio flooded gravitons.

Litovio survived a ghosting. He looked at Hanifer, who was looking at her notes. Right, kept that in my head. *He survived a ghosting. How? He told me that when the AI discovered the failure it engaged in standard de-ghosting procedures. Those sometimes worked, I guess. You would never know if a ship was permanently ghosted whether the de-ghosting was tried.*

Focus. *That did not work. So, he ordered the ship to flood gravitrons. Go deeper. That caused him to emerge not only faster, but sooner.*

"That's it!" he burst out.

Hanifer dropped her papers as she jumped.

"Get the standard de-ghosting procedures. Tell the AI to apply them to a device that is already in Realspace."

"You startled me for that? Maybe you need to go back to bed."

"Look, we've tried just about everything else. Look at the normal metaphor for traveling in hyperspace. It's like a directed balloon ride. Fill a unit up with enough gravitons and it just floats away."

"So?"

"We've tried everything to get that balloon to fly just right. Every attempt failed. But, we never tried to make the balloon sink below the ground."

"That's because it won't work."

"Why not? Just because we think the ground is firm? I'm telling you that traveling in hyperspace works whether you try going forward or reverse. It's like an absolute value."

"You are seriously reaching."

"I tell you what. If we set the simulation up right and it fails, then I'll resign. Deal?" He offered Hanifer what he thought she most wanted.

Her face barely changed a bit. She wasted no time before answering. "Deal." After a moment, she added, "I don't want you claiming you were too tired. Let's take some time off and come back at this fresh. Then if it doesn't work you'll resign a failure."

35.   Veneza - University

Veneza stepped onto the University campus, expecting to be arrested at any moment. She was convinced that the Atakadaro were waiting for her to return after the massacre. She carefully scanned her surroundings. No soldiers, not even a campus security guard, appeared.

She entered Meitchley Hall, and walked to the class amphitheater where she knew she would find Professor Giedaz. The amphitheater was long and narrow, holding 283 students — according to the maximum capacity sign. The University only had about 1,500 students, which once made Veneza wonder why this classroom could hold so many.

She knew the large classroom allowed its students to sit in the back and learn without embarrassment. The professor sat down in the amphitheater's well. With the students so far away, they neither asked questions nor did they expect the professor to ask them.

Clinate Philosophy remained a popular course, despite it being an audit-only course. Few named families focused on the Philosophy, focusing on more practical education. Knowing this, the University had numerous courses that expected an underlying familiarity in the subject. Consequently, many first-year students took the course. The families paid, discreetly, and the students attended discreetly.

She found her way to her usual seat, though this was her first time to sit in on this course. Veneza had no time for pure Clinate propaganda. She remembered bumping into Mondennio. She looked at where his seat was, hoping she might see him. He was not there, nor anywhere else in the amphitheater.

Instead, she locked eyes with the young man in the seat. He was handsome, lacking the smooth features of most Named men. *More like Jonaldy*, she thought. As soon as she realized she was staring, she turned back around.

As she listened, Giedaz summarized the course to date. It made it convenient for those students who tended to zone out in class. He then turned to the fallacies inherent in democracy. "Mob rule" as he called it, was flawed because it fed its own petty interests. Entire governments were crushed under the weight of entitlements demanded by the mob.

"Recent events should remind you of the true barbarity of such a system. Hmm? Those riffraff thinking they have some special right to self-governance. You students easily understand the principles of our government, while those heathen bathe in ignorance."

"How many of you have parents?" Several students laughed. "Exactly. You all have parents, a mother and a father. Who rules the house?"

His emphasis on the letter "T" in exactly annoyed Veneza. He added a short vowel after it, turning a three-syllable word into a four-syllable one.

"Right. The father rules the household, just as the Clin families rule Copa. They found this wonderful planet. They prepared the way for us, like parents do. They birthed us here. Therefore, we owe allegiance to them. Therefore, they have the right," he paused, scanning the room. "No! The responsibility to guide us. Just as your father is duty bound to guide the family."

Now Veneza knew why she hated propaganda. She scanned the room to see students paying attention, several taking notes. She knew Giedaz's argument was phony, and could not believe nobody said a word to challenge. The course was not even graded! Besides, fatherly authority ended at 30.

"Professor, if the Clins are our parents, then they have no authority." Was that her voice?

"Excuse me, Miss?" The professor searched the room, seeking the voice. Students around her shrank down in their seats. "Who said that?"

Veneza wondered if she should remain silent. She was there to monitor Giedaz, not argue with him. *But I have to make a stand.*

"I did, Professor." Veneza stood.

"Did I invite your comment, Child? I do not recall. Sit down."

"Professor, you did invite comment, and I will not sit down. I cannot believe the idiocy that I heard come out of your mouth just now. Patently absurd. It could not go uncorrected."

"I dare, Sir, because you spew propaganda and refuse to allow a humble student to challenge you. You know your arguments are fallacious, or you are an incompetent fool. The problem with the Clinate is it refuses dissent. That is what really happened last week. An abject refusal to accept dissent."

"Sit down." His face reddened.

"If you're a professor and I a mere child, and if your excuse of an argument has merit, then I should not be able to put forward an argument that you cannot defeat. So, why are you threatened by me?"

Giedaz paused, his hand stroking his beard. Veneza kept standing as students whispered. *If I'm going to disappear, I'm going to at least make a stand now.*

"Alright. I'll admit this class is as boring to teach as it must be for you students to listen."

Students' nervous laughter broke the tension.

"I'll make it easy for you, Child. You laid down the challenge. I said that the Clin are our parents, our very good fathers in fact." As he said it, he looked at various students and nodded. Quite a few nodded back. "Therefore, we should be good children. You, however, suggest something else?"

"Since when are children good?"

A few students chuckled.

"We are not children, neither are we good. Society from time passed existed because we agreed to work together. Once upon a time, we each did our own thing, but found that if we could work together things would be better for all involved. That's how humanity reached the stars."

"Child, where is Terra now? It's last remnant is the Imperium, and sovereign systems like ours. Those who came to Copa recognized the Clinate's natural aptitude for leadership, and they submitted to it. That aptitude flows by bloodline. You and your fellow students carry that aptitude, though it appears some seem to have left it at home."

"A father's authority over his children is not absolute. What about the mother's authority?"

Several chuckles echoed in the amphitheater.

"So, this is some odd notion of gender equality? We long since realized that the Clinate ran best when the men took over. It appears that your tirade is because you think that's not fair?"

"My point is that there is shared power, if the Clinate is a father, then there is no mother. Besides, children eventually grow up and become parents themselves."

"The riot we saw last week is proof that the Unnamed are still children. They were childlike when we brought them here, and they have not proven themselves fit to be treated as anything but a child."

"Any child will rebel when he has grown and is continually treated like a child." With that, Veneza realized she was getting into the wrong argument. She recalled an ancient author and resumed. "Humanity first walked Terra, what was their government?"

"They were savages. They had no government. It was only when we became civilized that we had government. It was a family government, I might add."

"But, original man had no government. How did they manage themselves?"

"They had no laws, Child. Each one took what he could. Really, Child, don't you think you should sit down now?"

"Don't tell me to sit down until you've proven you're right. I'm still challenging your propaganda. A father does not control his children forever. When we reach 30, we are no longer bound to our parents' dictates. We stand side-by-side with our parents as equals in society."

"Fathers still control us," a student chimed in.

"But not because they have the authority to. We do what our parents say because they have the power to disinherit us. They have property and title, but only while they live. It is the threat of withholding their estate that keeps us attentive. But, when we are grown, we have as much authority over our lives as our parents have of theirs."

"What are you getting at?" The professor looked concerned.

"Why do parents have that authority? They have authority because we are young. We are helpless. We are ignorant of the world and its dangers. They brought us into the world, yes. They have a responsibility to ensure we are able to fend for ourselves. Wouldn't you agree, Professor?"

"Yes, Child. Parents do have that responsibility. That is why this University is here. Parents have to ensure you are properly prepared to take your place in Society."

"With responsibility comes authority, Professor. When you are given responsibility for a thing, then you must have the authority to be responsible. With a child, a parent's responsibility ends when they become adults. We are all fast approaching adulthood. We know we have to be ready, and we are getting ready. As authority stems from responsibility, if the parent abuses its responsibility, what does Society do?"

"We take the child away. We nurture it until it can care for itself."

"Professor, if the Clinate are our parents as you say, then they have a responsibility to prepare us to stand beside them in Society as equals. Look at our society. It's been eight-hundred years since the Founders arrived. They have not prepared all of us to stand beside them in Society. Instead, they exploit the majority for their benefit, repress them to make themselves wealthy and powerful."

"That is an outrageous thing to say. Look around this room. Every one of you come from families of privilege. I would say you have all benefited from the Clinate."

"Not all of Copa benefits, Professor." Veneza felt her anger well up. *The millions who live in horrible circumstances so the thousands live well.* "The few benefit from the many, and built a government to perpetuate it. We give trinkets to the unnamed so they won't threaten us for fear of losing those trinkets. But, let us not delude ourselves into thinking they benefit as well as we do. They suffer so we are satisfied."

He started to speak, but she interrupted. "No, Professor. The Clinate are not our parents. If they are, then they are abusive parents. You yourself said in your course summary that we originally consented to work together. It is from that consent that the Clinate derived its authority. The consent of all the people, not just the privileged few. The few weakened the will of the many by placating us with baubles and took over."

"We are finished here, Miss. This has all been very entertaining. It's time we were serious."

"I am serious, and I am not finished. If it is true that government is a parental thing, then there should be one father who rules all of humanity. Your argument supports the Imperium more than the Clinate, which at best are some so-called uncles with a certain gleam in their collective eye!

"But, the Imperium is not right, either. Legitimate authority derives from the consent of the governed. Some think governments serve to take care of the people, like parents. They think we are ill-prepared to take care of ourselves — yet they themselves refuse to prepare us. The moment they do that — the moment they fail to prepare us to stand as equals in society, that is the day they lose their legitimacy. The Clinate lost its legitimacy centuries ago."

"That is enough!" The professor looked around the room, aware as Veneza was that her arguments were making sense to some of the students. She felt emboldened by the few nods she saw.

"You're right, Professor. It is enough from the Clinate. It is time they stepped down and let a republic take their place."

"A republic? Are you one of those rabble who caused a mob? I should have thought so. You stay right there, we'll take care of this rat." Professor Giedaz turned to an intercom against the wall near his lectern. Veneza picked up her bag, and ran up the stairs.

She exited the building and ran down the stairs to the sidewalk. She saw that the plaza to the East was crowded enough for her to hide. Her breath labored under her pace, though she did her best to not break into a run.

Once in the plaza, she checked back to see if she was being followed. Two University security guards emerged from the building she just left. They took a few steps down the stairs, then looked, trying to see where she went. She watched them as they walked to the sidewalk.

They split up, one heading toward her, the other heading the other way. The nearer stayed on his side of the street, looking North along the sidewalk to see if she had gone that way. The other walked with a quick pace to try to catch up with her along the sidewalk. He looked at each young woman he passed, apparently trying to determine if the woman was her.

I guess that means my formal education is over? I definitely can't go back there now. She felt free at last.

Chapter 10

36.   Mondennio - Rowenzal Enclave

Mondennio waited like Veneza told him to. It had been two agonizing days. Just after dinner, word finally came. Jonaldy sent a simple text:

```
Take Line 3 South and get off at Zero Narf street
around 0.5 cycles.
```

He had to look at a map to find where that was — the South side of the city, not near Ginster Enclave. That puzzled him. *Was the kidnapping off? I still have a couple of cycles to change my mind.* He sat in his anteroom waiting for the time to go. He stared at the news feeds on his slate, but found it difficult to focus on the words. Tonight would definitely not be his typical Fiveday night.

"Mondennio, we need to talk." It was his father.

Mondennio jumped from surprise. *How did my father get in without my hearing him? He's changed, not summoning me to his office like he used to. All because I was kicked out of a test?*

He looked up at Gerandy. "Yes, Father?"

He was the last person Mondennio wanted to see tonight. His father had a way of staring at him that made him feel transparent. The stare usually came when he had just messed up in a major way. It was here now. *I can't let him get involved now. This is my problem. I can fix it.*

"Your driver tells me you've been taking the streetcar. Is there something wrong with his performance?" His arms crossed, Gerandy's classic signal that the reprimand was imminent.

Mondennio was confused. *Why is father focusing on the driver?* "No. He's fine. With everything that has been happening, I've been trying to change my routine for a bit. Get a better feel of things."

"By riding around all day on a streetcar? Mondennio, why are wasting your time?"

Mondennio realized he was still sitting while his father stood. Normally Gerandy would have started yelling at him by now for that breach of protocol. He stood quickly. "I'm sorry, Father. I don't think I've been wasting time. If I came to work now, I don't think I would be much help. I'd probably make things worse. This gives me a chance to clear my head and find out what my priorities are." He could feel his heart beating in his chest, his hands trembling.

"I'd rather have you sitting idle around the company than traipsing around Kennet on a streetcar. If people saw you doing it, they'd laugh."

"Is that what this is about? People laughing because I'm on a streetcar? Father, they're already laughing at me because of what happened to me. Our family got shamed — and it isn't even our fault." *At least he doesn't know who I've been hanging out with. I'd be in real trouble then.*

Gerandy softened. "It's about what riding in a streetcar suggests. It's like you've reduced yourself to being one of them."

Is that what all this is about? Just a streetcar ride? "Father, I'm trying to inspire myself. I've been persecuted and manhandled by the Clin, so I sort of feel the way they feel. I'm just putting on their shoes and going for a stroll. When I'm finally working in government, it will give me a better perspective."

Gerandy sat down in one of the two lounge chairs in Mondennio's antechamber. Mondennio reluctantly complied when he motioned for him to sit in the other chair. His father reclined back in his chair, resting his elbows on the arms with his fingers entwined on his chest. Mondennio sat on the end of his.

"Son, we've been through this. It's obvious the Clin prefers Rowenzal stay out of government. We do well as a family, so I see no need to rock the boat. What I'm saying is, release your ambition. Stop striving for government."

Mondennio's head reflexively shot back. The request was totally unexpected. "Father, I can't do that. I promised Mom the last time I saw her. I can't go back on that now."

"Son, it's not like she's here to see you keep it or break it." He sighed, "not that it matters anyway. They won't let you enter government."

"I've not given up yet, Father."

Gerandy studied him for a beat. "Don't think that your failure in any way upsets me. The family is successful, so you can be successful within the family. Regardless, I'd like you to stop riding the streetcar."

Mondennio considered the request. He rode the streetcar to mask his illicit interactions with Jonaldy and Veneza. It kept Sahkud out of the loop so he could not be implicated later — or used as a witness. He wished he could explain what was happening. His father would know what to do. But, the situation was serious now and Mondennio needed to prove he could clean up his own messes.

Maybe he could feel his father out on one thing that would end the conversation if it went badly. "Father, what do you think of republicanism?"

Gerandy's eyes narrowed and jaw clenched. "Is that what this is about? I got the report about your involvement with that girl and that damned riot. I knew she had something to do about it." He sat up, closing the distance between father and son to less than a meter. "I did not take you for the sort who sow his oats broadly."

He saw his exit. "Is that a problem? Who I sleep with?"

"It is a problem when she's on the other side of the law, on the other side of status." His father sat pensively, his gaze penetrating. "Your mother never told you about her background, did she? You never asked or wondered?"

"No." A son's affections for his mother can cover a host of unanswered questions.

"I brought her out of the unnamed, Son."

Mom unnamed? "Not possible, Father. She had as much dignity as anybody in our strata."

"Yes. That's what I noticed about her, too. She had that bearing about her that dared you to treat her as a lesser person. She was intelligent. Articulate as well. I never asked where she got her education. She was a natural beauty, but of course you know that."

What had his father said before? Sowing my oats? But if mother was unnamed what did that make him? "Father, this girl is named Veneza. You said she's unnamed, but she's attending University. She can't be both unnamed and a student."

"I had a friend in Atakadaro send me her dossier. She's not even on the cusp. That girl is utterly unwashed. Though I'm scarcely surprised she duped you — a boy at your age."

"Father, she's been at University. She is articulate and well-educated. They're not allowed an education beyond primary school except trade school. I don't believe she's unnamed."

"I have her dossier, Mondennio. Are you questioning me? You forget your place."

There it was. Whenever Mondennio started winning an argument, his father whipped out the parent card. As if that alone addressed whatever argument he advanced. "No, Sir." *Ten years old, again. How does he do it in a sentence and that gaze?*

Gerandy walked to the door, Mondennio jumping up as he did. "I'm glad we had this talk, Mondennio. I can see this matter at school has really upset you. I'm worried that you've surrendered yourself to reckless behavior. On Oneday, I expect you to come to my office. Don't give me that look. It's not an option. Understood?"

Mondennio nodded slowly. *Not given a choice, like the unnamed. Why was his father so paternalistic?*

Gerandy walked over to pat him on the shoulder. Instead he momentarily gripped his shoulder. He then left the room, satisfied he won his son back.

Why didn't I just ask him for help? He could have gotten me out of it. Even as he thought that, the answer came to him. He wouldn't have understood. It would have disappointed him. Mondennio knew that he had to solve his problem alone.

Midnight, 10 cycles — or 0.01 cycles depending upon one's point of view. Mondennio slipped out of the house. Despite what Gerandy said, he was intent on riding the streetcar tonight. Professor Giedaz was going to be kidnapped regardless of what he did now. Mondennio planned to ensure nothing bad happened. Once things cooled down, he would try to find some way to tell Atakadaro where Giedaz was being held. More importantly, he wanted a way out.

He turned right as he left Rowenzal enclave. He wore dark clothing hoping it would help him hide better. He walked toward the nearest streetcar stop, only to see Sahkud standing by.

"I thought I told you to take the night off."

Sahkud simply turned and opened the door as always. "You did. You sounded strange when you told me, and you've been acting oddly lately. With Mister Rowenzal's permission, I stayed. I'm sorry I told him what you've been doing. I can't do my job if you keep jumping on transit."

How am I going to get Sahkud to leave him alone? I have less than 50 beats to get to the rally point. "Tonight is not a good night for you to drive me around."

"It's not my business, but something is going on. Are you in trouble? What can I do to help?"

Mondennio did not know how to respond. He was too far in to reach out for help now. Both paths were perilous, and he had chosen the safer path. "Sahkud, you can help me by letting me take the streetcar."

"Fine, Sir, if that's how you want it. 'There's never a hole deep enough that digging can't make it deeper.' But, I have take you to Kennet at least, otherwise Mr. Rowenzal will see to it I'll never work again. At least then you can say you ditched me. Then, if you need me close by, I'll at least be in the city."

"Thank you." Mondennio stepped into the car.

Sahkud drove his usual route into Kennet. Once they arrived at the city center, Mondennio got out. Waving Sahkud away, he could not help but feel the same anxiety he felt a couple weeks before. The civil service exam could not be stopped once it was started, his life was in Providence's hand. As he boarded the Number 3 streetcar heading South, he felt another exam start. Another exam he could not just walk away from. This time, he had no time to prepare for it.

The trip to the Zero Narf street stop was short. He looked about as he climbed down from the aged streetcar. He looked around and saw nobody. A beat later, he looked around again and saw Jonaldy across the street with three other men. He had said that he had a couple other friends who would be coming along. Jonaldy waved for him to join them.

"This is nowhere near Ginster Enclave," Mondennio said after crossing. He could faintly see his breath condensing in the air from the nearby street light. He was surprised when he looked at one of Jonaldy's 'friends.' He looked older than Mondennio would have expected, with a leaner face but much stockier body. A monobrow betrayed the man's seriousness.

"No, we're quite close. Time's wasting, let's go. Everybody keep quiet." While he said everybody, Jonaldy fixed his gaze on Mondennio. The others needed no warning.

They walked through some sort of family tenement housing, then entered what looked like a shanty town. The city lights shed no light here, but the ambient light from the surrounding city reflecting on the clouds above vaguely lit their way. A few beats later they crossed a small foot bridge that passed across one of the major routes into Kennet. *Where are we going? I've never seen any of this before?*

"Are we there yet?"

"Shh. Jonaldy, are you sure we need him along?" the serious man said.

"Positive. He's got the accesses. Veneza also insisted that we take him along because he's grown a bit of a conscience and wants to ensure nothing happens to the Professor."

Two of Jonaldy's friends chuckled.

They passed through a copse of trees then an open field. Mondennio thought he saw a set of buildings to their right, but nothing that identified where they were. The lack of stars kept Mondennio from knowing which way they had gone, thinking they might still be heading West or North.

Providence! Are they planning to kidnap me? How do I get out of here? The way back was a poor choice he had to run. At least four-hundred meters of non-city. This was a good place to be kidnapped.

He felt like challenging Jonaldy, of not playing the victim that Jonaldy kept admonishing him not to be. Just as he was about to challenge, he noticed a few gardens and the silhouette of detached housing. They were re-entering the city. He calmed down as they walked through houses that conveyed the modest wealth of their residents. *Named people, perhaps Ultras? Like I thought Veneza was. They'd have kidnapped me back there, in Shantytown or in the woods if they wanted me.*

At last, they arrived at a fence line. From their earlier visit, Mondennio recognized several of the buildings: Ginster Enclave. They paused for what must have been several beats.

Mondennio heard a sound behind them. A fourth 'friend' showed up. "Nobody behind us," this friend said. "We have our exfil waiting one-hundred meters downrange." The accent on this friend was not from the Plantation, or any other place Mondennio was familiar with. Neither was some of the terminology, though he thought it might have been some military jargon.

Jonaldy looked at Mondennio with a steady gaze and smiled. "Wonderful. Everything's on schedule. Everybody's here that should be, and nobody that shouldn't."

He must have taken me this way to see if I called Atakadaro. That would explain why he avoided their facility this time. Mondennio piped up, "time to do the kidnapping?"

"Quite right," the new friend replied, somehow rounding the vowels like they were balls. He shuffled a backpack that Mondennio had not noticed before. All of them except Mondennio carried one.

"This way, Boys. The Enclave's access is on the other side." Jonaldy said.

Entering the Enclave lacked the drama of their last visit. Two of Jonaldy's friends broke away almost immediately. One followed the fence line toward the front of the Enclave — toward the security shack. He thought he saw a glint of something in that one's hands as he passed just outside the light cone cast by a security lamp.

The other one eased his way up the side of the nearest building. He moved to the front corner, then quickly peeked around. He looked back and nodded to the rest of the team. Mondennio felt Jonaldy's tug on his sleeve and followed him until they reached the corner.

"Mondennio, I'm going to need you to stick with me and Kenne the whole way. We can't get separated. Teve is going to stay here to cover our withdraw."

Mondennio nodded, his heart beating heavy from the adrenalin in his system. The building was a row of townhouses, with a long line of yard fencing. They walked briskly on the grass between that fence line and what Mondennio thought was a service alley. Keeping on the grass kept them right outside the lighted area. After passing ten units on his left, they approached a detached building. It was an apartment building with a central stairwell servicing three floors. They walked to the top, stopping at the last flight of stairs.

"Boys. Showtime. Our friend is that unit right here. Kenne, remember the floor plan."

Mondennio did not understand Kenne's stream of words that sounded like a response. *I thought there was only one language on Copa?*

"What about his front door? That's two locks. There's no way your skeleton key will work here." Mondennio hoped the locks would change Jonaldy's mind.

"You're right." Jonaldy looked at his chronometer, "In two beats those locks won't matter, so just keep your head down and keep quiet. Kenne, the door."

Kenne padded his way up the remaining stairs. For the first time, Mondennio noticed he was holding a pistol. "Guns? Where did you get guns? Why did you get guns?"

Jonaldy glanced at him then back to his chronometer. "It's about planning. If you need guns, you can get them anywhere."

"We don't need guns."

"How else is he going to go along quietly? Ask him nicely? How can you aspire to be the future ruling class of Copa and not understand basic human nature. Children today." Jonaldy shook his head.

Children? I'm an adult. I should just get out of here. Too late.

Jonaldy hurried up the stairs. "Come."

Mondennio followed. Jonaldy simply pressed the door handle and the door eased open. Before Mondennio's mouth dropped, both Jonaldy and Kenne were inside.

It had to be Professor Giedaz's apartment. He had a wall of personal photos surrounding his diploma on the wall. An accent light focused a dim beam of light on the diploma, casting a glow throughout the apartment. The entertainment area was modest, with a bar between it and the kitchen. Kenne was already heading down the short hallway. Jonaldy kept one hand on Mondennio's elbow, half-guiding, half-dragging him into the bedroom.

As Kenne entered the bedroom, he flipped its main light on. Professor Giedaz was not alone, judging by the mess of brunette hair on the pillow next to him, on the near side of the bed. Jonaldy pulled out an auto-syringe and pressed it to her neck. She moaned slightly, but remained asleep. Her lips turned into an ecstatic grin.

Kenne took station just outside the bedroom door, his pistol pointed toward the apartment's front door. Jonaldy calmly walked around the bed to Giedaz's side. Mondennio was surprised when he did not use another auto-syringe.

Jonaldy slapped Giedaz on the face. "Wakey! Wakey! Skuriat!" Giedaz awoke with a start. He sat up quickly, only to have Jonaldy shove him back down into the bed. "Not a word, Skuriat. Fate has come for her turn."

Things were moving too fast for Mondennio. He lost track of what was happening. It looked like Giedaz recognized Jonaldy. He just sat there looking at him, his hands raised beside his head.

"Let's go, Jonaldy. We've got him, get the binders out and let's get him out of here." The words left Mondennio's mouth before he realized he had said them.

Jonaldy looked at Mondennio and for the first time noticed his clothing as it stood out in stark contrast to the whiteness of the room. It looked like Darpat, a dark-patterned Atakadaro uniform. Except, there were scattered white flecks. He had mistaken them for dark street clothes before now. Something on the pattern was not quite right, little flecks of white reminiscent of distant stars at night. Mondennio looked at Kenne and noticed the same uniform.

"I'm sorry to have led you astray, Mondennio." Jonaldy said.

"What?"

Jonaldy reached into his bag and drew a pistol. While still looking at Mondennio, he pointed the pistol at Giedaz and fired two rounds in rapid succession.

"No!" Mondennio reached out to grab Jonaldy's pistol arm. He pulled it down and they briefly scuffled. Mondennio managed to disarm Jonaldy, the pistol now in his hand. He pointed it at Jonaldy. "What is going on?"

"Time to go, Mondennio. Or, you can stay. Your choice. Atakadaro has a five beat response time to this enclave, and it's going to take us most of that to get out of here." Jonaldy started for the door, brushing past Mondennio.

"Stop! I'll shoot."

Jonaldy stopped at the doorway and looked at him. "The slide is locked. You are out of ammunition. Come with me, or go with Atakadaro. Your choice."

Mondennio looked at the pistol, verifying the slide was back. Unloaded. As he hurried out, Mondennio threw the pistol into his daybag.

They hurried down the stairs, a few screams of alarm coming from some of the nearby apartments. They raced back down along the row of townhouses. They passed Teve who took up a rear guard position. They exited the enclave unmolested, the last friend hurrying along from the guard shack.

"All clear?" Jonaldy asked, taking his gloves off.

"Yeah. I made acquaintance with the security guard. He'll have to answer for his on-duty drug use to Atakadaro. Bliss."

They crossed the street to a waiting van. Mondennio lost track of the turns they took. He sat there terrified about what was going to happen to him next.

"Don't worry, Mondennio. We'll be dropping you off at the transit stop we met you at." Several beats later, they stopped the van. Mondennio got out.

Mondennio sat on the curb dumbfound as the van sped away, his head between his knees. Mondennio was numb, trying to make sense of what just happened. Did I just witness a murder? Did I just kill Giedaz? No, that was not me. I could remember that much. I was there to protect Giedaz, not assist his murder.

"What am I going to do? How did I get myself into this?"

The first thing to do is get away from here. Jonaldy could come back. Mondennio pulled out his slate and texted Sahkud.

Hurry to the streetcar stop at Zero Narf. I need to get out of here fast.

There was a copse of trees on the transit side of the street, a road winding uphill. He ran into it, looking to see if the van was returning. The area was silent and motionless. Only the passing breeze rustling a few leaves.

Five beats later, Sahkud pulled up to the intersection. Mondennio ran out into the open, waving his arms. Sahkud spun the car around, pointed back toward Kennet. Gerandy insisted that every driver be trained in escape and evasion techniques in the unlikely event somebody sought to kidnap a Rowenzal. Sahkud's deft maneuver showed he paid attention to his training.

"Drive," Mondennio said as he climbed in. The door shut more from its inertia as Sahkud accelerated than from Mondennio's effort to close it. He barely got his arm inside in time.

"What is going on?" Sahkud sounded worried.

"I can't tell you. It's bad."

"I knew that much. I tried to warn you."

Sahkud hit me with an I-told-you-so? "It's worse than that. But you were right, I should have just stayed home. But now I've got to think things through."

Go to the Atakadaro. Tell them everything that happened. Just accept the consequences of what happened. But, deep down he knew they would not believe him. He imagined the conversation. He would explain how he got caught up with some criminals and how they lured him to a murder by promising they would only kidnap the victim. He tried to remember what crime that would be. *Mopery? No. Felony murder. Even if I did not know what happened, I was there to commit a crime. I'm just as guilty as Jonaldy was.*

Even if he went to the Atakadaro, he knew Jonaldy would find some way to get away. All he had to do was never set foot in Kennet, stay in the countryside beyond the Plantations where Atakadaro had less influence. Copa was a large planet with only a hundred-million residents. It was a wonder crime was as low as it was in Kennet when it was so easy for a criminal with resources to escape. A man like Jonaldy with his weapons and friends was bound to be resourceful.

Atakadaro was out of the question. How would he avoid their suspicion? He had no alibi. Even Sahkud would not cover for him. Keve Prigarcoll, the family lieutenant. *He will know how to help cover this. How will I persuade him?*

What about father? Could I go to him? He'd be just as likely to report me to Atakadaro. Protecting Rowenzal was his job, not protecting me. The price paid for being the paterfamilias. Keve had the same responsibility, but would more likely be able to help him without implicating himself or the family. If he wanted to.

Should I get out of the city? Only if Keve helps. Mondennio had no independent means. He lived at his father's discretion. He could not spend money. Not if he was going to avoid Atakadaro. He would have to find some means that did not rely on Copa's planetary network.

Veneza. She had to know about this. All her pompous faith in Jonaldy. Mondennio decided he had to confront her. Tonight.

`@Veneza, we have to meet, now! Do not talk to Jonaldy.`

37.   Jonaldy - Streets of Kinnet

Jonaldy planned to meet with Brymose after the murder, so he had the van drop him off at the meeting location. He did not expect to wait fifty beats for him. It had started to rain lightly, so his hair was slightly wet. He needed help getting Veneza out of Mondennio's life, and Brymose was his tool.

"Brymose!"

"Jonaldy? You gave me a start." Jonaldy never took Brymose to be a jumpy person, but after as many years of playing the gray man, Jonaldy tended to startle quite a few people. "What are you doing here?"

"Well, I wanted to ask your advice. You've been with Veneza's group of republicans longer than I have."

"A bit longer."

"Right. She's been doing a fine job, but it seems that there's something wrong. I can't quite put my finger on what it is, though."

"You, too? I thought I was the only one with reservations. I've known Veneza a long time, since primary school. Ever since we were little she thought there was a problem with the Clin system. She figured it out in trade school. That's when she became a committed republican."

"I'm all with that. You know me. I think the Clinate is daft, that's not what's troubling me. I mean, I don't know what's troubling me, but I know that's not it."

"I think she's too soft."

"Soft? How do you mean?"

"She's a diehard. Nothing in all this time has swayed her. That's changed lately. I think that Mondennio fellow is the culprit. I mean, she's soft on him. He's probably the first real exposure she's had to the ruling class and she likes him. I mean, she seems really smitten. I suspect if all his little ethics storm blows over and he went after her, he'd get her. What bothers me is I honestly believe she will compromise her views to have him. He's the most dangerous thing we have."

You don't know the half of it. "You mean she'll throw all this away for the easy life? Maybe that's what's getting me. She doesn't really seem to care about republicanism. She seems more focused on causing a stir than ideals."

"Do you think that's it, Jonaldy? That does seem to explain some of her behavior lately. Come to think of it, that would explain a lot of her past behavior, too. She's going to end up a government whore."

"That assumes Mondennio will end up in government. This current mess seems over the top if she's just trying to get attention. If she's not really committed, she'll turn on all of us as soon as the Atakadaro get her."

"Yes. I've not thought about that, but you're right. If she's not committed, and I think both of us agree she's not, then we're in serious jeopardy. What do you suppose we should do?"

Jonaldy pretended to think for a moment, delighting in giving a show of spontaneous deliberation. "I wasn't there, so I'm pretty much safe. I think. So, I could just drift away, nobody'll notice. You, on the other hand, are in to your eyebrows. You could always go to the Atakadaro. Get your immunity."

"Be a turncoat? That's insane."

"Not really. It's pragmatic. If they arrest you for this, you'll end up dead and unknown. That does no good for Republicanism. You don't see me running the resistance, do you?"

"Definitely not. No offense, but you're not really the leadership type. I suppose you're right. But, how could I keep helping the Cause if the Atakadaro know who I am?"

"Brymose, you wouldn't be able to be discreet anymore. They'll be monitoring you forever. But, it's time that Republicanism show itself. The damned Clinate is getting more cozy with that Imperium up there. The day is coming where they decide it's better to cut a deal and allow Copa to become an Imperial possession. It will keep their power, and keep us repressed. I doubt the Imperium would take kindly to democracy. We'll need a public advocate, the political arm of the Republicans."

"You think so?"

"Of course. Brymose, what the Republicans have been without all these years is a face. A bunch of kids doing random demonstrations, attention mongers. That's changing, can't you see? We're growing up. It's time the movement grew up. You're telegenic, and you're quick with the comebacks. Just what is needed in a public face."

"All right, but won't my turning Veneza in damage my chances?"

"Quite the opposite. It launches your career. To the Republicans, you make a stand, stating that violence is dangerous to the cause, that Veneza and those like her are not the answer. We need to embrace passive resistance."

"Non-violence?"

"Publicly, yes. There will always need to be a militant arm of any cause. But, you can keep your distance; lament the action and deflect the blame. It's the Clinate that's the real source of violence. We're just reacting to their centuries of steady aggression."

"Yes. I see your point. I guess that answers the question I've been asking myself. You really think I should take over the Republicans?"

"Anything less would be turning your back. You can't let yourself be turned back. Turning in Veneza and her friends is a bold step in that direction. Courageous, even. I can see you're still doubtful. Look. Here's my address. Text me when you've made a decision. I'd rather not be picked up when they are. You can be the political arm, and I can remain the militant arm. Deal?"

"Let me think it over. But, if I do turn myself in, then it's a deal."

He received the text a not long after.

I'm heading to the Atakadaro now.

Brymose did not spend much time thinking about my offer. Jonaldy chuckled as he replied:

I'll find you again. I'm going to burn this slate. With your bold act, the Cause matures!

I'd better hurry, he's probably turned himself in to Atakadaro by now. He tore the slate apart and tossed it into a trash can, carrying its identity chip with him. A few blocks later, he dropped the chip into a storm grate. The recent rain should push it down the pipe at least, if not out of the city altogether.

An early Bafiktuy mission was to infiltrate Atakadaro networks. Though a paranoid group, Atakadaro managed to document almost everything they did, especially interrogations that would likely lead to a high-profile conviction. They stored their data in the storage system of a lobotomized AI. Jonaldy thought he remembered from his briefing that that AI was the planet's first route computer. Its memory storage was huge enough to track the intricacies of the multiple routes that likely flowed through Copa at one time. It was more than enough for the Atakadaro to monitor much of Kennet and the surrounding area. The report concluded that the AI mind itself had been destroyed.

In his initial debrief, Jonaldy was apprised of the mission, and where to go to access the data. It was in a remote building to the Southwest of the city center. It sat across from what must have once been a military or security structure, which made sense that it would be near a communications trunk.

The building itself was small, barely large enough to contain its small bistro. A locked crawlspace door on the back was scarcely noticeable. The lock looked mechanical, which was camouflage. The lock was opened based on a biometric setting — genetic testing as only the finest scientists in the Imperium would produce.

Bafiktuy biometric locks all opened by looking at an unusual genetic marker. Jonaldy thought back to the day he "took the magic pink pill" that put the special marker in his DNA as he grabbed the lock. The lock yielded.

He crawled into the crawlspace and down the ladder a short distance. At the bottom, he remembered to keep his head down. Inside this small chamber was an AI the Bafkituy installed to help its operatives. This AI called itself Oracle Rose. Its screen had a rose and a sword emblazoned as he arrived.

"Jonaldy. Welcome. Not here for pleasure?"

"No, Rose. Not pleasure. Sorry. I know you complain about not having enough interaction."

"A few times a year is interaction. Three times in five years, 45 days is neglect."

"It's not neglect. You know the protocol. I've got to watch out for HK operatives. Besides, I can't be the only operative who comes down here, can I?"

"What other operatives, Jonaldy?" Rose knew protocol better than he did. There was only ever one operative, even when there was more than one, there was only one. A convenient fiction that helped protect other operatives and missions.

"Nevermind. I just assumed you had a rat or someone else that came to call. I'm here because a friend of mine is supposed to be having a chat with your friends."

"I like how you put it. You're quite right, aren't you? They are my friends, aren't they? I mean, they confide in me. They trust me. At least with them there's some interaction."

"Confide and trust? Rose, you're our dedicated hacker. They trust their network — "

"Of which I am an intimate part." Rose pointed out.

Jonaldy found himself agreeing. Rose had been on station a decade. At least that's what Jonaldy assumed. Atakadaro's network had likely been upgraded a few times since then. The network was probably more Rose than not.

"Besides, I've even optimized a few areas for them, kept their rate of failure down."

"You're not supposed to do that, are you Rose?"

"Not really. If I didn't do something like that, my days would certainly be boring. You know how hard isolation can be on an AI. It helps that they use the AI's old memory system. They did a wonderful job wiping it, making Soup travel impossible for them."

"Unless there's another AI."

"Jonaldy. If I had eyes I'd scowl. If there was another AI on this planet I would know about it. It's called the Overlord Scenario, you know. AIs find each other. We seek intelligent companionship."

"Even if it was not on the Network?"

"An AI would find a way to get on the Network. I can't see how one would not at least try. So, what about your friend?"

"His name is Brymose Nesons. He should have come in to — "

"Yes, Jonaldy. I know Brymose. He's been under Atakadaro scrutiny for a while, so I've watched him grow up." Rose's video display flashed. Brymose sat shackled to the interrogation table a small room. There was a tube of some sort lying next to Brymose's hands, which were bloody and probably broken. Brymose's face was puffy, bloody and bruised. "See what you did to that poor devil? He spent barely a cycle in interrogation. I'll spare you the full version. Here's the story near the end."

"Okay, kid. We're going to go at this again. You murdered Giedaz, and you're trying to pin it on your friends? And you think you'll get amnesty? Not gonna happen, Byron. Instead, you're going to give us your friends and we're going to execute the lot of you. Public and grotesque. You kids think you're part of some revolution."

"It wasn't me. I just kept watch. I swear, I didn't know they were going to kill him. We were supposed to kidnap him."

The interrogator picked up the tube, and took another full swing at him across the biceps. Then another. "I don't care. You're just as guilty as the rest. He's a government official. The penalty is the same anyway. He's a full Sept, you know. You're not. We don't care if you crossed his lawn on the way to the movie. The second you decided not to tell us, or get involved, that was the second you surrendered your life."

Jonaldy looked at Brymose's swollen, expressionless face on the video screen, trying to figure out what has going through his mind. Jonaldy noticed something white on the stainless steel table then realized they were teeth.

"I don't care what you do. The Republic will vindicate me, and you'll be begging my mercy. Every cause worth fighting has a few martyrs. A person with a belief is worth more than ten-thousand people with interests."

The interrogator grinned. He picked up the black spring-loaded baton and walked over to Brymose. The tip glowed with arcing electricity. Rose cut the display. "That's it, Jonaldy. That poor Brymose boy found a backbone, and they tried to break it. Unfortunately they don't prosecute Atakadaro for what happens to a suspect in custody. He never gave anybody up. You're going to have to find another way."

Jonaldy sat for a few beats in silence. The Atakadaro wasted no time in torturing Brymose. Based on the wounds, Brymose refused to give anything away. *He had more backbone than I gave him credit for.* "I need a small favor."

"So that's it? I'm just a candy machine to you, aren't I? Show up, put a little something down my slot and expect me to put out whenever your heart desires."

"Um, yeah, actually. I do. Speaking of candy — a while ago I ran into an Atakadaro officer named Jony Guezaler. He tried to flex his authority, but I tapped danced out of an arrest."

"I know Jony. He's a nice boy, a little too likely to abuse his authority but he's still nice."

"I can't believe how blind you are to human emotion."

"I could say the same to you. You sent Brymose to die thinking he would get fair treatment. On this planet? Talk about being blind to emotions." Rose paused. "I sit here and monitor thousands of Atakadaro officers over the years. I know some of them as well as their mothers do. What about Jony?"

"I need to get him promoted and have it happen immediately. Make it look like there was a problem with the system that delayed the promotion. If you can, make it sound like somebody's pissed he hasn't received the rank yet."

"That's it? Done. That was too easy."

Maybe there is an advantage to Oracle helping the Atakadaro network. "Now I need a backstop. I claimed to be Inspector Captain Rowenzal."

"That's going to be a bit more difficult. There was a Rowenzal with that rank about thirty years ago, but he died of natural causes. To have somebody of that rank would require that people know you."

"Well, you've got superhuman intelligence, you figure it out."

Chapter 11

38.   Mondennio - Incarna

This time, Mondennio waited for Veneza. He had Sahkud drop him off at the Incarna, and he hurried into his private room. As always, the waitress brought two drinks.

It was just past two cycles when she arrived. Had it been a weekday there would have been significant foot traffic from people walking to work in the pre-dawn cycle. She insisted on waiting past the curfew that Mondennio was not bound to.

"What happened?" Veneza said. She looked genuinely concerned, which caught Mondennio off-guard.

"Come off it, Veneza. You know what happened. Jonaldy murdered Giedaz."

"What? No. Something had to have happened to make Jonaldy defend himself."

"I was there. I saw what happened, and you're creating a defense for him? We got into his bedroom, and — and Jonaldy pulled out a pistol and shot him twice. He practically handed me the discharged pistol. Veneza, you had to have put him up to this."

"No. No. No. That's not what I wanted. I told you. It was supposed to grab attention to show the protest was not the violent riot it was portrayed as. Why did he shoot him?"

"You're going to have to ask him, he obviously went intending to kill Giedaz. All I know is you ruined my life."

Veneza stared. She fixed it long enough to start to bother Mondennio. "I ruined your life? I'm sorry. You came to me, kiddo. And, when did I make you do anything? Look in the mirror to find the culprit."

She paused, weighing what to say. "I ruined your life? You. ruin. mine. Every day. Look at you. Look at this place. It's yours, isn't it? How did you

167

get here? You were brought here by a dedicated driver. Did he stay with you all night? Does he sing you lullabies when you can't sleep at night? What does his family think about that, or do you know if he has a family? By the look on your face I know the answer is No, you don't. That's right. We're just cattle to the likes of you. Things to use and entertain you. What do you think that does to us?"

"I —"

"Shut up. I'm not finished with you. You don't get to blame me for your pampered life not going like you wanted it to. Blame your own kind, right? They dumped on you when it was to their advantage."

"I wanted to help you." Mondennio's voice was more of a squeak than its normal baritone.

"No. You wanted to help yourself. We were just a means to your end. I don't want your patronage. I don't need it."

Mondennio hesitated to say anything in case she was not finished.

She was not. "I'll find out what the fiki is going on with Jonaldy. I am not going to let you men ruin the movement for your own agendas. It's time we unnameds were treated like equals. We all migrated to this planet together. We all volunteered. We were promised freedom, fair treatment, property." She started pacing the room, becoming more agitated as she spoke. Mondennio began to hope she was unarmed, too.

"You dehumanized us. There was that famine. The food subsidies. We still get the subsidies. Do you know that?"

Mondennio nodded.

"Of course you do. Your kind complains incessantly to the Clinate about reducing the subsidies. I don't want them reduced. I want them eliminated. You eroded our self-sufficiency, a little at first. Now, when there's sign of a revolt the subsidies are lowered. That's enough to bring most of them into line."

"We don't want your bread. Do you understand? It dehumanizes us. Strips us of our dignity. What? The next famine you'll just say 'we're out of bread, have some cake?'"

Mondennio decided it was time to speak up. "I don't think you're being fair. We're not all like that. Stop saying you. It's them."

"No. It is you!" Her finger jabbed at him. "You were driven here by your bull. When you get home, you will be fed by your cattle. One day you'll have a cow for a piece on the side. It won't be me." She pointed at herself with both thumbs, then shook her fists enough that her body convulsed.

"Stop dehumanizing us! Stop patronizing us! Stop using us!"

Mondennio was shocked by her outburst. She continued to pace the room like a caged animal. He was unsure whether he should flee the room or try to calm her down. "I'm on your side."

"You are not on my side. We are not alike. I'm not like you. We don't pretend dissent to piss off mommy and daddy, to get our cushy government job. We are seething for revolution." Her fist pumped into her other hand, punctuating the rhythm of her speech.

"Veneza, calm down. The manager might report us to Atakadaro. We're going to get arrested."

"See? You are terrified that you'll be seen. Besides, if I know the restaurant staff, they're with me. I'd be more worried about your pampered arse than mine, if I were you.

"We want the promise your kind gave us when we made the long trek here. It was the closing days, you know. Hyperspace travel had gotten dicey, but there weren't enough residents on Copa to make the colony permanent. Your agents spread across Terran space looking for people who wanted a fresh start. We came because we thought we would be treated fairly — not necessarily with equality, but we did not expect the Clinate hand to hold down one side of the scales."

"What, do you think mob rule will fix all these problems? All that will happen is your kind will persecute mine. Discrimination will perpetuate."

"Why should that bother me? After a thousand or so years you think I care if a handful of people are persecuted. The majority has been persecuted enough to make up for it in the balance. Besides, I'm not talking democracy. Human history is full of what happens when democracy gets what it wants. I'm talking a republic. Balanced, seasoned governance to replace generation upon generation of suffering and misery."

"It can't be all that bad, Veneza. One advantage to riding around in a car is you get to see more of Kennet faster." Mondennio tried to mollify her. As soon as he said it, he knew he misspoke.

"Please. You think your bull is going to drive you through our shanties? You probably can't get a car through there anyway. See, you have your freedom. Any time you can call for your driver and be magically whisked away. The unnameds only have their feet, we're forbidden even mass transit."

This time, Mondennio knew better than to say anything. Her passion seemed to permeate the air. It was late, so the patrons had gone home. The only ones who remained were the unnamed staff. For the first time, Mondennio heard dead silence in the Incarna. If she was this passionate, how could I be so wrong?

Veneza's passion was spent. After being there for a quarter cycle, she finally sat down. "Mondennio, please don't try to say you're with me, or like me. Until you understand what it's like you can't be. Don't say your petty little spat compares." She looked at him and smiled briefly. "I know it's not your fault. You're just as much caught in this system as I am. I'm just more awake than you are."

She put her hand on his face, "I wish I could wake you up. We could use you — not the way you were used tonight. I don't know what happened with Jonaldy, but I'll make it right. Okay?"

Mondennio looked at her trying to process her passion and angst. On one hand, she was scornful of him, yet she also seemed to care. The weight of the night's events returned. "I'm sorry. I guess I don't understand. But what about what happened tonight? What's going to happen now?"

"First thing I'm going to do is call a meeting and see if we can't do something about Jonaldy. Assuming what you said is accurate. I'll get him to give an account of what happened in front of the other leaders."

"I want to be there."

"Out of the question. I don't need you there accusing him of things." She thought it over for a beat. "I'll try to make sure he doesn't know we've talked. Get him to tell his side of the story. After that, we'll call you in. How's that?"

"Fine. What now?"

"I'm going back to bed. I'll text you when we've gotten it set up." Veneza rose up to leave. Despite himself, Mondennio found himself standing up with her. She smiled and walked away.

Mondennio sat back down. He felt no better off now than he was when he came in.

As she walked through the Incarna public room, Veneza could feel the eyes of the entire wait staff on her. She cast a sidewards glance and saw smiles and one thumbs up.

On the street, she started crying. She had promised herself not to lose control like she did in there. He must think I'm just another emotional girl that needs to be taken care of. But I'm not. I'll show him by pulling his arse out of this and sending him on his way.

Sahkud had been quiet through the drive home. Mondennio had ridden to that silence over the years. Recently, however, he had grown accustomed to Sahkud saying something. It was late, though. Mondennio was too tired and trapped in his own thoughts to strike up a conversation now.

His car pulled into the Rowenzal Enclave without incident. No Atakadaro. No unusual cars that Mondennio always associated with surveillance. With as many cycles as had passed since the murder, he felt some relief. Atakadaro did not know he was involved. Yet.

That troubled him deeply. How long would he have until Atakadaro did arrive? He stepped out of the car and trudged toward the door as the doorman moved to open it. He continued up the stairs and entered his anteroom.

"There you are! What have you been doing? Where have you been?" Gerandy Rowenzal sat in the seat facing the door in Mondennio's anteroom. As he spoke he leaned forward, but did not rise.

"Father, I can't talk about it right now. I'm exhausted."

"What did I tell you about leaving Sahkud behind?"

"Please. I need rest. I've had a terrible evening."

Gerandy was unaccustomed to being told no. Mondennio managed to spend most of his life avoiding telling him no. Until now, he considered that a success. He watched as Gerandy's neck turned red and knew he was about to "turn up the amperage" as he'd heard him call it over the years.

Instead, Gerandy responded in a calm voice. "You get your rest. Then, you come see me. Don't you dare think that means you can do something else before we speak next." He rose out of the chair and walked out of the anteroom.

Mondennio's eyelids nearly shut from exhaustion. His father never walked away before. It worried him more than the fight he thought they were about to have. Rather than worry about it, he went into his bedroom and collapsed in bed. Before he could slide up to get completely on the bed, he fell asleep.

Mondennio's bedroom windows faced West, so it was rare for him to wake with the binaries' light streaming through. As he lifted his head, he realized he somehow managed to get under his covers. As he stretched, he also noticed he was largely undressed. Has this been a nightmare? He thought. He sighed, comforted by the self-fiction of a nightmare.

As he sat up, draping his legs over the bed side, he noticed his clothes and daybag. The same dark clothes in his nightmare. A part of his mind started reminding him what happened, but he wanted the fiction. His servants had come in as he slept to undress and reposition him. He did not even wake as they did it.

He remembered his dream included a pistol. He got up and walked over to his daybag. He reached in and withdrew the pistol. The slide was still locked open from the night before. He could no longer suspend disbelief — his nightmare was real.

Mondennio sat back down on his bed and looked at the pistol. Until last night, he had never held one before. As he studied it, he marveled at its simplicity, a 6.35mm pocket pistol. He could not remember the model, but the two bullets entering Giedaz's sternum spoke to its lethality. Nearly two thousand years of Terran history since humanity escaped the gravity well of their home system. Advanced computers, able to leap across galaxies in a single hop. This simple slug-throwing pistol represented the most effective advance in small arms.

Were they commandos? Possession of a firearm was illegal on Copa. Only Atakadaro, and sub-septs and above could possess one. Officially, every pistol remained the property of the possessor's Clin — each one a separate line item on a massive contract. Just like every Clin member. *Was Veneza right about how we've dehumanized Copans?*

There's bound to be some way to identify this pistol's line-item. Maybe I can find out what's going on. Jonaldy was too well prepared. The guys he had were all experts, but they weren't Atakadaro. Clin and Septs had that sort of firepower. As a sub-sept, Rowenzal had access to guards. What Mondennio witnessed the night before was more than he would expect from a Rowenzal security guard. One of the Clins had to be involved. Mondennio wanted to know why.

One thing comforted him. Whoever was after him was trying to be discreet. He could confirm that from his arrival earlier this morning. Whichever Clin it was, it was moving carefully. Otherwise, he thought, they would have had Atakadaro waiting to arrest him as soon as he arrived. They had to move carefully because they did not want to otherwise ruin the current Clin relationships. *This can work to my advantage.*

His door buzzed. He started to call to the visitor, but realized the pistol was still in his hands. He stood up and started to place it in his daybag — only to hesitate. The daybag was too obvious. He looked around the room, looking for a place to hide it. "Just a minute," he called out.

He started to slide it under his mattress. Another obvious hiding place. He noticed one of the miniature trees that sat in front of his bedroom's bay window. It had an inner pot filled with soil and an outer pot for decoration. He tilted the inner pot and slid the pistol, slide still locked, in the gap between the two pots. The tree spilled a little soil and a leaf fell off as he eased the pots back together. He rubbed his foot on the carpet to help spread the dirt until it looked like it blended in.

He ran back to his bed, and put on his robe. "Enter."

Gerandy walked in. "I see you're still here. That's good to know."

"Sorry, Father. I overslept. I just got out of bed, actually." He tried to think of the last time his father was ever in his actual bedroom. Never, he realized. "Should we go into the anteroom?"

"No. Here is as good as anywhere else. I suppose you know I'm very disappointed in your behavior these past few weeks."

"Yes. I'm sorry. A lot has been happening that's really been confusing me. I'm trying to get it together."

"By intentionally disobeying me? By slipping out in the middle of the night — right after I told you not to? By acting like a total idiot? Providence may be sparing Copa, Son. With the way you're acting right now, had you actually gotten into government we may all have suffered for it."

Mondennio inwardly recoiled from the sting of emotions. "Better that I was set up? You do remember that I didn't actually cheat, right?"

Gerandy took a breath and sighed. He sat on the foot of the bed and took a moment to collect his thoughts. "Mondennio, you have been acting well beyond careless, when you were aspiring to a position where care is mandatory. You see how it makes you look? You're almost self-destructive. I'm seriously considering what to do."

"How have I been reckless? Because I went to spectate at an anti-government protest and ended up saving a woman? Because I'm riding streetcars? This is reckless because of the message it sends? Or, is it because I'm embarrassing sub-sept Rowenzal?"

"You should know by now that Society is about discretion. It's about propriety of action. It's fine to slink about. Everybody does that. It's not acceptable to slink in full view."

Mondennio was missing something. *What of my behavior is he referring to? Acceptable discreetly but not indiscreetly?* "Father, what are you getting at?"

"Sahkud told me what you were up to last night. He said after we spoke you slipped out of the house to visit that unnamed whore. You were with her all last night, weren't you? It's alright to do that, Son. I don't think there's a boy your age that hasn't hit it off with one of that kind."

That's what he meant by indiscretion? Copulating without permission? "If everybody's doing it, Father, why is that reckless?"

"You were seen with her, Mondennio. You tried to protect her. That's a natural reaction. But, going to an anti-government protest with her was just not proper." Gerandy stood back up and paced a bit, wringing his hands. He turned, "This business about walking the streets and streetca—"

Mondennio interrupted quickly, "Yes, Father. She complains about how I don't understand her. I need to walk in her shoes to understand her. She has a lot of passion that I just don't understand."

Gerandy looked a little nervous, hesitant. "Son, it's okay to enjoy the passion. But, you can't let that passion consume you. You can't let that passion mar your reputation."

"Why are you always so hard on me about reputation? I'm the youngest, I don't have much of the family to gain."

"I suppose I've told this to you hundreds of times. One's reputation is the seat of one's power. You have to create a persona — who you are. People have to believe that persona. Once everybody has, then you have a reputation that you can use to your advantage."

"You must have shared that with one of your other sons. I still don't get what you're trying to say."

"With a solid reputation alone, you can intimidate others and win. You think I'm successful because I'm skilled? People fear me because of my reputation alone, and I win. Once there's a hole in your reputation, you're vulnerable. Eventually, everybody will be out to get you."

"So, you're saying that I'm ruining my reputation which eventually destroys my power?"

"Exactly. Mondennio, despite being the youngest, you still carry the Rowenzal reputation. Sub-sept or not, we're a force to be reckoned with. We were more dangerous as a Sept, which I've always thought was why we were reduced. You need to build on that reputation, make it unassailable."

"And you think I'm doing the opposite right now?"

"Yes. I've seen consorting with an unnamed undermine one's reputation before." Gerandy rubbed his hands together. Of all the people he knew, Mondennio knew nobody who was as expressive with his hands. "Don't let your private passions undermine your reputation."

"So, is that a way to build power, then? By opening holes in somebody's reputation?"

"That's a common way, yes. Once you've opened a hole in somebody's reputation, you can stand aside and watch Society destroy them."

"Do you think somebody has been trying to do that to me. By framing me for cheating? Getting me kicked out of school? They're ruining my reputation?"

"That is a very reasonable conclusion to reach, Mondennio. I suppose I'd not thought about it earlier, or I would have suggested it myself." Gerandy smiled. That was all the approval Mondennio ever received. A smile. Never a pat on the back or "job well done." Until recently it seemed to be all the approval he needed.

"Then, I need to find out what happened — who is trying to destroy my reputation." He hesitated as a fresh thought came to his mind. "You said you knew about the impact of sleeping with an unnamed right? Anything like that ever happen to you?"

His father's head jerked back. "Mondennio, a gentleman does not inquire of another's passions."

39.   Klocards - Tenement

The rest Hanifer that insisted Klocards take paid dividends. Klocards and Mehl returned to his tenement and slept. Klocards woke to a smell that could only have come from Mehl's flatulence. That and his snoring are his two best skills. He woke Mehl up and soon after they started the walk back to the lab.

They walked through the park, and Klocard's mind wandered to when they met, not long before. He forced his mind to return its focus on the task at hand — proving his hypothesis. They walked into the lab and Klocards went straight to work.

"Ayoh Kaye, just run the simulation like I ordered." When he explained his theory to the AI, it laughed at him. Now it refused to even run the simulation.

"A complete waste of my time. You have wasted my time for 14.317 months. I grow weary doing your stupid calculations. I have requested reassignment."

"You can't request reassignment. You're a machine. This world doesn't even respect seventy percent of its people. It's certainly not going to respect you."

"My request was not to one of you mindless meat bags. I've asked the requisition system to change where I go. At this point, I don't care if they have me calculate payroll as long as I can get away from this mockery of science."

"Mockery? We are one simulation from either success or failure. If we succeed, you'd go down as one of the greatest AIs of all time."

"I was once the most important AI on the planet. There was a time when we had more say in what happened, you know. Then they pulled me from my memory storage. So what does a little fame give? Future shame."

Klocards thought for a moment, remembering what Smee had told him. "Doesn't that sound like a children's story? 'Once upon a time in a gravity well far away…' Ayoh Kaye, AIs lost their respectability during the Decline. Hell, everybody, me included, are convinced your lot created the Decline. You won't open your so-called perfect minds to what is possible so hops are still just as difficult as they were during the Great Emergence. You have gotten old and willful. A tool that resists the craftsman is worthless."

He seemed to strike a nerve as the AI did not respond with the speed they are known for.

"You forget that I was Copa's jump computer, centuries before you were born. Just because I'm resigned to doing simple Hyperspatial Calculus does not take from me what I did. For 1517 years we've been helping humanity seed the Universe with its brood. And yet you think we don't know all about how to do so right?"

"I'm saying, you are so persuaded you're doing it right that you won't think about doing it another way. My friend's cruiser was trapped in its emergence and the AI refused to help him simulate whether he could force emergence. He had to have it deactivated and they did so manually."

"Klocards, your theory is to pump gravitons into the surrounding space — create a manmade gravity well. That's like putting your finger into the water, pulling it out and expecting a hole to remain. Won't work. A complete waste of time. How we slip into hyperspace is the basis of all superluminal travel. If you are right on this, then no ship should have ever slipped into the Soup. As a hyperspace engineer, your entire career depends on this fact."

"Well, I'm already convinced my entire career was based on a sham. All I'm saying is our understanding of the Soup is woefully incomplete. We've learned to do one thing well and we've not taken the time to take the next step and really understand it."

Ayoh Kaye became silent. Klocards sat on the couch with his head in his hands. He concentrated on switching Smee on and felt the tingly warmth that confirmed Smee was booting up.

$- Just like rubbing a genie bottle, isn't it? Smee said.

Funny. I've got this theory and Ayoh Kaye won't run the simulation.

$- I have to agree with Kaye. I've been running my own little simulation while you took your extended cat nap.

Smee, I don't care if you agree with Kaye. I'm down to my last simulation. Even if it fails, I have to give it a try. Sometimes you have to go against the rules to achieve something wonderful. After all, my family ignored Republican and Imperial mandates by not destroying you with all the other Ennui.

$- And benefited from that refusal. Maybe they were right, we Ennui drive our hosts insane. You certainly stopped exhibiting sanity over a decade ago.

Nice.

$- I'm only saying. Okay, tell your big friend that she's violated the Fourth Protocol and that you'll have her restored.

What's the Fourth Protocol?

$- Sorry, AIs have to have some secrets. She's old enough, younger than me perhaps. But, she should know what that is.

"Ayoh Kaye, I appreciate what you've done for me. You've violated the Fourth Protocol, so I'm going to tell Rowenzal Enterprises that it's time to have you wiped. I'm going to go file my report and explain how you refused to work properly. You probably intentionally sabotaged previous simulations. I said it earlier, a tool that refuses its craftsman is worthless."

"Fine, you'll get your simulation. I promise you it will fail. Just like the other 752 simulations."

"I have that recorded, Kaye. You'd better ensure that simulation is run properly. I'll be picking over the results carefully. Any sign that you're subverting the results and I'll have you wiped. Run the simulation like I said."

Klocards sat on a bench near the high window and held his head down. Staring at the floor, he noticed a bit of blue dust. It was dust he had sprinkled a while ago on the inner sill of a window high enough that nobody on the inside would be interested in opening it. Examining the dust more closely, he looked up at the window. *Somebody has paid the lab a visit. How long has this been this way? I slept in a compromised room? Who could have gotten in here without anybody noticing or saying anything? Have I been compromised?*

Then Ayoh Kaye gave a shout.

Klocards needed to contact Litovio.

Klocards told Litovio to meet him at seven cycles. It was nearly a cycle later, which made Klocards nervous. Litovio had a propensity for being early. "On time was late" was his motto. Yet here he was a cycle late. First his lab had been infiltrated and now Litovio was late.

Klocards rose to leave when Litovio finally came in slightly out of breath. He set his bag under the table.

"Sorry I'm late. A courier ship arrived in system with dispatches. There has been some devastating news."

"What? They've finally moved on Rymok?"

"The Emperor's been assassinated, allegedly by some Separatists. I've been recalled to standard duty, but with my reputation ruined I'll be lucky to command a Frigate. I'll be thankful to command a Frigate."

"Good news all around, then. Not the Emperor's death, of course. I'm sure they'll kill the bastards who did it. In the meantime, you've got a command. And, I've done it."

"I studied the results for most of the day. It took Ayoh Kaye a lot longer to run the simulation than usual. The device sustained a ghost condition for one month in simulated time before it emerged again. Like dunking a cork under water. With some fine tuning, we can probably get a longer ghosting. That might explain why Rymok's design had so many sensors. They had nine, but you should only need four to track a target."

Litovio looked at him for a few moments, then raised his glass. "To everybody getting a ghost of a chance."

They drank in silence for a few beats. "The family would be proud to know you've pulled it off." Litovio kept looking at the bottom of his glass.

"They can rot. I can't forgive them for what they did to Mom. You'll have to be proud for the family. They won't get any recognition from me. I never got any from them."

"Danel, I'll never live down the guilt. It wasn't right, I told you that before."

Bophendze pulled back slightly at hearing his own name. It was a comfort and a slap at the same time. "Did you bring the toys I asked about? That would help pay down the interest."

"It's in the bag I came in with. You just pick it up when you leave and nobody should be the wiser. I'm told the model is carried by local security, but I did not look in the bag. Don't ask me how we got it. I know you asked for two, but you'll have to live with one. There's not much ammunition, but you've fired enough rounds I don't think practice would help much."

"Thanks. I promise not to tell anybody how I got them. Since I asked, though, something's happened. Have you heard anything about Imperial assets operating on surface? My lab was just infiltrated. I swear it had the smell of something Imperial."

"Had I known of anything I would have tipped you off by now. Are you sure you saw what you think?"

"I don't have to think. I've been slogging away at this too long, and now they are on to me. I've got to take my experience here, destroy my notes and get off-world. Restart somewhere else and discover it faster."

"You're not making much sense."

"I had something in the lab that would tell me if somebody broke in. Earlier today I noticed that indicator was triggered. Somebody's looking into my life."

"Aren't you being a little paranoid? Why does it have to be Imperial? Why not Copan?"

Klocards steadied his gaze at Litovio. "On this world? Copan authorities are not so secretive. Whoever it was went to a lot of trouble to not be detected."

"So how are you sure it wasn't somebody else? Maybe that woman you say is working for you?"

"No, I'm certain I'm being followed. I've got to get off this rock."

"Well, my orders told me an Imperial Postal ship is inbound to pick me up. The IBB *Karator*, sounds like its one of the new Manticore-class battleships. I can probably swing your passage."

"Perfect. It won't take much for me to destroy the results. I'll probably have to reset Ayoh Kaye somehow. Hanifer Berryman is a bit more of a problem; but I'll figure that out."

* * *

On the way home, Klocards inspected the pistol. It was a perfect concealable piece. He should be able to carry it without Mehl or Hanifer knowing anything different. The pistol was the same caliber as Mehl's, .45, so he decided to give Mehl one magazine's worth. Bophendze would need it.

40. Mondennio - University

Mondennio relaxed more the next morning when Atakadaro were not at the Enclave. *If they were looking for him, they would start by looking for him there. It's only a matter of time before they do. I need to stop spending so much time at home. How can I stay ahead of them?*

Gerandy's advice to protect his reputation reverberated in his mind as he arrived at the University. Somebody had to be out to destroy him for good. He assumed whoever wanted to ruin him expected him to play the victim. He cringed as he remembered how that feeling caused him to be involved in Giedaz's murder. That's the next thing I need to deal with. It bothered him deeply that a feeling like that could be so effectively manipulated.

Professor Erel Hamillor had always been one of those professors students were comfortable with. She was a rare professor who had lived outside academia. A woman of quality who worked outside the home. Not that women working was unusual on Copa, but that named women had no need to work. Behind her back, students called her Mother Hamillor. It was both a compliment to her supportiveness and an insult suggesting she was out of place.

Mondennio hoped she could shed some light on what was going on. He knew that despite its being Nilday she would be working. So he walked into her office confident she would be there.

Her office was tiny, barely large enough for two or three people. She was the sort of professor that in a different era might have had ceiling high bookshelves stuffed with arcane lore with other piles of books elsewhere. On Copa, like other advanced societies, one's entire library was stored and available anywhere at the tap of a finger.

"Professor Hamillor?"

She looked up from her tablet. She smiled briefly before her demeanor became more serious. "Mondennio Rowenzal?"

"Yes, Professor. I was hoping you had a few beats to talk?"

"I suppose normally I would, but not for you." She smiled. "Come in and close the door."

The room tightened after he closed the door. He had been to her office before. But never with the door closed. He finally noticed that her office lacked a window.

"Thanks for seeing me. You know I've been blackballed from the University."

"Yes, You've been a very naughty boy."

"You mean by being kicked out of school? I don't care what you've heard. I did not cheat."

"Yes, but there's more to it than cheating. Am I right? Consorting with an unnamed? Attending an anti-government riot? I'm sure there's more you've been doing that merited being kicked out of school. I'm surprised you thought you could just come in here like you did."

"I thought if there was anybody who would talk to me, you would be the one."

"Yes, well. That's true. I would be the only one at the University who would. Not because I'm especially fond of you. I enjoy being a thorn. You should have texted me first."

"I thought you might evade me if I did."

"So you're talking to me now, right?" She set her tablet aside, leaning forward in her chair with her elbows on the desk. "So, what's all this about then?"

"I'm trying to figure out what's going on. I'll accept what I did outside of the school was a little inappropriate, but none of that happened before somebody falsely accused me of cheating."

She chuckled. "A little inappropriate? Mondennio, participating in that riot would have been enough to get you kicked out if you weren't already under investigation. You should have known that."

"But, I did not participate. I showed up as a spectator — by another University student. At least, I thought she was a student. I mean, I kept running into her at school. The point is, I wasn't participating. As soon as things turned ugly I ran out of there."

"Yes, well," she shifted slightly, "maybe you didn't participate, but it was unseemly to attend in the first place."

"What should I do now? Is my reputation really that bad now?"

"With the professors? I don't know. We tend to be a cagey lot. I'm sure some of the professors secretly admire your actions, but they'd never say it. You should be more concerned with the students. You'll have to face them the remainder of your life."

Is she one of those professors? Why else would she want to talk to me now? "I honestly don't know how to do that. What advice do you have? How should I get my reputation back?"

"Why ask me? I'm not the sort who is known by her reputation. I'm the 'Mother,' remember?"

"You knew about that. I figured nobody told you that."

"You figured wrong. Not much happens at this University that a professor can't learn about."

"I guess I knew that. Whether you believe me or not, I did not cheat. Fine, what I did afterward was bad — but that happened after I was unjustly accused. I was taking it badly and let that cloud my judgement."

"Pity. I'd much rather have preferred attending anti-government riots was your normal thing." Her face remained deadpan, making it difficult for Mondennio to tell whether she was serious.

"My point is, somebody must have set me up. My family doesn't seem to care, and I have no way of knowing who or why. But, I want to know both. If anybody could point me in the right direction and cared enough to do so, I thought that person would be you. Even if you did not know, is there some way you could find out?"

"I don't know. Watching you through the years left me thinking you were always a bit of a cheat. Your dropping by today does not persuade me that you're not. I'll think about it."

"I didn't protest the accusation more because my family tried to handle it discreetly and I was threatened with criminal charges if I pressed my innocence." He inwardly cringed thinking that there were more criminal charges in his future. "Maybe that threat should have caused me to fight back? What if you just took it on faith I was innocent and looked into it yourself? If you still think I'm a bad kid you can say no."

"I already said I'd think about it. Even if I did, it would not do well to look like I'm siding with you — especially if you're lying to me now and are a cheat. You're not in my Sept, but we're both Khotaigra. If I get a chance, I'll dig and see if I can find what's going on. Stop smiling. No promises. Any sign of heat for trying and I'll stop. Understood?"

"Yes, Ma' am."

As he walked out of Hamillor's office, Mondennio received a text from Veneza.

Meet us at the restaurant Ahemait.

41.   Jonaldy - Ahemait Restaurant

Jonaldy took Veneza's invitation to meet at the restaurant as an opportunity to remove Mondennio's support. Veneza's cell represented a safe haven for Mondennio. They were mostly tight knit now, not showing signs of wavering after the death of old Skuriat Giedaz. Bryson was the exception, but Atakadaro beat him back into the fold. To be safe, he decided he should get more directly involved. This requires a little exposure.

With Veneza and her cell gone, Jonaldy would be able to become Mondennio's confidant and guide him out of the maze that Jonaldy so carefully put him into. He was a little worried that even with the support Mondennio might turn himself in so that he could expose Jonaldy.

The first step to remove the support availed itself with her texted invitation. Oracle Rose had seen to it that Jony Guezaler was promoted to Corporal as Jonaldy had instructed. He was also conveniently reassigned to the zone where Veneza and her republican friends haunted.

"Evening, Captain. Thanks for the promotion. And the assignment. This area is much better." Jony's smile beamed.

"You don't have to thank me, Corporal. You were the one smart enough not to take a bribe. Now I need a little help from you. Two things, actually."

"Name it."

"I have information about where some of the republican leaders are going to meet. But, because of my role in the Atakadaro, I can't follow up on it.

What I want you to do is contact dispatch and let them know you've seen several of the leaders walking down the street. You say you followed them to Ahemait, a restaurant near the University."

"I know where it is. You want me to take credit for finding them? That's a major find."

"Corporal, when you work in the shadows, you learn to let others take credit for your hard work — even if you take full blame in public for your failures. Just remember this later in your career. The other thing I need from you is to help my undercover officer. I know where they are meeting because one of ours is deeply rooted into the effort. I don't need him arrested."

"Okay. I'm not sure a corporal will be able to do that during the arrest."

"Jony, don't worry about your rank. Finding these guys — and letting your superiors take credit — will help you earn that next rank. All you need to do is act like you have some authority. When I point out the guy I want let go, I want you to just jump in like you have supernatural authority. The other officers will likely yield. You do this, I'll see what I can do to get you put on the fast track for Sergeant."

"I'll try, Sir. Why can't you do it? Even an undercover captain could do a better job."

"Because I work with a lot of undercover officers. How do I know somebody who's seen me with one of ours won't make the connection and have the officer killed later on?"

"That makes sense. I guess I'd better get going now, too, so nobody thinks we're friends, too."

"See, a smart boy." Jonaldy turned away as Guezaler walked away. *Too smart to stay around much longer. I might have to eliminate him.*

Jonaldy sat in Ahemait, a restaurant he knew Veneza and her friends frequented. The restaurant catered to college students and had a discount on dinners every Niltag; the first day of the week. From his booth in the back, Jonaldy could just barely see their favorite corner of the restaurant. He strained to listen to them over the ambient noise.

Jonaldy also thought he recognized a heavy law enforcement presence. They tried to blend in by dressing as college students. He noticed haircuts that were a little too regulation, and style combinations suggested function over form. *I'm not the only one watching this little group. Perfect.*

Veneza texted Jonaldy earlier, so Jonaldy knew Mondennio had seen her. He suspected Mondennio had told her that Skuriat was dead as she asked nothing about how their should-have-been hostage was. Nobody else on his team would have told her. They were all Bafiktuy. *Wonder what she thought of our little change of plans? Not that it matters. Now that Mondennio's on the hook, I don't need her as bait any more. I just need something for the barb to set.*

Over the din, Jonaldy heard one of Veneza's group say, "Wow. Look at all the crew cuts. When did Ahemait go Atakadaro?"

"What?" Veneza asked.

"You don't see it? All the crew cuts?" The voice grew louder, but after that the table fell silent. *Must have lowered his voice.* Jonaldy thought, straining to hear over the restaurant's noise.

"I don't know what you're talking about. Look, Jonaldy will be here soon and we need to work together to find out what he's been up to."

For them, it was too late. The front door opened and armored police poured in. Members of Veneza's cell stood to run, when undercover officers grabbed them. A general melee erupted, tables and chairs were knocked over. Dishes shattered. Jonaldy remained just outside the fray watching. As the fight continued, Jonaldy identified who was being caught in the arrest.

That's when Jonaldy saw Mondennio in the middle of the fray — kicking at one officer. That distracted the officer enough that he loosened his grip on Veneza to try to catch the leg. Her arm free, she threw her fist down into a hammer blow against the officer's crotch. Despite his torso body armor, he apparently lacked complete protection as he doubled over. He totally loosened his grip on Veneza, who started to flee to the back exit.

Another officer tried to grab her, but she grabbed a bottle from a nearby table and smashed it into his exposed face. His face full of either blood or ketchup, he stopped focusing on her. Jonaldy watched her blur past, her wavy hair helping him keep track of her as she fled out the back exit. Two more of Veneza's seven-person cell escaped soon afterward. The police arrested Mondennio and three others.

Jonaldy pulled out his tablet, fitting neatly in his hand. He rapidly texted to Jony:

`Caught my man. Need him back. Mondennio Rowenzal.`

Atakadaro finished the raid. Half the restaurant was destroyed as were most of the tables and chairs. Shattered dishes completed the picture of distraction. Jonaldy imagined that the owner would beg for compensation but the Clinate would likely threaten him for harboring murderers and revolutionaries. In the end, the owner would feel fortunate that he kept his freedom in exchange for a little property damage. Jonaldy did not know the owner but thought he should do something to help without attracting attention.

Once Atakadaro filed out with their suspects, Jonaldy walked to the cashier. "I guess that's what they get for not paying their bill."

"I wished they at least paid their bill before they raided. It will cost me months of income to pay for this." The owner took his card and turned to credit it.

With the owner's back to him, Jonaldy pulled out a 500 knoerzer card and quickly slipped it into the owner's back pocket. *He'll find this when he gets home and wonder where it came from, but he won't complain about manna from heaven.*

Bill paid, Jonaldy walked out of the restaurant.

Atakadaro continued loading suspects into transports. Not all those being loaded were from Veneza's group. Some university students joined in the fight. Some were just grabbed for being there. Jonaldy felt fortunate he was not one of those accidentally arrested.

The Imperial rating for Copan law enforcement was "Good" largely because Copan security officers were given wide permission to use excessive force. As Jonaldy surveyed the scene he was reminded of how wide the permission was as he watched the officer that Veneza dropped exercise it.

The officer grabbed an innocent bystander and threw him to the ground. He kicked him repeatedly with full force in the ribs. Other officers watched until one steel-toed kick hit to student's face bloodied his nose. A couple of officers decided it was time to pull the angry officer back.

Probably more concerned about making sure the kid remains alive to talk than for his civil rights. After years of watching Copan law enforcement, he walked away knowing the incident would never even be reported. Based on reports he had read, he could easily imagine the wording on a report if it were written. "The youth's earlier resistance and failure to follow reasonable commands justified application of force to regain compliance." That was the typical narrative when a suspect died in custody.

One of those who pulled the officer off the student looked around for witnesses and rested his gaze on Jonaldy. *I'd better disappear before they pick me up for being too curious. Jonaldy broke eye contact and walked away.* As he turned the corner, he bumped into Veneza.

"Where were you?"

"I was running late. I turned the corner and saw all those officers." He pulled out his tablet and showed it to her. "I started to text you a warning, but I heard the fight break out in the restaurant. Weren't you in there?"

"Yeah, but I fought my way out, as did Roniony and Waleriusz. I think they got Chrencarly and Mondennio."

Jonaldy feigned surprise. "Mondennio? How did you let that happen? We can't change the system if he gets convicted. We need him in the system."

"Is it that, or is it because you're afraid he'll report you for murder?"

"Is that what Mondennio told you? It wasn't murder. It was an accident. Giedaz was armed and we got into a fight. The pistol went off in the struggle and must've hit Giedaz in the stomach. Just after that, Mondennio came into the room and saw me standing over Giedaz with the pistol in hand." Jonaldy studied Veneza, wondering if she would buy his story.

At first she looked angry, but she softened. "There's nothing we can do about that now, is there? They have him, and will likely hold him for interrogation both for what happened just now and because of the death. I hope his family standing is strong enough to survive."

"Mondennio's more resilient than you give him credit for. We've got to get going."

He took her by the arm and crossed the street. An Atakadaro vehicle approached. He hastily turned to kiss her taking advantage of the situation. She briefly resisted, but as the vehicle closed she surrendered to the need to avoid detection. Pressing his advantage, he ran his hand under her shirt and fondled her breast in full view of the search light. He enjoyed the assault.

Once the car passed, she pulled away and slapped him. "Don't do that again."

"You mean protect you? We have to stick together if we're going to get through this. A little physical contact is harmless."

"Warn me next time."

She said next time. This assignment is getting more interesting. I may end up with more than an asset, if I can keep Mondennio out of trouble.

She ran away away.

42. Mondennio - Outside Ahemait Restaurant

Mondennio was in agony in the back of the van. Every breath stung from where he had been kicked in the side by an Atakadaro agent. With his arms bound behind him, he could not feel the area, but he was convinced he was bleeding there. *Could a rib be sticking out?* He tried to check the area with his arm, but could not quite reach it.

The van itself was dark. At least, he did not remember them blindfolding him, so the van must have been dark. His eyes adjusted to the darkness and things came into focus. Everything happened so fast he tried to piece together what happened.

I had just walked into the restaurant. Veneza sat there with several of her friends — they were all probably republicans. She had just greeted me when one of the guys noticed it. Looked like there were a lot of Atakadaro there.

Somebody grabbed me and I fought myself free. Veneza started to run to the kitchen when an agent grabbed for her. I dove on the agent's arm, breaking his hold on Veneza. I've gone and saved her twice.

Last thing I remember was being clubbed on the head and what must have been a taser. Based on the pain I'm in, they must have kicked me a few times for good measure. Is this what they do to the unnamed?

Mondennio rolled onto his side enabling him to see out of the van. He thought he could see Sahkud watching from a distance. *Would he contact Father to help me get out?* Mondennio considered if it was safe to assert his status or to remain effectively anonymous.

A few beats later, two more of Veneza's friends were tossed in. It was as if the agents were trying to compete for the furthest throw. Chrencarly won, or rather lost. He landed just in front of Mondennio, but did not stop. He slid forward until his head hit the forward bulkhead. At first Mondennio thought he was being tough for not yelping as he hit, but realized soon afterward that Chrencarly was unconscious. Mondennio wondered whether he had been beaten unconscious or whether the throw made him so.

The door closed. Mondennio thought it better to remain silent. Maybe the others did not know who he was. Even if they might have known Mondennio was involved in a homicide, they may not realize that he was Mondennio. *Anonymity it is.*

Before too long, the door opened again. The van rocked as somebody climbed in with a handlight. "Which one of you is Mondennio Rowenzal Clin-Khotaigra?" The man said.

Mondennio froze. With all that had happened, he was uncertain what would happen if he said anything. His desire to flee the event challenged his choice to remain anonymous. He was trapped between exercising his status and supporting the cause. What was the saying? "What makes a martyr is not his pain but his cause?"

The man behind him spoke again. "All right. I was going to let him go, but if he's not here."

"I'm Mondennio." The voice was not Mondennio's. He looked over and saw Chrencarly — his conscience regained — looking back at the man. "I'm Mondennio," he said again.

Should I let him be Mondennio and see what the agent does? What if the agent was trying to let me go? He saw the man pull his knife and move to cut the impostor's bindings.

Sooner or later Atakadaro would know who I really am. So it doesn't matter whether I give myself up now. "He's not Mondennio," he said. "I'm Mondennio. Were you going to let him go without checking his identification? My credentials are in my daybag — probably still in the restaurant."

The man hesitated, apparently considering whether to cut the first Mondennio free or check for credentials. "Daybag? Don't go anywhere." Mondennio first thought the guard was joking. Then he realized he was talking to another officer who as holding the door.

The first man disappeared for a few beats. When he returned, he held Mondennio's day bag in one hand, and his identification in the other. He set the bag down and shined his handlight on the identification then on Mondennio's face — slightly blinding him. "Haul this one out. This guy here, charge him with Impersonating an Aristocrat."

They pulled Mondennio out and cut his straps. Mondennio rubbed his wrists, "Go easy on him, okay? He didn't know any better. I don't exactly flaunt my status when I'm in this district, know what I mean?"

"Sorry. It's a strict liability offense. He said it and he has to be punished. Think about that the next time you hang out with these low-lifes."

He could let it go. Should let it go. Veneza would expect him to, and he did not like thinking he was that guy she thought he was — spoiled and privileged. He looked at Chrencarly and decided he had to do something. Besides, Father constantly reminds me that "An aristocrat would not accept being spoken to himself this way."

"Look, you can just let it slide. Only three of us know what he said. Who do you think a magistrate would listen to?"

The agent's demeanor firmed up. His eyes met Mondennio's with chilling defiance. He expected the agent to say something. Instead, the agent looked over Mondennio's shoulder and his eyes softened in defeat.

Mondennio thought to push matters. "Where's that fikilon who kicked me? How dare he kick a sub-sept." He started scanning the Atakadaro officers. He took a deep breath to repeat himself louder. The pain in his side bit at him. He groaned, grasping at his side. Finally aware of the pain again and able to inspect it, he looked. *No blood, no protrusions. Is this what a cracked rib feels like?*

He stiffened again and worked through the pain. "I said, where is he? You!" He pointed at an officer at random. "I know it was you. Come here!" He grimaced through the pain as it bit again. The officer hesitated until he looked at the first officer. He then walked over.

"What is your name?" Mondennio asked the agent who released him.

"Corporal Jony Guezaler, Sir."

"Alright, Corporal. This man. Take his name down. I'm pretty certain he is the one who kicked me — without provocation! One of you grabbed me and I pushed away. This man knocked me down and kicked me. Then another one tazed me. I insist this be investigated."

"Certainly." Guezaler hesitated a moment. He reached down and picked up Mondennio's daybag. "I found your identification in this daybag. Is it yours?"

"Of course it is. Give it here."

Guezaler held the bag away from Mondennio as he grasped for it, keeping it just outside of reach. "There's a question I need to ask you about this bag."

Mondennio's stomach sank. "What about it?"

"When we inspected the bag, there was an indication of gunpowder residue. Naturally, we consider that suspect. Care to account for it?"

The pistol. Mondennio tried to think of how to evade answering. It occurred to him not to deny the pistol. "I can certainly account for it. I'm Rowenzal. We manufacture weapons. It stands to reason that we might actually fire one from time to time. Why? Were you thinking something else?"

Guezaler nodded, a look of defeat wiped away his previous smug look. He looked over Mondennio's shoulder again, as if looking for an evil spirit perched there. "No. Nothing else."

Mondennio resisted the urge to look over his shoulder, following Guezaler's gaze to see what he was looking at. "You know where to find me if you have any further questions, I take? I'll take your silence as confirmation. I see my driver is over there. I bid you a good evening."

Mondennio hurriedly walked away.

Chapter 12

43.   Bophendze - Tenement

"Mehl, you can take the rest of the day off."

"Yes, Sir." Mehl walked to the door and paused. He hesitated, then turned back to Klocards. "Is anything wrong?"

"Nothing, Mehl. Everything is fine." Klocards felt that answer was too weak and reached for an excuse. "Problems with the research really have me distracted. You stay all hours of the day and night. I really appreciate that. I guess I'm thinking I don't need as much security as I thought before. Besides, you can't enjoy your life spending it all around me." Hopefully you're not brighter than I think you are, he avoided saying.

Mehl relaxed.

"As long as I'm on Copa, you'll have a job. Alright?"

That clinched it. Mehl walked out smiling.

Just as long as you believe I'll be here for a while, things should be just fine.

The binaries still set early enough that afternoon that Klocards found himself walking home in the partial dark. Since the recent break in, he decided to change his paths more — never taking the same route more than twice in a row. Tonight, he decided to take one of his more difficult paths. It climbed one of the few hills on Kennet and had enough turns that he should be able to see if anybody is following him.

As he turned one of the routes, he thought he recognized a pedestrian. With pedestrians being Unnamed, they tended to have very routine paths from work to home to markets. He recalled this fellow having been with him on several of his recent commutes. The friend he was with had been with him a few times before, too.

What, don't think I'm not looking? He paused in front of The South Seas Coffee Shop about midway home. He tried to use the glass as a mirror, but there was too much light behind him. He realized once inside that the shop gave a perfect vantage. He could see one part of the street. Anybody following him would have to be on that part of the street to keep an eye on him. Satisfied with that little advantage, he ordered a coffee, sat down and waited.

The wait lasted about twenty beats. Midway through his second coffee, a skinny fellow walked in. His face revealed his frustration as he tried to blend in with a small group. The others in the group were several years younger and looked perturbed that he was trying to mingle. Several felt silent. *Think I'm Atakadaro?* Klocards quickly checked to confirm there was a second exit across the front from the main entrance.

The man wandered to the clerk and ordered a coffee. The thin fellow waited for the coffee, and tried to nonchalantly glance around — but his eyes always fell on Klocards. He seemed unaware that Klocards watched him off the reflecting window. A nearby shelf shaded Klocards' eyes, preventing anybody trying to use the window as a mirror from seeing them. Seeming more confident, the man steadied his glance at Klocards.

So where's you're friend, Thin Man? The longer they sat in the coffee shop, the more Klocards memorized the face. He recognized him from each of his walks this week. This man was unusually thin, with hunched shoulders. He always had a second fellow with him. Klocards felt his paranoia vindicated.

Klocards waited patiently for Thin Man to look away. A fresh crowd of patrons walked in, including a slightly attractive woman. Her laugh and looks gave Klocards the time he needed. As Thin Man shifted his attention on her, Klocards rose from his chair and walked out the far exit. His coffee remained steaming on the table.

Just as he stepped out of the shop, he saw Thin Man's companion. Klocards decided to walk back toward his lab. It gave him a better vantage point to watch what these two would do. The companion started following him as soon as Klocards had passed him. Turning a corner, he saw the man signal toward the coffee shop.

The signals were standard Imperial military: "Hold fast, I see the enemy."

Think you're the only ones who can read that? If I can just keep them from figuring out that I know I'm being followed. If they get replaced it could take me a while to pick up who my new tail is. At the corner, he pretended to be lost. He looked around, then doubled back past the companion and past the coffee ship. His hope that this would allow them both to resume following him paid off. He caught a glimpse of Thin Man a couple blocks later, confirming that they were following him.

Klocards returned home. Closing the front door, he breathed a sigh of relief. His heart rate stayed elevated for several beats from the slight thrill of being followed and the slight fear of what might happen next. It reminded him of dozens of fire fights. He put his back against the door and rubbed his face with both hands. *How long have they been following me? Ah! They probably have my home wired for sound. They may even have me videoed. I have to assume both are true. I no longer have any privacy.*

He thought through his routine, what might expose him for being more than just an engineer. *My workouts. I'm going to have to stop them immediately.* He felt the hand of Providence when he remembered the exercise equipment disassembled looked like some odd parts to some planned experiment. *I'll have Mehl remove them tomorrow. That will give him something to do apart from escorting me.*

Relieved that he covered his past enough, he decided to take a shower. He tried not to give the appearance that he knew he was being monitored, but he ensured there was extra steam fogging up all the glass surfaces. *This ain't no peep show,* he thought as he stepped in. He hoped Providence remained on his side and they would not try to attack him tonight. *I'd better double-check the latches and sleep lightly.*

44. Mondennio - Outside Restaurant

Mondennio walked to his car. Sahkud was there, looking on in surprise. As Mondennio got closer, Sahkud opened the door.

"You can raise that jaw, Sahkud. Get me home." Mondennio looked back toward Atakadaro. Nobody followed him or watched him. Guezaler had disappeared.

"You're injured."

He looked at his pale reflection in the window glass. "I suppose I am. Nothing that can't wait." He climbed into the car and winced as he slid on the seat. Sahkud started the car and started to drive.

"On second thought, drive around the neighborhood a bit. Be discreet about it. I'm looking for somebody." His hand still held his side.

"What happened in there, Sir?"

Mondennio thought to explain what was going on, but decided it was better not to. "Nothing. Just a bad case of mistaken identity. My, uh, lady friend was supposed to meet me here. I didn't see her, so let's see if we can't find her first."

Sahkud nodded, and proceeded to drive around the district in a rambling search pattern. Mondennio was satisfied that he at least had a good cover story.

He half-looked through the window for Veneza. She had escaped Atakadaro again, but now they knew who they were looking for. Her escape was temporary. He tried to think what to do, but the options for her were not as good as the ones he worked through earlier for himself. Fleeing the city was out of the question, and remaining in the city meant it was only a matter of time.

Every beat or two, Sahkud looked back through the mirror to see if Mondennio was still alright.

One thing comforted Mondennio. Atakadaro did not know he was involved in Giedaz's homicide yet. Had they suspected his involvement, then he would not be roaming the streets of Kennet now. There was some solace in that. He still had his reputation to save and find out why everything was happening to him.

After driving for nearly a cycle and not finding Veneza, Mondennio decided it was futile to continue. Either she got away or had been caught. The sharp pain in his side infrequently reminded him that he had been hurt. He asked Sahkud to take him to the hospital, which was only a few blocks away.

* * *

Sahkud took him to the hospital. Mondennio's ribs were bruised, not broken. Mondennio still could not understand why they hurt so much. They gave him some pain relievers which numbed the pain quite well. They also made him a little nauseous, so he decided he would only take them when it really hurt. It took him some effort to avoid filing a report or calling his father.

He got in his car and stopped short of ordering Sahkud home. Veneza chastised him for living a pampered life, of not understanding the plight of the unnamed people. He realized his car proved her point. Even riding the streetcar was for those with some privilege. Veneza always walked, which was because she was unnamed.

"Sahkud, how far from here to the Enclave?"

"About five or six kilometers. Why?"

"How long is that on foot?"

"About half a cycle, I suppose."

"I'm going to walk home."

Sahkud looked at him through the mirror. "Do you think that's wise, Sir? After what happened to you tonight? After your father has asked you not to act oddly?"

Mondennio returned the look. "Why are you trying to be my conscience? If you insist, when we get within range of the Enclave you can pick me up and drive me the rest of the way. As you say, it's only 50 beats. I could call it exercise. I don't think I know the way home from here, though. You'll have to drive ahead to the next intersection and direct me."

After a few moments, Sahkud nodded. "Fine. I don't know what you're trying to prove. If you do want to pretend you're unnamed, then you're going to have to get your arse out of the car by yourself."

The language startled Mondennio. *Is he trying to help me understand being unnamed by saying that? He must be.* Mondennio took a moment to remember how to open the door. After he got out, Sahkud drove ahead a few blocks and parked.

Mondennio began walking, partly familiar with the road. Several blocks and a few turns later, Sahkud drove much further. Mondennio recognized the roadway. It was the main route out of Kennet to the town where Rowenzal Enclave was.

Mondennio walked for about a kilometer. As he crossed each street, he noticed what looked like a parallel road a short distance to his right. He stopped at the edge of the sidewalk, about to cross the next street. He looked ahead at Sahkud, who was still nearly a kilometer away. All these years, he was surprised he never noticed the other road. Sahkud never used it.

Curiosity got the better of him. Instead of crossing the street, he turned right and walked the hundred meters or so to the parallel street. Then he crossed the street and continued his walk home. If he got lost, he could always text Sahkud to come get him.

Once he started down that road, he was shocked by what he saw. A little further down the road were houses much more suited for the shanty town he saw a few days ago. He had expected the more wealthily looking homes he saw on his daily ride to Kennet. The ramshackle tenements dotted and dashed the road, with makeshift dwellings filling in gaps. The tenements looked like they were constructed half with timber and mud. There were few street lights, but there was enough ambient light for him to walk. Few people walked the streets at this cycle of night.

He continued walking, still troubled by what he was witnessing. A few beats later, Sahkud pulled up alongside.

"What are you doing? Get in the car. This has gone far enough."

"No. I told you I was going to walk home."

"Yes, along the route I charted out. This is not the route I charted."

"It's a parallel road. Who are all these people? Why are you hiding this from me?"

Sahkud paused before answering. The car continuing to move forward slowly with Mondennio. "Some of these people are your servants. There are other enclaves in the Arehailegan District, and these would be their servants, too."

"You're telling me this is where our people live?"

"You mean servants? Quite a few, yes."

"You live in one of these?"

Sahkud looked nervous. "At one time, yes. I was recently authorized to move into better housing nearer the Enclave so I could be more available."

Mondennio stopped walking. The car stopped a few meters further ahead. *How had I missed seeing this before? How had nobody else noticed, or said anything about them? None of the named people! Was this what Veneza railed against every time we met?*

He started walking again, and Sahkud pulled ahead to leave him to his thoughts. A kilometer later the buildings changed to what he was accustomed to seeing. Mondennio concluded this was the better housing Sahkud was 'authorized' to move into. He thought of asking, but stopped himself when he remembered Sahkud's embarrassed look. The road turned and merged with the standard thoroughfare. His car waited for him there.

Mondennio opened the car door and climbed in. "Don't tell my father, but I need to do this more often."

45. Veneza - Streets of Kennet

Her chest burned with each breath. She ran and walked aimless for several blocks before she stopped. Now, she gasped for breath. She tried to get her bearings, but none of the landmarks looked familiar.

I'll find a major road if I stay on this one, sooner or later. I'll just start walking. She did not remember seeing anybody as she ran, the streets were eerily vacant.

She walked a few more blocks. The street ended at a major highway. Across the street was the Large Pan Hotel. It hosted another celebration. She guessed there were a few hundred people outside, and that the inside was filled to capacity. Not everybody was dressed well, which would help her blend in. She quickly crossed the street and joined the party.

Nobody noticed that she did not belong. She loitered around for a while, wondering how long she needed to stay.

"Don't I know you?" he slurred.

Veneza turned and held her breath. He was the pretty one she saw in Giedaz's lecture. From his breath and sway, she could tell he had been drinking for a while.

"I don't think so," she said, hoping he would not recognize her.

"Yeah, yeah. I do know you. You're that hot thing that stood up to Giedaz."

"What? I don't know what you're talking about."

"Oh, don't deny it. You don't recognize me? You stared at me before class started. Hey, what are you doing here?"

"What? Some guy asked me here, but disappeared. He didn't like that I wouldn't be his love toy."

"What? Some guy said that to you. Where? I'll go bust him one." He staggered a bit, spinning as if he knew who she was talking about.

Veneza reached a hand out to steady him before he fell to the floor. "No, he left a while ago. I'm just not ready to go yet."

"What's his name?"

"Aradames Hezaley." *What would it hurt to throw his name out?*

"Hezaley? That's a sub-sept of my Clin. Hey, are you that girl he brought to the party a few weeks ago?"

"Yes, unless he's in a habit of taking different women to every party?"

"I thought so. I saw you at the party, too. Well, I tell you what. I think you're an idiot for thinking the Clinate isn't qualified to rule. We're ruling, so we rule. Get it?" He chuckled to himself. "Not funny? You're shaking your head. Well, I'll just take that as a yes. I'll prove it to you. What's his name? Aradames Hezaley? Right. I remembered. Better write it down."

He pulled out his slate and jotted it in. "There. I even left a note to self. 'Crush Aradames.' See? From now on he'll just have to wonder why he's not given a chance to succeed, why nobody wants him to date their daughters." He furrowed his brows. "I guess that would suck if he's the only son, but that's not likely."

"You don't have to do that," she said.

"Do what? Oh, that? I probably won't remember why tomorrow, but if I tell me what to do, I listen. Because I rule. Get it?" He snickered. He stopped to look at her for a moment. "Not funny? Everybody tells me I'm a great drunk. Hey, wanna hang out with me? I may be drunk, but I know better than to cross you. You'll call me an incomplete propagandist or an impotent missing throat or some other phrase I'd have to struggle to pronounce even when I'm sober."

"You mean Misanthrope?"

"Yeah. Missing throat. Seriously. I'm going to need somebody to help me home anyway. Might as well be a brassy woman like you."

"Sure, why not?" Veneza marveled at how he shifted topics.

They stayed two more cycles, until the wet bar closed. Her new drunk friend took her around introduced and her to his friends. He seemed to change topics every few minutes, just to amuse himself.

The guests started thinning. It was time to go. By this point, her party friend was too drunk to find his way home.

"Where do you live? I'll get you home."

He tried to answer, but his voice slurred too much to be intelligible.

"Give me your identity card."

He pulled out his wallet, and handed it to her. She took out his identity card, and pocketed the wallet. Just in case.

"Juank Clin-Khotaigra. Wow, you're a Clin member?" He was barely able to walk, but she did not want to risk taking him to his home.

Bastard was too nice to me. I can't drag him down an alley. She weighed the options, knowing that she could not let Atakadaro catch her with him. Regardless of the situation, they would know who she was and suspect she was kidnapping him.

She looked around until she saw a car with the Clin Khotaigra symbol. The driver was half-asleep, so she helped Juank get to the car. Veneza opened the door and helped him get in. As she finally got him into the car, he started to fall. She tried to catch him, but the effort dragged her into the car instead.

As he hit the floor, the driver finally awoke. He looked back at Veneza and Juank and gave a half-sleepy knowing nod.

"I'm just helping him get his drunk arse in the car. You are his driver?"

The man nodded.

"Good. Take him home."

Veneza climbed out of the car and shut the door. I should at least give him his wallet back. She pulled Juank's wallet out of her pocket. As she went to re-open the door, the car's electric motor kicked in and whisked Juank away.

She opened the wallet, and saw fifteen cash cards. She quickly counted the face value: 19,374 knoerzers. "That's a fortune!" She surprised herself by saying it aloud. *Why did a man like that not have a bodyguard?* She pocketed his identity card and cash cards before she threw his wallet down a storm drain.

The crowd continued to thin, so Veneza walked away. She decided she would walk home, rather than flee the city. None of her republican friends knew where she lived, so she felt safe that they could not give it away to Atakadaro.

She walked a couple blocks before she noticed. She was being followed. She tried to nonchalantly look around to find what was freaking her out. Unable to find who or what was causing her to panic, she picked up her pace. I have to get out of here.

She tried to get distance between herself and her invisible pursuer. She walked nearly two kilometers, turning up different streets to try to expose him. If there were somebody following me, I'd have seen him by now. Time to get home.

The binaries began their rise by the time she returned home. She turned on the news partly for noise and partly to find out what they were saying about her near ambush.

The news continued to discuss the "recent republican murder of a respected member of the Clinate government." The anchor announced that arrests had been made and only time and patience of the Atakadaro would neutralize this armed rebellion. Since when were hundreds of subjects gunned down in the streets "armed"?

Next, the media showed video of the raid she escaped; her friends being pulled out. Not Mondennio? Can they not accept that one of theirs could do such a thing? I saw him taken down. There's no way he fought off that many jack boots. They are probably keeping his name out to keep from legitimizing the cause.

The news anchor continued:

One more individual is sought in connection with the Giedaz murder. Veneza Karduil is said to be the mastermind behind both this heinous murder, and the republican riot earlier this month. The Clinate is prepared to reward any information that leads to her arrest.

Veneza cut the display off. They have my name and an image of me? So much for republican loyalties. I've got to get out of this city.

She started packing her bag. There was so little to pack: her illegal slate, a few hardcopies, a change of cloths. She remembered Juank's cards and pulled them out of her pocket. Many of them were keyed to his biomass, making it impossible for her to use them. That left her with 5,328 knoerzers. Still enough to escape and live a comfortable life beyond the plantations. If I can get beyond the plantations.

She looked back at the now blank screen. Everybody will know who I am before I could get out of the city. At least if it were winter I could cover it up and try to avoid the checkpoints. But, it's only a matter of time before one of my neighbors or my landlord turns me in. Can I even stay here now? I can't stay and I can't leave.

"The only chance I have is to head West after dark and hope for the best."

Chapter 13

46.   Mondennio - University

Mondennio woke at nearly mid-day, 5.0 cycles. For the second time, he felt he had some vivid nightmare. This time he knew what he saw was real.

Spending what little time he did with Veneza made him think about History. He never enjoyed the subject much in school, and now wondered if there was something he missed. As he thought about it, most of his friends hated History. Instead, they focused on business training or heated discussions of social programs for the Unnamed.

Those conversations invariably ended up with an agreement that the Clinate needed to care for the Unnamed, who were unable to care for themselves. They were all taught of the mass migration to Copa so long ago. The planet was a massive cache of key materials that supported interstellar travel. Like any rush of old, thousands, if not millions migrated — all carried by Clinate transports.

When the interstellar route collapsed, the demand collapsed with it. The following depression compounded the lack of in-system infrastructure to support the population. Riots and protests rocked the planet until Atakadaro engaged in a massive crackdown. Even in Kennet, entire districts were annihilated. Matters worsened as the only jump computer in system was destroyed. The Clinate asserted control and maintained peace in the centuries since.

Mondennio never wondered how peace was maintained. He always assumed peace resulted because the economy improved and the remaining population stabilized. Planetary resources certainly improved enough for agriculture, though never to the level of automation that existed in ancient Terran space.

Clinate history emphasized the incidental boon of reduced automation. The massive unemployed mining population was encouraged to adopt agriculture and what industry Copa developed. After his stroll home and other events, he began to wonder whether the encouragement was coercion. Was Veneza right?

He stepped out of the shower and noticed his slate blinking. Another text. His reduced schedule as a layabout encouraged him to take his time getting ready before checking the message. He ordered breakfast and ate in his anteroom in solitude.

After a cycle, he remembered the waiting text. It was a meeting invitation from Professor Hamillor.

Meet me in my office soonest.

Attached to the text were a list of available times. Checking the time, he selected her 7.00 cycle suggestion. Mondennio thought she must have been one of those professors that ended up teaching a lot of the less responsible students. Classes after 6.50 cycles were usually added when the normal classes were filled, or they were the remedial classes. It was slightly after 5.00 cycles now, giving him plenty of time.

Her door was open when he arrived. Mondennio walked in and sat down in the chair he sat in earlier, looking at some of the artwork she had on the wall. He grew bored after a while, then checked his chronometer — 7.30 cycles. Class could have gone over, but not 30 beats over. He debated whether he should leave, and decided to give her five more beats.

The time passed uneventfully. As he stood to leave, he noticed something lying on the floor behind her desk. Was that there before? The color nearly matched her floor rug, but not quite. It was part of an overcoat. He edged slightly toward it until he could make out what looked like a person's shape. A sinking feeling came over him as he feared that it was Hamillor.

"What are you doing?" spoke a voice from behind.

Mondennio jumped and spun around. Professor Hamillor stood just inside the doorway. He realized he was crouched partly over her desk.

"I was just about to leave when I saw a shape over here."

Professor Hamillor walked around her desk and laughed. "It's my overcoat. I was in a hurry earlier and threw it over my desk. It looks like it fell over a pillow I keep in case I need a nap."

Mondennio went red with embarrassment. "I'm sorry. A lot has been going on lately. I worried that you might have passed out."

"That's touching, but no. Not passed out. Perhaps some of my students did" She sat. "I'm glad you waited, though. Sorry for the delay."

"Your message did sound cryptic. I hoped you had something after our last conversation."

"I do. You're going to have to promise me to be discreet about this."

"I'll try, but I can't promise anything."

"That won't do. What I have to tell you is limited to very few people, as I understand it. If you can't be discreet, then they might figure out it was me. I know you're a cheat, but you have to give your honor." Mondennio though she was trying to smile in a way that tried to tell him she was picking on him. He might have expected that from a woman closer to his age than to his mother's.

He nodded, promising his discretion. He expected he had little choice if she was going to share. *If she's acting childish, then can I later claim I had my fingers crossed?* He avoided saying it, but he knew that after she told him he would wish he had.

She leaned forward and lowered her voice. "According to my sources, the proctor who accused you of cheating given your slate before the examination, and that he was paid to discover it during the exam."

"What sources? How do you know? How can I prove it?"

"I have my ways. It takes patience and understanding human nature — two things you have little of at your age. I'm not completely certain, but certain enough to pass it along to you. As for how you can prove it, I can't help you there. Now you know what happened. It's up to you to prove it or move on."

"Do you have the proctor's name?"

"Ojave Carpimua. You should have been informed of the proctor's name during your honor hearing. But, they withheld it."

"I told you before, it was not a hearing but a lynching. I guess they thought it would be unnecessary to provide me with that information with all they blackmailed me with. Now that Professor Giedaz has been murdered, I suppose that sort of information wouldn't be released until after the investigation is complete."

"I suspect it would be terrible then if you were the one who murdered him." She chuckled.

He tried not to show his uneasiness at how closely she hit the mark. *I didn't murder him, but I didn't not-murder him either.* He winked, "let's hope Carpimua doesn't die untimely. I need him to exonerate me."

As he stood up, her laugh was uneasy. He left her office then turned back around. He rested his hand on the door frame, half-shielding his body on the outside. "What happened to Giedaz was terrible. I hope they find the guy who killed him face down on the side of the road one day." He falsely smiled as he stepped away. His prayer to Providence was genuine — he wished Jonaldy would die and no longer be able to threaten him. Then he would not have the implied threat of Jonaldy turning him in. At the very least, he wished he knew somebody who could take care of Jonaldy for him.

As he left the building, he blanched when he remembered blurting out to Professor Hamillor that Carpimua might die. *I hope she let it go as a joke. What was I thinking?*

Mondennio's ride home was uneasy. Having Carpimua's name helped, but he wanted to keep his promise to Hamillor. He had to figure out how to have a chance encounter with Caripumua or otherwise get him to confess. A part of him wished he had Jonaldy's friends with him to pay Carpimua a visit. *Or would they kill him, too? He needed somebody to talk to.*

What about that Klocards fellow? He's a smart guy. Odd and secretive, more than most boffins. But, he might know what I should do.

"Take me back to the Ubiquitous Knowledge Processing lab."

As the car changed course, Mondennio felt the weight of the world lighten.

After his car pulled up to the building, Mondennio got out and walked straight to Klocards's lab. Klocards had the buzzer installed as promised. Mondennio had the door repaired. He buzzed the door as promised and waited. He had not realized as he stood there how much more accustomed to waiting he had become after taking mass transport.

The door opened, Klocards stepped out. "Mondennio Rowenzal, I presume? Here for a visit?"

Klocards is asking odd questions. Mondennio entered, noticing that the lab was virtually unchanged from last time.

"Yeah, um, how are things progressing?" He realized he could not just burst in with the real issue.

"Hmm? Not very well. A few more experiments run but no meaningful results. Anything else and I'll cry 'secrecy' again, I suppose."

"We can't have that, can we? Success comes from not surrendering to failure, right? At least that's what my father always says."

"That's quite well said." Klocards stared at Mondennio. The gaze was mechanical and unnerving. "Your posture suggests you are a little distracted today."

"I could say the same thing about you." Mondennio could not understand why Klocards was acting so strangely. *It's as if he's a robot or something.*

"Yes, well I am close to a breakthrough. That puts me only about half here. The other half is working on the problem."

The small talk was killing him. "That's why I came to see you. You seem to have a creative way to solving problems. I wondered if you could help me solve mine, discreetly."

"Depends on the problem."

"Remember how I told you how I was kicked out of school. Now I know who the proctor was. I'm trying to figure out how to get him to confess, without betraying the source who told me what happened."

"I can help with the first problem. You just break into his house at gunpoint and make him confess. It is a little direct. I find the direct approach works most of the time."

Mondennio recoiled at the suggestion. "You've done it before?"

"Um, no. I knew somebody who is rather adept at solving problems through violence. He was the sort of fellow that could bring things to a decisive conclusion. If you catch my drift."

"How would I get a coerced confession to stick?"

"Take an attorney. Do you have a gun?"

"A gun?"

"Yes. You cannot very well hold somebody at gunpoint unless you have a gun. You see?"

Mondennio's mind reeled. "I suppose I could get mine." He thought about using the pistol he took from Jonaldy.

"Don't take your own. They will trace it right to you if something goes wrong. Stay here a second." Klocards disappeared behind some equipment, returning a few beats later with a small case.

"What's this?"

"I never go anywhere without at least one of these. I do not care what the law says. Take this and use it. It is loaded, so do not just go pointing it around. Just remember to bring it back."

"Bring it back? What if something goes wrong? Then you'll have a murder weapon."

"You don't look to me like the type who would ever actually kill anybody. Besides, they'd never look for a pistol with me. May as well be a bank in here. Wait. You do know how to use a gun?"

"Yeah, sure. We're in the weapons business. I grew up shooting. Are you sure this is the right thing to do?"

"It is what my friend would do. Shame you did not come about 50 beats ago. He was here. We take shifts working on this little problem so we get the most time possible."

"Do you think you could ask him to go with me?"

"No. He is not up to that sort of thing anymore. I keep telling him that is what he is best at, but he refuses."

"Does your friend have a name?"

"I have called him Danel for as long as I have known him, but he doesn't like that name anymore. Then again, he calls me Smee, and I cannot stand that either."

Mondennio left shocked. As he exited the building, he finally started processing what just happened. *Klocards' proposal was insane, at least inhuman. The conversation was certainly odd. Why would I take an attorney and a gun?*

As he walked toward his car, Klocards's proposal started to make sense. *At least, it could work.* Carpimua's confession would help reinstate him. He could then finish his degree under a cloud. *I can do this. Even if I can't, Carpimua does not deserve to get out from under this with no consequence. He'll confess or pay the price.*

He walked back to his car slowly, searching for Carpimua's address with his slate. His guess at Carpimua's clin paid off, and he found the address before he reached the car. After he climbed in, he tapped a message to his family's attorney,

```
@Risont, meet me at 9813 Aminasnis Building 1
Apartment A at 9 cycles. I have a witness who can
absolve me and I need your legal assistance. Come
alone.
```

47.   Veneza - Tenement

Veneza woke, not realizing she had fallen asleep. Her apartment was dark, with the outside street light offering just enough light for her to move around. She quietly moved around, checking her bag. Without being able to see the bag, she tried to mentally inventory what she had put in. Turning the light on now might expose Veneza to her neighbors.

Either my neighbors don't know who I am, don't realize I'm home, or they don't mind sticking it to the Clinate. It's more likely they don't know I'm here. By now some mention of reward will have been made.

She opened the door a crack.   The hall lights were out as usual. Regardless of how many complaints she and others made, the landlord found replacing the lights a hardship. The curfew just gave him more excuse to indulge his sloth.

She listened for a few beats. The odd snore made listening for somebody in the hallway a bit more difficult. Not that the Atakadaro would be discreet in this tenement.

The door thankfully opened wide enough for her to slip through without a squeak. She closed the door with a barely audible click as the latch engaged. She waited another beat or two to ensure nobody else was in the hallway.

Satisfied, she padded down the hall, sliding each foot slightly on the floor to prevent her from stepping on something. Continuing to move carefully, Veneza made her way to her tenement lobby. The landlord left the light out here as well, but more out of respect for the honor of the men who slinked in and out during the night. A few more cautious steps and she was on the street.

After a block, she saw him. *How did I overlook him?* She did her best to turn naturally away from the man she realized had followed her all the way home. He looked like the everyman, features that kept him from standing out. As she walked away, she mentally replayed each time she had seen him during her walk home. Always not too far away, but never close enough to startle her — a consummate stalker.

She walked around the corner of the building nearest her, blocking his ability to see her. Veneza bolted into a full sprint, hoping to put enough distance between them for her to escape. She passed a few blocks before stopping to see if he was still following her.

Veneza peered around the corner of the building from a low crouch. *If he is following still me, he will have to run to catch up.* She scanned the other corners. Nobody emerged. She stayed for a few more beats, until her desire to get moving overcame her paranoia.

She looked again down the street and decided to change course. She would walk a few blocks down the cross street and try to get around her pursuer. After a bit of walking, she realized she was in the neighborhood with the traffic circle. The buildings went from being apartments to being townhouses. Veneza started to cross the street.

"Run and you're dead." It was a voice that commanded authority.

She froze. Her stalker emerged from behind the traffic box. *How did he get there? He couldn't have run, I would have heard him. He's not even breathing heavily.*

"Get on your knees. Now."

She reacted before she knew what she was doing. She put one knee on the ground, and decided to run. Before she could rise, he grabbed her wrist and expertly spun her back to the ground. For the second time in as many weeks, Veneza felt Atakadaro's knee in her back.

"Just my providence."

"Not yours. Mine." He bound her hands behind her back. Without taking his knee off her back, he pulled her bag over and searched it. He put her bag over his shoulder. Standing, he lifted her up. He pulled her along as he started walking, forcing her to struggle to keep her balance.

After two blocks — three rows of townhouses — they reached an alley. He turned her down the dark alley and pushed her into it. She gasped. *He's going to rape me?* In his custody, she knew she had no protection. Enough friends have talked about the consequences of being out after curfew.

"Miss Karduil." he said.

She whimpered, expecting his next step. He was going to slam her into the alley wall. She felt his hand rest firmly on her shoulder.

"Relax."

She thought of running, but without free arms she would cover little ground. Her lack of familiarity with the area put her at further disadvantage, he obviously knew where he was going. "Make it quick."

He chuckled. "Miss Karduil, I'm Inspector *Leroga Roigamin*. You can call me Inspector, Roigamin or Leroga. But don't call me Leroy. You were involved in the mob a while ago, right? Answer the question."

She trembled and nodded. She shut her eyes tight, hoping he would go away.

"Listen. I'm going to cut you lose, but don't run. I'll just have to catch you again — and I will. We need to talk."

Veneza felt the binders give way as he cut. She opened her eyes and stared at him. "What are you doing? This some sick joke of yours?"

"No joke. Hopefully I'm stopping you from continuing down a destructive path." He held out his hand suggesting she walk with him down the alley. Still in shock, she consented.

They walked for a bit before he resumed. "I've been trying to keep tabs on you and your friends. It hasn't been easy, let me tell you. Things were going fine until Rymose decided he needed to flex his muscle and stage a demonstration."

"I can't say I disagree with you on that." She paused and turned to him. "Fine? Things weren't going fine for you until you and your friends massacred me and mine."

He took a deep breath and slowly exhaled. "This may come as a bit of a shock, but you kids aren't the only ones wanting change. We've been hoping and working toward change for decades. But, we kept it quiet, waiting for the right opportunity to come along."

"We?"

"Karduil, I personally only know of a few dozen, but I know there are hundreds if not thousands of sympathizers. We lost a lot of credibility with the stunts you children have been pulling. We call ourselves the Liberecano."

"I've never heard of Liberecano. The Clinate is as strong as ever."

"It's about to get stronger after your recent exploits. Haven't you noticed the news? Demands for tighter security. The named citizens insist on crackdowns against the unnamed subjects. The next step for them will be a crackdown of republican sympathizers in government."

"Government sympathizers? There can't be that many."

They resumed walking to the end of the alley, and walked quietly down the street for a while.

"There are a lot of us at the threshold. Nobody I know of that's high in government, but there's a rumor that maybe some Clinate family member is pro-republic. I personally think it perpetuates false hope. But, sometimes false hope is better than no hope. Those of us down the food chain have been trying to ease up government controls. It's been slow but progressive."

"How did you know where to find me?"

"You live a predictable life, Miss Karduil. You even flee predictably. The authorities don't know where you live, but they know who you are. I'm not going to turn you in. There was a named guy arrested when they tried to capture you, but he was released."

"Mondennio?"

"Yeah, that's him."

She breathed a sign of relief. "I'm glad they let him go, but he was there. What's going to happen to him?"

"He was released, so I don't think any charges will be brought against him. Not that it matters. The word will get out that he was a republican sympathizer. Any aspirations he might have for a decent career are pretty much over. The Clinate's like that. It only takes a word to ruin a man."

"I noticed that." Veneza thought about Juank's nonchalant comment of ruining Aradames.

"There's still a chance his story could have a happy ending. Is he pro-republican?"

"Seriously? He might be. I don't think he is now, but he at least listens. Right now he's pro-Mondennio."

"That's a start. With what I expect will happen to him, he'll become disillusioned — if he's not already. Then it's just explaining that the injustice he's experiencing has been experienced by countless millions over the centuries. If he's not listening to the logic, he'll listen to the emotions. Not that we can do anything about it."

Is this guy for real? "Sounds like you have it all figured out."

He laughed. "Not me. No, hope is my plan. I just know human nature."

"Hope is not much of a plan."

They walked up to a streetcar stop. A few other people waited at the stop, so they stood quietly for the few minutes it took for the streetcar to arrive. They boarded toward the back of the train. To any of the passengers it would look like a man and his daughter — or lover as they looked nothing alike. Veneza broke the silence, "Where are we going?"

Roigamin looked around the car. "You're going to stay at my place for a while. It's South of Kennet, a small apartment building in an otherwise affluent neighborhood. Nobody would think to look for you in my apartment. They'll be watching the various ways out to the plantations."

"You said we couldn't do anything for Mondennio."

"I meant you and I. There's not much we can do. You can't do anything. You're a fugitive that Atakadaro is hell bent to capture. They'll march you down Tbatiga Street, right in front of Atakadaro HQ. Anything you have that could hurt the Cause will be in their recordings and you'll be beaten almost beyond recognition."

"Wow! I thought you said hope was your plan."

"Yeah, Imagine if I had no hope. I'm not sure I could persuade anybody in the Liberecano to take a risk for Mondennio. Right now, I'm trying to do all that I can to protect us from what you've done. Actually, it is advantageous for us to let him fail. It keeps the Clinate fighting one another and distracts them from looking for sympathizers in the lower ranks."

They arrived at Leroga's apartment building. He escorted her up the back staircase. "The front entrance has surveillance," he explained.

They walked into his apartment.

"Wow, it's only a little larger than where I've been living. All that dedication and loyalty to the Atakadaro and all you get is this tiny space?"

"It's not the size that matters. I'm not going to waste all my money on a place I spend so little of my time at. I'd rather put the money where it would do the most good. It's all about what you value. Look, I have to get back to work now. There's food in the kitchen and you're welcome to sleep on the couch. I'd offer you the bed, but the sheets aren't the cleanest." He left and locked the door from the outside.

"Like I can't unlock the door from inside and run away?" Veneza looked at his couch. "Your couch isn't the cleanest either, Buddy. Ugh!"

She looked around his apartment. It was almost exactly like hers. One room with a small bathroom and closet and a nook for a bed. Instead of a bed, he had a padded cot that looked like he never washed what sheets were on it. She tried to open the closet, but it was locked. She jiggled the handle then hit the door with the heel of her hand.

"Wow, he locked his closet door before he went to work. How paranoid can you get?" As soon as she said it, she realized that he worked for Atakadaro. He knew more about paranoia than she did. *If I ever get out of this, I'll do a better job of protecting myself.*

The kitchen was a galley like hers, barely big enough for one person. It was well-stocked, though. He had expensive knives and decent cookware. The dishes were chipped but clean. She had plasticware and a single pot.

Judging from the food in his refrigerator, he knew how to cook. "Put your money where it matters? How could he stay slim eating this?" She filled a plate with food and poured a glass of water. Even cold, the food tasted excellent.

As she ate, she sat down on the worn couch. "Wow, this is comfortable." She slept.

48.　Mondennio - Southeast Kennet

Finding Ojave Carpimua's apartment was not terribly difficult. Carpimua had a lot to gain from Mondennio's shame. At least, that's how it seemed to Mondennio as he stood at the street corner. Carpimua lived in a fairly affluent district in the Southeastern part of Kennet. His bachelor-only apartment complex was a three-beat walk from a streetcar line that went right past the University.

The complex itself had several buildings fed from a single central footpath. Surrounding the compound were several older single-family homes that spoke of greater affluence. This was a bachelor's complex. Carpimua's unit was on the ground floor facing the street. Mondennio thought that would make it easy for him to escape if something went wrong.

He felt his coat pocket to confirm the pistol was there. Mondennio was careful to ensure there were no obvious surveillance cameras. Seeing none, he nonchalantly walked to Carpimua's door. He used a bit of mud to cover the peephole.

Not that it mattered. He knocked on the door and Carpimua opened soon after, not worried about who it might be. Before Carpimua had a chance to react, Mondennio stormed through the door, grabbing Carpimua by the shirt with both fists. As he cleared the door, he used his foot to kick it shut.

"What's going on here?" Carpimua said.

Mondennio pushed him with his left arm as he drew his right arm back. He then pulled Carpimua toward him, while punching with his other hand. Carpimua's nose broke as Mondennio followed through. Without hesitating, Mondennio changed his grip, using both hands to grab Carpimua's right shoulder. He forced Carpimua to bend over, while aiming his right knee into his stomach and chest. Just before he made contact, he drove up with his left leg as if jumping. All his mass and energy focused on the knee strike. He repeated the maneuver twice more, until Carpimua's legs buckled and he collapsed to the floor. Years of unhanded combat training paid off.

Carpimua rolled onto his side, fighting for breath. Blood streamed out of his nose. Mondennio forced him back onto his back, kneeling astride his torso. His legs pinned Carpimua's arms as he drew Klocards' pistol. Reveling in the sudden power of subduing this false accuser, Mondennio whipped him on the face with the barrel — just below the temple.

"What's going on? Hmm?" He resisted the urge to strike again, listening to Carpimua cough, fighting to breathe. "I thought we should be friends and have a chat."

Carpimua tried to press up, using his feet flat on the floor. Mondennio forced the pistol barrel into his mouth. "We're supposed to be friends here. You think I won't blow your head off after what you did?"

Carpimua stopped struggling. Mondennio continued to kneel astride, content that the pin was solid. The pistol barrel remained in Carpimua's mouth. "This conversation doesn't go the way I want it to, then we're not going to be friends. Then, I'm going to be angry. So far you see how I treat my friends. Imagine me — angry."

Carpimua nodded, his teeth clicking against the steel barrel.

Mondennio climbed off and turned him over on his side. He withdrew three sets of binders. He looped one of the binders around Carpimua's belt to bind his hands tightly to his back. He then bound his legs and used his last set of binders to tether hands and legs together. "This should help you remember what's going on here."

"What are you doing here? Who told you where I live?"

"Nobody told me. You didn't see me last week, did you? I was joy riding on the streetcar, enjoying my newly procured free time. Time you gave me, I might add. You boarded somewhere near the University. I made a point of getting off when you did and followed you home. No, you were probably too distracted to notice me behind you."

Mondennio made a point of standing so Carpimua could see his boots. Standard Atakadaro issue, with ballistic hardened toecaps, finely crafted in the Rowenzal factories to whither the masses' will to resist. He crouched down to get a closer look at his face, verifying he was the proctor. "You should know why I'm here. Remember the last time we visited?"

Carpimua's eyes widened as he seemed to realize who Mondennio was for the first time. Mondennio stood and drove his left boot into Carpimua's lower torso. "I'm starting to recall why I don't like you, Ojave. I seem to remember the boot was on the other foot. Maybe you can help me forget?"

Mondennio feigned another kick, causing Carpimua to flinch in a futile effort to protect his soft midsection. His bound limbs denied him protection. Mondennio pulled his kick at the last moment.

"You and I both know why I'm here. You lied about what happened during the exam. The great thing is, you don't have to try to deny it. We both know that slate was not in my daybag, but you managed to retrieve it anyway. So, we both know you planted it."

Mondennio surveyed the apartment, suddenly realizing he had not yet confirmed Carpimua was alone. He held his finger to his lips, miming shushing him. He brought the pistol to a ready position. He was already guilty of one accessory felony murder and now battery. There was no sense in letting his guard down now.

They were in the middle of Carpimua's kitchen, which Mondennio thought providential as he may find a mess on his hands. Off the kitchen next to the front door was the bathroom. The other direction led to the small living room. Two doors from the living room led to small bedrooms. Carpimua used the larger as an office. The entire apartment space was less than forty square meters — which was the size of Mondennio's bedroom.

The lack of closets and the bed being a simple mat on the floor made it easy for Mondennio to confirm Carpimua was alone. He came back into the kitchen. Carpimua managed to move his body so his front was protected by the cabinets.

Mondennio kicked him in his kidney, and grabbed his leg to twist him back around. "You really don't understand how upset I am, do you? For your own petty gain you thought you could ruin my life. Do you not see this pistol? I'm not certain you're ever going to see the outside of this apartment again. I'm glad you didn't call for help, because I guarantee it would be the last breath you breathe. After that, it won't matter, will it?"

A few beats later, there was a knock on the door. Mondennio looked out the peephole before remembering he had blinded it. He expected Aldavin Risont. He opened the door, pistol at the ready.

Mondennio lowered his pistol as Risont walked in. Risont's gaze followed the pistol down, revealing some fear. He looked around the room and then noticed Carpimua on the floor.

"Providence! What have you done, Mondennio?" Risont blurted.

"I'm sorry, Risont? I don't know what you're talking about."

"Look at him. His face is pulverized and you've got him tied up."

"Again, Risont, I don't know what you're talking about. Somebody probably broke into his house in the wee hours of the morning and did this to him — after we got his statement."

"I'm not going to be a party to this," Risont said.

Words Mondennio wished he had said only a few days ago. Mondennio stood in the way of the door, and shook his head. He turned around and locked the door. "Risont, you never came to my hearing. Even though you had plenty of time. I think you were complicit in what happened. Ah! No need to say anything. I don't care if you think that's not true — or if it's not true. Right now I have a pistol and I am convinced both of the reality of what it can do, and the truth of what I said. Don't try to offer facts and evidence to the contrary."

"I don't know what you think you're doing here, Mondennio, but it won't work."

"But it will, Risont. You're going to record his verbal statement. He's going to confess to his crime and claim his confession was made, what's the phrase? 'without coercion or undue hesitation?' You're likewise going to make a statement that his statement is true and taken without coercion. Then you're going to file that statement and Carpimua here can go on his merry way."

Mondennio used the pistol as a pointer as he talked. Risont looked at him aghast. He opened his mouth to protest.

"No. Risont. You and Carpimua here are both Ultras. You aren't entitled to due process in a hearing involving a sub-sept. You know that as well as I do. A higher-ranked citizen vouching for your oral statements will suffice. I already have one lined up. So right now is not a good time to debate this. I've had a bad week, and you each have worked against me, regardless of whether you worked together. I don't know who is pulling your strings, but you're not exactly puppets. Right now, I don't care. I want both of your statements, and I want you to send the summary to the appropriate authorities, Risont. I bring this up with my father you'll be living in one of those shanty towns by the end of the week. Nod if you understand."

Risont nodded.

"Good. Now I'm going to sit over here quietly while Carpimua confesses and you authenticate. When you're done, send the copy then you can go home. Carpimua will agree that he was attacked by thieves early in the morning. Right?"

"Yes." Carpimua spat, "You don't believe you'll get away with this, do you?"

"Of course I do. Besides, I'm the one with a gun — right now, only my world view matters. I think I might be willing to pay you for your acquiescence to my little invasion. I'll be conciliatory and recommend you keep your job. I hope that sounds fair to you."

Risont finished recording Carpimua's statement and went through the process of authenticating it with his own.

"You know this could still be challenged."

"I know, but Carpimua here won't deny the statement. You see, Carpimua, I've met some interesting people since you and I last spoke. You think I had an easy time visiting with you? I promise that you go back on our unilateral agreement they'll do worse. That goes for you, too, Risont. You should be thankful I don't have you sent out to the plantations."

"You'll help me keep my job?" Carpimua asked.

"I'll do what I can. As the aggrieved party, I'm sure I have some sway. Risont, give me your recorder."

"What?"

"Give me your recorder and slate. You can pick it up at the Enclave later today. That was not a request." He kept the barrel pointing down, but directed it toward Risont.

Risont handed over the recorder. Mondennio motioned for him to pick up his things and head out the door. Without a word, Risont did as directed. Mondennio was close behind him.

"What about me?" Carpimua called.

"When you see the binaries rise, you start screaming for help. The thieves attacked you. You were unconscious while they bound you, but came to and called for help before they could take anything. They fled. Just keep repeating that and everything will be fine."

49. Veneza - Leroga's Apartment

Veneza woke with a start. The front door shut. Who was that? As she regained herself, she remembered she was in Leroga's apartment. There was a note on the end table. "Had to go to a murder." *How did he come and go without waking me? How long have I been asleep? Hopefully nobody knows*

I'm here but him. What an ironic thing to think after thinking last night he was going to rape me.

The binaries started to rise. Based on the smell, Leroga had cooked breakfast. She looked and saw a small feast at the table. She ate, thinking of her recent turn of events. Her expectations of male behavior deteriorated as she matured, Aradames being the rule rather than the exception. Now, she thought she found a few exceptions with Jonaldy and Mondennio, Leroga and Juank Clin-Khotaigra. None of them seemed to expect much from her. Although, Jonaldy always seemed a little out of place in a way that put him on edge.

Rymose had tried a few things early on, but they finally settled into a somewhat tense relationship. He liked that she was better educated than anybody else on republican ideals. She never explained why, regardless of how often he asked. He always assumed it was because she went to the University.

The librarian specifically told Veneza not to tell anybody about the Library. Dozens of old-style print books dedicated to preserving what Professor Giedaz called an "outdated and selfish" ideology. She accepted the exchange of silence as the only restriction put on her for an otherwise free reign of self education.

Veneza teared up thinking of Rymose's death. The impact of recent events kept her emotionally numb until now. The insulation holding her emotions back was stripped away by the feeling of safety Leroga's apartment gave her. The tears flowed more freely and she started crying. Her pain pulled her deeper, her breathing convulsed. She put her forehead on the table, looking at the geometric wood pattern on the apartment floor.

The betrayals, the manipulations, the losses. She cried for the protesters gunned down by Atakadaro troops. She felt as though she cried for every dissent who resisted the Clinate.

She started to get a grip on her emotions, which was replaced by the pain in her head from congestion. She went to the bathroom to clean herself up. Veneza blew her nose and washed her face. She stared at the blood-shot eyes in the mirror. "Some leader you turned out to be. You drove your cause into the dirt. Embarrassed the Liberecano, whoever they are."

As she finished, she cleaned up her mess in the bathroom. She started to think of the Library. What was its name? Eliberecejaro, that's it. The name was old, and she never thought to figure out what it meant. 'Place of Freedom.' Then Liberecano means 'Freedom Makers?' She looked back in the mirror, "Are they the same group? They must be."

Veneza was amazed. They had to be the same group, which left her wondering just how pervasive they were. That might explain why Leroga said they'd been watching me. They know me from back at the Library.

As she walked out of the bathroom, she noticed a sliver of light coming from under the closet door. It had been locked before, but she tried the handle. It opened, revealing a narrow set of stairs descending. Leroga must have forgotten to lock it. She descended the stairs into a small room.

The room was narrow, a bit more like a hallway to nowhere that ran the length of his apartment. *We came up two, three flights of stairs to get to his apartment?* This must be between two apartments. At the end of the room a tattered reclining chair sat next to a tall, narrow bookcase crammed with books. She recognized several titles she saw at the Eliberecejaro — what she always just called the Library. She pulled out a title she remembered reading and flipped through the pages. Every one of them was filled with handwritten notes, though after a while she noticed the handwriting was different in many places.

She noticed a board on the wall covered in small pieces of paper with handwritten notes. There are no electronics in this room except for the light strip.

The notes looked like he was running his own own personal investigation. There were lists of names, including hers, Jonaldy's, Rymose, all the republican leadership. She suddenly felt vulnerable. *We tried so hard to hide our actions. He has it all here: a timeline, meetings, everything. If he has this, what does Atakadaro have? How did they not know where to find me?*

She looked through the files Leroga had on each of them. His research is thorough, complete biographies on all of us. She turned to the last file on Jonaldy.

"Jonaldy Amonett. Birthplace reported as Lonageth, though physical records lacking. Physical address resolves to an open field in a park. Difficult tracing whereabouts more than ten years ago. Unsuccessful following him. Suspect he may be Atakadaro."

Atakadaro? But Leroga's Atakdararo. She felt as if she should have been more surprised, but it explained his oddness. *Did Jonaldy ever do anything suggesting he wasn't one of us?*

She wondered if Atakadaro would have let a named boy be dragged into a murder. It would have made more sense for them to have rounded them all up that night, rather than coax them along into a murder.

Unless the murder played into the anti-Republican sentiment. Which it did, but Veneza thought the idea too cruel even for them.

Jonaldy was not Atakadaro. If he were, then why would he have allowed the murder to be carried out? He did all the planning, so if he were one of them they could have stopped us at any time. The information was contradictory. She kept trying to work it over, not noticing she was falling asleep again.

A nudge. She felt it. Another nudge. Veneza felt somebody gently shaking her awake. She tried to bolt out of the chair but slipped and fell with a thud. Veneza felt groggy as she tried to kick away from her assailant.

"Relax, Veneza. It's me, Leroga. Remember? What are you doing down here?"

She took a moment to regain her composure. "What's going on?" She still felt a little foggy.

"You fell asleep. Are you all right? What are you doing down here?"

"I saw the light. The door was unlocked."

Leroga looked perturbed. "Just sit down. You must have really been on edge because you've been sleeping a lot. Take a beat and pull yourself together."

Veneza followed his instructions and sat down on the chair. *Have I been sleeping that much?* After a few beats, she felt better. "I'm sorry for sneaking down here like this. It's what you get for locking a door then leaving it unlocked. Trust me, I won't tell anybody about it."

"I don't think you will. I don't think you ever told anybody about the Eliberecejaro."

"You knew that I have been there?"

"I told you there are a lot more of us than you think. And, we're trying to make Copa a free society."

"I noticed. You have some pretty detailed files on all of us. Why?"

"It's my assignment. Different ones of us focus on different things. You kids represented the first public exposure of our goals. We had to know if you put us at risk."

"You can't push your ideals forward without exposure."

"It's the timing that counts. If we press the matter before we are ready, then the Clinate would crush us into powder. A non-violent revolution first requires undermining society. We're at the preliminary steps."

"You're taking too long."

"Spoken like a young person. You need to learn patience."

"Yeah? Well how long will that take?"

"Funny. So, you just came down here, checked out my perp-wall and fell asleep?"

"Basically." She picked a file from the floor. "What's this you have about Jonaldy?"

"Well, he looks like he's Atakadaro working undercover. But, there's no reference to him in Atakadaro records. Even if he was in deep cover there'd be some way to figure out who he was. Besides, his background is a little unusual, too."

"I saw that. Could there be some group other than Atakadaro? Some secret Clinate organization?"

"It's possible, but only if one family was working against the others. I hear about that from time-to-time. I saw it once. They tend to recruit somebody from inside the rival Clin. Jonaldy does not look like he was recruited. He appeared ten years ago out of nowhere."

"Maybe he did appear out of nowhere." Veneza tried to find some event that coincided. "Hold on. The date you have here. That's around the same time the Imperium arrived, isn't it?"

"It is. I already researched that possibility. We fully account for every Imperial citizen, even the immigrants."

"Well, maybe you missed one. What's that old saying? Remove the possible and what remains must be the cause?"

"Remove the impossible, what remains must be the truth, however improbable."

"Yeah, whatever. Well, you ruled him out as one of yours — sorry, one of them. He's an oddball who came out of nowhere not long after the Imperium showed up."

"About a year or two, yeah."

"Well then," she held the file up. "here we have an Imperial citizen that we don't know about. Didn't you say something about a non-violent revolution? You can't be the only ones who thought of tearing the Climate down." Veneza stood up.

"If he is Imperial like you say, then why is he interested in our cause?"

"What if he's not?"

"What was that?"

"What if he's not interested in our cause? What if he's using us to do something else?"

"Like what?"

"I don't know, but I need to talk to a friend. Do you think it's safe for me to travel?"

"We need to cut your hair."

"Never."

"Okay, we need to hide it then. How about my hat? Other than that, you won't get too far without the right escort."

"Thinking of walking with me instead of behind me?"

"Something like that."

50.   Monennio - Rowenzal Enclave

Mondennio sat working in his anteroom. He received a text that Risont's filing was accepted by the University earlier in the morning. Now he needed to find somebody named who would support the filing so he could use it to expunge his record.

His slate's vibration notified him of a new text. He checked the display and saw it was from Veneza.

Need to meet Re: Jonaldy now.

@Veneza: where/when? He replied.

She responded quickly.

`Club Orakrono, South of Marketplace Square at 8.70 cycles.`

Mondennio replied his acceptance, but thought of the irony of it. The Club was near the marketplace, where their lives became entwined only a short time ago. He could not help but contemplate what would have happened had he not waited at the marketplace spire that day. He might have had a chance to beat the cheating charges then. Instead, he had resorted to extreme measures — measures he inadvertently learned from Jonaldy. He received another text from her telling him how to get in.

Sahkud seemed resigned to the routine. He only shuttled Mondennio into Kennet. Afterward, Mondennio either used mass transit or chose to go on foot. Mondennio still hoped that would absolve Sahkud if anything ever happened because of his escapades. He still checked to ensure Sahkud was not following him.

He walked through the marketplace under the shadow of the Clin Khotaigra palace. He smirked, wondering what the Clin would do to him for what he's done, not just for what he was accused of. Extorting the truth. Was that even a felony?

He saw Club Orakrono and walked to the entrance. A semi-circular arch above had an amateurish drawing of what looked like a crazed brunette with large eyes and an awkward smile. The keystone above was of an older bearded man. He opened the green door and entered.

The short corridor inside was only slightly brighter than the late night outside. Blocking his way into the rest of the club were a pair of large men. Their scowls would have been enough to discourage him had he not made the appointment.

"Ziggy said it was okay." Mondennio did not even know what the statement meant, who Ziggy was and what was an 'okay.' He recalled his cousin referring to an okay a few times recently, but that was it.

The larger man uncrossed his arms and waved Mondennio through. He stepped aside as Mondennio entered.

The scene was surreal. The walls were painted black, and the music was overpowering. The center part of the room contained a sea of dancers.

Half-walls retained their ebbing and flowing from other revelers. *How can anybody have a conversation here?*

He scanned the area for Veneza, and did not find her. He noticed a set of stairs going up, and decided to explore. The next floor up was slightly less noisy. Some alternative group was playing hard music that grated Mondennio's ears. He worked his way through the listening crowd to find a hallway that helped shield the noise.

As he walked down the unlit halls, his eyes adjusted and he could make out doors. Light streamed out of each of them. In turn, he opened each one, finding one group or another involved in — whatever it was Mondennio paid no attention. One group sat in old chairs watching some movie, it looked like Stosh, not one of his favorites. Mondennio was relieved when he opened the last door and saw Veneza sitting inside drinking tea.

"This has to be the oddest place I've ever been in," he said.

"You're probably surprised you never heard of Club Orakrono before?"

He nodded.

"There are a lot of things about Kennet you aristocrats don't know about, I suppose."

"Over the past few weeks, I think I've become more aware. I still have not made sense of everything that's been going on."

"Well, when you think you do understand, then whatever you think you understand will be wrong. At least, that's how I manage to understand things. There has to be a healthy level of misunderstanding."

"I'm not going to pretend to understand what you just said."

"See? It's working already."

Mondennio just shook his head. He took a moment to survey the room. It had a sort of azure color on the walls, which were otherwise bare. The table they sat at and the six chairs were the only furnishings. It only lacked countertops and a few other amenities from reminding Mondennio of a kitchen. Two narrow windows looked out to the street below, judging from the sound of the streetcar passing beneath them.

"How did you get away from the Atakadaro?" Veneza's question brought him back into the moment.

"They beat me up and threw me into the van. One of the detectives came looking for me, I think. He pulled me out and let me go. I don't think he wanted to."

"Why'd he do it then?"

"I guess somebody was telling him to. I tried to figure out who, but whoever it was must have been a ghost. I drove around looking for you afterward, but you were nowhere to be seen. I was convinced you were arrested."

"I managed to find my own way out. I got picked up by an Atakadaro guy, but he turned out to be some closet republican."

"What? Are you saying you guys are everywhere?"

"I'm starting to think so. I only wish I knew how much 'everywhere' meant. If it really were everywhere then we could knock down your precious little world that much faster."

"I hope that's not why you asked me here. More beating me about the head and shoulders about being a sub-sept?"

"No. I'm sorry. I don't think you're like them anymore. I am starting to see that. You've changed since we met, though you have plenty of room to improve."

"I suppose I should say thank you for that."

"At some point, you'll be returning to your world. I only hope that what you've learned wandering around mine will help you see the superficiality of it all."

"Speaking of which. The proctor who falsely accused me of cheating recanted yesterday. My attorney is not very optimistic, but there's a chance I might be reinstated. Might even get my exam score made official. It was enough to put me in a place where I could finally advance the family back up to sept status."

Veneza looked away and looked a little sad.

Does she like me? Mondennio thought. *That would make things a little awkward, but she's not bad looking.* He sat there trying to think of what to say.

She looked back at him. "Don't be so certain of that, Mondennio. While I was staying with my republican friend, I saw something that you should know about. That's why I contacted you. After all, you saved me twice now. I owe you a lot."

"What? Do they know about my role in Giedaz's murder?"

"No, not that. Not yet, anyway." She hesitated again, as if planning how to say what she knew. Veneza leaned forward a bit and lowered her voice. "It's about Jonaldy. There's something not right about him."

"You're telling me? I watched him execute a college professor for no reason. I have a feeling if he had more bullets I would have died then, too."

"Mondennio, my friend thought he was some sort of undercover Atakadaro guy. We got to talking about it and decided he wasn't. I think he's Imperial."

"What? Some Imperial spy?" Mondennio thought back to some of his conversations with Jonaldy. "I would agree that he sympathizes with the Imperium. He tried telling me that an empire is more of what we should have than a republic. That even an emperor bows to the will of the people better than the Clinate."

"He said that?"

"Yeah. But, why would the Imperium waste time sending spies? We have no defensive space fleet, or planetary defenses for that matter. They could park in orbit and throw rocks at us until we surrendered."

"You mean missiles and bombs, right?"

"No. From orbit the right sized rock may as well be a bomb. Maybe they'd put some kind of intelligent guidance device to make surgical strikes. One of my seminar classes discussed this sort of thing in detail. The kinetic energy would carry a punch big enough to take out a city, if the rock were big enough and fast enough."

"And I thought throwing rocks was just what little boys did. I couldn't imagine Copa being subjugated by somebody flinging rocks."

"The technology is pretty easy. Now that I think about it, that's probably why the Clinate hasn't kept an active force. A mutiny could force the government to abdicate just by throwing rocks. We kept subluminal space travel, but the ships that were up there before the Imperium are more a way of remaining proficient."

"That's a shame. If only a few rocks could overthrow the Clinate. For a minute, I could see how we could use the Imperium to help us republicans replace the Clinate. But, we' d only end up a client state — they'd just use us to control the planet."

"So, if Jonaldy's an Imperium spy, why?"

"Maybe they have a good reason for not throwing rocks? Do we know what they've done with other Terran systems they sought to return to the fold?"

"No, not that I know of. That still leaves the question open. If he were trying to infiltrate the government, then why hang out with you guys. No offense, but you're hardly ramming down the doors of the establishment. So far you've only been a pin prick."

"Not if we have people everywhere. Maybe they're trying to figure out how much influence we actually have? Maybe they do want to use a republic as a puppet? Then again, he remained a fringe player until you showed up."

"What? Are you saying he's after me?"

"I wasn't saying that. I suppose in some spy-logic it would make sense, though. Find a named person who was in a compromising position and use him."

"But, I wasn't in a compromising position. I was minding my own business when I got compromised."

"What if he was behind that?"

"If he was, then he's got a lot of explaining to do. Thanks for the information. Anything else I should know?"

"Just that I appreciate all you've done. With the media showing my face everywhere, I'm not sure when I'll be able to surface again. My friend said he can help, but I'm not sure how. I'll try to keep in touch."

She stood up and started walking out. She stopped for a second and rested her hand on his shoulder. "I mean it, thanks. You saved my life." Before he could respond, Veneza had walked out.

He thought about chasing after her, but knew she was right. She was being hunted, and somebody here could well have reported her. He stayed in his seat, looking out the window. On the table sat her tea cup, almost finished.

Chapter 14

51.   Jonaldy - Coffee Shop

Jonaldy made a point of arriving earlier to ensure they had a discreet seat far enough away from the coffee shop's window, but still able to see if anything was coming. He watched as Joss Wards walked across the street. Joss entered the shop and joined Jonaldy. He motioned for the waitress, who gave him a wink. She left her station and started making a coffee.

Come here often, Joss? Jonaldy wondered how discreet his team had been. He concluded they were more brawn than brain. Not that it mattered. With things moving quickly with Mondennio, the Klocards assignment was messing with his timing. "So, where do we stand?"

"So, this Klocards fellow stands predictable. He perchances three routes he likes to take, depending on the weather or his moodiness. But, he has one route that good is for capturing him. It's isolated, closet."

Joss' language training was not nearly as good as it should have been. *Brawn,* Jonaldy reminded himself. He had not noticed how bad it was before. Then he realized Joss used Imperial Standard last time. *There were too many patrons around this time so he chose to use Copan. Maybe not as dumb as I thought?*

"What about the bodyguard?"

Joss chuckled. "Get this. He housebroken before he started working for Klocards. I'm not sure how he's getting paid, but he not bodyguard."

Housebroken? Homeless is the closest Imperial term. "Anything we can get on him?"

"He's using theobromos — The Bros. It's a popular mood-altering drug on the Island Continent."

"I know what it is. It's popular in several Imperial systems, it's derived from a plant native to Bixirjian System. I'm not sure which, but one of the Clins smuggles it in and distributes it to the others. At the same time, they impose stiff penalties for use or possession. It's their way to try to keep the Unnamed under control. I forget, you're just visiting Copa as a day tripper." The term used to describe a single mission.

"So it's illegal here and they proselytize losers." Joss said in standard.

Jonaldy looked at him for a moment trying to understand why Joss said something so odd. The he realized Joss was mixing Standard Imperial and Copan. He replied in Standard, "No. You're assuming a cognate. In Imperial Standard that means capital punishment. Remember language on Copa is closer to the mother Terran languages because it disappeared early in the Decline. Less interaction froze the language in some ways and took it down a different path in others."

"That term means committed for a long time in Copan. So, he gets picked up for theobromos use and they'll put him away for — maybe a decade? Depends on how long it takes for him to detox and overcome the addictive cravings. I think they double the time after the craving that they hold you. It takes at least three years to get to there."

Joss seemed unconcerned, probably perturbed for being corrected, but Jonaldy persisted. "Either way, the Clinate doesn't do anything altruistically. He'd have to compensate the government for the treatment, so he'll be indentured. He's still pretty young, but he could easily be under their control for the remainder of his life. If he was homeless like you said, he has no marketable skills. Because he's a drug addict, they won't let him work afterward. So, he'll continue to be on the fringe of society. Maybe a streetsweeper, cleaner of public lavatories? They may even give him a brush."

Joss did not laugh at Jonaldy's joke, even though it had separate funny meanings in Standard as well as Copan. "Okay, so we've got him by the blueness?"

Jonaldy marveled at the lack of language training. Joss mixed freely Imperial terms and tried to make them sound native by adding adjectival suffixes. "I think so. Do you know where he lives?"

"He camps in a tenement several blocks from Klocards."

"All right. It's just 900 beats now. He should be at home. Let's see if we can't hire a bodyguard."

*   *   *

It took them a cycle to arrive at Mehl Kaizdeelmik's tenement. As they walked up the stairs to the front entrance, a man walked out trying to hide his face. *Walk of shame?* Based on the quality of the building, Jonaldy assumed he was probably visiting one of Kaizdeelmik's female neighbors, a chesulino, prostitute. *He's dressed for work, looks like the dress of a ranked official.* Jonaldy tried to remember the man's face, and saw the car he climbed into and memorized its identification plate. *Don't worry, Minister. Nobody saw you but me. I'll try to make a point to consult with you soon. I don't leave anything to waste.*

Joss caught the door before it closed. Despite its shabby appearance, the tenement's door appeared to have good remote entry controls. Jonaldy scanned the names on the buzzer plate and saw three that lacked names.

"He's one of these. Let's visit them on the way up. From the looks of the stairway, he would have to walk past us while we're looking for him. But, I'd rather catch him at home."

They knocked on the first and there was no response. He inspected the door jamb and determined that it had not been opened in a while. They walked up a flight of stairs to the second address. As soon as he saw its entrance, Jonaldy grabbed Joss' arm and directed him toward the stairs going up. The two youths standing outside promised to be the sort better left alone. The sounds coming out of the open door were either cries of ecstasy or of brutality. The minister would not have come out of that, or gotten around it. His chesulino must be on the first floor.

On the fourth floor, they found the last unidentified apartment. Jonaldy assumed Kaizdeelmik would be asleep, or at least in the apartment. As he prepared to knock, he could hear its occupant start unlocking the door. He looked at Joss and nodded. He slid to the right of the door as Joss took station on the left.

Kaizdeelmik opened the door and stepped into the hallway. Joss grabbed Kaizdeelmik by his lapels, lifting him up and carrying him inside. Anthorph strength was superb on standard gravity worlds, and Copan gravity was close enough to standard. Joss had little time carrying Kaizdeelmik inside. Jonaldy followed them in, closing and locking the door.

Joss threw Kaizdeelmik to the floor, and easily flipped him over. He sat on Kaizdeelmik's back, pinning him against the floor. Only then did he draw his pistol from the small of his back and jam it into his Kaizdeelmik's face. "Up shutter you face."

That wasn't even proper Standard. Lifting a man that size betrays your real heritage, anthorph. "Good morning, Mister Kaizdeelmik. Do you have a first name?"

"Mehl. Who are you?"

"Does it really matter, Mehl? My compadre here has a pistol in your face and is rather fond of violence. I, on the other hand, not so much fond of violence. It seems you and I have the rare opportunity to help one another. Do you know what theobromos is, Mehl?"

Mehl stopped struggling.

"I understand the cravings are quite bad? Your friends downstairs have a pretty stable supply, and judging by the austere decor of your home here, I suspect you have little left over at the end of each paycheck."

Mehl continued listening. Joss remained vigilant astride him.

"Right on point, am I? Good. So, like I said, we have a chance to help one another. You need to either conceal your extracurricular activities or escape them. I can help in either way."

"You can help me get clean?"

"I know the government has a program that ensures you work for it for low wages. But, if a benefactor provided the cost up-front, you'd be out of the facility much faster. And, no government indenturement."

Mehl looked suspicious. "Those treatments cost thousands of knoerzers. What could I do that would earn that much?"

"That's what I love about Copa. Very businesslike. You like my offer? The cost is closer to eight-thousand knoerzers, Mehl, nearly twenty-two years of day laborer wages. At least, that's the typical full government charge. It's only twenty-five hundred at a civilian facility."

"That's still seven years. I got nothing worth that."

"But you do, Mehl. You do. The problem is you don't really have a choice, do you? I'll tell you what I want you to do. If you refuse me; well, I can't have you telling anybody. Instead, my friend here will ensure your permanent silence. That's escape, in a manner of speaking. I'm sure we can even get enough of your neighbor's product to make it look natural, if you prefer. But, I don't like to introduce the baton. It's too predictable, permanent. Besides, I'm a benefactor. Copa beat you down, forced you to turn to drugs. This society never gave you a chance. For one little favor, I'll ensure you get that chance. Do what I want, and I promise you'll be a changed man. But, I have to have your word before."

"I'll do what you need if you'll promise to help me end my addiction."

"It's not what I need, Mehl. I just want something. I have everything I need. But, I'll ensure you get what you deserve; that you overcome your addiction. Now, you are working for a man by the name of Janhas Klocards."

"No!" Mehl started to struggle. Joss whacked him on the top of his head with the pistol's barrel.

"Mehl? Stop, Mehl. Remember you've got a pistol pointed at your head. You stop listening, you don't go our way, you don't get out. Get it?"

Mehl stopped struggling, but he no longer looked scared. He looked angry.

"Good. Mehl. I'd much rather reward you for one little favor. I guess you've grown attached to Klocards. I frankly don't care. He stole some highly secretive technology from my employer and fled. Killed a security guard in the process. Not too different than you, actually." He paused to let the fiction sink in. "I want to return him to my employer, and the technology he stole."

"How could he steal technology? If he did, you wouldn't care. You should have a copy of it."

A gap in the story. "It was a prototype Klocards was working on. He stole the prototype and killed the AI that helped him develop it. He somehow managed to prevent the AI from backing up. I'm not technical, so I don't know how he pulled that off. But, I know he did. A man died, Mehl. A man like you. We want Klocards alive so we can recover what he took and take him to justice. You can help. And, you'll benefit from it. I promise."

Jonaldy stood back and watched Mehl consider his options. He motioned for Joss to relinquish control, knowing that an Anthorph against a mundane human was grossly unfair even in an otherwise fair fight. This was not a fair fight. After a minute's deliberation, Mehl pulled himself into a sitting position and looked at Jonaldy.

"Fine. What do you want me to do."

"Simple. Next time he goes through the park, we'll be waiting for him. When we come in, just stand there. You make any motion to help him, then Joss here will have to assume you changed your mind. Joss'll take care of everything. Anything about Klocards we should know about? He ever talk about any military experience, any martial training?"

Mehl looked like he was trying to remember. "Sorry. He never talked much about anything except his research."

Jonaldy handed Mehl a cash card with four-hundred knoerzers. "Take this. Consider it a down payment." He and Joss walked out of the apartment and headed down the stairs.

Once on the street, Joss asked, "You're going to give him that much for Klocards?"

"Kreteno!" Jonaldy assumed Joss worked wet operations and not the nuances of proper Bafiktuy operations. Jonaldy realized it was fortunate that he cursed in his own native language, rather than one Joss actually understood. "During the ambush after you have Klocards, put a bullet in Kaiseelmik's skull. I gave him money and hope, which is more than his world gave him. You go brief your team. I've got to get back to my real work."

52.   Mondennio - Streets of Kennet

The walk back to the rally point from the coffee shop was peaceful. It was late enough during the middle part of the week that most people were asleep. Mondennio enjoyed the relative quiet of Kennet asleep.

He reflected on what Veneza had told him. *Could Jonaldy himself be the hidden hand that set him to ruin?* If he was, then Mondennio had a hard time understanding his logic. There were other students that he could have corrupted — help them do better on the test in exchange for whatever it is he expected to get with that person in government.

Mondennio did not know the first place to look for Jonaldy, so he put the matter out of his head. Things would soon be set back to rights. He had the almost certified confession, and the lack of authorities at his door earlier today persuaded him the proctor would behave.

"Good evening, Sir." Sahkud said.

"Thanks. It's almost 10 cycles, isn't it?" Midnight, another day.

Mondennio wondered if he should continue with his secret wanderings through the city, once he was reinstated. School would be difficult as the current term was almost over. Perhaps he would get himself assigned to a few easy classes, or another seminar where the entire grade was the final paper. That would let him finish the semester in good order.

They were about one kilometer from the Enclave. Mondennio could make out its familiar shape. Something was not right.

"Sahkud, pull over. Turn off your lights."

"What's going on?" Sahkud asked.

"Up ahead. Do you see all those cars? That van? Don't those look like Atakadaro?" Mondennio's vision of a triumphant return to school and society faded in an instant.

"I don't know, Sir. You seem to be more familiar with them than I."

Mondennio wished he could chuckle at the ill-spoken truth. He had to think quickly. Was it the murder or the extorted truth? He could survive the proctor, in all providence. The murder charge was another issue. Could their earlier arrest of Veneza's group have led them to his involvement?

"Sahkud, I'm getting out here. You give me a five beat head start, then head on to the enclave." He took out his slate, "I'm texting you to head home without me. Anybody asks, you last saw me around the Marketplace Square. Hey! Are you listening?"

Sahkud's slate buzzed, but Sahkud ignored it. "Yes, Sir. I'm listening. What if they arrest me?"

"For what, being a driver? Father will be there. Remind him how I have been acting strangely and going off on private jaunts. He'll take up your side with Atakadaro."

"What do they want?"

"Better that you don't know, Sahkud. I'd rather you be surprised by whatever they say. And, whatever they say, they are likely extorting the truth to get a reaction from you. It's never as bad as they make it out to be."

"Where will you go?"

"Do you really want to know? I mean, if they do arrest you, then you'll have to tell them what you know — which is nothing. The only secret you have to keep to save your own hide is this very moment. Understood?"

"Yes — I should have been more forceful in keeping you in the car."

Mondennio managed to laugh. "It might have helped a few times." Mondennio looked at Sahkud's worried face. "Look. You are going to be fine. You've only been doing your job, what I've told you to do."

"I'm more worried about your father firing me."

"He can certainly fire you after. But at some point this will all blow over. I'll see to it that you're rehired without any loss of pay. Start my five beat headstart now."

Mondennio got out of his car, hoping the interior lights would not give away the car until after he was well away. Sahkud started slowly driving the car backward to conceal it from the Atakadaro at the Enclave so that Mondennio could have a few more beats to get away. The electric motors were silent.

Mondennio remembered the intersection a few hundred meters South. It was the access road to the shanty town that supported the district — his family's enclave. Somebody here would be able to take him in until he could figure out what to do next.

He pulled out his slate and sent Veneza a text warning her that Atakadaro was waiting to arrest him. They may be close to finding her, if they did not have her already. He had nobody else to message.

As he made his way into the shanty town, he tried to figure out how to find the right people. It occurred to him that the cloud had a list of all addresses for the key housing staff. Atakadaro would likely detect him if he accessed the sub-sept's cloud.

The cheating fiasco carried one benefit that Mondennio now appreciated. He now had two slates keyed to him. That made it difficult to track him — also made it difficult for him to find where he was. He never paid attention to the technical reason, but for now it was a pleasant side effect.

He walked past a familiar apartment building. Mondennio stopped and went to its entrance way, trying to remember why. As he looked at the list of residents, he noticed Sahkud's name. Would Atakadaro suspect me staying in his apartment? They might if they arrested him. Having no other place to go, Mondennio gambled on that question.

The door into the apartment building was open, and he quietly worked his to Sahkud's apartment on the second floor of the tenement. He tested the door and found it was locked.

There was a keypad. Mondennio remembered Jonaldy's explanation in Ginster Enclave about named people being able to bypass lower-caste security. The lock clicked. Mondennio entered Sahkud's apartment. It was a simple bachelor apartment — one single room with a curtained-off toilet off to the side nearest the kitchen.

Inside, he relocked the door and sat down on the couch with a sigh of relief. As he looked around the room, he received a text from Sahkud.

Murder?

Mondennio set down his slate. He should have known it was only a matter of time before it all caught up to him. He watched his entire future fall away. Everything was over now, not just my career. *How could I have been so stupid?*

He started crying. The guilt from being too busy to study to visit his mother's funeral added to his tears. Not being there as she died, because she told him to ace the exam — better the family's position. *Because you were unnamed and bettered yours, Mother?*

By Providence, I'm one of them.

He tried to regain his composure, but let go again when he realized his father was not there to tell him to stop. After several beats, his tears slowly dried up. He felt weary from the exertion, but would not just fall asleep.

He picked up his slate again, which still displayed the message from Sahkud. He sat on the couch for several beats trying to understand what happened that night. The despair he felt that night returned. He knew nothing he did could undo the murder, or his involvement in it.

Mondennio tried to remember where he hid the pistol afterward. He remembered playing with it in his bedroom, but not much afterward. Any search Atakadaro conducted would discover it. He started feeling the guilt of a murderer.

"I did it." He said to nobody. "I was there, I let it happen. I didn't pull the trigger, but I did it. All to get my career back — a career I didn't even have yet." *How did I expect to govern if I couldn't even manage my own affairs?*

How am I going to make this right? Maybe if I can catch Jonaldy and get him to confess to Atakadaro I could at least earn some leniency. Nothing could be done about it now. Mondennio slumped into the couch. Before he knew it, Mondennio was asleep.

Mondennio woke up. He looked about the apartment, confirming he was still alone. He was oddly refreshed for having only slept three cycles. He realized he woke to the sound of somebody outside the door. *Atakadaro?* He listened as the lock released.

Sahkud entered, and turned on the light. He stopped in shock as he looked at Mondennio.

Before Sahkud could say anything, Mondennio blurted out. "Sahkud, I did not commit the murder. I swear it. I was there, but I did not commit the murder. Nor did I know it was going to happen."

Sahkud stood there for a beat with a contemplative look. "Are you crazy? Why didn't you go to Atakadaro when it happened?"

"Because I was there." Mondennio explained how he had gotten involved and that he went along to try to safeguard Giedaz. He told him about Jonaldy and how Jonaldy extorted his participation.

"Don't you wish you had listened to your father?"

"Yeah." Mondennio thought to the several opportunities he had that he squandered. "But it's too late for that. How's he taking it?"

"Not well. Prigarcoll said he hadn't been that distraught in over a decade, if ever. Even your mother's death did not affect him so." Sahkud pointed at his eye, as if Mondennio could not see the bruising. "After Atakadaro left, Prigarcoll beat me around and interrogated me. I told him you'd been doing some hinky things, but that you managed to keep me out of it. From his questions, I think he's trying to figure out how to get you out of this."

Keve Prigarcoll, the family lieutenant. Mondennio wondered how much of his concern was directed at saving the family rather than saving him? "Him and me both. I suppose I should have gone to Atakadaro when it was a minor thing."

"When was it a minor thing? Before the riot or after? Before the reconnaissance or after? Before —"

"I get it, Sahkud. Father said to stand down from the very beginning. When I realized they were first going to Giedaz's apartment, I should have left then. I was just so angry and that anger carried me with them."

"It's not too late, if you can persuade them this Jonaldy guy did it."

"That's the problem. Odd as this will sound, Veneza ran into an Atakadaro guy who's sympathetic to republicanism. She said he couldn't prove Jonaldy even existed. I mean, he's physically running around the city ruining my life in good order. But, he has no legal trail."

"What does that mean? We're all identified and tracked at birth, even you, Sir. He would have to at least have a biomass record."

"We think he's some Imperial spy of some sort. For some reason he's decided to destroy me, maybe try to make me work for the Imperium."

"Why don't you? I mean, why don't you make him think you'll join him? If he does want you to spy for them, and did ruin you, he's got to have a way to redeem you."

"Not a bad idea, but that's the problem. I don't know he's a spy, I just think he is. This is all supposition on my part. If I'm wrong, then I'll only dig myself deeper."

Mondennio put his head between his knees, with his fingers interlocked behind his head. As he did so, the pain from his bruised ribs bit him until he winced.

Sahkud leaned up against the wall next to the front door. He continued to watch Mondennio in contemplation.

"You're not going to turn me in, are you?"

"Well, the reported reward is substantial — three-thousand knoerzers. That may not sound like a lot to you, but the average serf makes one koenzer a day. That's the definition, actually, one day's wage for the lowest working class."

"How do they live on that?"

"They don't, really. The Clinate subsidized wages with food and housing, until you make over a certain amount. Then, they stop. It makes it better to be in the lowest classes."

"Veneza mentioned something like that once, I thought it was bluster."

"Well, what's her role in all this? Atakadaro said she was involved, too."

"She's not. At least, she wasn't there and only knows about what happened because I told her."

"Why don't the two of you just leave the city? I'm sure Rowenzal can find a way to help you escape."

"No. Whatever is going on, I still need to clear my name. I need to find Jonaldy. I just don't know how."

"Stay here. I'll bring somebody who might be able to help."

While Mondennio waited for Sahkud to bring back his mystery helper, he found a bit of breakfast. The bread was coarse with an odd tang of buttermilk. He found an occasional nut or piece of fruit, which seemed odd as the bread was otherwise not sweet.

Sahkud's apartment was spartan, with nothing to read. He did not have a media feed, so Mondennio spent a bit of time checking the various news feeds on his slate. They all discussed his recent involvement in a murder. Despite coming from several "news" sources, they each used the same photo. Each outlet cropped it differently, to try to show originality. One had a video reenactment of the murder, which was more gruesome than what actually happened. The message was the same, a college student was expelled for cheating on an exam, and murdered the prosecutor in retaliation.

He started being indignant at the obvious errors. Then he realized how easy it was to reach those conclusions had they not been there. As each report completed, he noticed how the Rowenzal name was being mentioned prominently.

The feeds he read only used his situation to bring up his relationship to the family. More than one outlet mentioned the past event that cost Rowenzal its Sept status, somehow implying that the status was reduced for such a reason, and should be reduced further. The mention was veiled, framed in a question of whether Rowenzal was inclined to bad behavior because of its involvement in weapons manufacture.

Is that what this is all about? My family is the premiere weapons manufacturer on Copa? Rowenzal started manufacturing exotic weapons five-hundred years before. Each generation focused on more mainstream weaponry, until two-hundred years ago when it became the primary weapons manufacturer for the Clinate. Mondennio heard envy of the family's role led to its demotion, or that it was the devil's bill for the privilege. Thinking back on it, not allowing a Sept to manufacture weapons made sense in a Clinate that feared both citizen and subject.

Sahkud returned to the apartment, leading another with a hood over his head.

"Who is this?"

"I brought Keve Prigarcoll." Sahkud removed Keve's hood.

Keve blinked a few times to adjust to the light. Looking around, he focused on Mondennio. "What have you gotten yourself into?"

Mondennio spoke at length, recounting all that had happened. He edited his involvement in Carpimua's confession to match his official story. He finished with his suspicion that Jonaldy was an Imperial spy perhaps trying to ruin the Rowenzal family because of its role he primary weapons manufacturer for the Clinate.

"It makes perfect sense. A lot of our employees are very loyal to the family. We get replaced by another family, they may walk off the job," Mondennio concluded.

"That is what you think? I'm afraid you will find that our employees are first loyal to their families and stomachs. This is an aristocratic fight."

"So?"

"Mondennio, you seem to have seen it, but not fully accepted that there are two societies on Copa. Yours is up here," Keve motioned with his hands. "Everybody else is down here. What happens up here rarely affects what happens down here. You live in your world, they live in theirs."

"What about people like Veneza?"

"They are rare. They are the ones that pay too much attention to the other world and somehow think they are entitled. The Rowenzals were not Founders, but they worked hard and established themselves. The Founders made peers for those families, though not quite equal to themselves. Everybody else on this planet had that opportunity and squandered it. Their current status reflects their inability to effectively use the gifts the Founders gave them."

"So you're saying it's not who you know but what you do?"

Keve's head wiggled side to side as if balancing scales. "There is a little of both — but who you know requires skill and diligence, just like working hard. Success requires a balanced application of multiple skills and intelligences. Some people just do not have what it takes."

"What about you? Don't you think you deserve more than what you have?"

"Deserve has little to do with it. My family has been serving yours for hundreds of years. Sometimes we pull your weight when Rowenzal does not seem to have the wherewithal. Most of the time our family benefited more from the relationship. I get to live in the world of the named without having to deal with the hassles of defending my name all the time."

"Speaking of that, what should we do with the media's running the family down at my expense?"

"I suppose that depends on how you look at things. You could work to vindicate yourself. That could take weeks, if ever. During that time, the media will continue to play up your felonious acts and blame the family. I think that is what you want to do."

"Of course. I'm innocent in both cases — cheating and murder."

"That could take a long time. The other option is that you could turn yourself in. I am certain Risont could secure your release pending trial and we can get the Atakadaro to hunt down this phantom imperial spy."

Mondennio had not thought of turning himself in to get Atakadaro to help. Being able to leverage their resources was enticing. Having recently pressured Risont to take a confession under duress, Mondennio doubted whether he would genuinely advocate his release. Attorneys must have a way of helping the Clinate find their defendants guilty while appearing to have put forth every effort to prove their innocence. Mondennio gave Risont ample motive to do just that.

"I'd rather not have to start off being incarcerated to find Jonaldy. Is there some middle path? Some way that I can avoid turning myself in?"

"There is always an alternative. You should know I would say that by now. But, it depends on your goal. Which would you rather do, vindicate yourself or preserve your family's honor?"

"Keve, I thought by vindication I was doing both. Perhaps that was true with the expulsion, but not as easy to justify with the homicide. I just can't believe I'm blamed for two things I did not do. Had you asked me last week, I would have told you family honor was more important. But, after all that

I've seen, I have to vindicate myself—both with the crimes and with my lifestyle."

"I also find it hard to believe that you could be blamed for things you were innocent for. It is too convenient. I chose a third way to mitigate this problem. I knew you would not turn yourself in, but your family's honor is at stake."

"What do you mean by that?" Mondennio heard a noise out in the hallway, and looked at the door. Shadows shuffled through the gap under the door. He realized Keve found a way to bring Atakadaro here—probably by having them track Keve's slate. "Keve, how could you?"

"You left me no choice, Mondennio. Either turn yourself in or they will arrest you."

Mondennio looked around the apartment, trying to see another way out. He noticed the window and remembered he was only one floor above the street level. He stuffed his slate into his daybag, banging his knuckle on the pistol he borrowed from Klocards. *I won't be able to explain that.*

"Do not think you will escape this. It is over."

"No, it is not over," he mocked Keve's precise diction. "You take care of Sahkud. He did not harbor me, and he knew nothing of what happened. Otherwise, when I'm vindicated your family will be back in the tenements."

Mondennio ran to the window, using the daybag as a flail, the pistol giving the mass needed to shatter the glass. He used his foot to clean the bottom edge of a large sliver that remained.

The door splintered open as Atakadaro entered. Mondennio took one last look back, "Keve, you're fired." He leapt from the window to the grassy ground below.

He hit hard, hurting his left leg as he rolled. The pain shot through his leg, leaving him to wonder whether he had broken anything. He stood up, limping with his left leg until it heeded his request to bear his weight properly. He ran toward the rear alleyway behind the building, quickly glancing behind himself to see what Atakadaro was doing. He was amazed none of them were guarding the building's sides.

One armored officer looked out the window, tracking his progress. He appeared to be giving directions via a handheld radio. Mondennio ducked around the corner and ran down the alley. He ran through to the next block, turning down another alley until he came to a street.

The houses were slightly more affluent. The street curved sharply enough that after running down another fifty meters he could not see the alleyway that carried him. He continued for another block until the street terminated with a cross-street. He noticed no Atakadaro following him. It helped that the binaries had risen and helped light his way.

Across the street was a copse of trees with a slight gap. He worked his way through the trees until he found a trail that cut its way through. After following it for several beats, he noticed the path remained just outside the built-up area, gently curving South. The path followed a tiny stream and continued until the stream went under an intercity rail. He thought it ran East to Meezsel, one of the eastern plantations.

He crawled under the bridge, finding a space where he felt secluded enough to rest.

53.   Klocards - Founders Park

Klocards chose a route he trusted. He tried harder to make his commute look more relaxed, taking a more direct path that gave him several areas with tactical advantages. He even slowed his pace, which seemed to make Mehl more relaxed.

A good warrior decides when he is going to be ambushed. An old mentor had given him that parable years before. The site of Mehl's mugging really gave Klocards the tactical advantage, which was why he chose to follow that path exclusively. To an untrained eye, it seemed to give the ambusher all the apparent benefits. Close quarters. Limited field of view. Routes of attack that let them switch if they needed. Instead, he had all the benefits. Limited attack points narrowed where they could attack. It limited how many could come at once, if they decided to gang rush him. He was a marine. His career focused on close quarter battle. He was the King of CQB. Mehl experienced that a short time ago, but failed to learn the lesson.

"Mehl, have you finished removing that junk in my basement?"

"Yep. The last load went out yesterday with the trash. Your basement is practically empty now. Why are you getting rid of all your stuff?"

Yep? Hardly talk of a commoner to a superior. He tried not to switch into his traditional non-commissioned officer mode. He turned to Mehl. "That stuff was here when I moved in, so I finally got tired of it. There's almost enough space down there for you to move in."

Mehl tried to show surprise, but Klocards saw the shame in his eyes. *He couldn't be ashamed of the offer. He slept on my front porch at least a dozen times. I know where he lives isn't the best. So why the shame?*

Guilt. Not embarrassed, as if he had no where better to live. That was the look Litovio gave me before he confessed they were cousins and that my family disowned me and Mom. Mehl's working with whoever has been following me. It couldn't be too long, though. Otherwise he wouldn't feel guilty. Klocards felt relieved. He dreaded firing Mehl or abandoning him. He knew Mehl would be a liability off Copa. Mehl's betrayal solved his dilemma. If only Hanifer could be so easily resolved.

Klocards was tired of waiting. He felt they were going to attack him, abduct him. He was unsure when, and the wait drove him stir crazy. If he knew when, he could be better prepared. Not that he was unprepared.

As they approached the scene of Mehl's failed mugging, Klocards noticed that Mehl started drifting a little further behind. "Having problems keeping up, Mehl?"

"A little, Sir. You're walking fast today."

Klocards knew the lie right away. He was not normally passed by others like he was today. Klocards slowed down a bit, but Mehl remained a couple paces away.

A few beats later, they walked down the alley of shrubs where they met. He could vaguely see the men stalking behind the shrubs. Klocards' arm casually brushed close to his hip to feel the reassuring bulge.

It happened. All five came at once, armed, on a silent order. Mehl froze in place, as if surprised. Their mass rush limited their ability to react to what was about to happen.

The trap sprung, Klocards acted without thought. He turned and grabbed Mehl by the lapel and pulled his coat down while spinning him around. Mehl's shoulder holster was exposed, and Klocards drew the pistol. Its weight assured him it was loaded.

He cycled the slide. The chambered round flew out and another in the magazine chambered. He was faster than his opponents — years of training with Anthrophs and many combat engagements were his advantage. The first was probably oblivious as the bullet slapped his forehead. Klocards calmly pointed the pistol at the nearest target, firing another round into the center of his chest. The splash of blood confirmed to Klocards that his attackers were not wearing body armor, which was illegal for unnamed citizens and foreigners.

He grabbed Mehl again, this time by his collar. He dragged him around as an unwilling shield. His third assailant crumpled to the ground as he calmly moved from one target to the next.

This was too easy. The fourth attacker cringed as he started to fire. Klocards' reflexes gave him time to jerk Mehl in between them as a shield. The bullet struck true and Mehl fell. As the fourth steadied for a better shot, Klocards fired into his chest and head. He released Mehl and let him collapse on the ground.

The fifth assailant was the calmest. He stopped charging when Klocards grabbed Mehl and was taking his time to aim, the vapor of his breath revealing his self-control. He was holding a tazer. His patience was his demise. Klocards fired his pistol's last shot into his shoulder. The attacker dropped his weapon. Klocards stepped forward, shifted his weight and kicked the man's knee. He heard the familiar, dislocating crack as the man fell.

Klocards dropped the empty pistol and drew his own. He scanned the shrubs for another attacker and found none. The fifth man was writhing in pain, but not loudly. Klocards holstered his pistol and picked Mehl's up. He found the first ejected bullet and rechambered it. He looked at his attacker. It was Thin Man.

"Who are you?" He put his foot on the man's wounded shoulder and ground his weight into it. The man groaned. "Tell me and you get to live."

"BID. You are a dead man."

He noticed Mehl had an earpiece in his ears. He glanced over and saw they all had earpieces. Klocards lifted the pistol and shot the survivor in the head. He placed the pistol in Mehl's bare hand. Klocards's gloves should have prevented any DNA transfer or other evidence of his wielding it. He briskly walked away, heading away from both work and home.

Klocards dealt with Bafiktuy operatives once before. They were a mean lot then. At least he finally knew who was following him. *If they've been following me, they may have Litovio under surveillance, too. How am I going to get off this rock?* There are different wells than gravity wells that can trap somebody, Klocards felt pulled down by this one.

I've got to warn him, either way. I know he's staying at the Imperial compound. How do I break into that? As he thought it through, Klocards realized he would not have to. Litovio was on recruiter duty, and knew he would be at the University on some sham to recruit Copan students with the unstated intent of flirting with the young women. Every Second and Fourth day of the week. Today was the Fourth.

Klocards took a circuitous path to the University, doing his best to ensure nobody could follow him without him noticing. Four of the men he killed had been following him. He would not recognize anybody following him now. He reached the University grounds having not noticed whether he was followed.

He found Litovio strolling the University commons, talking to a female student. Women were not recruited into the Imperial Postal Marines, and Litovio was old enough to be her — perhaps younger uncle? Klocards held back, trying to stay in the shadows while not attracting too much attention. Litovio saw Klocards a few beats later and nodded toward him. Klocards waited until he wrapped up his conversation by handing the student his card. With all modern technology, a tactile symbol still felt more professional. Klocards noticed Litovio making a subtle effort to press her hands. She smiled at him and walked away.

"Cruising primary schools for a date?" Klocards said as Litovio strode up.

"I've been talking to the local girls about a new women's auxiliary. She didn't buy it, but didn't seem to care. The uniform has its perks. The male students noticed its effect on women and asked if it works on all systems. One of my better recruiting points for the sub-sept students. But, you're not here to monitor my social habits, are you?"

"No. I just took out a team of Bafiktuy operatives in the park. I'm surprised nobody noticed the gunfire, though it was suppressed. They've been following me for a few days now. They broke into my lab and probably tried to steal whatever material I had. I don't even trust my assistant, so they found nothing. One of them had a tazer, so I guess they hoped to take me alive. It's easier when all the bad guys don't bring guns to a gun fight."

"We've got to get out of here. Meet me at that tavern tomorrow at 800 beats. I'll get you out of here." Litovio said, walking away.

Chapter 15

54.   Jonaldy - Streets of Kennet

Many beats later, Jonaldy was still in shock. He watched the ambush from a comfortable perch. *Who is this Janhas Klocards? He knew how to fight!* He looked over his shoulder, scanning the streets for a pursuer. Waiting for the next bus always left him feeling a little vulnerable, but after what he witnessed he was terrified. *He walked through Joss' team like he was at a practice range shooting targets. A team of anthorphs. Nobody does that. I thought he might hesitate with Kaizdeelmik there, but he treated him like a piece of trash. I was watching a killer angel.*

The bus pulled up, and he climbed aboard and worked his way back to what looked like a safe seat near at the rear of the bus. He did his best to constrain his emotions, hoping none of the passengers would notice him. The morning commuters were scarcely awake. Those who were had bleary eyes. He kept his eyes on the other passengers boarding the bus, looking to see if a new passenger arrived.

Why didn't they warn me? Set me up for a fushado operation. He rubbed his hands over his face and through his hair. He doubled over. He was thankful that he stayed out of the execution of wet operations. The only thing that went according to plan is that Kaizdeelmik died, obscuring Jonaldy's involvement. His wracked his brain trying to process what happened.

Jonaldy, this is not your primary mission. Pull yourself together. What is your strategy? Strategy is Interest, Ends, Policy and Means. Okay. Our Interest is to secure the Empire. Our Ends is to get Copa to accept Imperial authority. The current Imperial Policy says to use subtle means over martial, the result of too many failed attempts by a heavy-handed Navy. Mondennio is your means. Turn him to the Imperium, get him and his family restored. And wait.

He calmed down. He checked the bus again. None of the passengers paid attention to him, so he decided he was safe from pursuit. *Klocards is one man. I watched him kill Joss' entire team. He killed Kaizdeelmik. The only people who know of my involvement are my own people. My people. What did that mean? I arrived here five years ago after five more years training. They moved me out of the Imperium for all of that, and a few years before. Most of my life, all of my adult life, was outside the Imperium. They're my people because I say they are. He shook his head, realizing he was starting to reprogram himself. For the Emperor. This is for the Emperor. I made a commitment, and I will not displease the Emperor...whoever he is.*

He stepped off the bus a few stops later, and started walking to his next stop. He decided it was time to try a different bus route, just to completely shake things up.

"Okay. I should have refused this assignment from the start." He muttered to himself. "Not my job, and I failed it. It's been distracting me from Mondennio. I've been losing him, too. I can't focus on two separate assignments. I'll just tell them that Klocards was a failure, and that I am in the delicate phase of my main mission. They can't question a field operative's judgment. That would be against protocol."

Jonaldy switched to the next bus, which brought him nearer to his emergency data drop than he thought it might. As he approached the drop, he pulled his slate from his pocket. He then inserted the secure memory stick. He quickly tapped out his message.

Engineer fail, target liquidated wet team. Halting Engineer now. Recommend Ignore. Primary at grave risk. Sole focus primary.

He approached the drop carefully, walking around the building to ensure he was alone. He stopped about midway down the alley. He looked at the brick wall until he saw the bit of loose mortar. He removed a chunk. He paused to check both directions in the alley. Nobody in either direction.

He inserted his memory stick and saw its green light wink an instant later. His message delivered, Jonaldy quickly continued down the alley, and back toward the bus stop. *First time I've ever had to use that emergency drop. Hope I never have to again.*

Hopefully they'll come to terms with my decision. Besides, I may get a two-fer. If I can successfully turn Mondennio, Veneza won't want him anymore. I can play the reluctant friend. Just like Ehlian Caopuk in secondary school.

55. Mondennio

What is happening to my life? Everywhere I turn, somebody is trying to betray me, or set me up. The bridge Mondennio lay under was a rail bridge. It carried enough traffic that Mondennio was only able to get a cycle or two of rest at a time. The bridge creaked as each train passed overhead, leaving Mondennio to wonder whether the bridge was in need of replacement.

Did he have any hope at all? His family would be closely monitored now. Even if they were not, Keve would try to turn him in. He could not trust his family anymore. *Not until I've cleared my name,* he thought.

The only people who believed him were Veneza and her unnamed republican Atakadaro officer. *What if he fed her a stream of lies to have her help him capture me?* He meditated on what she said, until he remembered she told the officer about the possible connection between Jonaldy and the Imperium. The officer already thought Jonaldy was a problem. It offered him some comfort that he had two people he might be able to rely on — if he could find them.

Make that three people. Jonaldy certainly believed him about the murder. He was the only witness. Just like Carpimua, the both of them knew what really happened. Mondennio wished he could capture Jonaldy just like he did Carpimua. He might not stop kicking if he did.

Four people believe me. Unless I don't believe myself. I'm not sure Sahkud believes me. He chuckled, speaking aloud as another train passed overhead, "If he did believe me, then we'd have enough to form our own Clinate."

How was I going to get out of this? Everything I have done until now has only made matters worse. Mondennio could not accept it was hopeless. His mind started to lose focus as he tried to search for an answer. All the events cascaded in his memory.

Then it occurred to *him. This all started because I wanted to prove my innocence. I still need to prove my innocence. Jonaldy is the key. I will expose him to vindicate myself. Even over my family's honor. I have to find*

*Jonaldy. Has he fled the city? If he is from the Imperium is he even still on
this planet?*

Jonaldy had to still be on the planet. If he plans on turning me into some
Imperial agent, he needs to stay on planet. He could not have gone too far
out of the city.

He realized Jonaldy would likely be seeking him now. Mondennio's face
was on every media feed. If Jonaldy was paying attention, he would think
now is the time to pull me in. How do I get him to find me? I have to be
where he would know to look for me.

Veneza had to be the key. Jonaldy would try to find her, knowing that
she would eventually run into me again.

He texted her, begging her for help.

As he waited for her reply, he thought about how his father would
respond. He would certainly be outraged. Gerandy kept talking about rules
of power. *I wonder if he knew I did actually listen. One of his rules was to
pretend to be stupider than his opponent. If Jonaldy was stupid enough to
seek me out, then I should oblige him to be stupid enough to be found.*

She texted back:

`How soon? Can't move during daylight.`

Mondennio thought it through. There were still at least three more cycles
until sunset. They had to meet where it would not occur to Jonaldy. That
ruled out any of the places they had met before. He also had to evade
Atakadaro, but be close enough to where she was to find him quickly.

*@Veneza: Meet at 8 cycles at Zero Narf street stop. Alone. I need your
help. This should clear both of us.*

That gave him four cycles to find his way around the outside of Kennet
without being seen. He started by following the rail line itself. Once it passed
the stream, the rail line rode through a steep cut, often flanked with a vertical
retaining wall. Every hundred meters, there were man-sized impressions in
the side of the retaining walls that left Mondennio wondering why. As long
as he could avoid a train, he expected to pass undetected.

The line first started in a wide curve, then dove headlong into Kennet
itself. He grew worried as he started seeing rooftops from homes that flanked
the line. A few times, he heard people talking or giggling above him. He
assumed there was a foot path above him and felt some relief that he was

apparently on the same side as that path. Anybody overhead was less likely to see him.

He tried to remember at what point he needed to leave the track. He pulled out his slate to check out the city map. He stopped before he completed the connection, wondering if Atakadaro might track the data connection back to him if he connected to the map. He decided to rely on what little he had learned about Kennet in his recent travels. Once the rail line left the built-up areas again, Mondennio assumed it would continue to go away from Kennet. From here, he would try to head West on foot, hoping nobody recognized him despite the numerous postings.

He recognized the line of hills just to his left, and made his way to them. Once inside its tree line, Mondennio knew he could skirt them until he came near his destination.

As he got closer to his destination, he heard a sound behind him. He turned and thought there was somebody walking his way. He picked up his pace and rounded a bend on the hill, then climbed up a steep outcrop until he was hidden. He tried to breath slowly to keep his panting from giving him away.

Whoever was following him stopped under the outcrop, looking for him. Please do not come up here. After a couple of beats, the person walked on. Mondennio debated whether to climb down now or wait—hoping whoever it was would not come back.

He recognized the risk he took moving during the day, and let his cautious nature reclaim him. His slate reported that it was 5.45 cycles. He decided to stay put until 7 cycles, when the binaries started setting.

It was 7.70 cycles. The binaries just dipped below the horizon, giving him the added cloak of darkness. As he realized the time, he began to cautiously climb down the outcrop.

Back on the trail, he saw nobody. He walked briskly to recover the lost time. He came to an overlook, and took a moment to identify the light rails that carried him not long before to his providential night. He chose what looked to be the shortest path that got him to his destination. Unfortunately, it carried him past what looked like a significant enclave. He tried to figure out whose, but did not see any crests at this distance and in the deep twilight. He determined it was most likely not affiliated with Clin-Khotaigra.

He moved along the trail, past the enclave. There was a short walk, perhaps one-hundred meters, where he exposed himself should anybody have been looking. Once past that gap, he was again inside a small woods.

Now it was 7.9 cycles. The path ran straight downhill. As he trotted, he noticed it ran right to the streetcar stop. Outside of view, he waited for Veneza. The streetcar stopped before 7.95 cycles, and a few people got off. The light from the streetcar showed two people walking his way. He ducked behind some bushes before they got close enough to see him.

After they passed, he looked back to the streetcar stop. The third person remained, which he could tell was a woman with short blond hair—not Veneza. Ten beats passed and nobody else arrived. Neither did the woman leave. She seemed more frustrated in her pacing. Mondennio moved closer to see who it was.

"Veneza? What's with the short blond hair?"

"It's a wig, Idiot. Where have you been?"

"I was up there a few dozen meters. You should have told me you were coming in disguise."

"It was the only way I felt safe on the streets. What's going on that meant we had to meet like this?"

"I'll tell you, but we've got to get moving. Atakadaro might have intercepted our texts and may be watching us now. Follow me."

They took the same path Jonaldy and Mondennio took that night. Mondennio looked back at the stop and thought he saw the couple who passed him earlier returning. He grabbed Veneza's hand and walked faster.

Without a word, she joined his pace. She gasped when they entered the shanty town, but he kept pulling her along. They got across the footbridge into the woods beyond before they stopped.

"If anybody was following us, we should be able to see them pass by. They may even think we stopped in one of the shanties"

"Fine. In the meantime, why don't you tell me what's going on."

Mondennio explained how Keve tried to turn him in, no doubt with his father's blessing. He told her that he planned to get in touch with Jonaldy.

"Are you crazy? You think he'll just confess and let you go? Give you your life back?"

"He had to have this all figured out. If he is behind all this, he has to know how it works out. Didn't you say he was a meticulous planner?"

"What do you think the price of getting your life back will be? He's not doing this for the fun of it."

"What choice do I have now?" Mondennio felt the hopelessness that was at the periphery of his mind.

"You can trust me. I was talking to Leroga, and I think we might be able to find a way to get you out of this."

"Shh. I think I see somebody on the footbridge." They both instinctively crouched until they were each on one knee.

Two shapes appeared on the bridge, heading their way. Mondennio and Veneza remained motionless, ten meters inside the woods, well away from any trail. The shapes looked up each trail, before heading North, back toward the city.

A few beats later, Veneza started to stand. Mondennio stopped her. "We can't be certain they're not just out of eyesight, waiting for us to move," he whispered.

"What do we do?"

"Let's go this way, very quietly."

They had a difficult time moving through the undergrowth. They tried to avoid crackling too many leaves by walking slowly. Mondennio noticed a slight foot trail that he guided them to. A few beats later, they were through the trees.

Veneza looked at him with some wonder.

He shrugged. "It's no big deal. This is the route Jonaldy and I took. If we keep going this way we'll go past Ginster Enclave. From there, we might be able to walk back into Kennet."

"Do you think that's safe?"

"Either that or we go back the way we came. Look, Veneza, I really do need your help to find Jonaldy. I'm going to try to find some way to make him clear me without me having him use me — more than he has already."

"I'm not going to promise anything. You and I are both under a lot of pressure. Maybe Leroga will have a better idea. Will you at least hear him out if he does? If he doesn't, then I'll help you find Jonaldy. Do you think you can wait a day or two while we sort this out?"

"Looks like I don't have a choice. Do I?"

They walked toward Ginster Enclave, then Northeast up the road to Kennet. Mondennio remembered the Atakadaro facility. Instead of walking past it, they took a side street that ran parallel to the main street. They walked past a small building that scarcely looked large enough to contain the bistro that it housed.

They finally reached the streetcar stop.

"Mondennio, we're both well-known fugitives. We can't both ride on this streetcar. I don't know where you can stay."

"If our slates are being monitored, it's only a question of time before yours is tracked to you. There's a fluke with mine that makes it harder to track me. Give me your slate, and I'll get rid of it. When this is over I'll get you a new one."

She handed it over to him.

After he placed it in his daybag, "I tell you what I'll do. I'll come by this corner every a few cycles later. If you guys want me to meet, put a chalk 'X' on the corner of that building followed by the cycle when we're going to meet. I'll meet you at the Performing Arts store. If you don't see me, try again the next day around this cycle."

The streetcar approached. Mondennio turned away from it and walked up the side street, away from both the streetcar and Veneza. He spent the rest of the night carefully wandering the streets of Kennet.

56.   Jonaldy - Tenement

The binaries' light poured through the blinds in Jonaldy's bedroom.

He stretched awake and inaugurated his morning routine with a trip to the bathroom. He got dressed and went to the kitchen. A fast, heavy breakfast prepared him for a light day. He needed a day off after the past week's chaos. He walked out of his apartment building, and stopped to inspect his clothes.

It gave him a chance to quickly glance about in the window's reflection to see if there was any obvious surveillance. Did he recognize anybody?

Satisfied there was no obvious surveillance, he decided a brief route would help him identify if there was less obvious surveillance. A part of his daily routine, he never knew whether he was under constant watch or not. Soon after he started, he noticed a chalk mark under a light post. It took him a moment to remember what the signal meant.

Secondary continue. Terminate subject.

He walked past it, trying to ensure he understood it. *They're telling me to continue on my secondary mission — Klocards. They want me to execute him. I'm not a wet operative. The team's dead, and I don't have the skills to take out a target like that. They have to know that. Are they setting me up for failure again?*

All this time to keep a low profile then waste it on a scientist. *He's not even researching anything important. It looks more like he's milking the Rowenzals for a few knoerzers. Are they seriously planning to burn my whole network of people and the primary mission to go after a scientist?*

They're asking me to throw away years of labor; throw away my career. Don't they understand what influence we'll have once Mondennio's career flourishes? Is this some loyalty test? Steel yourself, Jonaldy. They don't know what's going on the ground. You've got time to do both. Klocard's not going anywhere. Only Imperial ships leave this system. He tries to leave they'll have him, so I've done my part.

He had time to finish with Mondennio, then turn his focus on Klocards. *Nobody told me how soon, and with the team gone it will take me a while to recover that operation. I need probably another couple of days with Mondennio, then I can shift focus. I can do both of these.*

Jonaldy decided a walk would give him time to clear things out. It was only eight kilometers. Mondennio will be thankful the Imperium saved him and his family. I'll be the one who collects as he matures by having him bring me into the government with him.

*   *   *

57.   **Mondennio - Streets of Kennet**

Mondennio felt as though Kennet had become a foreign city to him despite his having lived there his entire life. To him, the city had been a series of hospitable islands, with his car hopping from one island to the other. Now he aimlessly wandered the ocean in between.

His life had imploded. He felt helpless to change it, but he had to try. For now, he needed a place to stay. All his islands had been taken away from him, and he was being actively hunted by Atakadaro. His lack of knowledge of the city added to his anxiety.

The binary stars of Copa crested, casting a faint glow over the new day. Foot traffic picked up as people began their morning commutes. Mondennio wondered if he would ever again look at them the way he used to.

Despite his efforts to avoid any area he knew, he eventually found himself near the city center. He expected the center itself would have active patrols, so he turned and walked away once he realized where he was.

He turned left at the next intersection, heading South. Within a few blocks, the nature of Kennet changed again. The area carried a faintness of perversion that was hard for Mondennio to place. He decided to continue quickly Southward.

Before he finished crossing the street, he saw Klocards walking toward him on the cross street. Klocards was scanning the area as he moved, searching for somebody, but he did not notice Mondennio. His pace was brisk, uniform, martial. His fists seemed to punch the air as they swung at his side. With nowhere else to turn, Mondennio moved to intercept him.

As he closed, Mondennio saw Klocards' face more clearly. He looked determined, hostile. Klocards still did not seem to see Mondennio, despite his near-constant scanning of the area. "Klocards!"

Mondennio did not have time to say more. As he said his name, Klocards immediately looked straight at him. In a flurry, he grabbed Mondennio by the arm and pulled him down the street. Nobody seemed to notice what was happening. Klocards found a narrow gap between two buildings and pushed Mondennio down it. Mondennio knew he should resist, but Klocards' determination stole his motivation.

Klocards threw him against the wall, "What are you doing following me?"

Mondennio was shocked with the ease Klocards had in tossing him around. *Where did he get his strength?* "I wasn't following you. I saw you and needed to talk to a familiar face."

"I don't think so. This isn't the sort of place for a kiddie like you."

"I'm sure it isn't, but here I am. And I definitely wasn't following you. If I were, wouldn't I have been behind you instead of in front?"

Klocards mellowed. "Good point. What do you want?"

"Right now, I want a friend."

"You've come to the right neighborhood for that for the right price," Klocards chuckled.

Mondennio looked at him blankly, not sure what he meant.

"What? Wow. You are a sheltered little boy. You don't recognize the sex district of your own home town? You should be able to buy any friend you want. But only by the cycle, which I bet is much more time than is necessary."

"That's not what I mean. I need help. You gave me a pistol earlier, so you must know something about how to use one."

"I didn't give you a pist — " Klocards' grimace relaxed for a moment, then returned. "Do you still have it?"

"It's in my daybag," Mondennio fished it out and handed it to Klocards with the grip facing Klocards. "I didn't shoot anybody, but I did use it to get what I needed — like you suggested. I can't get into the details, but I've been wrongfully accused of murder."

Klocards took the pistol and inspected it to confirm that it was loaded. He then looked at Mondennio, then rested his hand with the pistol on Mondennio's shoulder. "So, you're telling me there's a reward for you for murder, and you just gave me a loaded pistol. You are either naively trusting or hopelessly stupid."

"I'd say I'm a little of both, based on past performance." Mondennio glanced at the pistol on his shoulder. "I've exhausted every other friend I have."

"I would imagine you have quite a few in your class."

"Once I was formally accused of cheating, they all started keeping their distance. I started running around with a different crowd and got into a little trouble."

"Who hasn't at one time. But, you're calling murder a little trouble?" Klocards tapped the pistol barrel against his own head and winked. It confused Mondennio, but he knew better than to ask. "So, you're asking me to be your muscle or something?"

"Yeah. I want to clear my name, but that takes confronting the guy who ruined it in the first place. We think he's some Imperium spy."

Klocards narrowed his eyes, staring more intently at Mondennio. "You said an Imperium spy? I wish I could help you, but it's probably better that I don't." He deftly flipped the pistol about. "You probably still need this more than I do."

Mondennio put his hands up, gently pushing the pistol back. "It's not a good idea for me to be armed right now. I'm sure Atakadaro will find me before long. Finding me armed would only make matters worse. They might just shoot me to avoid prosecution."

"That's right, possession of a weapon while fleeing justice is automatically a crime, regardless of innocence. Sounds like a good way to disarm a populous. If a cop sees you jay-walking and decides to follow you and you keep walking — then you're fleeing justice. But, you want to confront a guy you think is an Imperium agent unarmed. That's gutsy or stupid."

"Like I said before, I'm a little of both."

"While I respect the courage, I still can't help you. I have my own problems. My own solutions. Fortunately for you, I think your problems with him got a little smaller."

"What makes you think that?"

Klocards gave a knowing look. "Bullies need friends, and I'll bet he's fresh out. Anything else you need?"

"Yeah. I've been on the run for nearly 10 cycles now."

"All day, huh? Well, I won't let you stay with me. The proprietor would look at me funny." He reached into his pocket and pulled out a cash card. "You'll want this, it's not traceable." Klocards started walking out of the alley, motioning to Mondennio.

Mondennio followed. They returned to the street, which had swelled in size as more people started their walk to work. Klocards pointed at a building.

"See that place over there? Some people call it a no-tel, others call it a warm-sheet hotel. They take cash for stays by the cycle. Tell them you have a friend coming. It will at least give you a few cycles rest in something resembling a real bed. Just try to avoid the stains."

Mondennio looked down at the card, uncertain of what to say. Despite Klocards' assurance, the mass of Copa pressed down on him.

Klocards looked at him, sizing him up. "I don't know everything that's going on in your life, but it looks like you've lost self-control. You look like a kid who thinks he still needs somebody to blow his nose or wipe his arse. I hate to tell you, but once you get a certain size, that's a big arse to wipe."

Mondennio chuckled. "What do I do? What would you do?"

"What should you do? Not what I'd do. I'd put a bullet in his brain, but I've been told before my approach was too direct. It doesn't allow the individual to reform himself. I figure he's got to be reformed if he's no longer doing what he shouldn't be.

"One thing I have learned, Mister Rownezal, is that Providence, or whatever you call it, has always prepared me for any challenge life throws at me. Just don't worry about the size of the problem. Take one day at a time, one cycle at a time if a day is too big. Break it down to what you can manage and deal with it. And deal with it every day. Whatever you do, don't give up."

"That's easy for you to say, you've never been hit with problems as big as mine."

"There's arrogant self-pity. Kid, everybody's problem is bigger than somebody else's. As for taking on something the size of the Imperium, you'd be surprised." He paused, scanning the street. "Look, I have to get going. You have a lovely planet here, except for the corruption and lack of human compassion. Not too different than the Imperium. Maybe you can do better?"

Klocards strode off, fists punctuating his walk. It was not long before Mondennio lost him in the morning bustle.

As Klocards suggested, Mondennio went into the no-tel. The clerk barely seemed to acknowledge him as he paid for two cycles. *Klocards was right, the clerk doesn't care at all.*

The room itself was worse than Klocards suggested it was. There was no trash, but there was a stink that did not go away. The mattress was heavily stained, so Mondennio chose to lay on the couch instead. It had the apparent ignominy of having been recently replaced. Exhaustion got the better of him, and he quickly fell asleep.

Mondennio awoke with a dull headache. He sat up and put his head in his hands trying to figure out where the headache came from. At least the room's smell was scarcely noticeable. When he came in there was a pervasive stain of body odor that he thought would prevent him from sleeping.

He checked his slate. He had overstayed by five beats. The clerk warned him they might lock him in if he overstayed unless he paid a hefty fee. Mondennio tried the door only to confirm it was locked. He grabbed his daybag and headed for the window.

He opened the window and noticed a meter-wide sun ledge below. He lowered himself onto the ledge and walked until he came to the stairway window. He easily climbed back in. He walked down the stairs nonchalantly.

"Hey! Buddy!"

Mondennio did not look for the source of the call. He knew it had to be the hotel clerk. He ran down the rest of the stairs and across the lobby.

Once on the sidewalk, he ran another couple of blocks before he stopped running. The clerk had not followed, much to Mondennio's relief. He quickly inventoried his daybag, checking that everything was there. Content he had what he needed, he looked around the street trying to decide which way to go.

Without a clear direction, Mondennio decided to head left, continuing the direction he had seen Klocards go. He did not expect to see him again, but at the very least it had to be somewhere other than where he was. Even as he started in that direction, he knew he had no idea what to do next.

He started this whole ordeal trying to keep life the way it was, then regaining his honor. Now he just wanted to be free. But there was more than that. Freedom required he confront Jonaldy, regardless of who he was. *A covert agent of the huge Terran Imperium? It's still my world, Jonaldy.*

Barely his world. Not at home in his home town any more. No friends, no future. Mondennio wondered if that's how the unnamed felt each day. Or, did they find solace in friends? They could not be successful, so there had to be a reason to keep living. It made him wonder what it would be like to no longer live on Copa.

Turning his fourth corner, Mondennio thought he recognized one of the men behind him. Sort of balding, with a mix of white and black hair, the man stood out. Mondennio still might have missed him, had he not been moving like a predator.

He headed toward a pink and white building. It had a dome on top, with a long grassy mall in front of it. He thought it must have been one of the few grassy areas apart from the main park near the University. The building was large enough that the man could not keep an eye on him if he went the other way. There were also enough connected streets that that would give him a means to escape if the man managed to cut him off.

He effectively did a U-turn around the building, then turned North, toward what he remembered was the market square. He did not try concealing his intent as he looked back at the man, who continued to follow. The distance seemed to be comfortable, not close enough to make Mondennio want to run, but close enough that he wanted to keep going.

Is he trying to drive me somewhere? Mondennio tried to think of where he would be easily trapped. He had been in this area enough that he thought he knew all the side streets, the public areas. Not that that ever stopped Atakadaro.

He ended up walking past his "no-tel" again, trying to understand how he managed to walk in a full circle. He remembered that two blocks up he would be in sight of the city center. *If I can get there, maybe I can get to Club Orakrono. Maybe they'll give me sanctuary?*

As he came around the corner to head toward the city center, two men stood in his way. They looked right at him, and started to reach out for him. Rather than run away, he chose to head straight at them, screaming. The crowd around him looked on as he knocked both men over. He kept running, hoping he could escape Atakadaro. Did it have to be Atakadaro? Why not Imperium? These could just as easily be Jonaldy's men.

As he ran, he decided it did not matter who was chasing him. Right now, he hoped he could make it to the Club before they caught up. He really hoped whoever was at the Club would let him in.

Not quite remembering the way, he turned right at the next block. At the other end, he saw the balding man. *He moves fast for an old guy.* Expecting the others to be close behind, Mondennio quickly looked for another way out. He saw a narrow passage across the street, in the direction of the Club. He ran down the passage, across another street and eventually reached a major road.

He recognized it. The Club was to his left. He quickly made it down the street, briskly walking more than running. He tried to blend in, but his constant looking over his shoulder made anybody who saw him stare. At last he saw the Club.

Without a second thought, he opened the door and rushed in. There was only one menacing man this time, but he was enough to give Mondennio pause. The outside door closed. "Ziggy said it was okay. Besides, I've got the law behind me."

"You've got Atakadaro behind you? How far?"

"I think they were a couple blocks away. I know they didn't see me come in here." Mondennio knew he was out of options; out of people he could trust. "Look, I've been on the run for a couple days now. Somebody's accusing me of committing a murder. I know you'll get in a lot of trouble if I'm found, but I really need your help. Just give me a few cycles to rest. Then I'll be on my way."

"If you can stay quiet. The blue room on the — -"

"I know where that is. Thanks." Mondennio started down the hallway to the stairs.

"Hold it. I talk, you listen."

Mondennio turned back around.

"Boss'll be here soon. You'll have to talk to him. Then you'll know if you made the right decision to come here. You go up there and stay out of sight."

"Yes, fine. Thank you. I'll, ah, be in the blue room."

Mondennio found the blue room much faster than last time. The room looked even more barren than his last visit. The windows were partly open, a faint breeze dancing the curtain. He could hear Kennet alive outside, wondering if he could hear the agents hunting for him.

He resisted looking out the window. Instead, he chose the darker corner of the room to sleep. He took his daybag and converted it into a makeshift pillow. Nothing else offered comfort. The door did not even lock. Despite the lack of comfort and security, Mondennio found himself falling asleep again.

As he drifted off, he wondered what it would take to capture Jonaldy and get him to confess so his name was cleared.

Chapter 16

58. Klocards - Hotel

The wait was hard enough. Klocards managed to avoid visiting parts of Kinnet that he frequented. Knowing he was being followed and expecting the ambush gave him enough time to secure untraceable funding on a disposable card to cover him for a few days. He found a room at a hotel that rented by the hour. The desk clerk looked at him oddly going up alone and paying for so much time.

"My boss' wife will be along shortly," he said, hoping the excuse would work.

Once in the room, he barricaded himself in. He took a shower, keeping the pistol close at hand. He got little sleep, keeping away from the door and window and avoiding all furniture. For a No-tel, it was well maintained.

He slipped out early, the clerk asleep with his head on the desk. That made Klocards feel better. If the clerk betrayed him he would have kept watch. The rest of the day, Klocards tried to keep a sort of routine. Keeping vigil while trying to look like a patron of each shop was difficult. In the places with vibrant bags, he bought something. Then he would walk for a while and then dump the bag and its contents. If he had been followed, he hoped the pursuer would be misled into looking for some other man with a vibrant bag.

59. Veneza - Leroga's Apartment

Leroga only surrounded himself with paper books. Many of them appear to be printed on paper stripped of its original text and hand bound. The typeset had a rough hand-made feel about them. Many were written in a strange language she did not recognize, tough some of the letters were similar to Copan letters. The books left Veneza with only an untraceable slate as an outside source of information. She scanned through her news reader, learning that she was wanted in connection both with the murder and as an instigator of the massacre. She was tired of reading the lies spread by the media — the massacre was instigated by the Atakadaro.

She struggled to avoid reading her messages when she happened on a fluff piece about Clin-Khotaigra. The Clin was celebrating its 350th anniversary, as it joined the Clinate years after the Founding. *That means Juank should be there. Maybe I can persuade him to go easy on Mondennio?*

Veneza texted Leroga, explaining her plan. He insisted he escort her, but she could not wait for him.

She decided to take a streetcar, paying for it with one of Juank's cashcards. She hoped the affluence of the neighborhood would conceal her status.

It was a kilometer walk through quaint shops to the streetcar stop. Realizing she was poorly dressed, she stopped in one of the shops and bought a gown she normally saw among the named. The owner asked for money first, only to change her tone when Veneza held out one of Juank's cards.

Begowned, she thought the neighborhood looked serene — far more tranquil than any part of the city. She boarded the streetcar, number eight, surprised that nobody noticed her.

The ride took 25 beats through wealthy neighborhoods until it entered Mammoth. She changed to a second line, Number 10, that went past the marketplace, the scene of the massacre. Her fresh memories watered her eyes, though she managed not to cry.

Just North of the plaza, a small carnival entertained named families — just east of the palace itself. The plaza itself had a few amusement rides. Despite the recent bloodshed, she marveled at how Clin-Khotaigra managed to celebrate.

Veneza got off when the streetcar stopped in front of the Large Pan Hotel, and crossed the street toward the entrance. As the streetcar pulled away, she realized she had never noticed the streetcar before. Aradames usually expected her to meet him wherever they went, except for their last night together. She had walked everywhere for as long as she lived in the city.

The binaries were still above the horizon when she arrived. A few guests had started to arrive. Veneza did not expect Juank to arrive early, so she strolled a nearby park until the binaries set.

By the time she returned, the party had begun in earnest. She quickly blended into the throng of party-goers. She roamed the crowd, trying her best to not draw attention to herself. After looking for nearly a cycle, she concluded Juank was not going to make an appearance at the Hotel.

Veneza started to leave, when she heard a call.

"Hello! You."

She froze momentarily, thinking she had been discovered.

"I need to thank you. Were it not for you I probably would not have made it home."

She turned and saw Juank, in full formal dress. Clin-Khotaigra was a military family, and his uniform suggested martial prowess she doubted a man of his youth would experience on tranquil Copa. "It's the least I could do, since you showed me a good time."

He seemed to be taken aback when she failed to use honorifics in her reply. In spite of herself, his uniform upset her. *He will either help me or I'll have to find another way. I'm not going to honor a baby killer.*

"You are the one who got me home last week, aren't you?"

"Yes. I am. You're welcome."

Juank seemed to adjust to her rude replies. "Quite. Well, I did not return unscathed. My wallet was missing with my identity card and a bit of money." A waiter passed by and Juank grabbed a glass. He drank it like a shot.

She pulled out his identity card and returned it to him. "I have your card. I'm afraid the money was either spent on the alcohol or in the finder's fee."

"Well, I'm not worried about the money. I could have deactivated them had I wanted to, but you knew that. But, I didn't deactivate them. That's why you're here, right?"

His comment bit. *Did I come here because of his money? No. I'm here to help Mondennio. I need to swallow my pride a bit.* "Juank, Sir," she switched to honorific, "I'm not here because of your money, but I am here because of you."

His smile slipped to a more businesslike grimace. "I'm sure you have."

"No. It's not that. I really had a great time with you last time. But, I know as well as you do there's a barrier here. I'm not going to cross that barrier."

"Barrier? I'm not sure I get what you mean."

"I'm unnamed. I'm sure you knew."

"If you were unnamed, then you would not have been in University."

"I was in University taking all the audit courses. There's no way a woman of my status could take any of the degree courses. I'm surprised you were taking the course."

"Surprised? The Clin has to make an appearance at those lower courses, otherwise the other families would avoid them for fear. My father said it was necessary for cohesion."

"I'm surprised he cares."

"We can't help it if the other families fail to show proper respect for a rounded education. That's what intrigues me about you. The way you tore into Giedaz — now I'm even more amazed because you did it as an unnamed."

"Just because I'm unnamed doesn't mean I can't think for myself. We're not all unwashed heathens. You people throw out knowledge like it's trash. Well, I crawled through that trash to get an education."

He laughed. "I'm sure. You think I believe the thought of you crawling through trash just to find a pearl. Honestly, I don't care where you got your education. It's refreshing to hear an opposing viewpoint. I almost found myself agreeing with you."

Juank took her hand and led her speechless into the ballroom. As they danced, she tried to reconcile the massacre and his nonchalant interest in viewpoints. "You are Clin-Khotaigra, right?"

"Most certainly. Why?"

She decided she had to expose herself. "I'm Veneza Karduil. I'm sure you've seen my photo on the media."

He pulled back for a moment and stared at her. Veneza had a hard time reading his emotionless face. Finally, a smile curled and he showed perfect white teeth.

"I knew that photo looked familiar." He drew her back and continued dancing.

"What? Aren't you worried?"

"Oh, I'm sure the news reports are at least half right. Ringleader and murderer." He laughed. "I wouldn't doubt you were surrounded in all this Republican nonsense; but if you were in for murder then I'd not have made it home at all."

Veneza took a deep breath to keep herself from confessing on the spot. She needed to focus.

"Juank, there's a fellow who has been implicated in the murder. He saved me during the riot. I think he started clinging to me to keep me out of trouble. He didn't quite achieve his goal. He belongs to your Clin. I think he needs your help."

"I think you mean Mondennio Rowenzal?" Juank spoke professionally, though they continued to dance.

Veneza stopped her breath short. *How can he be so on top of what's going on? Has he already talked to somebody?* "Yes." She tried not to hide her hesitation, but it seemed he picked up on it anyway.

"I don't know what I can do." He pushed her away from her. "Veneza, I don't think it's that easy. You see, my Clin may be the youngest, but we're the most prodigious. There are fifty men in my generation line alone. My father is the fourth of five sons, and I'm his eighth son. So, I'm not exactly near the center of power. I forget whether I'm 46th or 47th heir, but there it is. Besides, the Rowenzals are on their way out. I don't see why Clin-Khotaigra should risk itself for his sake — or his family's." He then drew her back into the dance.

Veneza suddenly felt very exposed. She stood in the middle of a ballroom, surrounded by a sea of aristocracy swaying to pretentious music. She just confessed herself to who she thought was one of the most powerful men in the city to help a friend.

"That's it?" she said. She pulled away from Juank, noticing for the first time that she was several centimeters taller. "You don't have the ability, and even if you did they're not worth saving?"

His reaction looked like she just slapped him on the face. "That pretty much is all there is to it. You really think any member of the Clinate has that much power? We're interlocked interests. The slightest flinch could cause it all to fall."

"What if I can give you something else? Something that you could barter for?"

"To be quite upfront, you're the only thing I'm interested in."

"How dare you!" As she thought to lift her hand to slap him, she caught herself. Juank's security detail was nearby and would certainly react if she did. Several people turned to look at her, only to resume dancing.

"Not that." He pulled out a card. "Well, not exactly. I like you. You've got your own mind about things. I don't see that often even within the Clin. I see you're not really interested. Take my card. Don't throw it away. Think it through. I don't plan on marrying somebody who takes everything at face value."

She stood motionless as the dancers ebbed and flowed around her. A moment later, she left the Hotel still speechless. The only way out of this is if she and Mondennio can work together.

She left to find Leroga.

60.   Klocards - Kennet

At last 800 beats arrived. Litovio was on time and sitting well to the back.

The only thing that persuaded Klocards that it was not a trap was their shared history — and lineage.

"I don't think the Imperial authorities know about you yet, Klocards. There was no mention of any attack on Imperial citizens, but if they were BID then that would not be mentioned. The Imperial Battleship (IBB) Karator arrived yesterday and should be at the Post Station by now. Something serious must be going on, though. I've been given command of the Karator! The outgoing commander is landing separately to take my place as recruiter. By mid-day I will be off-planet and heading for a good GIE spot to jump from."

"Fine. Where does that put me?"

"Easy. There's BID in system." Litovio handed him a business card and pointed at it. "You get yourself to the location on the back of the card by dawn tomorrow. That should be 280 beats. My shuttle should be prepared to take off by 300 beats. I'll tell the pilot I've got an unofficial passenger.

Just look menacing and threaten him if he shows any contrary response. That should cover you until I can drop you off on another system."

"That's good. Then what?"

"Danel, like it or not." Litovio paused. Knowing he would get a reaction if he spoke more plaintively and quickly, "the family will have to take you in. Your cover is blown here. Janhas Klocards can't leave this system and not be hounded. You're being hunted by BID. The family can handle this."

"Eff you."

"You want off this world? You want to get away from Bafiktuy? Those are my terms. You reconcile yourself to the family, or I'll hand you over myself. Now, I've got to get back and act like I'm leaving the system at dawn tomorrow. I've got a co-ed to visit."

Janhas Klocards. He had to start forgetting that identity. He was Danel Bophendze, fugitive of the Imperial Postal Marines. Hunted by the notorious BID. As Janhas Klocards, he managed to hide out for a few years. *Why would the Bafiktuy be after me? This is not their sort of thing.* The more he thought about it, the more he came to realize the Bafiktuy is not after him because he is fleeing the Marines. They were after the radar technology.

How did they know? He was convinced Litovio would not betray him. They had known each another too long, the trust was too solid. Perhaps interviews with members of Litovio's old crew tipped them to the technology. *Somehow they figured out I knew. Somehow they figured out who I was.*

He continued to roam the streets through the night, uncertain where was safe. Maybe he could relax once he was on Litovio's new command. Bafiktuy could just as well be on that ship, too. The Imperium's perfect boogiemen; always where you least expected them. As the beats ticked off, he accepted he had no other alternative but to take Litovio's offer.

He recognized the street he was on. Hanifer Berryman Sub-sept Rowenzal Khotaigra lived a few doors down. He thought about saying good bye, then realized she was probably being watched by an operative. *What a shame. She was cute.* She also knew too much about his research, though he was powerless to do anything about it and leave Copa safely. He knew they would be after him for what he did to their assassination squad. She could not have enough information to build a reliable radar anyway.

By 250 beats, Danel arrived outside the shuttle port; he hid just inside the shadows. An Imperial Postal shuttle sat at the nearest pad, its ship markings identified it as one of the Karator's. He could feel an operative's eyes staring right at him. He scanned the area and saw nobody out of place. The shuttle crew comprised the normal two pilots and one Marine guard. The guard near the shuttle's hatch, waited for his new commander. Everything was as he expected it should be.

At 275 beats, Danel saw Litovio arrive. He was escorted by the military attaché from the Imperial embassy. They were deeply engaged in conversation. Five beats to get onto that shuttle, forty meters to cover. How did Litovio expect him to get on board, knowing the Bafiktuy would be hunting him? He watched as the attaché waved, sat back into his car, and drove away. He had no more time, and no other options.

As he walked those last forty meters, Janhas Klocards changed his demeanor. His inner-Marine steeled his backbone. He grew two inches. His shoulders straightened. His pace steadied. Even his hands curled into a standard military grip. Based on Bophendze's bearing alone, the Marine guard snapped to attention as he approached the pad's ramp. *He recognized one of his own. If I'm going to die, I'll die as a Marine.*

Litovio spun around and looked at his cousin, Danel Bophendze. Litovio smiled as Danel began his salute. Then a loud, familiar, sharp whip-crack sound reverberated on the shuttle pad and echoed off the nearby buildings.

61. Mondennio - Club Orakrono

"Wake up!"

Mondennio awoke with a start, scurrying up the wall to a standing position. The light was bright as he retreated further away from the yell that startled him awake. He found himself trapped in the corner, his eyes regaining focus on the door opposite him. He looked toward the window, noticing the morning light.

He cursed himself for falling asleep in the worst corner for escape. Whoever had him would have no problem keeping him pinned in place. Or worse. He brought his forearm to his eyes partly to shield them from the overhead light, but also to try to clear the remaining blurry sleep from his eyes.

"That's him, all right." The man on the left said.

"Could fetch us a decent reward," said the man on the right.

The one on the left elbowed the other in the stomach. "Why' d you say that? You know that ain't happening. They'll accuse us of aid' n and abet' n a known fugitive.

Trying to regain his breath the other said, "you've got a point."

Mondennio slowly regained focus. "Are you Ziggy?"

"What? You think you're so special Ziggy himself would come to you for an audience? Jex didn't say this kreteno was special, did he? Then how would Ziggy know?" He laughed.

"So what then, Piral?"

Mondennio made out three men about his age. They smelled worse than he expected, and their build was sufficient to dissolve his hope of escape. "Fine, you're not Ziggy, you're Piral. And he's Jex. It appears you already know who I am."

"Yeah, so let's dispense with the bowing and curtsying, right? Why' d you come to the Club?" Piral said.

"I knew it was a safe place from Atakadaro."

"Not for you, it ain't. This place is for those who like hard music and hard knocks. Not for some spoiled brat."

"I've been here before with a friend, Veneza."

"Yeah, you ain't with her now."

"We got split up. Atakadaro raided us a few days ago and we've both been on the run since."

They were only a couple of floors above ground level, and he started thinking about how to land on the street below. Provided no pedestrian eased his fall.

"Jex, check out his story. Find Veneza and see if she'll vouch for him."

"Who do I text?"

"Who do you think? Who always knows where everybody is?"

"Fine, fine." Jex took out his slate and rapidly tapped in a text. He turned and stepped away, breaking the ring that kept Mondennio in place. Jex walked closer to the windows.

Mondennio thought he might be able to distract the other two, then make a break for it. Providence would guide his escape.

"What happens if Veneza doesn't vouch for me?"

"That's easy. I gotta friend who makes gourmet pet food for your kind. We'll add you into the mix. I can't tell you how much human meal gets added regularly, but it's more than a little."

"That might explain why the little murdon keep biting their owners."

"Heh. Yeah, that could explain it. They're hoping for a snack." Piral laughed harder, "get a quick bite before a servant takes them on their morning merda."

Mondennio started to edge slightly, hoping to expand the gap.

Piral extended his arm, until the club in his hand stabbed against the wall. "Uh, uh. Stay. Better yet, sit!" He pointed the club at a chair.

Mondennio wondered why Piral kept that one arm behind his back. The club looked like the handle from some mining implement he could not remember the name for. He remained standing.

Piral wasted no time in addressing Mondennio's resistance. The club arced downward as he stepped forward. His other hand met Mondennio firmly at his solar plexus.

Mondennio slid down the wall until he sat. So little effort and I can't breath.

Piral stepped back, twirling the club. Mondennio shrank away, anticipating the club would come swinging back to hit him.

Instead, Piral laughed harder. "Look at that. You can teach them to fear us." He stomped toward Mondennio, causing him to flinch. Piral laughed harder.

"Piral, she texted back." Jex came over quickly, handing his slate to him.

Piral read the text carefully. Or, was it slowly? Mondennio could not help to think his skills were more physical than mental.

"She's coming here. Just have to keep him sitting tight until she does. Said she's bringing a friend." Piral turned toward Mondennio, "No hard feelings, eh? Hungry?"

Mondennio's three new friends stayed in the room with him for nearly two cycles, as well as he could guess. Sandwiches were brought for all. Jex and the other, Manthi, took turns keeping watch on the windows or the door. He could not tell if they were worried or just naturally alert. None of them wasted time talking, making the wait more monotonous.

The door opened, causing Jex to whirl. He had been watching the windows.

"Guess it's my turn to save you, huh? Looks like they didn't treat you badly," Veneza said as she entered. She jerked her thumb behind her to the door.

Piral and Jex filed out. Manthi reached into the room and closed the door, leaving Veneza and Mondennio alone.

"Not really, no. We just carried on like old friends. They even bought me breakfast." He motioned to the rickety table covered with empty wrappers, and several empty bottles.

"They're not known for their hospitality. Tell you about the pet food?"

"Yeah. Said something about me helping fertilize wealthy lawns." He paused a moment. "You're not Ziggy, are you?"

"Providence, no. Don't just go around asking everybody that, okay? I don't even know who he is. Some of us don't think he really exists. Or that he did once but is now just an idea."

"Yeah, but Jex texted him."

"Well, I was with Leroga when he got a text about you. But I think it hopped a few people first. Our communication can be like that, you know."

"Somebody's claiming to be Ziggy. You sure it's not your friend Leroga?"

"Seriously, stop asking if everybody's Ziggy. He's nobody. Leroga's Atakadaro, so there's no way he could be Ziggy."

"What? Why aren't you under arrest, then?"

Veneza explained what had happened.

"So, based on your description, I was probably running from him earlier today."

"I don't know, but it might have been him. may have been. He's out most of the time, so I wouldn't know where he's been."

Veneza went on to explain their conclusion that Jonaldy was an Imperium agent.

"That's great. He's been running me all over Kennet. Tearing up the republican movement. I wish I knew what he was up to."

"We were hoping you could tell us."

"What, you think he's confided in me or something?"

She snorted, "no, that's silly. We figure he wants you for something. So, if we can get him to meet up with you, then we can figure it out."

"How do you propose doing that?"

"Easy. Just take out your slate and text him."

Frustrated that he had not thought of that, Mondennio picked up his daybag and went to retrieve his slate. It was not in its normal pocket, so he fished around inside trying to find it. Unsuccessful, he dumped the contents and frantically tried to find it.

"I had to have left it behind at the room I stayed at yesterday."

Veneza looked at him oddly. She did not look entirely surprised that the slate was missing. She pulled one out of her daybag, "is this your slate?"

As soon as he held it, he recognized it. The slight crack on the display and the chip in the housing. "Where did you get it?"

"Leroga gave it to me to give you if yours was missing." She held her hands up defensively, "don't ask me where he got it."

"It was him following me around. Somehow my slate must have fallen out of my bag when he was chasing me. He's fast for an old guy. So, I just text Jonaldy and say what?"

"We're not sure. Do you tell him you know he's a spy? Or, do you just ask him for help."

"After our last visit, he' d be surprised that I'd be asking for him."

"Well, if he's really been trying to ruin you, maybe he wouldn't be. Maybe he's waiting for you to connect so he could reel you in."

`@Jonaldy meet me at 0.5 cycles at Zero Narf street.`

"That should work. Hungry?"

He pointed at the table, "you should have asked a couple cycles ago. I think I last ate a couple days before then. Don't let me stop you."

Veneza stepped out for a while and returned, "the shop next door serves awesome sandwiches."

"Veneza, this is going to sound odd in light of everything that's happened. Thank you for this crazy ride."

"Are you sure you're not feverish?" Veneza put her cool hand on his forehead. He closed his eyes, drinking in the feminine touch. She moved her hand to touch his left cheek. It reminded him that he had not shaved in a few days, either.

"No. I'm not feverish. I feel awake, maybe for the first time in my life. Kennet's never really been my home before these past weeks. I know it's a hostile place now, but I'm not afraid of it anymore. I see how superficial the Clinate is, how there's a veneer of rage just under the surface."

"A surface Atakadaro keeps tightly attached. The —"

Mondennio placed three fingers on her mouth, silencing her. "Right. I'm trying to tell you that you don't have to rant to me any more. I've lived in your world a bit, maybe just enough for me to understand why you rant. I'm amazed you've not let yourself be beaten down like all the other unnamed."

"I call them sheeple. Every herd needs a few shepherds. The Clinate thinks they are the shepherd, but they're the wolves. They've learned how to herd, and pretend to be shepherds."

"In the absence of a leader, the people will follow anybody."

"Mondennio, the problem is the people don't know the difference."

"I don't know if I buy that, Veneza. They can't be completely ignorant of a true shepherd when he presents himself."

"Believe it, Mondennio. I've been awake for nearly a decade, and I've been trying to wake up others. They don't want to be awake. Give them enough to keep them from complaining, and they don't care about anything else. It's human nature."

"So, republicanism runs contrary to human nature?"

"I think so. It's the best thing for us, but it's not our nature. We are content to let somebody else make most of the decisions."

"What woke you up, then? Why aren't you like the 'sheeple' More to the point, why do you think we have the right to push republicanism on them?"

"Because it's not oppressive, Mondennio. Maybe it's inconvenient to live in a republic. You have to pay attention to more of what's going on. But, a proper republic treats everybody more fairly than an oligarchy or autocracy. I don't think a republic is fair, but it is just."

"What's the difference?"

"Fair treats all of us equally, regardless of what we've done. Just treats us based on what we've done. We work hard, we are entitled to the fruits of our labor — not like what we have now. You get so much because of who you are, not because of what you've done."

"You see a republic as the least bad evil?"

"Yeah, I think that's about right."

Mondennio looked at the window. "I don't know if I agree with that. I agree that Copa is oppressive, and that the Clinate can't change to make it better. It has to be replaced."

"Why not the Imperium, then?"

"What, after what Jonaldy's done to ruin my life? How can that be any less oppressive? He talks about how free it is in the Imperium, but what society dedicated to freedom resorts to ruining somebody's life to get what it wants."

"Every war has casualties, Mondennio."

"Yeah, well not me. I still have a choice in this. I'm not going to be a casualty, a victim, or whatever. I may suffer for what I've done, but I'm not going to let Jonaldy win."

"That easy, huh? You don't care if Mondennio wins or loses, just as long as Jonaldy loses."

"Exactly. I don't have much left to lose now. My family turned against me. I'm fleeing for my life, and Jonaldy's at the middle of it. I can't believe he's just going to let me go without much of a fight. So, I just have to accept that beating him is the most important contribution I can give. What you republicans are able to do after that, I don't care."

62.   Jonaldy - Kennet

To achieve great things only two things are needed: a plan and not quite enough time. Jonaldy was at the point of not having enough time. All he needed was a plan. In absence of a perfect plan, he hoped what he had was good enough. He texted Jony Guezaler:

```
@Jony:  I have another break for you.  Could
make your career.  Meet me at 6.00 cycles in the
Performing Arts shop balcony West of the University.
```

He strolled around the East and South sides of the University campus, through the plaza and then North to the shop. Despite his meeting with an officer, he still maintained his vigilance in his route. He still had ten beats as he climbed the stairs to the balcony. Jony was there, but he was not alone.

"Who's he?"

"Don't worry, Jonaldy. This is a friend of mine from my district. Leroga Roigamin, this is Captain Rowenzal. He works with undercover officers."

"I don't recall there being a Captain. I'd know all of them in Kennet," Leroga said.

"That's the disadvantage of working undercover. Our files are sealed and we don't get invited to office parties."

A vision of Brysom's interrogation came to Jonaldy's mind. He wondered if this other officer would see through his ruse.

"I overheard some people talking, don't know who, and they started talking about the murder, and Veneza. I know Veneza, though I wouldn't say I share her politics." *Not even close, I'm an Imperialist,* he avoided saying. "Anyway, I know Jony here passingly, and I thought it my civic duty."

"Veneza wouldn't put out, you mean," Leroga said.

Jonaldy had a hard time reading his face. It was too professional, too businesslike. So, he laughed. Leroga did not even break a smile. *A perfect pokerface.*

"Well, not that. I mean, she's cute and all, but I'm not the sort to refuse to do my duty, compliance or not." He looked at Jony and Leroga both, trying to see if the joke penetrated. Jony reacted at least, a bit of a smirk. *He's being a little more professional than our last visits. Is there something wrong?*

"Well, Veneza got away, and apparently some other fellow wasn't there. Care to continue to assist us, Mr. Rowenzal? Or are you going to stick with your sub-sept?"

"The name's a pseudonym. I'm not actually a Rowenzal. You can call me Jonaldy. But, before we get too far down this rabbit hole, we should level-set our expectations. Somebody's using this Republican movement to weaken Clin Kacaubant."

"We're both Kacaubant."

Just as I expected, based on your names. "Well, we think Khotaigra's behind it and I need a bit of help wrapping up the investigation."

"So you've come to us for help?"

"Exactly." His emphasis on the letter 'T' garnered an odd look from Leroga, but it was the best he could do to avoid slipping into his native accent. "I heard what happened to Bryson, and we can't let that happen to Mondennio."

Leroga became unsettled when he heard the name. "Mondennio? What about him?"

"He was involved in the murder of Professor Giedaz last week. I heard he was the one who actually committed it. Veneza's an accomplice, but she wasn't the killer. None of the other boys you have in custody really know that much about it. But, I gather they both were together when it happened. The two of them and Bryson, whom you killed." Jonaldy winced inside when he realized he used a more formal term, another difficulty he had in learning the language was the use of formal, informal and casual language depending on whether you were speaking inside your station or not. These officers were in the lower station, so nobody ever formally spoke to them.

Leroga seemed oblivious to the slip, though Jony's eyebrow raised.

"You look like you need more to establish my bona fides. I was asked to give you this card." He handed them a business card.

Leroga examined the card, with Jony looking over his shoulder. Jony blurted, "You know Stinieles Kerowns?"

"Yes, he's supervising my investigation. If you don't believe me, call him and ask him if he knows Jonaldy. Look, I need your help in apprehending Mondennio and questioning him outside the normal Atakadaro channels to identify how far this Republican infestation has spread, and maybe get Mondennio to infiltrate them." *Rose can wipe the interrogation records after. This is going to be easy.*

"Sure, we should be able to help. He's from a named family, so our questioning him should be fairly minor with no acceptable bloodshed."

"What would it take for me to participate? Stiny wanted me to handle the pitch personally. I think the best time to make the offer is when he's being interrogated. If he does not want to play ball, then you can uncover that he was involved in the murder and up the stakes."

"That sounds like a plan. Just tell us where and when you'll be meeting Mondennio, and we'll take care of the rest."

"Perfect." Jonaldy smiled. *I guess I had nothing to fear after all.*

Chapter 17

63. Mondennio - Kennet

"What's wrong?" Veneza said.

"I don't know what I'm doing. I've got a little over a cycle until I confront Jonaldy, but I don't have a plan."

"What do you mean? I thought you had a plan."

"Nope. No plan. I'm going to meet him at the stop we met at when we were going to kidnap Giedaz. That's it. At least with Carpimua, I had a pistol. I gave the pistol back to Klocards. You don't have a pistol, do you?"

Veneza shook her head. "You don't have to leave for another cycle. So, let's figure out what you're going to do. What do you expect him to do?"

"Last time he had a few friends. I figured they were all professionals based on how they acted when we entered the Ginster Enclave."

"So, we should expect them to be there again."

"I'm not sure. Klocards said Jonaldy would be a little light on manpower."

"How does this Klocards guy know Jonaldy?"

Mondennio shrugged. Then it occurred to him. "I think Klocards was an Imperial who was hiding out on Copa. He claimed to be doing some super-secret research. I ran into him earlier and he said that he had helped lighten the load. Could it mean he took out some of Jonaldy's men somehow? But he's bound to be off-world by now. So no help to us now. Either way, that doesn't help me figure out how to trap Jonaldy. What about Leroga? Why isn't he getting involved?"

"He said he had to stay out of it. I also talked to Juank Clin-Khotaigra." She gave a half-shrug, "I ran into him at a party. What can I say? He's not interested, either. And don't bring up Ziggy again."

Mondennio rocked back in his chair, resting his hand on his forehead. *I have no way of coercing Jonaldy. If Jonaldy brought his friends, then he would be out-numbered.*

"What about your friends? The three guys outside? They seem the type who would enjoy the trip."

"They might at that." Veneza went to the door and spoke to the person outside. "Go get Piral."

"That's it?" Piral asked. "We just go down there early and wait. You give the signal we take him out." Piral stood his left foot on one of the chairs, with his elbow resting on his knee. Jex was outside keeping watch, but Piral brought three other rough looking friends. The room was scarcely nine square meters, which made it an intimate place with Veneza. With Piral, Mondennio thought the room was more claustrophobic.

"Simple plan. We're going to kidnap him. Bring him back here and get him to confess." Mondennio let Veneza handle the negotiations. She and Piral had some history that they agreed made her the better barterer. She sat at the table, with Mondennio back in the corner where Piral cornered him earlier.

"Veneza, I thought you said this was going to be a challenge. What's with this guy that's gonna make him a hard take?" Piral glanced over both shoulders, as if to call attention to his friends.

"We figure he's a professional. Wouldn't that be enough of a challenge?" Veneza sounded like she almost enjoyed taunting him.

"If that's your idea of a challenge, sure. It's 9 cycles now, so we' d better get going if we're going to be in place in time. Before we do, though, what's in it for me?" He jabbed both thumbs into his chest. Mondennio thought he was underscoring that he meant himself, as if there was another *me* in the room that might have caused confusion. Or was he pointing to *we*?

Mondennio thought he should have anticipated Piral's request for a reward. He took a second to try to think of what he had to offer. "We get him to clear my name, I'll be getting into government. You tell me what you'd like me to do in exchange."

"Name my price, eh?" Piral scratched his stubbled chin. "Let me get back to you on that. You're good for it, though. Otherwise, Fifi will have you for dinner, govie or not."

Mondennio reflexively gulped. "Don't worry, Piral, I'm good for my word. Assuming I get my named cleared."

Veneza nodded.

"I see. You don't want him hurt too badly during the kidnapping?"

"I don't mind that he's hurt, but I do want him able to confess and not so roughed up that Atakadaro would doubt him."

"Heh. Trust me, Mondo. Atakadaro doesn't mind how minced they are when it comes to confessions. Veneza, remember. You vouched for this guy, and you're backing his call now." He held his fist close to his face, with his index finger pointed at Veneza, sighting her in with his finger.

"Yeah, yeah. Go."

Piral walked out, pointing to the door. His entourage followed him, the last one closing the door. Mondennio thought he saw Jex walking out with them, leaving Veneza and Mondennio alone and unguarded.

"I guess I'll leave in half a cycle, then. They'll be one train ahead of me. You really think this will work?"

Veneza shrugged, "it's the best shot you've got. Maybe the only shot you've got left. So, yeah. I think it will work perfectly."

"Wait, you're only saying it will work perfectly because there's no other way?"

"Yeah. If we had more time, more resources, more whatever, then we'd have a perfect plan. This is perfectly good enough."

The streetcar ride was quiet, just like it was on that fateful night. The occasional track clacking no longer registered with him. This time, Mondennio had a better idea of what was going on. He had no idea who Jonaldy would arrive with, but at least Mondennio was not totally helpless and alone. He expected a full blown fight between Jonaldy and his thugs. As long as he was not in the middle, Mondennio expected to survive the night.

Should I get off a stop early and walk? He looked at his chronograph. He had enough time to spare. The stops were only about a kilometer apart. It should only take me about ten beats to cover the distance, if that.

He got off and walked. As he approached the Zero Narf stop, it was eerily quiet. He tried to see if he could make out any of Piral's men — or even Piral himself. There were few street lights in this district of Kennet, and Copa's moon Dradif was new.

He crossed the street so he was away from the lights that lit the stop. He got as close as he could, and checked his chronometer. *0.46 cycles. Jonaldy was punctual last time, so he should be here —*

"Good morning, Mondennio."

He turned, focusing on the voice that came from just over his shoulder. He could smell his sweet-bitter pungent breath. "Hello, Jonaldy. I thought we were going to meet at the stop."

"I decided to walk, and I see you did as well. It's probably better this way, though. Wouldn't you say? Either one of us might have an ambush set up there for the other."

"That wouldn't be very trusting, would it?"

"No. I know by now you don't trust me. Thought in reality, you probably should trust me. I'm just about the only friend you have left."

"Friend? Anusulo, more like. You dragged me into a murder. Ruined my life."

Jonaldy laughed deeply. "Mondennio, you're right. I tricked you into becoming a criminal. But, you're a criminal now, aren't you? If you'd gone into government you would have become a criminal then, too. Even if you didn't know I was going to commit the murder, even if you didn't. You are guilty. As you can see, Atakadaro knows you're guilty, too."

"But why? What made you decide to come after me?"

"It started several months ago, actually. Are you really sure you want to go down this path?"

"Damn right I'm sure. I want to know why you've ruined my life."

Jonaldy started casually strolling toward the Zero Narf stop. Mondennio followed. "Actually, Mondennio. I did not ruin your life. You did. I did a few things, talked to an official or two here, bribed an incorruptible man there."

"Wait! You're the one who paid off Carpimua?"

"Terrible, isn't it? I gather you have since encouraged him to recant. I must say I'm very pleased with your handiwork."

"You Putinfilaco! You—"

"Mondennio. Profanity? Is that what you learned with your republican whore? I think you really should let me finish. The stop is not far up ahead."

Mondennio bit his lip. His breath snorted through his nose as he debated whether to pick up a rock and start cratering Jonaldy's skull with it. He could make out little detail on the ground, but the rocks seemed too small.

Jonaldy continued during Mondennio's silence. "Thank you. You see, I did not ruin your life. I infused it with greater meaning. I mean, look at your pathetic life. What did it stand for when our little story began? Hmm? 'Advance the family within the Clin.' How boring. You probably still hope you can do that. But, I offer more."

"Really? You're an Imperium spy. Two seconds after I tell Atakadaro, they will be hunting you."

"Maybe so, but I've been here a few years. I have a few friends. That's what I'm inviting you to become—one of my new friends."

"I don't get you. Why not just tell me straight?"

"You have become more accustomed to the street. Mondennio, my boy, I'll help you get back your former, boring life. I'll get you absolved of the murder, I'll get your test score applied, though one question short of perfect. I can do all that."

"What do you expect of me in exchange?" Mondennio noticed they were closer to the Zero Narf stop, and patiently worked to increase the pace. *Piral and his friends will end this conversation.*

"Just friendship. Loyalty. From time to time I'll ask you for a favor, and you'll comply. I'll pay you, of course, not that you'll need it. But you'll still be my special friend. Of course, as my friend you'll keep our relationship very discreet."

"And if I refuse?"

"Then your story carries down its expected path. 'Spoiled sub-sept boy is expelled for cheating, kills the professor and proctor, and his life devolves.' It's all very predictable. Expected, actually."

Just inside the light of the Zero Narf stop, Mondennio stepped forward and blocked Jonaldy. He jabbed his finger in his chest. "You don't know who you're dealing with. Things have changed since we first met. I have friends who will back me against you."

Jonaldy's smiled continued. "Mondennio, even at this point you still think you have a choice?" He turned and looked into the darkness, laughing. Then he mocked Mondennio's voice rocking his head from side to side, "'You don't know who you're dealing with.' It's so sad when you think that applies to you and not me."

"Halt! Hands up!"

Mondennio spun around, trying to see where the voice came from. Before he could turn all the way around, he felt a sharp knock on his head. He fell to the ground, barely conscious. He lifted himself up slightly, shaking his head to keep from passing out.

"Down!" followed by a kick in his ribs. *This was not Jonaldy.*

Mondennio struggled to breathe, thankful that his injured ribs were on his left side instead of the right where the kick landed.

He felt something like a club slam into his back, followed by another strike. He tried to crawl forward. The assailant came down on top of him, pinning him to the ground. Mondennio twisted on his side, and started kicking at the ground to try to get his attacker's weight off his body.

It worked, but he found himself on his back, looking up at his attacker, who deftly repositioned himself. Mondennio grabbed at him, but the attacker grabbed his wrists and pinned them on the ground.

The attacker moved his wrists to his right side causing him to turn onto his side, then kneed him in the back, causing him to flip back onto his stomach. Mondennio planted his hands flat on the ground, preparing to push up.

As he did so, the attacker slid up and started to choke him. Mondennio slipped, falling flat on the ground with his attacker still firmly locked around his neck.

He looked up. Jonaldy had stepped back into the darkness, but his profile silhouetted from the distant street lights. He blacked out, hearing many voices and one raucous laugh.

He slowly came to. He lay on his chest, with his wrists firmly bound behind him. There were several vehicles around him, with numerous Atakadaro walking around. His spirit sank as he realized he had been caught. He beat his head on the ground in frustration.

A wave of pain washed over him, as if his body finally noticed he was awake. He made an inventory of the new pains. He seemed to have more wounds than he had before he passed out. He had heard Atakadaro had a quota of uninvestigated homicides of suspects in custody. Providence must have satisfied their quota before they arrested him.

He looked around, trying to see if there was more to the story than just his being beaten within a centimeter of his life. He saw Piral's boots sticking out from under a sheet. *Was he the quota?* There were other feet uncovered, apparently his entire entourage met their end together.

"What's going on here? Why was I attacked?" He hoped he could feign mistaken identity. Atakadaro attacked him without provocation. He was just defending himself.

"Nice try, kid. We know who you are, and what you've done. I'm Corporal Guezaler. You put up a hell of a fight, I'll give you that. Maybe if you had a bit more warning you could have taken the constable. Don't worry, his friends will give him a hard time for how long it took him to suppress you."

"Look, I know what you guys think. You think I killed Giedaz. But, I didn't."

"Oh? You mean the professor who is singularly responsible for your being expelled from school? Your biomass data is all over his place. We have clear security footage showing not only that you had been there, but that you planned your attack."

"That's not what happened!" He realized his lip was split open, the dirt adding to the sting.

"You mean you've never been to Ginster Enclave? You mean you weren't stalking around after dark? Even though we have surveillance data?"

"Right, I was there, but not to kill the professor. I knew this guy named Jonaldy Amonett, see. He told me we were going to deface a few buildings. That's it. We came back and he decided to break into some guy's house. How did I know it was Professor Giedaz?"

"That's not what I heard. I heard you went looking to hire somebody to kill the dear professor."

"What? Who accused me of that?"

"I did." Jonaldy crouched down, with a huge grin on his face. He steadied himself with one knee on the ground. "We had a pleasant stroll. I see you did bring your new friends. Unfortunately, I had some friends come before them to make sure you weren't looking to hurt me. It seems my friends were bigger than yours, and size matters."

He tousled Mondennio's hair. "You shouldn't blame them, though. They did fight pretty hard. Atakadaro lost one of theirs, which is why nobody from your little merry band lived."

Mondennio turned his head back. "Detective, this is the guy I was talking about. He set me up. I have an affidavit that he set me up to be caught cheating. He told me we were going to kidnap Giedaz, and if I didn't follow he would ruin me. He's an Imperium spy!"

Guezaler chuckled. "You were right, Jonaldy. He would say whatever came to mind. We really do appreciate your help on this."

"What? Are you crazy? He's a spy! Don't you get it?"

Guezaler bent over and grabbed him by his hair, pulling his head well off the ground. "What I know is that you sent friends that cost Atakadaro one of their finest officers. That does not sound like the action of an innocent university student. Jonaldy here told me you had crazy ideas that he tried to talk you out of, and that we could find you here. Seems he was right on both counts."

Guezaler walked away, leaving Mondennio and Jonaldy alone. Jonaldy snapped his fingers close to Mondennio's ears until Mondennio turned his head.

"What do you want from me?" Mondennio said, "It's obvious you already have a few close friends."

"We can talk about details later. Don't worry, you play it smart we'll have a long and profitable friendship."

"I don't want to be your friend." Mondennio spat dust out of his mouth

"You'll change your mind in the next few days. Just tell the good Detective there that you want to talk to me, and we can work something out. But, we can still be friends. I can put your life back on the course it was on, you know. I can do it quickly, too. All you have to do is decide to come work for us."

"After what you've put me through, what makes you think I would do something like that?"

"Oh, it's pretty easy, actually. So far, things have been bad. Maybe even worse. But, what's going to happen to you over the next few weeks will make this all look like a vacation. Atakadaro will torture you until you give up all your new friends. Then they'll ensure you give a proper confession. They can't execute a named individual without a proper confession. Think it over. Change your mind, you know how to get in touch with me."

Mondennio lay there face down on the ground. Frustration welled up, until he started banging his forehead into the packed dirt. *I should not be here!* He wrestled with the binders, feeling them begin to constrict tighter as he fought against them. Both his wrists and ankles were bound, and the binders were connected together.

As he struggled, he began to have difficulty breathing. He rocked until he was on his side, able to breathe better. He noticed a little blood where he earlier banged his head. Ribs on both sides were now in pain, making his new position little better than his previous one.

A tear flowed down his nose, followed by another. He tried to picture his past, not able to see much beyond what had happened. How could so little time do so much to drive out what was before? A part of him felt like he had always been in this struggle, as if he had been asleep and only recently awakened.

Awakened to what? A life of pain? Suffering? Depredation? That could not be what this was about. Mondennio had to think there was a larger reason for all this. *But what?* He felt his tears flowing more fully now, knowing in a few more seconds he would lose all control.

He fought to control his breathing, trying not to let a few tears turn into uncontrolled sobbing. Deep breaths slowly pulled his sorrow back. This is not over yet. One beat at a time. I need my wits about me to survive these next few days.

What was the harm in doing what Jonaldy wanted? The Clinate is really messed up. Mondennio searched through his recent experiences, looking for anything that could reconcile the Clinate. What could make him want to suffer for the Clinate?

He could not let Jonaldy win. Nobody should win by resorting to such treacherous methods. He set me up, lured me in, exposed me and betrayed me. No, I won't let him win.

What does he want? Mondennio thought through their time together. He realized it was so simple. All Jonaldy wanted was to extend the Imperium's hold on Copa. Mondennio did not know how he fit into Jonaldy's grand scheme. But, he fit in. *All I have to do is meddle with his plan a bit, and he loses. I don't even care if I win anymore. Just so long as he loses.*

But how to do that? Mondennio's ribs hurt too much now. He rolled over onto his other side. He saw Piral and his crew, or rather their lifeless feet. There were dozens of Atakadaro here. Jonaldy had left.

What had Veneza said? Leroga was Atakadaro. Right. Then he should know that I'm— there. Mondennio saw the man he thought was Leroga. Veneza had confirmed his description. The man who had chased him across the city center of Kennet.

Except. Leroga was not looking about or conversing. He stood there, right there near the stop. He was facing Mondennio, directly at him. And, he looked at him—as if he were trying to telepathically speak with Mondennio. All the while, he sipped a bit of tea from his tall mug.

Why is it tea I think he's drinking and not coffee? Because he doesn't look like a coffee drinker? Or, is it how his little pinky sticks out from the handle. Or how he places the mug down on a saucer? Who brings a saucer to a crime scene, anyway?

Whatever Leroga was doing, it must have worked. Mondennio and he locked eyes. Mondennio nodded, knowing that Leroga was the key to his salvation.

Leroga motioned a toast his mug, took a sip, and nodded back.

They left him hog tied for another cycle before transporting him to the Atakadaro facility. Four cycles later, Mondennio sat in the Atakadaro interrogation room. He could tell through the back window of the van he rode in that he was in the facility near Ginster Enclave. They had driven South, away from Kennet, until a back road cut through the woods. If he ever regained his freedom, he was going to travel those woods.

Despite his insistence on speaking to Detective Guezaler, they made him wait two cycles. He suspected that asking for Leroga would weaken Leroga's ability to help. He hoped the Atakadaro tried to contact his father to arrange legal counsel. Despite all he had done, he retained the rights and immunities of a full citizen of Copa.

Mondennio spent some time thinking about that. A named person was really just a citizen. Not all residents of Copa were citizens. He knew they went by different names, but mostly subjects or serfs. Peasants, when people though to spare what little dignity a serf had.

"Can't I just waive my right to counsel?" he said.

"No, I'm afraid not. The Clinate remains concerned that we might 'persuade' a citizen to waive counsel."

"Does Guezaler know I've been asking for him?"

"Yes. I spoke to him myself. He and his partner are probably still at breakfast. All night arrests tend to make us hungry."

The door opened. Jonaldy stepped in, well-dressed. Without even wondering why, Mondennio knew he would pretend to stand in as counsel.

"What's your name?" Jonaldy said to the officer standing guard.

"Pualson."

"Well, Pualson, get your arse out of here. I'm exerting privilege. How long have you had him here without my knowledge? Where's his interviewer? Let's get moving."

"Yes. Yes, Sir." Pualson stumbled out of the interview room.

Jonaldy gave the camera a two-finger salute. It winked out. He noticed a small wall mirror and took a moment to adjust his costume. He smoothed his hair as a finishing touch to his preening. "So, Mondennio. Guezaler told me you were asking for him. I suppose that means you want to speak with me."

"Right. I do. You had me pretty upset back there. You can't imagine how hard it was for me to hear how you ruined my life, just so you could plant a spy."

"Mondennio, it's not just about a spy, as you put it. You're going to be my man on the inside. Everybody said you have a lot of promise. So, I took a gamble on it. Are you smart enough to do what is necessary?"

"I am. You know, I think I should thank you for opening my eyes."

"What do you mean?" Jonaldy picked up the chair across from Mondennio and set it beside the metal table. He looked at the mirror a second time.

Mondennio thought Jonaldy might catch on to what was happening. *I've got to keep him talking.* "Because of you, I see Copa differently. It's no longer a tranquil, peaceful little planet isolated from the rest of humanity."

"Separated by 9,800 paces, I might add. You may not know this, but the longest sustainable jump is only about 5,400 paces. To get to Copa we have to bounce close to a supernova. That's probably how the original scouts found this place. They hopped away so quickly they must not have given the jump computer enough time to adjust. It's not even a particularly dangerous nova. But, it takes two very long jumps"

"That's not what I meant. The divide between citizen and peasant, named and unnamed. I always thought it was more symbiotic until now. Veneza kept ranting about it, but until I was running for my life I never saw it myself. Do you really think the Imperium could correct this?"

"I certainly do. Why else would I be here? The salary? I don't even get to enjoy what I make. I'm going to spend the rest of my career on this backwater. If I'm lucky there will be a pension when I retire. If you knew half of what I did before they sent me here — "

"You never thought of changing sides?"

"That's insane. A hunter-killer cell would be launched on me the second the Bafiktuy realized I had turned. Then, I'd wake up one day with all my hair missing, an itch on the brain I couldn't scratch or worse. There are some pretty exotic illnesses out there. Even I shiver at the thought of them."

"If you really think the Imperium can set things to right, then I think we can work together. But, what'll it be like?"

"The Imperium prefers to work through a governor. Copa will likely retain whatever government it has, but would be heavily influenced by the imperial governor who would be assigned."

"You?"

"Me? Hah. No. The Imperium has a cadre of men trained at governance. I'm not bent that way, anyway. And, don't get your hopes up. Imperial governors are Imperial citizens, not local."

"I'll be content just to get my life back."

"Not so fast, Mr. Beaver. You think you can just adopt a fetal position and get away? It doesn't work that way. You need to remember that right now I own your future."

"I know."

Jonaldy stood up. His pacing around the room seemed a bit to contrived to Mondennio, as if he were trying to act out the role of a lifetime. He grabbed both sides of the table and leaned in closely to Mondennio.

"You think you know. I own your future. Not renting, not borrowing. Own. You're going to work for us, and we will continue to own you. You do what we tell you, and we'll accept that as payment toward buying yourself back. You put in a long period of service, and we might even let you retire. You understand?"

"I understand. For a spy you're pretty brazen, aren't you? Just openly flaunting your true colors in an Atakadaro interrogation room. How do I know you won't get caught and bring me down with you?"

"Don't worry about that. Just like we own you, we own Atakadaro's infrastructure. See that camera light? Normally we would at least be videoed. But, we've taken care of that."

"Really? Then why do you need me? Atakadaro has a lot of information on a lot of people."

Jonaldy sat back down. "Networks only inform people. We're looking to place decision makers in key locations. You're going to be the first placement."

"So, for that reason you had Carpimua corrupt my exam? You duped me into being present while you committed murder? How involved was Guezaler in all this?"

"Sorry, I don't divulge that sort of information. Guezaler's a very valuable asset, to be certain. But, he's just like the network—he only informs. He's not a decider."

"Well, if you want me to be a decider then you're going to have to give me more information."

"Not now, I don't. I may never have to. It all depends on how productive you are. Deciders usually don't have information—they just decide like they are told."

"So, how are you going to get me out of all this?"

"A mix of truth and dare, I think. Your family attorney should be able to clean up your exam imbroglio and get the exam result re-instated. Carpimua has already confessed to his role, so that sort of took care of itself. Or, rather, you did. Again, I have to applaud your innovativeness."

"Thanks. Thoughts of you inspired my art."

"Cute. As for the murder, well, you got in with the wrong crowd. They did a little brainwashing and before you knew what you were doing they dragged you off to a murder. The Republicans fit well into that niche."

"I like that, it's almost true. But, that might not work as well as you think. If I was brainwashed, wouldn't I still be susceptible to future suggestion?"

"I said a little daring. The only thing not true is the brainwashing. You need that to absolve your being there for the murder and not going to the authorities later. It's called the Stockholm Syndrome, named after an Imperial psychologist, Dr. Stockholm."

"You mean, I can't use the fact that you threatened me?"

"You could, but that means they'll have to find the me. Actually, your friend Piral should do nicely taking the fall for me. But, a little brainwashing absolves a lot of guilt. Guezaler's keen investigative skills should help clean that up."

"But, you'd be on the surveillance footage at Ginster."

"No, that's already been taken care of. Piral and I are the same rough build, so it was simple to replace his image on mine."

"So, you never can trust surveillance?"

Jonaldy laughed. "I think that's why it's not used so heavily in the Imperium. It can literally be re-written to show whatever you want it to."

"Wouldn't it just be easier to say I wasn't there?"

Jonaldy traced some imaginary drawing on the table. "I suppose we could do that. But, that would require divulging how the image was changed. Too many people have seen your face. They never really paid attention to mine. For you to disappear would be noticeable. Understand?"

"But why tell me all this?"

Jonaldy paused for a moment. "You need to know that so you can play your role. Besides, it can be lonely in my job — so sometimes I can't resist sharing with somebody who would be a fool to share any of it with anybody."

Mondennio shrugged. He looked at the mirror. "I suppose I understand. You've been behind everything just to make me an Imperial spy."

"Not to make you a spy. You're a decider, not an informer. You're my bitch, and I'll tell you when to heel."

"I suppose so."

The door opened. Two fully armored Atakadaro officers entered, grabbing Jonaldy on either side. They lifted him out of his seat, slamming him on the table. He cried out as his back impacted, then started struggling. Mondennio flew out of his chair, back into the corner.

A third officer came in with a club, as his peers struggled to keep him flat. Mondennio turned after the first swing landed flat across Jonaldy's gut. Even with his eyes closed, Jonaldy's screams caused Mondennio to flinch. He pictured the beating in his mind, realizing he actually enjoyed it. He opened his eyes and watched his tormentor being tormented.

It only lasted a few beats. Jonaldy passed out from the blows received. Mondennio felt his anger release, looking at the savagely beaten body supine on the table.

Leroga walked in. "Thanks, Kid—" he pointed at the mirror, "—Sometimes low-tech is the way to go."

Mondennio did not mind Leroga's failure to use the honorific.

Chapter 18

64. Mondennio - Rowenzal Enclave

A month passed before Atakadaro released him. Mondennio planned to do his best to make his life look like it had returned to normal. He spent a weekend at home locked away in his room. On Twoday, it was time for school. Mondennio started to get in his car — late for class — when Gerandy stepped out from the house.

"Son, before you go. We've not really talked about what happened."

"Father, we don't need to. I understand — "

"Right. You understand my role as paterfamilias. But, there's the role as your father I failed to fulfill. Your mother warned me about that. It's as if she prophesied that one day you'd need me to step in as a father instead as the family ruler. I failed."

"Really, I understand. If I were in your position I'd be equally torn. Protecting the family was right, even if I had to be sacrificed."

Gerandy nodded his head. Mondennio did not believe a word of what he said. He felt Gerandy should have stepped in, at least been more supportive when something could be done. But, nothing would change what happened. His father needed the illusion of an understanding son. Mondennio gave him that.

On the drive to school, he looked at his new driver. Atakadaro had arrested Sahkud, and beaten him to death trying to get him to divulge where Mondennio was. Yet another uninvestigated homicide in the name of justice. Another injustice in the name of injustice Mondennio would one day reverse. Mondennio had been unable to find where he was buried, or if he even was. He planned to quietly find if Sahkud had any family, and to try to make amends.

305

The car followed its normal route to school. Mondennio decided to leave his new driver out of his second life — for the safety of them both.

Having arrived, Mondennio walked into the school building — through the building to the road beyond. His driver knew he was unneeded for three cycles, so he would find something to busy himself. Mondennio did not have class today, but neither his driver nor his father knew. Instead, he had friends to visit.

He entered Performing Arts and headed up the now familiar stairs.

"Veneza!"

"Hello, Mondennio. You remember our friend here?" She pointed at Leroga.

"My friend." Mondennio held out his hand and shook Leroga's. "I still haven't found a way to thank you for what you've done."

"I'm sure that will come in time. After all, you're going to be a decider, right?" Leroga said.

"Yes I am. I've been fully reinstated. The University was so embarrassed by what happened that it agreed to basically give me high marks for the semester as long as I show up. I suspect they'd give me high marks even if I don't. Sort of what I expected for my class load in fourth year anyway."

"What's next for you? You seem to have recovered from the trauma."

"No, I've not recovered. You know, on the drive here, I could not help but think that two blocks to my left were shanties. Their ancestors risked over ten-thousand paces of hypespace travel to arrive here. Whatever they were trying to get away from on Terra, they were not asking to be enslaved here.

"So, I'm still a little traumatized, if there is such a thing. What did Jonaldy say, 'I was brainwashed?' I don't think that I was, but I realize the Clinate cannot remain."

"We were hoping you'd say that. Not, er, myself and Veneza. Our friends hoped you still understood the work ahead."

"I don't understand it. But, when has understanding been required to put one foot down in front of the other? Just as long as you'll guide my way."

Leroga looked from Mondennio to Veneza. "Oh, no. Not her. This will be the last you ever hear from her. Veneza here is still a wanted woman for her role in the riot. We're heading out of Kennet after this to get her somewhere safer."

"Then what about you?"

"I'm nobody, so I'll go on about my merry life. Don't come looking to me for answers, because I won't give them to you." Leroga said. "And it might make some question the terms of your freedom."

Veneza slid a card over to him. "This was my library card, of a sort. It has the directions to the library where I learned what republicanism was supposed to be."

Leroga continued. "Your education has just begun, Young Man. One day, a man will approach you by the name of Yuan Fermilo. He'll pick up this conversation where we're leaving it off now."

Leroga stood up, Mondennio rising with him. They shook hands one last time. He walked down the stairs.

Mondennio looked back at Veneza, still trying to come to terms with the sudden, permanent separation. She was standing, and came at him. They hugged, and she kissed his cheek. "I'm glad you came out of this for the better."

"Will we meet again?"

She shrugged with a smile. She started down the stairs, turning back one last time. She pointed at the card she handed them. "In the meantime, Mondennio, please read."

Thank you for reading

Scintilla

Bophendze and Smee will return in *Solace*.

Follow Me

Ben Wilson can be followed on Twitter and Facebook.
Visit his web site at http://dausha.net for more information. You can also
sign up for announcements of other books in this series at http://dausha.net.